Oh, why do I not possess the secret of lofty, powerful language, of the sublime style, to describe these grand and edifying moments of human life, which seem created expressly to prove that virtue sometimes triumphs over ingratitude, free-thinking, vice and envy!   (from *The Double*, page 32)

"In vain the dreamer rakes over his old dreams, as though seeking a spark among the embers, to fan them into flame, to warm his chilled heart by the rekindled fire, and to rouse up in it again all that was so sweet, that touched his heart, that set his blood boiling, drew tears from his eyes, and so luxuriously deceived him!"   (from "White Nights," page 197)

I am a sick man . . . I am a spiteful man. I am an unattractive man.   (from *Notes from Underground*, page 233)

What is a man without desires, without free will and without choice, if not a stop in an organ?
                   (from *Notes from Underground*, page 255)

Every man has memories which he would not tell to everyone, but only to his friends. He has other matters in his mind which he would not reveal even to his friends, but only to himself, and that in secret. But there are other things which a man is afraid to tell even to himself, and every decent man has a number of such things stored away in his mind.
                   (from *Notes from Underground*, page 266)

Furtively, timidly, in solitude, at night, I indulged in filthy vice, with a feeling of shame which never deserted me, even at the most loathsome moments, and which at such moments nearly made me curse. Already even then I had my underground world in my soul.   (from *Notes from Underground*, page 276)

We are oppressed at being humans, humans with our own real bodies and blood; we are ashamed of it, we think it a disgrace, and we keep trying to be some sort of fairy-tale universal beings. (from *Notes from Underground*, page 351)

I am a ridiculous man. Now they call me a madman. That would be a promotion if it were not that I remain as ridiculous in their eyes as before.

(from "The Dream of a Ridiculous Man," page 407)

Dreams seem to be spurred on not by reason but by desire, not by the head but by the heart, and yet what clever tricks my reason has played sometimes in dreams, what utterly incomprehensible things happen to it!

(from "The Dream of a Ridiculous Man," page 413)

"On our earth we can only love with suffering and through suffering. We cannot love otherwise, and we know of no other sort of love. I want suffering in order to love."

(from "The Dream of a Ridiculous Man," page 417)

NOTES FROM UNDERGROUND, THE DOUBLE AND OTHER STORIES

Fyodor Dostoevsky

WITH AN INTRODUCTION AND NOTES

BY DEBORAH A. MARTINSEN

GEORGE STADE

CONSULTING EDITORIAL DIRECTOR

BARNES & NOBLE CLASSICS

NEW YORK

ℐℬ

BARNES & NOBLE CLASSICS

NEW YORK

Published by Barnes & Noble Books
122 Fifth Avenue
New York, NY 10011

www.barnesandnoble.com/classics

Notes from Underground was first published in the original Russian in 1864, The Double in 1846, "White Nights" in 1848, "The Meek One" in 1876, and "The Dream of a Ridiculous Man" in 1877. The present texts follow Constance Garnett's translations.

Published in 2003 by Barnes & Noble Classics with new Introduction, Notes, Biography, Chronology, Inspired By, Comments & Questions, and For Further Reading.

Introduction, Notes, and For Further Reading
Copyright © 2003 by Deborah A. Martinsen.

Note on Fyodor Dostoevsky, The World of Fyodor Dostoevsky, Inspired by Notes from Underground, The Double and Other Stories, and Comments & Questions
Copyright © 2003 by Barnes & Noble, Inc.

Notes from Underground, The Double and Other Stories
ISBN-13: 978-1-59308-037-2
ISBN-10: 1-59308-037-9
LC Control Number 2003102763

Produced and published in conjunction with:
Fine Creative Media, Inc.
322 Eighth Avenue
New York, NY 10001
Michael J. Fine, President and Publisher

Printed in the United States of America
QB
5 7 9 10 8 6 4

FYODOR DOSTOEVSKY

Fyodor Mikhailovich Dostoevsky was born in Moscow on October 30, 1821. When he was fifteen, his mother died, and his father, a strict former army surgeon, sent him and his older brother, Mikhail, to preparatory school in St. Petersburg. Fyodor continued his education at the St. Petersburg Academy of Military Engineers and graduated as a lieutenant in 1843. After serving as a military engineer for a short time, and inheriting some money from his father's estate, he retired from the army and decided instead to devote himself to writing.

Dostoevsky won immediate recognition with the 1846 publication of his first work of fiction, a short novel titled Poor Folk. The important Russian critic Vissarion Grigorievich Belinsky praised his work and introduced him into the literary circles of St. Petersburg. Over the next few years Dostoevsky published several stories, including "The Double" and "White Nights." He also became interested in a radical group known as the Petrashevsky Circle, headed by the charismatic utopian socialist Mikhail Petrashevsky. In 1849 Tsar Nicholas I called for the arrest of several members of the group, including Dostoevsky. He was kept in solitary confinement for eight months while the charges against him were investigated, and then, along with other members of Petrashevsky's group was sentenced to death by firing squad. At the last minute Nicholas commuted the sentence to penal servitude in Siberia for four years, and then service in the Russian Army. This near-execution haunts much of Dostoevsky's subsequent writing.

The ten years Dostoevsky spent in prison and then in exile in Siberia had a profound effect on him. By the time he returned to St. Petersburg in 1859, he had rejected his radical ideas and acquired a new respect for the religious ideas and ideals of the Russsian people. He had never been an atheist, but his Christianity was now closer to the Orthodox faith. While in exile he had also married.

Dostoevsky quickly resumed his literary career in St. Petersburg. He and his brother Mikhail founded two journals, *Vremya* (1861–1863) and *Epokha* (1864–1865). Dostoevsky published many of his well-known post-Siberian works in these journals, including *The House of the Dead*, an account of his prison experiences, and the dark, complex novella "Notes from Underground."

The next several years of Dostoevsky's life were marked by the deaths of his wife, Maria, and his brother Mikhail. He began to gamble compulsively, and he suffered from bouts of epilepsy. In 1866 his fortunes changed; while dictating his novel *The Gambler* to meet a deadline, he met a young stenographer, Anna Snitkina, and the two married a year later. Over the next fifteen years Dostoevsky produced his finest works, including the novels *Crime and Punishment* (1866), *The Idiot* (1868), *The Possessed* (1871–1872), and *The Brothers Karamazov* (1879–1880). His novels are complex psychological studies that examine man's struggle with such elemental issues as good and evil, life and death, belief and reason. Fyodor Mikhailovich Dostoevsky died from a lung hemorrhage on January 28, 1881, in St. Petersburg at the age of fifty-nine.

CONTENTS

THE WORLD OF
FYODOR DOSTOEVSKY AND
NOTES FROM UNDERGROUND,
THE DOUBLE AND OTHER STORIES

1821   Fyodor Mikhailovitch Dostoevsky is born on October 30 in Moscow. The second of seven children, he grows up in a middle-class household run by his father, a former army surgeon and strict family man.

1833   Aleksandr Pushkin's novel in verse *Eugene Onegin* is published.

1837   Fyodor's mother dies. He and his older brother Mikhail are sent to a preparatory school in St. Petersburg.

1838   Dostoevsky begins his tenure at the St. Petersburg Academy of Military Engineers, where he studies until 1843. He becomes acquainted with the works of such writers as Byron, Corneille, Dickens, Goethe, Gogol, Homer, Hugo, Pushkin, Racine, Rousseau, Shakespeare, and Schiller.

1839   Dostoevsky's father, according to rumor, is murdered on his country estate, presumably by his own serfs.

1842   Part 1 of Nikolay Gogol's novel *Dead Souls* is published.

1843   Dostoevsky graduates from the Academy as a lieutenant, but instead of pursuing a career in the army, he resolves to dedicate his life to writing. His first published work appears, a Russian translation of Honoré de Balzac's 1833 novel *Eugénie Grandet*.

1844   Dostoevsky begins work on his first novel, *Poor Folk*.

1845   On the basis of *Poor Folk*, Dostoevsky wins the friendship and acclaim of Russia's premier literary critic, Vissarion Grigorievich Belinsky, author of the scathingly critical "Letter to Gogol" (1847).

1846   *Poor Folk* and "The Double" are published. "The Double" is the first work in which Dostoevsky writes about the psychology of the split self. Dostoevsky meets the utopian socialist M. V. Butashevich-Petrashevsky.

1847   Dostoevsky publishes numerous short stories, including "A Weak Heart," "Polzunkov" and "The Landlady."

He is diagnosed with and treated for epilepsy for the first time.

1848   He publishes the short story "White Nights." The *Communist Manifesto*, by Karl Marx and Friedrich Engels, is published. Revolutions break out in France, Germany, Hungary, Italy, and Poland.

1849   Dostoevsky is arrested for his participation in the socialist Petrashevsky Circle, only a discussion group but, in the revolutionary climate of the time, considered subversive. He is condemned to death, but first spends eight months in solitary confinement. Tsar Nicholas I commutes his sentence to penal servitude in Siberia, but orders this to be announced only at the last minute.

1850   Dostoevsky begins his four-year internment at Omsk prison in western Siberia. His experiences there will influence many of his later works. While imprisoned he abandons the radical ideas of his youth and becomes more deeply religious; his only book in prison is a copy of the Bible.

1852   Part 2 of Gogol's *Dead Souls* is published.

1853   The Crimean War breaks out, the cause being a dispute between Russia and France over the Palestinian holy places.

1854   Still exiled in Siberia, Dostoevsky begins four years of compulsory military service.

1857   He marries the widow Maria Dmitrievna Isaeva.

1859   Dostoevsky and Maria are allowed to return to St. Petersburg.

1861   He and his brother Mikhail establish *Vremya* (Time); the journal publishes Dostoevsky's *The House of the Dead*, a work based on his experiences in Siberia.

1862   Dostoevsky travels to England, France, Germany, Italy, and Switzerland, a trip that engenders in him an anti-European outlook. He gambles heavily at resorts abroad, losing money.

1863   Dostoevsky makes a second trip to Europe and arranges to meet Apollinaria Suslova in Paris; he had published a story by her in *Vremya* the previous year. The two have an affair. The progressive Nikolay Chernyshevsky publishes the utopian novel *What Is to Be Done?*, which Dostoevsky will react against a year later in "Notes from Underground." *Vremya* is banned for printing a potentially subversive article regarding the Polish rebellion. Tolstoy publishes the first six books of *War and Peace*.

1864   Dostoevsky and his brother Mikhail establish *Epokha* (Epoch), the short-lived successor to *Vremya*; the journal publishes "Notes from Underground," the first of Dostoevsky's masterworks. Dostoevsky's wife, Maria, dies from tuberculosis. His brother Mikhail dies three months later.

1865   Burdened with debt, Dostoevsky goes on another failed gambling spree in Europe. He proposes to Apollinaria Suslova, but she turns him down.

1866   *Crime and Punishment* starts serial publication at the beginning of the year. Dostoevsky interrupts the writing in October in order to work on *The Gambler*; by meeting the contract deadline for that book, he retains the rights to his published works, including *Crime and Punishment*. He dictates *The Gambler* to a stenographer, Anna Grigorievna Snitkina, over the course of a month. He and Anna, who is twenty-five years his junior, become romantically involved.

1867   Dostoevsky marries Anna Snitkina; the alliance is one of the most fortuitous events of his life. To avoid financial ruin, the two live abroad for the next four years, in Geneva, Florence, Vienna, Prague, and finally Dresden. Dostoevsky's epilepsy worsens. He begins work on his novel *The Idiot*, in which the protagonist is an epileptic.

1868   *The Idiot* is published in installments.

1869   The last of the six volumes of Tolstoy's *War and Peace* is published.

1871   The Dostoevskys return to St. Petersburg. Serialization of his novel *The Possessed* begins.

1873   Dostoevsky begins writing for the conservative weekly *Grazhdanin* (The Citizen); "The Diary of a Writer" becomes a regular and popular feature of the weekly.

1875   Leo Tolstoy begins publishing *Anna Karenina*.

1876   *The Diary of a Writer* is published as a monojournal—that is, it was written and edited entirely by Dostoevsky; in it he publishes "The Meek One."

1877   "The Dream of a Ridiculous Man" is published in *The Diary of a Writer*.

1879   Serialization begins of *The Brothers Karamazov*, widely considered Dostoevsky's greatest novel.

1880   Six months before his death, Dostoevsky delivers his famous speech on Pushkin at the dedication of the Pushkin memorial in Moscow.

1881   Dostoevsky dies from a lung hemorrhage on January 28 in St. Petersburg. His epitaph, also the epigraph to *The Brothers Karamazov*, is from the Bible (John 12:24); it reads, "Verily, verily, I say unto you, Except a corn of wheat fall into the ground and die, it abideth alone: but if it die, it bringeth forth much fruit" (King James Version).

1886   The German philosopher Friedrich Nietzsche, who was greatly influenced by Dostoevsky's treatment of human psychology, publishes *Beyond Good and Evil*, which borrows dogma directly from *The Possessed*.

1912   Constance Garnett begins her translations of the works of Dostoevsky, introducing his writing to the English-reading world.

INTRODUCTION

Master psychologist, social critic, and metaphysical thinker, Dostoevsky continually surprises readers with his dramatic and penetrating insights into the human mind and heart. The stories collected in this volume span most of Dostoevsky's career, yet their protagonists are similar—all of them solitary men living in St. Petersburg, Russia's capital from 1712 to 1917. St. Petersburg was Tsar Peter the Great's planned city, his "window on the West." Yet Peter achieved his vision at great human cost. Located on hostile swampland, this "Venice of the North" was built on the bones of the laborers who hauled granite to shore its riverbanks and canals. Popular rumors of Peter as Antichrist warred with the official version of Peter as world builder and gave rise to a myth of duality that came to surround the city as well as the tsar.

By the mid-nineteenth century, when Dostoevsky began his writing career, Aleksandr Pushkin and Nikolay Gogol had already immortalized St. Petersburg's duality in verse and prose. In Pushkin's narrative poem *The Bronze Horseman* (1833), a devastating flood symbolizes the revolt of the elements against the city and its inhabitants. The flood serves as a backdrop for the conflict between the impersonal, imperial state and a humble individual who loses everything, including his mind, as a result of the natural disaster. Gogol's St. Petersburg tales focus more on the city as Russia's administrative and social capital and highlight the disjunction between its attractive appearance and its cruel realities. Dostoevsky evokes his predecessors' contributions to the myth and provides additional psychological and philosophical depth. St. Petersburg, in the words of the underground man in "Notes from Underground," "is the most abstract and premeditated city on the whole earth." In the tradition of Dickens and Balzac before him, Dostoevsky makes his city emblematic of Western urban civilization and also of Russia's self-consciousness vis-à-vis the West.

The protagonists of these collected stories are all St. Petersburg loners whose isolation marks their alienation from human community and what Dostoevsky called "living life." They are narcissists who suffer from shame and feel excluded from communities to which they long to belong. They feel inadequate and out of place. They fear rejection or failure, and choose isolation as a defense against their fears. In "The Double," Golyadkin, whose name derives from the Russian word for "naked" or "insignificant," voices shame at his very identity: "What a little fool you are, what a nonentity (Golyadka)—that's the kind of last name you have!" (p. 36). The St. Petersburg dreamer calls himself a "type . . . an original . . . a ridiculous man!" (p. 187). The underground man calls himself "sick," "spiteful," "unattractive" (p. 233). The pawnbroker refuses to defend his regiment's honor for fear of appearing "stupid" (p. 396). The dreamer of the final story in this collection calls himself "ridiculous" (p. 407).

By exposing his protagonists' deep sense of personal shame, Dostoevsky gives readers a key to understanding their stories. We see that their solitude is their major defense, but not their only one. They also protect their fragile egos by objectifying themselves, dreaming, rationalizing, dominating others, and adopting a shell of numbing indifference. In deploying these standard defenses against shame, they become not only realistic, nineteenth-century St. Petersburg "types" but also our contemporaries.

The Double

"The Double" (1846) was Dostoevsky's second published story. Although critics acknowledged its psychological acuity, they also criticized it for being wordy and fantastic. Yet Dostoevsky clung to the truth of the story's idea, and twenty years later he revised and shortened it, giving us the version in print today.

"The Double" is the only story in this collection written as a third-person narrative; not coincidentally, it alone names its protagonist. As mentioned, Golyadkin's name means "naked" or "insignificant," expressing the character's dual sense of being exposed and invisible. His first name comes from the biblical twin Jacob, the younger son who cunningly cheats his brother Esau of his birthright. Fittingly, in Dostoevsky's story, Golyadkin Junior uses his social cunning to usurp his elder's position. Golyadkin's patronymic Petrovich (literally, "son of Peter") marks him as part of the tribe of Peter the Great, the tsar who modernized and secularized Russia. Golyadkin Senior and Junior both serve in the extensive bureaucracy of Peter's modern state. Peter's Table of Ranks, designed to curb the power of the hereditary aristocracy by basing promotion on service rather than rank, provides the backdrop for the drama. A grade nine in a ranking of fourteen (one being the highest; see endnote 1 for "The Double"), Golyadkin decides to overcome his insignificance and invisibility by marrying his superior's daughter. This decision precipitates the identity crisis dramatized in the story.

"The Double" recounts the events of four days. The story opens as Golyadkin prepares to skip work and attend the nameday party of his superior's daughter. He has hired a carriage and rented livery for his servant. He drives along Nevsky Prospect, the main street immortalized by Gogol as a symbol of St. Petersburg's duality. Yet, as encounters with fellow clerks and his boss reveal, Golyadkin's desire to hide matches his desire to be seen. Dostoevsky thus provides readers with an early clue about the role of shame in Golyadkin's story. Shame involves seeing and being seen. Like shame itself, seeing and being seen function paradoxically to connect and isolate individuals. On one hand, Golyadkin associates seeing and being seen with power, a sign that he is in control or that others recognize and admire him. On the other hand, he associates seeing and being seen with powerlessness, a sign that he is exposed and vulnerable or that others have objectified and thus diminished him. Three times in the first three chapters, in moments of self-doubt, Golyadkin defends himself with a powerful gaze "calculated to reduce all his foes to ashes": first, after he encounters "the magnetism of his chiefs eyes"; second, while he sits in uncomfortable silence at his doctor's office; third, after his fellow clerks mock him. In chapter IV, Golyadkin loses the ability to conjure up this magic, protective gaze. Instead he employs a series of other defenses that mark the progression of his madness.

As early as chapter I, Golyadkin objectifies himself. After encountering his fellow clerks, he mutters to himself: "Why, what is there strange in it? A man in a carriage, a man needs to be in a carriage, and so he hires a carriage." After his superior catches sight of him, Golyadkin huddles into the corner of his carriage and mutters: "It's not I, it's not I—and that is the fact of the matter." This last verbal tic speaks volumes: Golyadkin not only considers himself nothing, he dissociates from himself. The first chapter's events prepare for his ultimate self-objectification: a midnight encounter with his double.

While Dostoevsky's story is psychologically compelling, it is also delightfully self-conscious of its literary construction. The subtitle "A Petersburg Poem" points to Russian literary tradition, particularly to two works: Pushkin's *The Bronze Horseman* and Gogol's novel *Dead Souls*, both of which are subtitled "poema." Dostoevsky's original subtitle for "The Double"—"The Adventures of Mr. Golyadkin"—was more limited, evoking only Gogol's satiric novel, which bears the subtitle "The Adventures of Mr. Chichikov." By subtitling his story a "poema," Dostoevsky broadens his field of reference as he evokes Pushkin's poem, thereby introducing the theme of madness and stressing the role of St. Petersburg, the setting for Pushkin's poem.

Dostoevsky also struts his literary mastery by inscribing Golyadkin's compulsion for repetition into the story's structure. Twice Golyadkin takes a carriage from his midlevel bureaucratic neighborhood to the Izmailovsky Bridge district, home of upper-level bureaucrats. Both times he crashes parties being held by his superior, Olsufy Ivanovich. Honored guests at both parties include his immediate boss, Andrey Filippovich, and Andrey's nephew, who has the job and the girl Golyadkin aspires to. Twice Golyadkin dismisses his carriage and, while waiting to contact Klara, spends long periods huddled in a small space outside the sphere of action: first in a corner inside Olsufy Ivanovich's house, next behind a woodpile outside the house. Twice he shakes his double's hand, only to be humiliated by him: first privately, then publicly. Repeatedly he confides personal secrets to Golyadkin Junior, who then betrays him. Golyadkin's repeated attempts to win the attention of his superior's daughter and the friendship of his double only expose his obsessive nature.

The larger repetitions of the story mark another progression, that of Golyadkin Senior's increasing exposure and exclusion. At the beginning of the story he is in active control, hiring a carriage and directing the driver; at the story's end, he is passively placed in a carriage and driven to the madhouse. Moreover, Golyadkin becomes marginalized geographically as well as socially. Initially a resident of St. Petersburg, he ends his adventures on the road to Peterhof, Peter's summer home.

The psychological action also repeats itself with variations that mark a progression: In response to humiliation, Golyadkin asserts himself and is again humiliated; he flees, reasserts himself, and is again humiliated. His exhibitionism inevitably leads to exposure and shame; shame disorients him and renders him extremely self-conscious. Golyadkin responds by physical and mental flight: He tries to both hide his body and deny his identity ("it's not I"), and he indulges in rescue fantasies. He then reasserts himself, only to be exposed, shamed, and removed once again. Golyadkin's fragile identity at the story's beginning becomes completely disintegrated by its end.

This pattern of repetition characterizes individual scenes as well as the story's general action. In chapters III and IV, for instance, the butler Gerasimich denies Golyadkin entry to Olsufy Ivanovich's house. Golyadkin responds to this shame with his two standard defenses of self-consciousness and flight. Returning to his carriage, Golyadkin "inwardly uttered a desire to sink into the earth or to hide in a mouse hole together with his carriage. It seemed to him that everything in Olsufy Ivanovich's house was looking at him now out of every window. He knew that he would certainly die on the spot if he were to go back" (p. 30). Despite his crushing rejection and humiliation, Golyadkin returns, this time on foot, and manages to enter the house through the servants' entrance. After a long, tormenting wait in

the wings, he thrusts himself into the room, walks up to Klara
Olsufyevna, and stumblingly congratulates her. As earlier, he is
annihilated by Andrey Filippovich's stare and attempts to disappear. Gerasimich again comes to eject him, but Golyadkin manages to escape the butler and retreat to a corner; he then invites
Klara to dance.

The movement is the same: advance, defeat, retreat and re-
group, advance. Each time Golyadkin goes a little further until
he oversteps the bounds of the permissible. Klara screams; the
orchestra stops; all eyes fix on Golyadkin as he is escorted from
the house. The clock strikes midnight. The narrator notes: "Mr.
Golyadkin did not want only to run away from himself, but to
be obliterated, to cease to be, to return to dust" (p. 45). Completely shamed, Golyadkin wants to die. From the ashes of his
humiliation, however, his double arises. Golyadkin will now repeat the pattern again and again, at home and at the office. Finally, when he once again oversteps the bounds of the
permissible at Olsufy Ivanovich's home, his fear of being seen
from "every window" is realized, and he is taken away altogether.

Dostoevsky's construction of "The Double" is a self-
conscious display of his literary mastery. His choice of the
double as a subject recalls the work of E. T. A. Hoffmann and
Edgar Allan Poe, as well as many works from the 1830s and
1840s, when doubles were a literary commonplace. The thirteen chapters recall the apostle Judas, the thirteenth guest who
betrayed Jesus at the Last Supper, which reflects Golyadkin's repeated betrayal by his double. Finally, the theme of pretender-
ship evokes a long tradition in Russian history, which witnessed
numerous popular uprisings led by men pretending to be the
"true" tsar.

Dostoevsky also inscribes the story's psychological dynamics
into its narrative strategy. Golyadkin has boundary problems,
manifest in his inability to distinguish where reality ends and
his paranoid fantasies begin. Accordingly, Dostoevsky's narrator
blurs the boundaries between himself and Golyadkin by going
in and out of his hero's head without telling readers when he

is doing so. Golyadkin has a number of characteristic verbal tics, such as, "I can take care of myself," "I'm an unimportant man," "well, it's no matter," "perhaps it will all be for the best." The narrator sometimes identifies Golyadkin as the source of these phrases by using reported speech: "I'm on my own account here. This is my private life, Andrey Filippovich" (p. 29). But sometimes he adopts Golyadkin's language for himself to indicate his hero's thoughts: "He was here also, gentlemen— that is, not at the dance, but almost at the dance; he was 'all right, though; he could take care of himself' " (p. 35). While mixing reported speech with indirect speech became a common narrative strategy in the early twentieth century with such writers as Virginia Woolf and Franz Kafla, Dostoevsky's experiments unsettled readers accustomed to clear boundaries between characters and narrators.

Despite this blurring of boundaries, Dostoevsky's narrator maintains enough of a narrative distance from his hero to provide readers with increasingly more clues on how to read the story. Early on, he exposes Golyadkin's statements about himself as projective denials. For instance, Golyadkin swears to Dr. Rutenspitz, his junior colleagues, Anton Antonovich, and himself, "I am not one to intrigue, and I'm proud of it"; then, after several drinks, he confides to Golyadkin Junior, "We shall be like brothers; we'll be cunning, my dear fellow, we'll work together; we'll get up an intrigue, too, to pay them out. To pay them out we'll get up an intrigue too" (p. 72). Golyadkin reveals his negative behavior as he disavows it. Readers learn that the more Golyadkin protests, the more we must pay attention.

In chapter XI Dostoevsky has Golyadkin explain his rhetorical strategy. Golyadkin Senior, who had earlier written an accusatory letter to Golyadkin Junior, attempts to persuade Golyadkin Junior to return the letter, declaring: "Give me that letter that I may tear it to pieces before your eyes, Yakov Petrovich, and if that is utterly impossible I entreat you to read it the other way before—precisely the other way before—that is, expressly with a friendly intention, giving the opposite sense to the whole letter" (p. 136). While Golyadkin Senior unconsciously reveals the duality of his words, Dostoevsky consciously exposes his character's verbal and psychological duality. When Golyadkin Senior asks his double to read his letter in the opposite sense, Dostoevsky shows that grandiosity is the other side of his narcissistic vulnerability. When Golyadkin Senior proclaims that the letter reproaching Golyadkin Junior with betrayal can be read as an overture of friendship, Dostoevsky shows that Golyadkin Junior is Golyadkin Senior's alter ego—a projection both of his ambition and his fears of displacement.

Dostoevsky also signals his literary mastery by creating a narrative ambiguity around Golyadkin Junior's objective existence: All the events after midnight on the first day could be happening in Golyadkin's head. And yet, like the ghost figures in Henry James's "The Turn of the Screw," Golyadkin's double does seem to have an objective existence, since other people see and interact with him. In crafting this ambiguity, Dostoevsky pays tribute to Pushkin's story "The Queen of Spades" and Gogol's story "The Nose"; both of these St. Petersburg tales can be read either as dreams or as actual events.

By raising questions about Golyadkin Junior's existence, Dostoevsky distracts readers from the power of his satire on Russia. Golyadkin's central conflict reflects a larger phenomenon, that of the split between the ideal and the real in Russian public life. A midlevel clerk with ambition, Golyadkin lacks imagination and aspires to be like his superiors in all ways. He wants higher rank and social standing, more power, more money, a better address. He paradoxically yet tragically chooses Russia's corrupt bureaucrats as his ideals. Golyadkin's dilemma plays out in the gap between his actual and ideal selves: He resolutely refuses to recognize that he does not fit into the world he longs to join. Dostoevsky's focus on Golyadkin's psychological splitting causes many readers to overlook the humor of his hero's ambition to be a mediocre bureaucrat.

Dostoevsky skillfully portrays Golyadkin as both victim and predator. Golyadkin may suffer, but he also causes suffering. He thinks only of himself and treats others as a means to an end. We know from his visit to Dr. Rutenspitz, for example, that he had encouraged his German landlady, and then abandoned her once he decided to court Klara. Likewise, he intends to marry Klara without consulting her. Dostoevsky thus cannily demonstrates how Golyadkin's narcissism sabotages his social interactions. Golyadkin's personal story can be read as a case study of shame. More importantly, it reflects a larger social problem: Narcissism subverts personal integrity and social harmony, which means that shame of oneself can harm others. Dostoevsky dramatizes this problem in the four other stories in this collection.

The White Nights Dreamer

The protagonists of the other stories collected here suffer from a crippling narcissism similar to that of Golyadkin. Their anonymity stresses their typicality. The white nights dreamer lives in fantasies fabricated from the romantic literature popular in the 1840s; the underground man polemicizes with the radical intelligentsia of the 1860s; the pawnbroker and the ridiculous man emblemize Dostoevsky's journalistic polemics of the 1870s. Dostoevsky emphasizes their narcissism by choosing a first-person narration. By making them all dreamers, he highlights the costs of their social alienation. The white nights dreamer is the most positive of the four protagonists. He is a young idealist whose shame manifests itself in timidity rather than pride. He dreams of approaching young women and telling them his story, and hopes they will understand and appreciate him. His dream comes true when he rescues Nastenka from a drunkard's predatory clutches; he gets to tell her his story and receives the positive affirmation he seeks. Even when her fiancé returns to marry her, Nastenka wants to keep in touch. The white nights dreamer, however, chooses isolation, a choice that anticipates the near-solipsism of the other three first-person narrators in this collection.

"White Nights" was written in 1848 and bears the imprint of Dostoevsky's early journalism. The "White Nights" dreamer, who roams the streets of St. Petersburg giving life to the city itself, is a narrative persona Dostoevsky developed in many of his 1840s feuilletons. He is a dreamer, which signals Dostoevsky's engagement with romanticism. The story takes place over four nights and a morning, which follows the Russian romantic tradition of the stories in Pogorelsky's *The Double, or My Evenings in Little Russia* (1828) and Odoevsky's *Russian Nights* (1844). Dostoevsky also deliberately refers to the storytelling tradition of *The Arabian Nights' Entertainments*, a reference he flags as the dreamer begins his story. The story's title, "White Nights," is a reference to the lightness of northern late spring and summer nights. In keeping with Dostoevsky's dual roots in the romantic and realist traditions, the title reflects both St. Petersburg's climate and the dreamer's habits. Dostoevsky exploits both the literal and figurative dimension of this extraordinary natural phenomenon by setting his dreamer's only contact with real life in nights full of light and eerie beauty.

Dostoevsky emphasizes his dreamer's solitude in several ways. First, the dreamer develops relationships with buildings rather than people. For instance, he delicately avoids one of his favorite buildings after it is painted canary yellow, so as not to embarrass it. Second, the dreamer confesses his social alienation to Nastenka. Before telling his story, he compares himself to a djinn that has been locked in a bottle for 1,800 years. The dreamer thus acknowledges that he has bottled up the contents of his mind and heart. Finally and most significantly, the dreamer tells his story to Nastenka in the third person, a narrative strategy that reveals his defense mechanisms. By objectifying himself in this way, the dreamer reveals his poetic proclivity for fashioning life into art. This strategy allows him to control the shame experience by situating himself as observer rather than observed; it also serves to distance his speaking self from his experiencing self. Sharing his story with a sympathetic listener like Nastenka is healing for the dreamer: "I expected Nastenka, who listened to me opening her clever eyes, would break into her childish, irrepressible laugh; . . . but to my surprise she was silent, waiting a little, then she faintly pressed my hand and with timid sympathy asked—'Surely you haven't lived like that all your life?' " (p. 196). Nastenka's empathic response provides him a way out of his self-enclosure. She invites him to open up rather than shut himself in.

Dostoevsky overcomes the limitations of a first-person narrative by exposing his narrators through their own speech. The white nights dreamer, for instance, tells Nastenka that he would give up all his years of fantasy for a single day of real life. Yet at the story's end, when she writes to offer continued friendship, he refuses, unwilling to accept a relationship that doesn't conform to his fantasies. As is true of the protagonists in the stories that follow in this collection, the dreamer's interaction with a young woman is material for his fantasy. However, unlike the bitter men in the later stories, the white nights dreamer remains grateful, concluding, "My God, a whole moment of happiness! Is that too little for the whole of a man's life?" (p. 228).

While the dreamer clearly expects his imaginary interlocutors to answer yes, Dostoevsky, behind his dreamer's back, clearly answers no. The dreamer may be sympathetic, but his decision to withdraw reveals a serious problem: the desire to control life by viewing himself and others as literary characters. This problem also manifests itself in Dostoevsky's later solitaries: They all attempt to script roles for themselves and others, a strategy that allows them to remain within the boundaries of the known and familiar. By defending themselves against shame with narcissistic self-enclosure, they employ an age-old, universal response to shame, one that characterizes the contemporary period. Dostoevsky's penetrating insights into the dynamics of shame ensure his characters' immortality.

The Underground Man

"Notes from Underground" is another Dostoevskian study in shame. While Golyadkin protects himself by splitting and the white nights dreamer by fantasizing, Dostoevsky's underground man intellectualizes. The three protagonists differ as radically as do their defenses, but they all expose their narcissistic limitations by treating a young woman as a literary construct.

Golyadkin fantasizes about rescuing and eloping with Klara, the object of his ambition (although he only causes the real Klara a few unpleasant moments). The chivalric white nights dreamer casts off his protective shell in order to help Nastenka. The underground man, on the other hand, engages in savior fantasies, yet intentionally insults and injures the real Liza. The underground man's deliberate cruelty, as he himself acknowledges, springs from deep shame—which he then passes on to others.

Dostoevsky shows in this story how shame can shade into guilt, a dynamic he was to explore for the rest of his life. Shame relates broadly to human identity, guilt more narrowly to human action. Shame arises from negative self-assessment, which arouses feelings of inferiority or inadequacy; or from feeling oneself to be the object of another's attention; or from a feeling of exclusion from the social realm. In contrast, guilt arises from a transgression of personal, moral, social, or legal norms. Shame and guilt can be related, but need not be. The underground man is ashamed of his face, for example, but he does not feel guilty about the way he looks. In part II the underground man passes on his shame, and in doing so harms Liza. He thereby compounds his original shame with the shame of knowing he is the kind of person who has harmed another. The underground man's shame leads to evil action and thus to haunting guilt. He writes partly to relieve his guilt, but he cannot—largely because he cannot escape the prison of his shame.

While the underground man dominates the text, Dostoevsky retains control of the story, from the very outset providing readers with many clues to the underground man's psychology and how it shapes his narrative. The underground man's famous first lines—"I am a sick man . . . I am a spiteful man. I am an unattractive man" (p. 233)—reveal his negative self-image. The lines also reveal Dostoevsky's authorial hand, for they expose the underground man's painful self-consciousness and thus the presence of shame. When the underground man announces that he is "sick," readers may surmise physical or psychic illness. When he declares that perhaps his liver hurts, he indicates physical illness. However, Olga Meerson demonstrates that Dostoevsky uses the underground man's diagnosis to suggest metaphysical illness by alluding to the Old Testament book of Lamentations. While the underground man remains resolutely earthbound, Dostoevsky suggests that he suffers from metaphysical desolation due to separation from God (Meerson, "Old Testament Lamentation in the Underground Man's Monologue"; see "For Further Reading").

The underground man's second statement, that he is "spiteful," reinforces the story's metaphysical dimension, for he uses the Russian word *zloi*, which also means "evil." By emphasizing his spitefulness in what follows, the underground man encourages a psychological reading. Dostoevsky, on the other hand, evokes the concepts of "good" and "evil," thereby underscoring the story's ethical dimension and showing how the underground man's spite leads to evil. Dostoevsky exposes the underground man's statement that he has succeeded in being neither "evil" nor "good" as a harmful neutrality; he will revisit this concept when he tackles the ethical implications of the ridiculous man's indifference.

The underground man's third adjective, "unattractive," blurs the boundaries between the physical and the moral; it also emphasizes his painful self-consciousness and thus his sensitivity to shame. His next lines reveal his self-conscious defiance of his audience's opinion. This is a startling narrative strategy that paradoxically underscores the very emotional vulnerability the man is attempting to conceal. Dostoevsky has his underground man protest too much; his anxious attempts to demonstrate how little he cares about the opinions of others expose his obsessive concern. With these opening lines, Dostoevsky the author instructs us to read more into the underground man's words than his narrator himself intends.

In the second paragraph, Dostoevsky provides another critical clue for readers: The underground man reveals that he is ashamed of his emotional neediness, which he perceives as weakness. This revelation prepares readers for the narrator's narcissistic rages: He first lashes out at those who witness his weakness and then flagellates himself for expressing his anger. His inability to control his public image exacerbates his shame. The underground man acknowledges the near-impossibility of his task—he writes partly to relieve himself of oppressive memories (hoping, pre-Freud, to effect a talking cure), but he refuses to acknowledge wrongdoing, for to do so would be shameful. The underground man's shame stifles his attempts to relieve his conscience.

In the same paragraph, the man boasts that he can repress his positive emotions. By having him acknowledge this defense, Dostoevsky signals readers to look for repression in the unusual structure of the text: The underground man lays out his ideology in part I but withholds most of his biography until part II. However, it is only after reading part II that we realize that the underground man's theorizing in part I derives from his painful experiences of twenty years earlier. The underground man, we understand, is generalizing his personal experiences into metaphysical pronouncements. For example, in part I he compares the laws of nature and the theory of determinism to a stone wall. He argues that men of action accept the existence of stone walls and work around them, while men of consciousness bang themselves against stone walls, deliberately causing themselves pain in order to protest the laws of nature. In part II we discover that the source of this analogy is the underground man's servant Apollon, a rigid man who withstands the man's attempts to bend him to his own will. Apollon remains the same; the underground man ceaselessly battles, loses, and suffers. The underground man's metaphysical truth turns out to be a psychological particular.

The structure of parts I and II also reveals the underground man's desire for control. While he states that he is going to talk about himself, the man carefully controls his public image, concealing or delaying some facts as he reveals others. In both parts he delays the pain of self-exposure for as long as possible. It is only at the end of his theorizing in part I, for example, that he reveals that he began his writing project to gain relief from an oppressive memory. In part II he writes first about his coworkers, his sidewalk duel, and his former schoolmates, and only then recounts the haunting story of Liza. The underground man's delaying tactics reveal his defenses: He conceals his emotional vulnerability by constructing an abrasive exterior.

The man also aggressively assaults his readers in a narrative strategy that imitates his behavior in the story: Just as he passes his shame on to Liza, so he tries to pass his shame on to his readers. The underground man periodically exchanges his habitual first-person singular pronoun "I" for the collective "we," projecting his beliefs or habits onto his audience. His extended use of "we" near the end of his "notes" reveals his narrative strategy:

> Excuse me, gentlemen, I am not justifying myself with that 'all of us.' As for what concerns me in particular I have only in my life carried to an extreme what you have not dared to carry halfway. . . . We are oppressed at being humans, humans with our own real bodies and blood; we are ashamed of it, we think it a disgrace, and we keep trying to be some sort of fairy-tale universal beings (p. 351).

The underground man claims that we are all fallen creatures, we are all ashamed of ourselves, we are all seeking to be other than what we are. In short, he hopes to alleviate his shame by sharing it, a strategy that Camus borrowed when writing his novel *The Fall.*

The underground man's assault on his readers explains his eventual failure to relieve his conscience. As Robert Belknap has noted, the underground man does not repent (Belknap, "The Unrepentant Confession"). He cannot escape his bad conscience because he refuses to give his audience the authority to forgive him. Confession can provide relief for both guilt and shame, but only if the one confessing gives his audience the authority to either forgive his transgression (guilt) or to accept him as he is (shame). But the underground man will not relinquish authority. As he repeatedly demonstrates, he prefers self-enclosure to egalitarianism. His psychological defenses become ethical defects and leave him no exit.

Though the underground man has entered the pantheon of literary and philosophical classics as a universal type, at the very outset of his text Dostoevsky grounds him in a particular sociopolitical climate. In his authorial footnote (p. 229), Dostoevsky insists that his underground man is both a literary construct and the product of Russian reality in the mid-nineteenth century. Twentieth-century readers know Dostoevsky for his fiction, but he was also an active journalist. He wrote "Notes from Underground" in 1864 as part of his journalistic polemic with Russia's radical intelligentsia. The underground man directly challenges the Russian nihilists' theory of "rational egoism," which denied the existence of free will and held that human beings act in accordance with what they consider their own best interests. This theory found its most famous statement in a novel by Russia's leading radical, Nikolay Chernyshevsky. Written in 1863, *What Is to Be Done?* became a classic of the Russian revolutionary movement (embraced by the Communist leader Vladimir Lenin, among others). The main characters of this didactic novel see themselves as "enlightened" egoists acting in their own best interests, which, it turns out, are also the best interests of others. As a consequence, their actions benefit others. As the philosopher James Scanlan masterfully shows, Dostoevsky has his underground man attack the theory of rational egoism from the perspective of a real egoist (Scanlan, *Dostoevsky the Thinker*, p. 62). Dostoevsky debunks the cardboard realism of Chernyshevsky's altruistic heroes by creating a more psychologically compelling, if repelling, personality. Like Dostoevsky, the underground man is a man of the 1840s, educated on German idealism and European romanticism. Yet, whereas his polemics are Dostoevsky's, his arguments are not. In Dostoevsky's text, the man is the message.

So what does it mean to be an underground man? Above all, "the underground" has come to signify a state of mind, a self-consciousness that the narrator brands a "disease." In Dostoevsky's view, self-consciousness and its attendant egoism come from the modernizing West, a land of fragmentation, individualism, and alienation. Most important, Dostoevsky views separation from God as a Western import to Russia, part of Peter the Great's legacy. By contrast, he sees an unmediated love of Christ in the Russian people. In both glorifying and vilifying self-consciousness, the underground man exposes himself as someone who both embraces and reviles Western modes of thought.

Readers understand "underground" figuratively but also interpret the word in a literal sense. Generations have envisioned the underground man as someone who lives in a basement apartment, ignoring evidence at the end of part II that he lives on an upper floor! In part I, the underground man declares his marginality by announcing that he lives in a "corner," an apartment at the edge of St. Petersburg. He calls St. Petersburg "the most abstract and premeditated city on the whole earth," but also claims that it is bad for his health. By describing his city simultaneously as a physical place (bad for his health) and a mental construct (Tsar Peter's vision imposed from above), the underground man muddies the distinction between the two.

Even after the underground man runs down the stairs after Liza, we persist in thinking of the underground as a basement. Dostoevsky, however, packs the underground man's upper-story lodging with meaning. On a sociological level, an upper floor indicates poverty, while on a psychological level it indicates alienation, a mental life divorced from Russian soil. Dostoevsky thus identifies the underground man, like the pawnbroker and the ridiculous man in the stories that follow, as a product of Peter's Russia: His reality is a mental construction, divorced from the world around him. Dostoevsky draws on the myth of St. Petersburg to enhance the metaphysical dimension of "Notes from Underground." He evokes Peter's ambiguous legacy of duality, the myth in which Peter was seen alternately as Creator and Antichrist and St. Petersburg as the cosmic battleground for human souls (see the first page of this introduction). The underground man proves himself to be Peter's son—an abstract thinker alienated from the Christian faith of the Russian people.

Although he returns to the earth to seek Liza, he stops to reflect, abandons his search, and returns to his upper-story apartment; the apartment becomes a symbol of his alienation.

To be an underground man is to be a divided, self-conscious, modern self. At the opening of part II the underground man admits, "I hated my face, for instance: I thought it disgusting, and even suspected that there was something base in my expression. . . . And what was worst of all, I thought it actually stupid looking" (p. 271). The underground man feels a terrible disjunction between his actual and desired appearance. Consequently, he expends great energy controlling his public image: "So every day when I turned up at the office I tried to behave as independently as possible, and to assume a lofty expression, so that I might not be suspected of being abject" (p. 271).

The underground man suffers shame at this basic fact of his own identity. He suffers further shame from his inability to control his public appearance: "But I was positively and painfully certain that it was impossible for my face ever to express those qualities" (p. 271). The underground man embodies shame's paradox, which is its capacity to isolate yet relate. The underground man's shame isolates him and makes him feel unworthy to be a self-presenting agent; at the same time it emphasizes his dependence on others for his sense of self. Shame reminds individuals of the community they have lost by exacerbating their self-consciousness and therefore their isolation. The underground man lives in self-imposed alienation, yet he longs to belong. As he admits, "I could never stand more than three months of dreaming at a time without feeling an irresistible desire to plunge into society" (p. 285). After visits to his department chief, his "only permanent acquaintance," he states, "I deferred for a time my desire to embrace all mankind" (p. 286). The underground man suffers the consequences of his earlier decision to break completely with his past. In giving up the prestigious job he was offered and accepting an insignificant post, he has diminished his world.

Part of the underground man's shame derives from anxiety

over exclusion from the social realm. As he makes abundantly clear, he may exercise his free will to isolate himself, but when he exercises his free will to enter the social realm, he wants to be included. He is torn between the desire to crush and humiliate his classmates and the desire to attract and dominate them. Yet his long stretches of solitude and fantasy deprive him of social skills, and he makes gaffs that exacerbate his shame. Shame in turn exacerbates his awkwardness and leads to exclusion; exclusion enrages him. His inability to control his rage leaves him feeling more exposed than before and thus redoubles his shame. His writing exemplifies this catch-22: He hopes to escape isolation by writing, yet he sticks his tongue out at his readers. Such antithetical impulses explain why the fictional editor at the story's end calls the underground man a "paradoxalist."

The underground man's paradoxical nature also reveals itself when he exerts his free will. In part I he argues that exerting free will in defiance of the laws of nature may be irrational and provides as examples his refusal to see a doctor or a dentist. While he demonstrates that exercising free will in an irrational way may harm him, he argues that it also proves his individuality, thereby elevating him above those who act unthinkingly; thus, despite its seeming disadvantage, it is actually "the most advantageous advantage." Throughout part II, however, the underground man provides more examples of how he has harmed himself through exercising his free will, thereby undermining his argument: He chooses to live with Apollon, the servant who torments him. He engages in a one-sided duel. He invites himself to dinner with Zverkov and behaves badly.

In all these cases, the underground man chiefly harms himself. But in both encounters with Liza, he inflicts deep suffering on another—a socially humiliated and defenseless woman. While he preaches free will in part I, in part II he reveals that his irrational choices are largely driven by shame and therefore are not "free." When he feels vulnerable and out of place, he responds by becoming defensive and irrational. Instead of protesting the laws of nature, the underground man is protecting his fragile ego. Dostoevsky demonstrates that his antihero reacts more than he acts. He may propound free will, but he does not act freely; he is motivated more by his emotional defenses than his intellect. He calls free will a force of life, yet his own choices and actions are mechanical. He continually rejects the social bonds that can save him from himself.

Dostoevsky clearly shows that the roots of the underground man's tragedy lie in his narcissism. The underground man cannot conceive of a world in which other individuals think or act differently from him. This tragedy expresses itself most vividly in the story of Liza. He meets her, as mentioned, after a series of humiliations that are largely self-inflicted. He arrives at the brothel prepared to challenge Zverkov to duel, but his classmates have dispersed, and he goes with Liza instead. After he wakes from his sex-and-alcohol induced sleep, the underground man plays out his revenge—not on the men who have witnessed his humiliation, but on a woman who suffers daily humiliation.

Here Dostoevsky pulls out all stops. At this moment, while lying naked and vulnerable in a brothel bed, his antihero bares his own psyche. While their bodies are exposed, Liza's emotional defenses are up, and the underground man takes this as a challenge. Using his rhetorical skills, his ability to create "pictures" and talk "like a book," he penetrates her defenses and reduces her to tears. But then, carried away by his own success, he demonstrates his dependence on literature as a model for life. Inspired by contemporary tales of redeeming prostitutes, the underground man gives Liza his address. This begins a second shame scenario.

His first encounter with Liza occurs just after he has been humiliated. Then, under the guise of compassion, he exposes to her the full horror and humiliation of her position and offers her a way out. Over the next days, he suffers paroxysms of shame, fearing that she will accept his offer and see for herself the gap between his rhetorical and actual selves. Far from being able to help her, he is mired in poverty and spiritual inertia. His worst fears are realized: Liza arrives at a moment when he is physically and emotionally exposed. She witnesses both his poverty and his impotent rage at his servant Apollon.

Their second encounter begins, once again, with his humiliation. But the script has changed. They are in his space, not hers. This time Liza expects something from him—hope, human kindness, a way out. He experiences her gaze as humiliating, her expectations as a restriction of his free will. He resolves to punish her. Describing their silence over tea, the underground man writes: "I was obstinately silent. I was, of course, myself the chief sufferer, because I was fully conscious of the disgusting meanness of my spiteful stupidity" (p. 342). Behind the narrator's back, Dostoevsky reveals his character's insufferable egoism. Overwhelmed by shame, the underground man refuses to see that Liza suffers as much or even more than he does. Despite the clear inequality of their positions (as he earlier observed, he is free to degrade himself, while she no longer has a choice), he claims that his suffering surpasses hers.

As she moves to leave, he lashes out, explaining to her the dynamics of passed-on shame:

> You've come because I talked sentimental stuff to you then. . . .
> So you may as well know that I was laughing at you then. . . . I
> had been insulted just before, at dinner, by the fellows who
> came that evening before me. I came to you, meaning to thrash
> one of them, an officer; but I didn't succeed, I didn't find him;
> I had to avenge the insult on some one to get back my own
> again; you turned up, I vented my spleen on you and laughed
> at you. I had been humiliated, so I wanted to humiliate; I had
> been treated like a rag, so I wanted to show my power (p. 342).

The underground man is explaining here how shame turns into guilt. He is shamed by others, so he shames Liza. In the brothel he relents and displays some kindness. Once Liza witnesses his further shame, however, he resolves to punish her. In the end, spurred on by his shame, he inflicts real and potentially lasting hurt on her. He explains, in clinical detail, the causes of his narcissistic rage:

Well, anyway, I know that I am a blackguard, a scoundrel, an egoist, a sluggard. Here I have been shuddering for the last three days at the thought of your coming. And do you know what has worried me particularly for these three days? That I posed as such a hero to you, and now you would see me in a wretched torn dressing-gown, beggarly, loathsome. I told you just now that I was not ashamed of my poverty; so you may as well know that I am ashamed of it; I am more ashamed of it than of anything, more afraid of it than of being found out if I were a thief, because I am as vain as though I had been skinned and the very air blowing on me hurt. Surely by now you must realize that I shall never forgive you for having found me in this wretched dressing-gown, just as I was flying at Apollon like a spiteful cur. The saviour, the former hero, was flying like a mangy, unkempt sheep-dog at his lackey, and the lackey was jeering at him! And I shall never forgive you for the tears I could not help shedding before you just now, like some silly woman put to shame! And for what I am confessing to you now, I shall never forgive you either! (p. 344)

Instead of responding to his words, Liza responds to the anguish behind them. She stuns him because she does not act according to a clichéd script. Furthermore, by acting with compassion she reverses their roles. The underground man cannot bear this turn of events. Earlier, when he brought Liza to tears in the brothel, she had revealed to him her treasure, a love letter from a student, which she held as proof of her worth. When he bursts into tears himself, he suffers shame, which arouses his self-consciousness. Thus, even as his emotions overwhelm him, his mind starts to calculate. To protect his exposed feelings, he turns the act of lovemaking into an act of power. Instead of accepting Liza's love, he chooses to humiliate her. In this final act, he reveals the full tragedy of the underground. Dostoevsky's champion of free will demonstrates that he is trapped by the defenses he has erected to protect himself.

In rejecting life and love, the underground man reveals the poverty of his imagination. He cannot respond to others with spontaneity or generosity. He sees love as an act not of reciprocity but of subjugation: "With me loving meant tyrannizing and showing my moral superiority. I have never in my life been able to imagine any other sort of love. . . . Even in my underground dreams I did not imagine love except as a struggle" (p. 347). His view of love as a power struggle locks him into a dynamic that permits only two outcomes: mastery or submission. His final words reveal the crux of his tragedy: "I began it always with hatred and ended it with moral subjugation, and afterwards I never knew what to do with the subjugated object" (p. 347). This stunning statement exposes the underground man's greatest limitation. By choosing to see others as objects rather than equals, he denies himself the possibility of meaningful relationships. He also deprives himself of the possibility for self-knowledge. In creating the world in his own image, he perpetuates his self-enclosure. The underground man's shame drives him to solipsism.

The underground man demonstrates his desire to escape his self-constructed prison through his writing. In chapter XI he gives his reason for writing by posing a question: "How can a man be left alone with nothing to do for forty years?" (p. 265). The question contains three key concepts: isolation, idleness, and exile. By stressing his isolation, the underground man expresses a mute desire for community. In confessing idleness, he expresses a need for meaningful activity. Forty years refers to his age. Forty years also alludes to the biblical period of exile—forty years in the desert; the underground man is unconsciously expressing a metaphysical longing for a spiritual home. This reveals the impulses behind his writing: He wants to be part of the human community, to engage in meaningful activity, and to find his place in the physical and metaphysical worlds.

The underground man also wants to test his ability to tell the truth about himself. He thus engages in Dostoevsky's ongoing polemic with Jean-Jacques Rousseau. Rousseau's autobiographical work, *Confessions* (1781), shocked the reading public with its revelations of shame. It was a literary project that mirrored Rousseau's private vice: visiting dark alleys to expose his private parts, at a distance, to young women. Like Rousseau, Dostoevsky's underground man writes a literary confession that exposes his shame. Like Rousseau, he hopes the process of confession will provide him relief. But in both cases, vanity undermines the project. Rousseau cannot obtain relief from his shame because he takes pride in it. The underground man cannot obtain relief because he has locked others out. As the psychologist Michael Lewis observes, confession allows the shamed person to distance himself from the emotional experience of shame by providing him with the opportunity to join others in viewing himself (Lewis, *Shame: The Exposed Self*, p. 132). Confession only provides release from shame, however, if the shamed person chooses a confessor (an audience) that possesses the ability to forgive and love. The underground man claims that he wants to tell the truth about himself, but he also denies that he's writing for an audience. He claims that he's addressing his notes to readers for "form's sake," hinting that there are things one cannot admit to others, or even to oneself.

> Every man has memories which he would not tell to every one, but only to his friends. He has other matters in his mind which he would not reveal even to his friends, but only to himself, and that in secret. But there are other things which a man is afraid to tell even to himself, and every decent man has a number of such things stored away in his mind. The more decent he is, the greater the number of such things in his mind. Anyway, I have only lately determined to remember some of my early adventures. Till now I have always avoided them, even with a certain uneasiness (p. 266).

Here the underground man reveals his dilemma: He wants to confront some of his repressed memories, but doing so will be painful and shameful. He thus denies the presence of an audience as he comes to terms with his own past. And yet he can only release himself from shame's pain by reaching out to others. As Robin Feuer Miller points out, for Dostoevsky "the genuine confession always serves to reunite man with other men and with the whole universe" (Miller, "Dostoevsky and Rousseau: The Morality of Confession Reconsidered"). The underground man both courts and rejects forgiveness. This goes one step beyond Rousseau, who engages in an *apologia* rather than a confession. As Belknap explains, an Augustinian, repentant confession takes the form "I did it, and it was wrong;" a Rousseauist *apologia* takes the form "I did it, and it was right." Dostoevsky's underground man engages in what Belknap calls an "unrepentant" confession, which takes the form "I did it, and it was wrong, but that's how I am" (Belknap, p. 121). The underground man confounds all expectations. But his choice also explains his failure, for he admits that he is writing as a form of therapy. Readers understand that he cannot stop writing because he still needs to express himself, that he is still seeking self-knowledge, and that he is still in pain.

The underground man's pain persists because he refuses to admit his wrongdoing. After he abandons his search for Liza, he rationalizes:

> Will it not be better that she should keep the resentment of the insult for ever? Resentment—why, it is purification; it is a most stinging and painful consciousness! To-morrow I should have defiled her soul and have exhausted her heart, while now the feeling of insult will never die in her heart, and however loathsome the filth awaiting her—the feeling of insult will elevate and purify her . . . by hatred . . . h'm! . . . perhaps, too, by forgiveness. . . . Will all that make things easier for her though? (p. 349)

As he attempts to justify his behavior, the underground man bares his soul, indirectly arguing that the feelings of insult he has experienced will elevate and purify him—by hatred. Sensing that his logic may not apply to Liza, however, he adds, "perhaps, too, by forgiveness." His encounter with Liza, who responds intuitively rather than logically, provides the underground man a glimpse of a way out of his self-enclosure.

Forgiveness, however, entails reciprocity, and the underground man prefers to inflict his pain on others. His writing project resembles his toothache. He does not want to suffer in silence; he wants others to feel his pain and suffer with him. He finds sensual pleasure in his moans because they indicate that he is in control. He may have no control over the pain, but he controls its expression: He knows "that he might moan differently, more simply, without trills and flourishes, and that he is only amusing himself like that from ill-humour, from malignancy. Well, in all these recognitions and disgraces it is that there lies a voluptuous pleasure" (p. 244). The underground man reveals that his pleasure in writing derives from being able to embellish his pain to sharpen others' awareness of him. Faced with isolation and exclusion, he chooses to expose himself. Like Rousseau, he forces others to acknowledge his presence. Like Rousseau, he acts out a script in which he is the only actor. His discourse on toothaches reveals his egoism: Instead of seeing himself as part of a community whose members all suffer a toothache at some time, he takes the toothache personally.

In Liza, Dostoevsky shows an alternative to the underground man's self-enclosure. Liza is also isolated, humiliated, and poor. She also erects barriers. Yet when she sees the underground man's pain, she reaches out to him as a fellow sufferer and freely offers to share his pain. Her compassion provides an answer to the underground man's discourse on the egotistical adage "the most advantageous advantage."

Unlike the underground man, Liza sees herself in relation to others, not opposed to them. She breaks out of the role he would cast her in. As Dostoevsky repeatedly shows, the underground man's insistence on superiority rather than reciprocity exposes his greatest limitation. To escape from the underground, he needs to see himself not as an isolated individual but as part of a community. He needs to overcome the limits of his rationality by listening to his heart.

Dostoevsky wrote "Notes from Underground" to demonstrate that theory cannot wholly account for human behavior. To debunk contemporary theories of rational or enlightened egoism, Dostoevsky proposes acts of love and compassion. He also undermines the underground man's championship of free will by showing not only that it is driven by shame, but that it causes him to harm himself as well as others. By refusing to acknowledge and repent his evil actions, the underground man loses all hope of relief. The first-person narrators of the stories that follow face similar predicaments. They are also narcissists jolted out of their defensive inertia by encounters with young women in distress. The pawnbroker in "The Meek One" eventually acknowledges his guilt; the ridiculous man embraces his guilt, sheds his shame, and becomes a prophet of love.

The Meek One

"The Meek One" first appeared in the November 1876 issue of Dostoevsky's journal *The Diary of a Writer*. One of the most popular journals of its day, the *Diary* combined social and political commentary, reports on contemporary court cases, reminiscences, and fiction. It began as a column in *The Citizen*, a journal that Dostoevsky edited from 1872 to 1874, and became an independent journal in 1876. Dostoevsky suspended its publication to work on *The Brothers Karamazov* and produced a few issues later on in 1880 and 1881. Dostoevsky's diary writer was a chatty persona who attempted to make sense out of current events, and who spoke frequently, but not always, for Dostoevsky the author. This unique narrative strategy of the *Diary* appealed to a broad range of readers, liberals as well as conservatives, and earned Dostoevsky the title of Russia's prophet.

In "The Meek One" and "The Dream of a Ridiculous Man" (April 1877), two of the most famous stories published in the *Diary*, Dostoevsky contrasts alienated, isolated, Western-educated men with young girls in crisis. Both stories reflect many of the oppositions that were addressed by their host publication: West vs. Russia; rationality vs. intuition; atheism vs. belief; alienation vs. rootedness in one's native soil; isolation vs. community; apathy vs. "living life"; linear thinking vs. contextual thinking; complacency vs. anxiety. These oppositions operate on psychological, sociopolitical, and metaphysical levels and reflect two dominant underlying metaphors—those of separation and union. Read individually, each of these masterpieces transcends its Russian setting; read as part of Dostoevsky's *Diary*, each reflects it.

"The Meek One" demonstrates Dostoevsky's commitment to examining contemporary life. In October 1876 he read a short newspaper article about a young seamstress who jumped to her death from a sixth-floor window while holding an icon. Haunted by this paradoxical image of despair and belief, Dostoevsky wrote his haunting story. Its placement in the *Diary* reflects Dostoevsky's interest in the broader issues of suicide, broken families, self-enclosure, and women's rights.

Dostoevsky embedded the paradoxical elements of shame into the real-life paradoxical image that inspired "The Meek One." Once again he chose an anonymous, first-person narrator. Like the white nights dreamer and the underground man, the pawnbroker is a loner whose encounter with a young woman in distress changes his life. Like the white nights dreamer, he fantasizes about love and happiness; like the underground man, he has fled a shameful past. Unlike either, the pawnbroker meets a woman who is twenty-five years younger, an age disparity that contributes to the tragedy.

In "The Meek One," Dostoevsky reprises the theme of gender inequity and its social consequences seen in "Notes from Underground." The underground man and the pawnbroker are both poor but independent agents with some career options. Liza and the meek one are both young women driven to desperation by families who plan to sell them. In them Dostoevsky illustrates the dilemma of many young women of his time: Where do they go when there is nowhere to go? The meek one's initial choices are bleak: Marry a wife-beating widower or find a position that compromises her. Each time she advertises for a job, she lowers her requirements. The pawnbroker sees that her next option will involve compromising herself and, at the eleventh hour, offers to marry her. The meek one accepts his unexpected proposal; however, she is unprepared for the daily humiliations she suffers as his wife. He rebuffs her affection, restricts her movements, pinches pennies on household expenses, and imposes a reign of silence. The meek one thus moves from an overtly hostile and exploitative household to a covertly repressive one. Ironically, while posing as her liberator, the pawnbroker limits his young wife's independence.

While the first-person narrative focuses on the pawnbroker's personal tragedy, Dostoevsky's choice of title reveals a broader sociopolitical agenda. *Krotkaya* is Russian for "meek one," a term that has biblical references to Christ's Sermon on the Mount ("Blessed are the meek, for they will inherit the earth," Matthew 5:5, New International Version). Meekness also forms part of a paired opposition conceived by Apollon Grigoriev, a Russian writer who collaborated with the Dostoevsky brothers on their journals *Vremya* (Time, 1861–1863) and *Epokha* (Epoch, 1864–1865). As chief critic of *Epokha*, Grigoriev developed a theory of "organic criticism," which argued that all art must spring from its native soil. He saw "meekness" as a native Russian trait that was opposed to the "predatory" quality of Europeans. Dostoyevsky thus fuses gender politics, organic criticism, and a Christian message in the story's title.

Early in the story, the pawnbroker reveals his pleasure at the disparity in age, class, and education between himself and the meek one. He is a member of the hereditary nobility who served in an elite military regiment, and he reveals his European education by citing Goethe's *Faust*. In contrast, the meek one, orphaned at the age of twelve or thirteen, had to supplement the little schooling she received as the daughter of a nonhereditary nobleman by taking courses while she worked for her aunts. The pawnbroker is born to privilege and rank; the meek one loses all when she loses her parents. As soon as the pawnbroker learns of the future awaiting her, he confesses, "I looked upon her then as *mine* and did not doubt of my power" (p. 362). The pawnbroker attempts to mold the meek one into his ideal wife, and, in so doing, curbs her freedom. He represses all her spontaneity, generosity, independence, and love. While he has a goal, he never shares it with her; his actions make sense to him, but are senseless tyranny to her.

The pawnbroker's strictness drives the meek one to revolt. She first generously helps the captain's widow, causing the pawnbroker to banish her from the shop. She next defies him by flirting with an old enemy of his, from whom she learns of his past shame. After spying on her, the pawnbroker reveals himself, and, like a jailer, brings her home. Finally, one evening she takes his revolver and puts it to his forehead without firing. He wakes, sees her, and closes his eyes. In his view, this act proves his courage, thereby allowing him to regain the honor he'd lost when he had declined to fight for his regiment. From that night on, they sleep separately.

When his wife becomes seriously ill and the pawnbroker realizes that she may die, he expends money and care to save her. She recovers but remains distant from him. He realizes that she has locked him out when she starts singing to herself. Frantically, he throws himself at her feet and tells her of his past shame as well as his plans for their future. This radical reversal drives her to suicide.

As in his earlier first-person narratives, Dostoevsky focuses on the pawnbroker's shame as a major motive for his action. As the meek one perspicuously notes, the pawnbroker is "revenging" himself on society (p. 360) for his past humiliations. After refusing to fight a duel to defend his regiment's honor, he pre-emptively resigns his commission. Since his brother-in-law had squandered his inheritance, the pawnbroker is plunged into dreadful poverty. Saved from homelessness by a small legacy from an aunt, he chooses a profession that gives him personal and financial independence. He loses social status but gains power.

The pawnbroker's shame also shapes his interaction with his wife. Having constricted his own world, he proceeds to constrict hers. When she rebels, he punishes and subdues her. When she initiates their sexual separation, he formalizes it by buying her a separate bed. This, however, provides her with an independence that proves his undoing—she chooses her own

form of protective self-enclosure. Wracked by guilt, she promises to be a faithful wife. Yet she remains scarred by his abuse
and withdraws into herself so completely that at times she forgets him. Her withdrawal elicits an hysterical confession from
him:

> I did not even hide what I had hidden from myself all my
> life. . . . I explained to her that I really had been cowardly that
> time in the refreshment bar, that . . . I was not afraid of a duel,
> but of its being stupid . . . and afterwards I would not own it
> and tormented every one and had tormented her for it, and had
> married her so as to torment her for it (p. 396).

Like the underground man, the pawnbroker fears ridicule. His
touchy pride thus dictates his actions. Like Liza, the meek one
realizes that he is exaggerating out of pain. Like Liza, this humiliated child tries to calm the wounded man before her.

The meek one cannot give her husband what he demands
because his narcissistic wound goes too deep. Under the guise
of love, he uses her. He had hoped to alleviate his shame and
isolation by marrying her:

> But when I brought her into my home I thought I was bring-
> ing a friend, and I needed a friend so much. But I saw clearly
> that the friend must be trained, schooled, even conquered.
> Could I have explained myself straight off to a girl of sixteen
> with her prejudices? . . . And though no one knew about it [the
> incident with the revolver], she knew, and for me that was every-
> thing, because she was everything for me, all the hope of the fu-
> ture that I cherished in my dreams! She was the one person I
> had prepared for myself, and I needed no one else (p. 388).

Like the underground man, the pawnbroker responds to his
own deep shame by trying to control the world. He scripts roles
for others. From his wife he demands the impossible: that she
understand him without explanation and that she be *everything*
he needs. In addition to showing how the pawnbroker's shame

drives his possessiveness and will to power, Dostoevsky demonstrates how he underestimates the meek one's ability to understand his shame. Instead of appealing to her love and intuition, the pawnbroker chooses to dominate her. His defenses against shame shackle them both.

Like the underground man, the pawnbroker views others as literary constructs rather than as flesh-and-blood individuals. The silent duel with his young wife satisfies him. Even after she recovers from her illness, the pawnbroker withholds his plans for their future: "In fact, I purposely deferred the climax: what had happened was, meanwhile, enough for my peace of mind and provided a great number of pictures and materials for my dreams. That is what is wrong, that I am a dreamer: I had enough material for my dreams, and about her, I thought she could *wait*" (p. 388). Behind his narrator's back, Dostoevsky once again demonstrates narcissism's destructive power. The pawnbroker views his wife as material for his own fantasies.

His self-enclosure is not lost on the meek one, who quietly mutters "*I thought that you would leave me like that*" (p. 394), a heartrending statement that reveals the spiritual hell he has created for her. He has been slowly murdering her soul, depriving her of every outlet for the good in her heart. He does not see the selfishness of his love. Even when he changes the script, he acts on his own fantasies. He decides that he must take her to Boulogne, to a "different sun," before they return to a "new life" in St. Petersburg. By deciding to take her abroad, the pawnbroker plans to rip his wife from her native soil.

Faced with the prospect of complete isolation in a foreign country with a husband who plans to reassert his conjugal rights and focus his relentlessly narcissistic attention on her, the meek one chooses death. Instead of accepting her husband's embraces, she clasps her family icon to her breast and steps out the window. The icon represents the Mother of God holding her divine son, thereby symbolizing familial love. Dostoevsky thus artfully contrasts the pawnbroker's predatory love with the meek one's love of family. He also charges her choice with a political message: The child of Russia refuses to be uprooted from her native soil. Leaving only "a teaspoonful of blood" (p. 402) as a sign of her internal wounds, she eludes the pawnbroker's predatory clutches.

As Dostoevsky explains in his preface to "The Meek One," he chooses a fantastic frame, the stenographic transcription of the pawnbroker's thoughts, to convey the highly realistic internal dialogue of a man confronted with his wife's corpse. Citing Victor Hugo's novel *The Last Day of a Condemned Man* as his narrative model, Dostoevsky argues that the fantastic frame allows him to convey an otherwise inaccessible realism. Faced with the cold, hard fact of his wife's suicide, incontrovertible evidence that she was not a fictional construct but a flesh-and-blood woman, the pawnbroker comes to understand the "truth." Unlike the underground man, who persistently denies wrongdoing, the pawnbroker eventually accepts responsibility for his actions: "I worried her to death, that is what it is!" (p. 402). In doing so, he takes a step out of his narcissistic self-enclosure. The story ends with the pawnbroker's anguished cry, "What will become of me?" (p. 403), leaving readers to wonder whether a moment's truth can change a lifetime of narcissism.

The Ridiculous Man

With "The Dream of a Ridiculous Man," Dostoevsky returns to the fantastic realism of "The Double." The last piece of fiction published in the *Diary*, it exploits all of Dostoevsky's ideological oppositions as it engages his lifelong polemic on suicide. In the story's first six paragraphs, the ridiculous man associates himself with European atheism and rationality, confesses to isolation and apathy, and demonstrates his desire to maintain a solipsistic, complacent life. Yet real life intrudes in the form of a little girl begging for his help. He brushes her off but then loses his complacency, a loss that shakes his resolve to commit suicide. While he is contemplating his feelings, the ridiculous man has a fantastic, life-saving dream.

Like Dostoevsky's other solitaries, the ridiculous man is a divided self whose emotions war with his reason; unlike them, his apathetic melancholy leads him to seek philosophical relief. He conforms to the psychological type identified by William James as susceptible to sudden conversions (James, *The Varieties of Religious Experience*). The little girl's cry for help pierces his armor of apathy and sends him on a journey of conversion. His defenses against shame thus prepare him for radical change!

Dostoevsky flags the role of shame in this story with the first sentence: "I am a ridiculous man" (p. 407). In the second sentence, the narrator reports how others perceive him: "Now they call me a madman." He then reveals that these labels no longer cause him to suffer because he has seen "the truth." With this opening paragraph, Dostoevsky indicates the way in which moral insight shapes identity.

As he tells the story of his conversion, the ridiculous man creates a distance between his telling self and his experiencing self. He notes that he responded to shame by withdrawal and ratiocination. Throughout his adolescence, for example, the ridiculous man locked himself in a protective shell. Nonetheless, he worried obsessively that he might confess his knowledge of his own ridiculousness to someone else, an act that would weaken his defenses and cause him to commit suicide (p. 407). This fear reveals the pathological nature of the ridiculous man's earlier shame: He associated self-exposure with self-annihilation. The persistence of his fear also demonstrates how strongly he wanted to confess. Like Dostoevsky's other solitaries, the ridiculous man was rent by conflicting desires for isolation and community. Like them, he chose the safety of isolation. He went even further, however; once he concluded that life is meaningless, he adopted a protective indifference that narrowed his perceptual field. He jostled people on the street, for example, because he simply didn't notice them (a striking contrast to the underground man's sidewalk duel). He withdrew so completely from the world that he contemplated leaving it by committing suicide.

The ridiculous man's encounter with the little girl delays his suicide. He stomps at her because she arouses his pity, thereby reminding him of his own vulnerability and challenging his philosophy of necessary indifference. Like the underground man, the ridiculous man translates his experience into metaphysical and moral speculation: Does his decision to commit suicide absolve him of moral responsibility to others? His solipsistic speculation inspires the ethical test case that dictates the action in his dream:

> If I had lived before on the moon or on Mars and there had committed the most disgraceful and dishonourable action and had there been put to such shame and ignominy as one can only conceive and realise in dreams, in nightmares, and if, finding myself afterwards on earth, I were able to retain the memory of what I had done on the other planet and at the same time knew that I should never, under any circumstances, return there, then looking from the earth to the moon—*would it matter to me or not*? Should I feel shame for that action or not? (pp. 412–413).

The ridiculous man is repeating a question raised by Nikolay Stavrogin in Dostoevsky's 1871 novel *The Possessed*. By setting the action on another planet, both men distance themselves from their abuse of a young girl, turning their actual "disgraceful and dishonourable action" into an abstract speculation. While pondering this question, the ridiculous man unexpectedly falls asleep. His intuitive thought processes then take over, allowing his dream to answer.

By locating the ridiculous man's dream in the Garden of Eden, the mythic site of the fall of Eve and Adam, Dostoevsky introduces a metaphysical dimension to the story. The biblical myth couples knowing and seeing as well as knowing and feeling. After Eve and Adam eat the fruit, their eyes are opened; they learn they are naked, and they cover themselves. Then they hide from God. In learning that they are naked, Eve and Adam become conscious of themselves. In covering themselves, they reveal an intuitive understanding of the world outside themselves. The myth demonstrates shame's intimate connection to identity as it explains the divided self. Eve and Adam lose their spontaneous connection to the world when they become conscious of themselves and others. Moreover, they are exiled from the Garden of Eden, which ends their unity with God.

In the biblical myth, a transgressive, and thus guilty, act results in shame and separation. In "The Dream of a Ridiculous Man," Dostoevsky follows the biblical model. Agitated by stomping at the little girl, the ridiculous man initially asks whether he will feel shame for a despicable action committed on a distant planet. Does he feel shame, or guilt, or both? Dostoevsky clearly demonstrates that defenses against shame motivate his act, but the act causes moral qualms, a sign that apathy has stifled but not extinguished his ethical self. As compensation for his earlier denial of responsibility, in his dream the ridiculous man claims responsibility for the fall from Eden. He asserts that the presence of a self-conscious being like himself, a man whose rationality dominates his intuition, corrupts the innocent inhabitants of Eden. He notes that their first sin is lying—a betrayal of the trust that creates and sustains community.

Taking responsibility for the fall demonstrates his grandiosity, which is the other side of his narcissistic vulnerability. It also demonstrates his acceptance of himself as a moral being with an ethical responsibility to the entire human community. He asks his fallen friends to crucify him, a form of punishment that would alleviate his guilt. Instead, they laugh at him, thereby repeating the humiliations he suffered on earth. But the dream has provided him with a critical distance from the earlier pain of his humiliation. He no longer sees his tormentors as antagonists, but as equally fallen beings. His dream changes the way he sees others and thus the way he sees himself.

Throughout his career, but particularly in the 1870s, Dostoevsky agonized over the mounting number of suicides in Russia. For him, self-annihilation most clearly evidenced an individual's lack of belief in God (thus his fascination with the story of the woman jumping to her death holding an icon). The ridiculous man belongs to a group of Dostoevsky's fictional, westernized, atheistic men who use their minds to protect themselves from their feelings. Dostoevsky reveals the thoughts and feelings behind their words and actions through their dreams. As the ridiculous man notes, the dream state integrates mind and heart (p. 413). In his dream, the ridiculous man is not a divided but an integrated self. Although he had planned to shoot himself in the head, in his dream he shoots himself in the heart. He calls out, not with his voice, but "with my whole being" (p. 415). He retains his atheistic view of life as meaningless and humiliating: "If I have got to be again . . . and live once more under the control of some irresistible power, I don't want to be vanquished and humiliated" (p. 416). He still suffers extreme self-consciousness: " 'You know that I am afraid of you, and you despise me for that,' I said suddenly to my companion, unable to refrain from the humiliating question which implied a confession, and feeling my humiliation stab my heart as with a pin" (p. 416). But then he sees the sun, and he knows "with my whole being" that it is "exactly like ours, a repetition of it, its double" (p. 417). This sight resurrects his love of life. His dream reveals to him "a different life, renewed, grand and full of power!" (p. 417).

The ridiculous man is saved not through ratiocination but through revelation. His dream returns him to an Eden whose inhabitants are not divided or self-conscious, but integrated, intuitive beings living in harmony with one another and with all of nature. Once he sees and experiences such love and unity, he understands that his own self-division and separation from others are humanity's postlapsarian heritage (that is, humanity's legacy of exile from paradise). Being loved in the dream releases the ridiculous man from his fear of rejection. As he comes to love the members of the utopian community, the ridiculous man realizes that love can heal the wounds caused by his narcissism. His dream reveals that excessive rationalism provides both a defense against emotional vulnerability and an escape from the hard work of love—that is, active commitment to human community.

Following his dream, the would-be suicide concludes: "The main thing is to love others as oneself, that's the main thing, and that's everything; nothing else is needed" (p. 427). The story illustrates a point Dostoevsky makes and argues repeatedly elsewhere—belief in God leads to love of life. In the story, the reintegration of the ridiculous man's psyche leads to love for the earth: "I cried out, shaken by irresistible, ecstatic love for the old familiar earth which I had left" (p. 417). Personal reintegration also leads to love for others: "Moreover I love all those who laugh at me more than any of the rest" (p. 426). By unlocking his capacity for love, the dream restores him to the earth and human community. By showing him how he is connected to all humanity, the dream liberates him from his self-imposed alienation.

Dostoevsky's story functions in the same way as the ridiculous man's dream. Both demonstrate how awareness of others saves individuals from isolation and self-enclosure. Both engage our minds with moral and metaphysical speculation yet create images that haunt our hearts. The little girl who "saves" the ridiculous man is one of numerous desperate children and young women who haunt Dostoevsky's journalism, his fiction, and his readers' memories. As the underground man notes, "little pictures" have a penetrating and lasting emotional power. The ridiculous man is particularly haunted by the memory of the little girl's wet and torn shoes (bashmaki), an image that links her to Akaky Akakievich Bashmashkin in Gogol's story "The Overcoat." With this realistic detail, Dostoevsky amplifies his social message. By evoking the image of Gogol's poor clerk—a victim of social injustice who haunts the streets of St. Petersburg as a spectral social conscience—he intensifies his portrait of the little girl as social conscience, a poor and defenseless being whose call for help jars readers out of their complacency. Unlike his underground man, Dostoevsky uses his creative gifts to create community.

The stories in this collection can be seen both as studies of shame and as narrative experiments. With "The Double," Dostoevsky for the first time combines a fantastic frame with a penetrating psychological realism. Golyadkin is a divided self, whose conflicting desires to exhibit and efface himself lead to self-objectification, splitting, and madness. The narrator moves in and out of Golyadkin's head, recording his interior monologues and portraying him from the outside as he talks to himself. While such a strategy became common in the twentieth century, it was highly unsettling to nineteenth-century Russian readers. This 1846 story was preparation for Dostoevsky's narrative experiments in "The Meek One" (1876) and "The Dream of a Ridiculous Man" (1877).

"White Nights," "Notes from Underground," "The Meek One," and "The Dream of a Ridiculous Man" can be read, as Robert Belknap notes, as a four-part novel that almost exists. Their anonymous narrators are self-conscious and self-centered. They also grow older as Dostoevsky their creator does (Belknap, *The Gentle Creature* as the Climax of a Work of Art that Almost Exists," p. 35; ["The Gentle Creature" is an alternate translation of the Russian title that in this collection is given as "The Meek One"]). As we have seen, their stories also can be read as a continuous case study of shame. Starting with the idealistic young dreamer of "White Nights," they tell a story of increasing self-enclosure. To defend their narcissistically vulnerable selves from the potential ridicule of others, these four men isolate themselves. The white nights dreamer, the underground man, and the pawnbroker all spend significant amounts of time living in a fantasy world of their own creation. The ridiculous man has almost perfected his narcissistic self-enclosure. He speculates:

> The world now seemed created for me alone: if I shot myself the world would cease to be at least for me. I say nothing of its being likely that nothing will exist for any one when I am gone, and that as soon as my consciousness is extinguished the whole world will vanish too and become void like a phantom, as a mere appurtenance of my consciousness, for possibly all this world and all these people are only me myself (p. 412).

His withdrawal represents the outcome of choosing, like the white nights dreamer did thirty years earlier, to remain alone,

and to script roles for imaginary others rather than risk spontaneous action in a world where other people act on their own
needs.

In this four-chapter portrait of a dreamer, Dostoevsky shows
how a narcissistically vulnerable type chooses to fantasize about
life rather than to live, a decision that depresses him, harms his
moral sensibility, and eventually destroys his desire to live. The
profile of the solitary man progresses from the white nights
dreamer who helps one young woman, to the underground
man and the pawnbroker who abuse and prey on one young
woman, to the ridiculous man who first dismisses a young girl
and then resolves to save her and everyone else he encounters.

Dostoevsky provides all four men the chance to escape their
isolation through contact with a young woman. With each
story, the men grow older and the women younger. The
dreamer and the underground man are both in their twenties
when they meet the seventeen-year-old Nastenka and the
twenty-year-old Liza, young women of marriageable age. The
pawnbroker is forty-one when he meets the almost sixteen-
year-old meek one. The ridiculous man's age is not specified,
but if he follows the pattern of the narrator aging with Dostoevsky, he is probably a year older than the pawnbroker when he
meets the little girl on the street. By increasing the age gap, Dostoevsky highlights gender inequity. The men, who have more
education and more mobility, worry only about themselves. The
white nights dreamer selflessly helps Nastenka but then withdraws from the world. The upper-class underground man and
the pawnbroker, on the other hand, prey upon younger, less
educated women. The ridiculous man dismisses the young girl's
cry of distress as a nuisance. Dostoevsky shows that these privileged men do not accept responsibility for the well-being of
others.

Dostoevsky's solitary men respond to shame by isolating
themselves, and even by committing cruel and indifferent acts.
Their narcissism impedes genuine dialogue and love. They try
to retain control of all situations by scripting roles for others.
By placing themselves first, these men harm others. The shame

that spawns their narcissism leads them to commit guilty acts. Their guilt opens them up to self-examination. The young women in these stories act as catalysts for action. Their age and gender emphasize their vulnerability. They are the poor or the meek; they are less educated; yet they all attempt to improve their lives. Moreover, unlike the narcissistic men, the young women reach out to their fellow sufferers. Their own shame sensitizes them to the shame of others. Vulnerable themselves, they respond with compassion to the suffering of others. They serve as contrasts to Dostoevsky's solitary, passive, reactive men.

Dostoevsky embeds his message into the action of the stories. He shows his readers that love and compassion can liberate us from the prison of shame, our postlapsarian heritage. He achieves this by providing what the Russian critic Mikhail Bakhtin calls "surplus vision" (Bakhtin, *Art and Answerability: Early Philosophical Essays*, p. 22). By portraying these men as extreme egotists, Dostoevsky encourages us to see their limitations. By showing us the disjunction between their thoughts and feelings, their desires and their actions, Dostoevsky teaches us to view them critically. Most important, by demonstrating how shame drives their actions, Dostoevsky exposes the high personal and social costs of their shame defenses. In the young women, Dostoevsky presents alternative responses to shame— acts of love and compassion. These alternative responses, he shows, promote social harmony and community through shared suffering.

With this four-chapter portrait of increasing self-enclosure and gradual self-liberation through contact with others' suffering, Dostoevsky shows the radical potential of moral insight. Reading Dostoevsky is not easy—he demands that we read with our minds and our hearts. His psychological realism grips us, but it also pushes us into a metaphysical dimension. Confronted with the suffering of a young girl, for instance, the ridiculous man of Dostoevsky's story has a revelatory dream that literally and figuratively broadens his field of vision. Liberated from his solipsistic indifference, he sees others as equally worthy and needy individuals. His awakened compassion inspires him to serve others. With this story, Dostoevsky teaches us that world-view is a matter of life and death.

Deborah A. Martinsen is Assistant to the Director of the Core Curriculum at Columbia University and Adjunct Associate Professor of Russian and Comparative Literature. Her book on Dostoevsky's work is titled *Surprised by Shame: Dostoevsky's Liars and Narrative Exposure*. She is Executive Secretary of the North American Dostoevsky Society, Treasurer of the International Dostoevsky Society, and a corresponding member of the Russian Dostoevsky Society. She is currently researching shame in Russian literature and culture.

NOTE ON TRANSLATION

We have chosen to use Constance Garnett's groundbreaking translations, the first in English, for all the stories in this volume. For the sake of contemporary readers, we have modified her transliteration system (for example, "Petrovitch" becomes "Petrovich"). In places, we have also modified the text to reflect Dostoevsky's intentional repetitions, which Garnett did not always heed.

NOTES FROM UNDERGROUND, THE DOUBLE AND OTHER STORIES

THE DOUBLE

A PETERSBURG POEM

CHAPTER I

It was a little before eight o'clock in the morning when Yakov Petrovich Golyadkin, a titular councillor,[1] woke up from a long sleep. He yawned, stretched, and at last opened his eyes completely. For two minutes, however, he lay in his bed without moving, as though he were not yet quite certain whether he were awake or still asleep, whether all that was going on around him were real and actual, or the continuation of his confused dreams. Very soon, however, Mr. Golyadkin's senses began more clearly and more distinctly to receive their habitual and everyday impressions. The dirty green, smoke-begrimed, dusty walls of his little room, with the mahogany chest of drawers and chairs, the table painted red, the Turkish divan covered in reddish oil cloth with little green flowers on it, and the clothes taken off in haste overnight and flung in a crumpled heap on the sofa, looked at him familiarly. At last the damp autumn day, muggy and dirty, peeped into the room through the dingy window pane with such a hostile, sour grimace that Mr. Golyadkin could not possibly doubt that he was not in the land of Nod, but in the city of Petersburg, in his own flat on the fourth storey of a huge block of buildings in Shestilavochny Street. When he had made this important discovery Mr. Golyadkin nervously closed his eyes, as though regretting his dream and wanting to go back to it for a moment. But a minute later he leapt out of bed at one bound, probably all at once grasping the idea about which his scattered and wandering thoughts had been revolving. From his bed he ran straight to a little round looking-glass that stood on his chest of drawers. Though the sleepy, short-sighted countenance and rather bald head reflected in the looking-glass were of such an insignificant type that at first sight they would certainly not have attracted particular attention in any one, yet the owner of the countenance was satisfied with all that he saw in the looking-glass. "What a thing it would be," said Mr. Golyadkin in an undertone, "what a thing it would be if I were not up to the mark

5

to-day, if something were amiss, if some intrusive pimple had
made its appearance, or anything else unpleasant had happened;[2] so far, however, there's nothing wrong, so far everything's all right."

Greatly relieved that everything was all right, Mr. Golyadkin
put the looking-glass back in its place and, although he had
nothing on his feet and was still in the attire in which he was
accustomed to go to bed, he ran to the little window and with
great interest began looking for something in the courtyard,
upon which the windows of his flat looked out. Apparently
what he was looking for in the yard quite satisfied him too; his
face beamed with a self-satisfied smile. Then, after first peeping,
however, behind the partition into his valet Petrushka's little
room and making sure that Petrushka was not there, he went on
tiptoe to the table, opened the drawer in it and, fumbling in the
furthest corner of it, he took from under old yellow papers and
all sorts of rubbish a shabby green pocket-book, opened it cautiously, and with care and relish peeped into the furthest and
most hidden fold of it. Probably the roll of green, grey, blue, red
and particoloured notes[3] looked at Golyadkin, too, with approval: with a radiant face he laid the open pocket-book before
him and rubbed his hands vigorously in token of the greatest
satisfaction. Finally, he took it out—his comforting roll of
notes—and, for the hundredth time since the previous day,
counted them over, carefully smoothing out every note between his forefinger and his thumb.

"Seven hundred and fifty rubles in notes," he concluded at
last, in a half-whisper. "Seven hundred and fifty rubles, a note-
worthy sum! It's an agreeable sum," he went on, in a voice weak
and trembling with gratification, as he pinched the roll with his
fingers and smiled significantly; "it's a very agreeable sum! A
sum agreeable to any one! I should like to see the man to whom
that would be a trivial sum! There's no knowing what a man
might not do with a sum like that. . . . What's the meaning of
it, though?" thought Mr. Golyadkin; "where's Petrushka?" And
still in the same attire he peeped behind the partition again.
Again there was no sign of Petrushka; and the samovar stand-

ing on the floor was beside itself, fuming and raging in solitude, threatening every minute to boil over, hissing and lisping in its mysterious language, to Mr. Golyadkin something like,
"Take me, good people, I'm boiling; and perfectly ready."

"Damn the fellow," thought Mr. Golyadkin. "That lazy brute
might really drive a man out of all patience; where's he
dawdling now?"

In just indignation he went out into the hall, which consisted of a little corridor at the end of which was a door into
the entry, and saw his servant surrounded by a good-sized
group of lackeys of all sorts, a mixed rabble from outside as
well as from the flats of the house. Petrushka was telling something, the others were listening. Apparently the subject of the
conversation, or the conversation itself, did not please Mr.
Golyadkin. He promptly called Petrushka and returned to his
room, displeased and even upset. "That beast would sell a man
for a halfpenny, and his master before any one," he thought to
himself: "and he has sold me, he certainly has. I bet he has sold
me for a farthing. Well?"

"They've brought the livery, sir."

"Put it on, and come here."

When he had put on his livery, Petrushka, with a stupid
smile on his face, went in to his master. His costume was incredibly strange. He had on a much-worn green livery, with
frayed gold braid on it, apparently made for a man a yard taller
than Petrushka. In his hand he had a hat trimmed with the same
gold braid and with a feather in it, and at his hip hung a footman's sword in a leather sheath. Finally, to complete the picture,
Petrushka, who always liked to be in his night-clothes, was
barefooted. Mr. Golyadkin looked at Petrushka from all sides
and was apparently satisfied. The livery had evidently been
hired for some solemn occasion. Petrushka watched him with
strange expectancy and with marked curiosity followed every
movement he made, which extremely embarrassed Mr. Golyadkin.

"Well, and how about the carriage?"

"The carriage is here too."

"For the whole day?"

"For the whole day. Twenty-five rubles."

"And have the boots been sent?"

"Yes."

"Dolt! can't even say, 'Yes, sir.' Bring them here."

Expressing his satisfaction that the boots fitted, Mr. Golyadkin asked for his tea, and for water to wash and shave. He shaved with great care and washed as scrupulously, hurriedly sipped his tea and proceeded to the principal final process of attiring himself: he put on an almost new pair of trousers; then a shirtfront with brass studs, and a very bright and agreeably flowered waistcoat; about his neck he tied a gay, particoloured cravat, and finally drew on his coat, which was also newish and carefully brushed. As he dressed, he more than once looked lovingly at his boots, lifted up first one leg and then the other, admired their shape, kept muttering something to himself, and from time to time made expressive grimaces. Mr. Golyadkin was, however, extremely absent-minded that morning, for he scarcely noticed the little smiles and grimaces made at his expense by Petrushka, who was helping him dress. At last, having arranged everything properly and having finished dressing, Mr. Golyadkin put his pocket-book in his pocket, took a final admiring look at Petrushka, who had put on his boots and was therefore also quite ready, and, noticing that everything was done and that there was nothing left to wait for, he ran hurriedly and fussily out on to the stairs, with a slight throbbing at his heart. The light-blue hired carriage with a crest on it rolled noisily up to the steps. Petrushka, winking to the driver and some of the gaping crowd, helped his master into the carriage; and, hardly able to suppress an idiotic laugh, shouted in an unnatural voice: "Off!" jumped up on the footboard, and the whole turnout, clattering and rumbling noisily, rolled into Nevsky Prospect. As soon as the light-blue carriage dashed out of the gate, Mr. Golyadkin rubbed his hands convulsively and went off into a slow, noiseless chuckle, like a jubilant man who has succeeded in bringing off a splendid performance and is as pleased as Punch with the performance himself. Immediately after his access of gaiety, however, laughter was replaced by a strange and anxious expression on the face of Mr. Golyadkin. Though the weather was damp and muggy, he let down both windows of the carriage and began carefully scrutinizing the passers-by to left and to right, at once assuming a decorous and sedate air when he thought any one was looking at him. At the turning from Liteyny Street into Nevsky Prospect he was startled by a most unpleasant sensation and, frowning like some poor wretch whose corn has been accidentally trodden on, he huddled with almost panic-stricken haste into the darkest corner of his carriage.

He had seen two of his colleagues, two young clerks serving in the same government department. The young clerks were also, it seemed to Mr. Golyadkin, extremely amazed at meeting their colleague in such a way; one of them, in fact, pointed him out to the other. Mr. Golyadkin even fancied that the other had actually called his name, which, of course, was very unseemly in the street. Our hero concealed himself and did not respond. "The silly youngsters!" he began reflecting to himself. "Why, what is there strange in it? A man in a carriage, a man needs to be in a carriage, and so he hires a carriage. They're simply good-for-nothings! I know them—simply silly youngsters, who still need thrashing! They want to be paid a salary for playing pitch-farthing and dawdling about, that's all they're fit for I'd let them all know, if only . . ."

Mr. Golyadkin broke off suddenly, petrified. A smart pair of Kazan horses, very familiar to Mr. Golyadkin, in a fashionable droshky, drove rapidly by on the right side of his carriage. The gentleman sitting in the droshky, happening to catch a glimpse of Mr. Golyadkin, who was rather incautiously poking his head out of the carriage window, also appeared to be extremely astonished at the unexpected meeting and, bending out as far as he could, looked with the greatest curiosity and interest into the corner of the carriage in which our hero made haste to conceal himself. The gentleman in the droshky was Andrey Filippovich, the head of the office in which Mr. Golyadkin served in the capacity of assistant to the chief clerk. Mr. Golyadkin, see-

ing that Andrey Filippovich recognized him, that he was looking at him open-eyed and that it was impossible to hide,
blushed up to his ears.

"Bow or not? Call back or not? Recognize him or not?" our
hero wondered in indescribable anguish, "or pretend that I am
not myself, but somebody else strikingly like me, and look as
though nothing were the matter. Simply not I, not I—and that's
all," said Mr. Golyadkin, taking off his hat to Andrey Filippovich
and keeping his eyes fixed upon him. "I'm . . . I'm all right," he
whispered with an effort; "I'm . . . quite all right. It's not I, it's
not I—and that is the fact of the matter."

Soon, however, the droshky passed the carriage, and the
magnetism of his chief's eyes was at an end. Yet he went on
blushing, smiling and muttering something to himself . . .

"I was a fool not to call back," he thought at last. "I ought
to have taken a bolder line and behaved with gentlemanly
openness. I ought to have said 'This is how it is, Andrey Filippovich, I'm asked to the dinner too,' and that's all it is!"

Then, suddenly recalling how taken aback he had been, our
hero flushed as hot as fire, frowned, and cast a terrible defiant
glance at the front corner of the carriage, a glance calculated to
reduce all his foes to ashes. At last, he was suddenly inspired to
pull the cord attached to the driver's elbow, and stopped the
carriage, telling him to drive back to Liteyny Street. The fact
was, it was urgently necessary for Mr. Golyadkin, probably for
the sake of his own peace of mind, to say something very interesting to his doctor, Krestyan Ivanovich. And, though he had
made Krestyan Ivanovich's acquaintance quite recently, having,
indeed, only paid him a single visit, and that one the previous
week, to consult him about some symptom. But a doctor, as
they say, is like a priest, and it would be stupid for him to keep
out of sight, and, indeed, it was his duty to know his patients.
"Will it be all right, though," our hero went on, getting out of
the carriage at the door of a five-storey house in Liteyny Street,
at which he had told the driver to stop the carriage: "Will it be
all right? Will it be proper? Will it be appropriate? After all,
though," he went on, thinking as he mounted the stairs out of

breath and trying to suppress the beating of his heart, which had the habit of beating on all other people's staircases: "After all, it's on my own business and there's nothing reprehensible in it. . . . It would be stupid to keep out of sight. Why, of course, I shall behave as though I were quite all right, and have simply looked in as I passed. . . . He will see, that it's all just as it should be."

Reasoning like this, Mr. Golyadkin mounted to the second storey and stopped before flat number five, on which there was a handsome brass door-plate with the inscription—

KRESTYAN IVANOVICH RUTENSPITZ[4]
Doctor of Medicine and Surgery

Stopping at the door, our hero made haste to assume an air of propriety, ease, and even of a certain affability, and prepared to pull the bell. As he was about to do so he promptly and rather appropriately reflected that it might be better to come to-morrow, and that it was not very pressing for the moment. But as he suddenly heard footsteps on the stairs, he immediately changed his mind again and at once rang Krestyan Ivanovich's bell—with an air, moreover, of great determination.

CHAPTER II

The doctor of medicine and surgery, Krestyan Ivanovich Rutenspitz, a very hale, though elderly man, with thick eyebrows and whiskers that were beginning to turn grey, eyes with an expressive gleam in them that looked capable of routing every disease, and, lastly, with orders of some distinction on his breast, was sitting in his consulting-room that morning in his comfortable armchair. He was drinking coffee, which his wife had brought him with her own hand, smoking a cigar and from time to time writing prescriptions for his patients. After prescribing a draught for an old man who was suffering from hæmorrhoids and seeing the aged patient out by the side door, Krestyan Ivanovich sat down to await the next visitor.

Mr. Golyadkin walked in.

Apparently Krestyan Ivanovich did not in the least expect nor desire to see Mr. Golyadkin, for he was suddenly taken aback for a moment, and his countenance unconsciously assumed a strange and, one may almost say, a displeased expression. As Mr. Golyadkin almost always turned up inappropriately and was thrown into confusion whenever he approached any one about his own little affairs, on this occasion, too, he was desperately embarrassed. Having neglected to get ready his first sentence, which was invariably a stumbling-block for him on such occasions, he muttered something—apparently an apology—and, not knowing what to do next, took a chair and sat down, but, realizing that he had sat down without being asked to do so, he was immediately conscious of his lapse, and made haste to efface his offence against etiquette and good breeding by promptly getting up again from the seat he had taken uninvited. Then, on second thoughts, dimly perceiving that he had committed two stupid blunders at once, he immediately decided to commit a third—that is, tried to right himself, muttered something, smiled, blushed, was overcome with embarrassment, sank into expressive silence, and finally sat down for good and did not get up again. Only, to protect himself from all contingencies, he looked at the doctor with that defiant glare which had an extraordinary power of figuratively crushing Mr. Golyadkin's enemies and reducing them to ashes. This glance, moreover, expressed to the full Mr. Golyadkin's independence—that is, to speak plainly, the fact that Mr. Golyadkin was "all right," that he was "quite himself, like everybody else," and that there was "nothing wrong in his upper storey." Krestyan Ivanovich coughed, cleared his throat, apparently in token of approval and assent to all this, and bent an inquisitorial interrogative gaze upon his visitor.

"I have come to trouble you a second time, Krestyan

Ivanovich," began Mr. Golyadkin, with a smile, "and now I venture to ask your indulgence a second time. . . ." He was obviously at a loss for words.

"H'm . . . Yes!" pronounced Krestyan Ivanovich, puffing out
a spiral of smoke and putting down his cigar on the table, "but
you must follow the treatment prescribed you; I explained to
you that what would be beneficial to your health is a change of
habits. . . . Entertainment, for instance, and, well, friends—you
should visit your acquaintances, and not be hostile to the bottle; and likewise keep cheerful company."

Mr. Golyadkin, still smiling, hastened to observe that he
thought he was like every one else, that he lived by himself, that
he had entertainments like every one else . . . that, of course, he
might go to the theatre, for he had the means like every one
else, that he spent the day at the office and the evenings at
home, that he was quite all right; he even observed, in passing,
that he was, so far as he could see, as good as any one, that he
lived at home, and, finally, that he had Petrushka. At this point
Mr. Golyadkin hesitated.

"H'm! no, that is not the order of proceeding I want; and
that is not at all what I would ask you. I am interested to know,
in general, are you a great lover of cheerful company? Do you
take advantages of festive occasions; and, well, do you lead a
melancholy or cheerful manner of life?"

"Krestyan Ivanovich, I . . ."

"Hm! . . . I tell you," interrupted the doctor, "that you must
have a radical change of life, must, in a certain sense, break in
your character." (Krestyan Ivanovich laid special stress on the
word "break in," and paused for a moment with a very significant air.) "Must not shrink from gaiety, must visit entertainments and clubs, and in any case, be not hostile to the bottle.
Sitting at home is not right for you . . . sitting at home is impossible for you."

"I like quiet, Krestyan Ivanovich," said Mr. Golyadkin, with
a significant look at the doctor and evidently seeking words to
express his ideas more successfully: "In my flat there's only me
and Petrushka. . . . I mean my man, Krestyan Ivanovich. I mean

to say, Krestyan Ivanovich, that I go my way, my own way, Krestyan Ivanovich. I keep myself to myself, and so far as I can see am not dependent on any one. I go out for walks, too, Krestyan Ivanovich."

"What? Yes! well, nowadays there's nothing agreeable in walking: the climate's extremely bad."

"Quite so, Krestyan Ivanovich. Though I'm a peaceable man, Krestyan Ivanovich, as I've had the honour of explaining to you already, yet my way lies apart, Krestyan Ivanovich. The ways of life are manifold. . . . I mean . . . I mean to say, Krestyan Ivanovich. . . . Excuse me, Krestyan Ivanovich, I've no great gift for eloquent speaking."

"H'm . . . you say . . ."

"I say, you must excuse me, Krestyan Ivanovich, that as far as I can see I am no great hand at eloquence in speaking," Mr. Golyadkin articulated, stammering and hesitating, in a half-aggrieved voice. "In that respect, Krestyan Ivanovich, I'm not quite like other people," he added, with a peculiar smile, "I can't talk much, and have never learnt to embellish my speech with literary graces. On the other hand, I act, Krestyan Ivanovich; on the other hand, I act, Krestyan Ivanovich."

"H'm . . . How's that . . . you act?" responded Krestyan Ivanovich.

Then silence followed for half a minute. The doctor looked somewhat strangely and mistrustfully at his visitor. Mr. Golyadkin, for his part, too, stole a rather mistrustful glance at the doctor.

"Krestyan Ivanovich," he began, going on again in the same tone as before, somewhat irritated and puzzled by the doctor's extreme obstinacy: "I like tranquillity and not the noisy gaiety of the world. Among them, I mean, in the noisy world, Krestyan Ivanovich, one must be able to polish the floor with one's boots . . ." (here Mr. Golyadkin made a slight scrape on the floor with his toe); "they expect it, and they expect puns too . . . one must know how to make a perfumed compliment . . . that's what they expect there. And I've not learnt to do it, Krestyan Ivanovich, I've never learnt all those tricks, I've never had the time. I'm a simple person, and not ingenious, and I've no external polish. On that side I surrender, Krestyan Ivanovich, I lay down my arms, speaking in that sense."

All this Mr. Golyadkin pronounced with an air which made it perfectly clear that our hero was far from regretting that he was laying down his arms in that sense and that he had not learnt these tricks; quite the contrary, indeed. As Krestyan Ivanovich listened to him, he looked down with a very unpleasant grimace on his face, seeming to have a presentiment of something. Mr. Golyadkin's tirade was followed by a rather long and significant silence.

"You have, I think, departed a little from the subject," Krestyan Ivanovich said at last, in a low voice: "I confess I cannot altogether understand you."

"I'm not a great hand at eloquent speaking, Krestyan Ivanovich; I've had the honour to inform you, Krestyan Ivanovich, already," said Mr. Golyadkin, speaking this time in a sharp and resolute tone.

"H'm!" . . .

"Krestyan Ivanovich!" began Mr. Golyadkin again in a low but more significant voice in a somewhat solemn style and emphasizing every point: "Krestyan Ivanovich, when I came in here I began with apologies. I repeat the same thing again, and again ask for your indulgence. There's no need for me to conceal it, Krestyan Ivanovich. I'm an unimportant man, as you know; but, fortunately for me, I do not regret being an unimportant man. Quite the contrary, indeed, Krestyan Ivanovich, and, to be perfectly frank, I'm proud that I'm not a great man but an unimportant man. I'm not one to intrigue and I'm proud of that too, I don't act on the sly, but openly, without cunning, and although I could do harm too, and a great deal of harm, indeed, and know to whom and how to do it, Krestyan Ivanovich, yet I won't sully myself, and in that sense I wash my hands. In that sense, I say, I wash them, Krestyan Ivanovich!" Mr. Golyadkin paused expressively for a moment; he spoke with mild fervour.

"I set to work, Krestyan Ivanovich," our hero continued,

"directly, openly, by no devious ways, for I disdain them, and leave them to others. I do not try to degrade those who are perhaps purer than you and I . . . that is, I mean, I and they, Krestyan Ivanovich—I didn't mean you. I don't like insinuations; I've no taste for contemptible duplicity; I'm disgusted by slander and calumny. I only put on a mask at a masquerade, and don't wear one before people every day. I only ask you, Krestyan Ivanovich, how you would revenge yourself upon your enemy, your most malignant enemy—the one you would consider such?" Mr. Golyadkin concluded with a challenging glance at Krestyan Ivanovich.

Though Mr. Golyadkin pronounced this with the utmost distinctness and clearness, weighing his words with a self-confident air and reckoning on their probable effect, yet meanwhile he looked at Krestyan Ivanovich with anxiety, with great anxiety, with extreme anxiety. Now he was all eyes: and timidly waited for the doctor's answer with irritable and agonized impatience. But to the perplexity and complete amazement of our hero, Krestyan Ivanovich only muttered something to himself; then he moved his armchair up to the table, and rather drily though politely announced something to the effect that his time was precious, and that he did not quite understand; that he was ready, however, to attend to him as far as he was able, but he would not go into anything further that did not concern him. At this point he took the pen, drew a piece of paper towards him, cut out of it the usual long strip, and announced that he would immediately prescribe what was necessary.

"No, it's not necessary, Krestyan Ivanovich! No, that's not necessary at all!" said Mr. Golyadkin, getting up from his seat, and clutching Krestyan Ivanovich's right hand. "That isn't what's wanted, Krestyan Ivanovich."

And, while he said this, a queer change came over him. His grey eyes gleamed strangely, his lips began to quiver, all the muscles, all the features of his face began moving and working. He was trembling all over. After stopping the doctor's hand, Mr. Golyadkin followed his first movement by standing motionless, as though he had no confidence in himself and were waiting for some inspiration for further action.

Then followed a rather strange scene.

Somewhat perplexed, Krestyan Ivanovich seemed for a moment rooted to his chair and gazed open-eyed in bewilderment at Mr. Golyadkin, who looked at him in exactly the same way. At last Krestyan Ivanovich stood up, gently holding the lining of Mr. Golyadkin's coat. For some seconds they both stood like that, motionless, with their eyes fixed on each other. Then, however, in an extraordinarily strange way came Mr. Golyadkin's second movement. His lips trembled, his chin began twitching, and our hero quite unexpectedly burst into tears. Sobbing, shaking his head and striking himself on the chest with his right hand, while with his left clutching the lining of the doctor's coat, he tried to say something and to make some explanation, but could not utter a word.

At last Krestyan Ivanovich recovered from his amazement.

"Come, calm yourself!" he brought out at last, trying to make Mr. Golyadkin sit down in an armchair.

"I have enemies, Krestyan Ivanovich, I have enemies; I have malignant enemies who have sworn to ruin me . . ." Mr. Golyadkin answered in a frightened whisper.

"Come, come, why enemies? you mustn't talk about enemies! You really mustn't. Sit down, sit down," Krestyan Ivanovich went on, getting Mr. Golyadkin once for all into the armchair.

Mr. Golyadkin sat down at last, still keeping his eyes fixed on the doctor. With an extremely displeased air, Krestyan Ivanovich strode from one end of the room to another. A long silence followed.

"I'm grateful to you, Krestyan Ivanovich, I'm very grateful, and I'm very sensible of all you've done for me now. To my dying day I shall never forget your kindness, Krestyan Ivanovich," said Mr. Golyadkin, getting up from his seat with an offended air.

"Come, give over! I tell you, give over!" Krestyan Ivanovich responded rather sternly to Mr. Golyadkin's outburst, making him sit down again.

"Well, what's the matter? Tell me what is unpleasant," Krestyan Ivanovich went on, "and what enemies are you talking about? What is wrong?"

"No, Krestyan Ivanovich, we'd better leave that now," answered Mr. Golyadkin, casting down his eyes; "let us put all that aside for the time. . . . Till another time, Krestyan Ivanovich, till a more convenient moment, when everything will be discovered and the mask falls off certain faces, and something comes to light. But, meanwhile, now, of course, after what has passed between us . . . you will agree yourself, Krestyan Ivanovich. . . . Allow me to wish you good morning, Krestyan Ivanovich," said Mr. Golyadkin, getting up gravely and resolutely and taking his hat.

"Oh, well . . . as you like . . . h'm . . ." (A moment of silence followed.) "For my part, you know . . . whatever I can do . . . and I sincerely wish you well."

"I understand you, Krestyan Ivanovich, I understand: I understand you perfectly now . . . In any case excuse me for having troubled you, Krestyan Ivanovich."

"H'm, no, I didn't mean that. However, as you please; go on taking the medicines as before. . . ."

"I will go on with the medicines as you say, Krestyan Ivanovich. I will go on with them, and I will get them at the same chemist's . . . To be a chemist nowadays, Krestyan Ivanovich, is an important business. . . ."

"How so? In what sense do you mean?"

"In a very ordinary sense, Krestyan Ivanovich. I mean to say that nowadays that's the way of the world. . . ."

"H'm . . ."

"And that every silly youngster, not only a chemist's boy, turns up his nose at respectable people."

"H'm. How do you understand that?"

"I'm speaking of a certain person, Krestyan Ivanovich . . . of a common acquaintance of ours, Krestyan Ivanovich, of Vladimir Semyonovich. . . ."

"Ah!"

"Yes, Krestyan Ivanovich: and I know certain people, Krestyan Ivanovich, who don't quite keep to the general rule of telling the truth, sometimes."

"Ah! How so?"

"Why, yes, it is so: but that's neither here nor there: they sometimes manage to serve you up a fine egg in gravy."

"What? Serve up what?"

"An egg in gravy, Krestyan Ivanovich. It's a Russian saying. They know how to congratulate some one at the right moment, for instance; there are people like that."

"Congratulate?"

"Yes, congratulate, Krestyan Ivanovich, as some one I know very well did the other day!" . . .

"Some one you know very well . . . Ah! how was that?" said Krestyan Ivanovich, looking attentively at Mr. Golyadkin.

"Yes, some one I know very well indeed congratulated some one else I know very well—and, what's more, a comrade, a friend of his heart, on his promotion, on his receiving the rank of collegiate assessor. This was how it happened to come up: 'I am exceedingly glad of the opportunity to offer you, Vladimir Semyonovich, my congratulations, my *sincere* congratulations, on your receiving the rank of assessor. And I'm the more pleased, as all the world knows that there are old women nowadays who tell fortunes.' "

At this point Mr. Golyadkin gave a sly nod, and screwing up his eyes, looked at Krestyan Ivanovich. . . .

"H'm. So he said that. . . ."

"He did, Krestyan Ivanovich, he said it and glanced at once at Andrey Filippovich, the uncle of our Prince Charming, Vladimir Semyonovich. But what is it to me, Krestyan Ivanovich, that he has been made an assessor? What is it to me? And he wants to get married and the milk is scarcely dry on his lips, if I may be allowed the expression. And I said as much. Vladimir Semyonovich, said I! I've said everything now; allow me to withdraw."

"H'm . . ."

"Yes, Krestyan Ivanovich, allow me now, I say, to withdraw. But, to kill two birds with one stone, as I twitted our young gentleman with the old women, I turned to Klara Olsufyevna (it all happened the day before yesterday at Olsufy Ivanovich's), and she had only just sung a song full of feeling. 'You've sung songs full of feeling, madam,' said I, 'but they've not been listened to with a pure heart.' And by that I hinted plainly, Krestyan Ivanovich, hinted plainly, that they were not running after her now, but looking higher . . ."

"Ah! And what did he say?"

"He swallowed the pill, Krestyan Ivanovich, as the saying is."

"H'm . . ."

"Yes, Krestyan Ivanovich. To the old man himself, too, I said, 'Olsufy Ivanovich,' said I, 'I know how much I'm indebted to you, I appreciate to the full all the kindness you've showered upon me from my childhood up. But open your eyes, Olsufy Ivanovich,' I said. 'Look about you. I myself do things openly and aboveboard, Olsufy Ivanovich.' "

"Oh, really!"

"Yes, Krestyan Ivanovich. Really . . ."

"What did he say?"

"Yes, what, indeed, Krestyan Ivanovich? He mumbled one thing and another, and 'I know you,' and that 'his Excellency was a benevolent man'—he rambled on. . . . But, there, you know! he's begun to be a bit shaky, as they say, with old age."

"Ah! so that's how it is now . . ."

"Yes, Krestyan Ivanovich. And that's how we all are! Poor old man! He looks towards the grave, breathes incense, as they say, while they concoct a piece of womanish gossip and he listens to it; without him they wouldn't . . ."

"Gossip, you say?"

"Yes, Krestyan Ivanovich, they've concocted a womanish scandal. Our bear, too, had a finger in it, and his nephew, our Prince Charming. They've joined hands with the old women and, of course, they've concocted the affair. Would you believe it? They plotted the murder of some one! . . ."

"The murder of some one?"

"Yes, Krestyan Ivanovich, the moral murder of some one. They spread about . . . I'm speaking of a man I know very well."

Krestyan Ivanovich nodded.

"They spread rumours about him . . . I confess I'm ashamed to repeat them, Krestyan Ivanovich."

"H'm." . . .

"They spread a rumour that he had signed a promise to marry though he was already engaged in another quarter . . . and would you believe it, Krestyan Ivanovich, to whom?"

"Really?"

"To a cook, to a disreputable German woman from whom he used to get his dinners; instead of paying what he owed, he offered her his hand."

"Is that what they say?"

"Would you believe it, Krestyan Ivanovich? A low German, a nasty, shameless German, Karolina Ivanovna, if you know . . ."

"I confess, for my part . . ."

"I understand you, Krestyan Ivanovich, I understand, and for my part I feel it . . ."

"Tell me, please, where are you living now?"

"Where am I living now, Krestyan Ivanovich?"

"Yes . . . I want . . . I believe, you used to live . . ."

"Yes, Krestyan Ivanovich, I did, I used to. To be sure I lived!" answered Mr. Golyadkin, accompanying his words with a little laugh, and somewhat disconcerting Krestyan Ivanovich by his answer.

"No, you misunderstood me; I meant to say . . ."

"I, too, meant to say, Krestyan Ivanovich, I meant it too," Mr. Golyadkin continued, laughing. "But I've kept you far too long, Krestyan Ivanovich. I hope you will allow me now, to wish you good morning."

"H'm. . . ."

"Yes, Krestyan Ivanovich, I understand you; I fully understand you now," said our hero, with a slight flourish before Krestyan Ivanovich. "And so permit me to wish you good morning. . . ."

At this point our hero made a scrape with the toe of his boot and walked out of the room, leaving Krestyan Ivanovich in the utmost amazement. As he went down the doctor's stairs he smiled and rubbed his hands gleefully. On the steps, breathing the fresh air and feeling himself at liberty, he was certainly prepared to admit that he was the happiest of mortals, and thereupon to go straight to his office—when suddenly his carriage rumbled up to the door: he glanced at it and remembered everything. Petrushka was already opening the carriage door. Mr. Golyadkin was completely overwhelmed by a strong and unpleasant sensation. He blushed, as it were, for a moment. Something seemed to stab him. He was just about to raise his foot to the carriage step when he suddenly turned round and looked towards Krestyan Ivanovich's window. Yes, it was so! Krestyan Ivanovich was standing at the window, was stroking his whiskers with his right hand and staring with some curiosity at the hero of our story.

"That doctor is silly," thought Mr. Golyadkin, huddling out of sight in the carriage; "extremely silly. He may treat his patients all right, but still . . . he's as stupid as a post."

Mr. Golyadkin sat down, Petrushka shouted "Off!" and the carriage rolled towards Nevsky Prospect again.

CHAPTER III

All that morning was spent by Mr. Golyadkin in a strange bustle of activity. On reaching Nevsky Prospect our hero told the driver to stop at the bazaar. Skipping out of his carriage, he ran to the Gostiny Dvor,[5] accompanied by Petrushka, and went straight to a shop where gold and silver articles were for sale. One could see from his very air that he was overwhelmed with business and had a terrible amount to do. Arranging to purchase a complete dinner- and tea-service for

fifteen hundred rubles and including in the bargain for that
sum a cigar-case of ingenious form and a silver shaving-set, and
finally, asking the price of some other articles, useful and agreeable in their own way, he ended by promising to come without
fail next day, or to send for his purchases the same day. He took
the number of the shop, and listening attentively to the shopkeeper, who was very pressing for a small deposit, said that he
should have it all in good time. After which he took leave of the
amazed shopkeeper and, followed by a regular flock of shop-
men, walked along the Gostiny Dvor, continually looking round
at Petrushka and diligently seeking out fresh shops. On the way
he dropped into a money-changer's and changed all his big
notes into small ones, and though he lost on the exchange, his
pocket-book was considerably fatter, which evidently afforded
him extreme satisfaction. Finally, he stopped at a shop for
ladies' dress materials. Here, too, after deciding to purchase
goods for a considerable sum, Mr. Golyadkin promised to come
again, took the number of the shop and, on being asked for a
deposit, assured the shopkeeper that "he should have a deposit
too, all in good time." Then he visited several other shops, making purchases in each of them, asked the price of various
things, sometimes arguing a long time with the shopkeeper,
going out of the shop and returning two or three times—in fact
he displayed exceptional activity. From the Gostiny Dvor our
hero went to a well-known furniture shop, where he ordered
furniture for six rooms; he admired a fashionable and very ingenious toilet table for ladies' use in the latest style, and, assuring the shopkeeper that he would certainly send for all these
things, walked out of the shop, as usual promising a deposit.
Then he went off somewhere else and ordered something
more. In short, there seemed to be no end to the business he
had to get through. At last, Mr. Golyadkin seemed to grow
heartily sick of it all, and he began, goodness knows why, to be
tormented by the stings of conscience. Nothing would have induced him now, for instance, to meet Andrey Filippovich, or
even Krestyan Ivanovich.

At last, the town clock struck three. When Mr. Golyadkin finally took his seat in the carriage, of all the purchases he had made that morning he had, it appeared, in reality only got a pair of gloves and a bottle of scent, that cost a ruble and a half. As it was still rather early, he ordered his coachman to stop near a well-known restaurant in Nevsky Prospect which he only knew by reputation, got out of the carriage, and hurried in to have a light lunch, to rest and to wait for the hour fixed for the dinner.

Lunching as a man lunches who has the prospect before him of going out to a sumptuous dinner, that is, taking a snack of something in order to still the pangs, as they say, and drinking one small glass of vodka, Mr. Golyadkin established himself in an armchair and, modestly looking about him, peacefully settled down to an emaciated nationalist paper.[6] After reading a couple lines he stood up and looked in the looking-glass, set himself to rights and smoothed himself down; then he went to the window and looked to see whether his carriage was there . . . then he sat down again in his place and took up the paper. It was noticeable that our hero was in great excitement. Glancing at his watch and seeing that it was only a quarter past three and that he had consequently a good time to wait and, at the same time, opining that to sit like that was unsuitable, Mr. Golyadkin ordered chocolate, though he felt no particular inclination for it at the moment. Drinking the chocolate and noticing that the time had moved on a little, he went up to pay his bill.

He turned round and saw facing him two of his colleagues, the same two he had met that morning in Liteyny Street,— young men, very much his juniors both in age and in rank. Our hero's relations with them were neither one thing nor the other, neither particularly friendly nor openly hostile. Good manners were, of course, observed on both sides: there was no closer intimacy, nor could there be. The meeting at this moment was extremely distasteful to Mr. Golyadkin. He frowned a little, and was disconcerted for an instant.

"Yakov Petrovich, Yakov Petrovich!" chirped the two collegiate registrars; "you here? what brings you? . . ."

"Ah, it is you, gentlemen," Mr. Golyadkin interrupted hurriedly, somewhat embarrassed and scandalized by the amazement of the clerks and by the abruptness of their address, but feeling obliged, however, to appear jaunty and free and easy. "You've deserted, gentlemen, he—he—he. . . ." Then, to keep up his dignity and to condescend to the juveniles, with whom he never overstepped certain limits, he attempted to slap one of the youths on the shoulder; but this effort at good fellowship did not succeed and, instead of being a well-bred little jest, produced quite a different effect.

"Well, and our bear, is he still at the office?"

"Who's that, Yakov Petrovich?"

"Why, the bear. Do you mean to say you don't know whose name that is? . . ." Mr. Golyadkin laughed and turned to the cashier to take his change.

"I mean Andrey Filippovich, gentlemen," he went on, finishing with the cashier, and turning to the clerks this time with a very serious face. The two collegiate registrars winked at one another.

"He's still at the office and asking for you, Yakov Petrovich," answered one of them.

"At the office, eh! In that case, let him stay, gentlemen. And asking for me, eh?"

"He was asking for you, Yakov Petrovich; but what's up with you, scented, pomaded, and such a swell? . . ."

"Nothing, gentlemen, nothing! that's enough," answered Mr. Golyadkin, looking away with a constrained smile. Seeing that Mr. Golyadkin was smiling, the clerks laughed aloud. Mr. Golyadkin was a little offended.

"I'll tell you as friends, gentlemen," our hero said, after a brief silence, as though making up his mind (which, indeed, was the case) to reveal something to them. "You all know me, gentlemen, but hitherto you've known me only on one side. No one is to blame for that and I'm conscious that the fault has been partly my own."

Mr. Golyadkin pursed up his lips and looked significantly at the clerks. The clerks winked at one another again.

"Hitherto, gentlemen, you have not known me. To explain myself here and now would not be quite appropriate. I will only touch on it lightly in passing. There are people, gentlemen, who dislike roundabout ways and only mask themselves at masquerades. There are people who do not see man's highest avocation in polishing the floor with their boots. There are people, gentlemen, who refuse to say that they are happy and enjoying a full life when, for instance, their trousers set properly. There are people, finally, who dislike dashing and whirling about for no object, fawning, and licking the dust, and above all, gentlemen, poking their noses where they are not wanted. . . . I've told you almost everything, gentlemen; now allow me to withdraw. . . ."

Mr. Golyadkin paused. As the collegiate registrars had now got all that they wanted, both of them with great incivility burst into shouts of laughter. Mr. Golyadkin flared up.

"Laugh away, gentlemen, laugh away for the time being! If you live long enough you will see," he said, with a feeling of offended dignity, taking his hat and retreating to the door.

"But I will say more, gentlemen," he added, turning for the last time to the collegiate registrars, "I will say more—you are both here with me face to face. This, gentlemen, is my rule: if I fail I don't lose heart, if I succeed I persevere, and in any case I am never underhand. I'm not one to intrigue—and I'm proud of it. I've never prided myself on diplomacy. They say, too, gentlemen, that the bird flies itself to the hunter. It's true and I'm ready to admit it; but who's the hunter, and who's the bird in this case? That is still the question, gentlemen!"

Mr. Golyadkin subsided into eloquent silence, and, with a most significant air, that is, pursing up his lips and raising his eyebrows as high as possible, he bowed to the clerks and walked out, leaving them in the utmost amazement.

"What are your orders now?" Petrushka asked, rather gruffly; he was probably weary of hanging about in the cold. "What are your orders?" he asked Mr. Golyadkin, meeting the terrible, withering glance with which our hero had protected himself twice already that morning, and to which he had recourse now for the third time as he came down the steps.

"To Izmailovsky Bridge."

"To Izmailovsky Bridge! Off!"

"Their dinner will not begin till after four, or perhaps five o'clock," thought Mr. Golyadkin; "isn't it early now? However, I can go a little early; besides, it's only a family dinner. And so I can go *sans façon,** as they say among well-bred people. Why shouldn't I go *sans façon*? The bear told us, too, that it would all be *sans façon*, and so I will be the same. . . ." Such were Mr. Golyadkin's reflections and meanwhile his excitement grew more and more acute. It could be seen that he was preparing himself for some great enterprise, to say nothing more; he muttered to himself, gesticulated with his right hand, continually looked out of his carriage window, so that, looking at Mr. Golyadkin, no one would have said that he was on his way to a good dinner, and only a simple dinner in his family circle—*sans façon*, as they say among well-bred people. Finally, just at Izmailovsky Bridge, Mr. Golyadkin pointed out a house; and the carriage rolled up noisily and stopped at the first entrance on the right. Noticing a feminine figure at the second storey window, Mr. Golyadkin kissed his hand to her. He had, however, not the slightest idea what he was doing, for he felt more dead than alive at the moment. He got out of the carriage pale, distracted; he mounted the steps, took off his hat, mechanically straightened himself, and though he felt a slight trembling in his knees, he went upstairs.

"Olsufy Ivanovich?" he inquired of the man who opened the door."

"At home, sir; at least he's not at home, his honour's not at home."

"What? What do you mean, my good man? I—I've come to dinner, brother. Why, you know me?"

"To be sure I know you! I've orders not to admit you."

---

*Without ceremony, informally (French).

"You . . . you, brother . . . you must be making a mistake. It's I, my boy. I'm invited; I've come to dinner," Mr. Golyadkin announced, taking off his coat and displaying unmistakable intentions of going into the room.

"Allow me, sir, you can't, sir. I've orders not to admit you. I've orders to refuse you. That's how it is."

Mr. Golyadkin turned pale. At that very moment the door of the inner room opened and Gerasimich, Olsufy Ivanovich's old butler, came out.

"You see the gentleman wants to go in, Emelyan Gerasimich, and I . . ."

"And you're a fool, Alexeich. Go inside and send the rascal Semyonich here. It's impossible," he said politely but firmly, addressing Mr. Golyadkin. "It's quite impossible. His honour begs you to excuse him; he can't see you."

"He said he couldn't see me?" Mr. Golyadkin asked uncertainly. "Excuse me, Gerasimich, why is it impossible?"

"It's quite impossible. I've informed your honour; they said 'Ask him to excuse us.' They can't see you."

"Why not? How's that? Why?"

"Allow me, allow me! . . ."

"How is it, though? It's out of the question! Announce me. . . . How is it? I've come to dinner. . . ."

"Excuse me, excuse me. . . ."

"Ah, well, that's a different matter, they asked to be excused: but, allow me, Gerasimich; how is it, Gerasimich?"

"Excuse me, excuse me!" replied Gerasimich, very firmly putting away Mr. Golyadkin's hand and making way for two gentlemen who walked into the entry that very instant. The gentlemen in question were Andrey Filippovich and his nephew, Vladimir Semyonovich. Both of them looked with amazement at Mr. Golyadkin. Andrey Filippovich seemed about to say something, but Mr. Golyadkin had by now made up his mind: he was by now walking out of Olsufy Ivanovich's entry, blushing and smiling, with eyes cast down and a countenance of helpless bewilderment. "I will come afterwards, Gerasimich;

I will explain myself: I hope that all this will without delay be explained in due season. . . ."

"Yakov Petrovich, Yakov Petrovich . . ." He heard the voice of Andrey Filippovich following him.

Mr. Golyadkin was by that time on the first landing. He turned quickly to Andrey Filippovich.

"What do you desire, Andrey Filippovich?" he said in a rather resolute voice.

"What's wrong with you, Yakov Petrovich? In what way?"

"No matter, Andrey Filippovich. I'm on my own account here. This is my private life, Andrey Filippovich."

"What's that?"

"I say, Andrey Filippovich, that this is my private life, and as for my being here, as far as I can see, there's nothing reprehensible to be found in it as regards my official relations."

"What! As regards your official . . . What's the matter with you, my good sir?"

"Nothing, Andrey Filippovich, absolutely nothing; an impudent slut of a girl, and nothing more. . . .

"What! What?" Andrey Filippovich was stupefied with amazement. Mr. Golyadkin, who had up till then looked as though he would fly into Andrey Filippovich's face, seeing that the head of his office was laughing a little, almost unconsciously took a step forward. Andrey Filippovich jumped back. Mr. Golyadkin went up one step and then another. Andrey Filippovich looked about him uneasily. Mr. Golyadkin mounted the stairs rapidly. Still more rapidly Andrey Filippovich darted into the flat and slammed the door after him. Mr. Golyadkin was left alone. Everything grew dark before his eyes. He was utterly nonplussed, and stood now in a sort of senseless hesitation, as though recalling something extremely senseless, too, that had happened quite recently. "Ech, ech!" he muttered, smiling with constraint. Meanwhile, there came the sounds of steps and voices on the stairs, probably of other guests invited by Olsufy Ivanovich. Mr. Golyadkin recovered himself to some extent; put up his raccoon collar, concealing himself behind it as far as possible, and began going downstairs with rapid little

steps, tripping and stumbling in his haste. He felt overcome by
a sort of weakness and numbness. His confusion was such that,
when he came out on the steps, he did not even wait for his
carriage but walked across the muddy court to it. When he
reached his carriage and was about to get into it, Mr. Golyadkin
inwardly uttered a desire to sink into the earth or to hide in a
mouse hole together with his carriage. It seemed to him that
everything in Olsufy Ivanovich's house was looking at him now
out of every window. He knew that he would certainly die on
the spot if he were to go back.

"What are you laughing at, blockhead?" he said in a rapid
mutter to Petrushka, who was preparing to help him into the
carriage.

"What should I laugh at? I'm not doing anything; where are
we to drive now?"

"Go home, drive on. . . ."

"Home, off!" shouted Petrushka, climbing on to the footboard.

"What a crow's croak!" thought Mr. Golyadkin. Meanwhile,
the carriage had driven a good distance from Izmailovsky
Bridge. Suddenly our hero pulled the cord with all his might
and shouted to the driver to turn back at once. The coachman
turned his horses and within two minutes was driving into Olsufy Ivanovich's yard again.

"Don't, don't, you fool, back!" shouted Mr. Golyadkin—
and, as though he were expecting this order, the driver made
no reply but, without stopping at the entrance, drove all round
the courtyard and out into the street again.

Mr. Golyadkin did not drive home, but, after passing the Semyonovsky Bridge, told the driver to return to a side street and
stop near a restaurant of rather modest appearance. Getting out
of the carriage, our hero settled up with the driver and so got
rid of his equipage at last. He told Petrushka to go home and
await his return, while he went into the restaurant, took a private room and ordered dinner. He felt very ill and his brain was
in the utmost confusion and chaos. For a long time he walked
up and down the room in agitation; at last he sat down in a

chair, propped his brow in his hands and began doing his very utmost to consider and settle something relating to his present position.

CHAPTER IV

That day the birthday of Klara Olsufyevna, the only daughter of the state councillor, Berendeyev, at one time Mr. Golyadkin's benefactor and patron, was being celebrated by a brilliant and sumptuous dinner-party, such as had not been seen for many a long day within the walls of the flats in the neighbourhood of Izmailovsky Bridge—a dinner more like some Balthazar's feast,[7] with a suggestion of something Babylonian in its brilliant luxury and style, with Veuve-Clicquot champagne, with oysters and fruit from Eliseyev's and Milyutin's,[8] with all sorts of fatted calves, and all grades of the government service. This festive day was to conclude with a brilliant ball, a small birthday ball, but yet brilliant in its taste, its distinction and its style. Of course, I am willing to admit that similar balls do happen sometimes, though rarely. Such balls, more like family rejoicings than balls, can only be given in such houses as that of the state councillor, Berendeyev. I will say more: I even doubt if such balls could be given in the houses of all state councillors. Oh, if I were a poet! such as Homer or Pushkin, I mean, of course; with any lesser talent one would not venture—I should certainly have painted all that glorious day for you, oh, my readers, with a free brush and brilliant colours! Yes, I should begin my poem with my dinner, I should lay special stress on that striking and solemn moment when the first goblet was raised to the honour of the queen of the fête. I should describe to you the guests plunged in a reverent silence and expectation, as eloquent as the rhetoric of Demosthenes; I should describe for you, then, how

Andrey Filippovich, having as the eldest of the guests some right to take precedence, adorned with his grey hairs and the orders that well befit grey hairs, got up from his seat and raised above his head the congratulatory glass of sparkling wine— brought from a distant kingdom[9] to celebrate such occasions and more like heavenly nectar than plain wine. I would portray for you the guests and the happy parents raising their glasses, too, after Andrey Filippovich, and fastening upon him eyes full of expectation. I would describe for you how the same Andrey Filippovich, so often mentioned, after dropping a tear in the glass, delivered his congratulations and good wishes, proposed the toast and drank the health . . . but I confess, I freely confess, that I could not do justice to the solemn moment when the queen of the fête, Klara Olsufyevna, blushing like a rose in spring, with the glow of bliss and of modesty, was so overcome by her feelings that she sank into the arms of her tender mamma; how that tender mamma shed tears, and how the father, Olsufy Ivanovich, a hale old man and a privy councillor, who had lost the use of his legs in his long years of service and been rewarded by destiny for his devotion with investments, a house, some small estates, and a beautiful daughter, sobbed like a little child and announced through his tears that his Excellency was a benevolent man. I could not, I positively could not, describe the enthusiasm that followed that moment in every heart, an enthusiasm clearly evinced in the conduct of a youthful collegiate registrar (though at that moment he was more like a state councillor than a collegiate registrar), who was moved to tears, too, as he listened to Andrey Filippovich. In his turn, too, Andrey Filippovich was in that solemn moment quite unlike a collegiate councillor and the head of an office in the department—yes, he was something else . . . what, exactly, I do not know, but not a collegiate councillor. He was more exalted! Finally . . . Oh, why do I not possess the secret of lofty, powerful language, of the sublime style, to describe these grand and edifying moments of human life, which seem created expressly to prove that virtue sometimes triumphs over ingratitude, free-thinking, vice and envy! I will say nothing, but in silence—which will be better than any eloquence—I will point to that fortunate youth, just entering on his twenty-sixth spring—to Vladimir Semyonovich, Andrey Filippovich's nephew, who in his turn now rose from his seat, who in his turn proposed a toast, and upon whom were fastened the tearful eyes of the parents, the proud eyes of Andrey Filippovich, the modest eyes of the queen of the fête, the solemn eyes of the guests, and even the decorously envious eyes of some of the young man's youthful colleagues. I will say nothing of that, though I cannot refrain from observing that everything in that young man—who was, indeed, speaking in a complimentary sense, more like an elderly than a young man—everything, from his blooming cheeks to his assessorial rank seemed almost to proclaim aloud the lofty pinnacle a man can attain through morality and good principles! I will not describe how Anton Antonovich Setochkin, a little old man as grey as a badger, the head clerk of a department, who was a colleague of Andrey Filippovich's and had once been also of Olsufy Ivanovich's, and was an old friend of the family and Klara Olsufyevna's godfather, in his turn proposed a toast, crowed like a cock, and cracked many little jokes; how by this extremely proper breach of propriety, if one may use such an expression, he made the whole company laugh till they cried, and how Klara Olsufyevna, at her parents' bidding, rewarded him for his jocularity and politeness with a kiss. I will only say that the guests, who must have felt like kinsfolk and brothers after such a dinner, at last rose from the table, and the elderly and more solid guests, after a brief interval spent in friendly conversation, interspersed with some candid, though, of course, very polite and proper observations, went decorously into the next room and, without losing valuable time, promptly divided themselves up into parties and, full of the sense of their own dignity, installed themselves at tables covered with green baize. Meanwhile, the ladies established in the drawing-room suddenly became very affable and began talking about dress-materials. And the venerable host, who had lost the use of his legs in the service of loyalty and religion, and had been rewarded with all the blessings we have enumerated above, began walking about on crutches among his guests, supported by Vladimir Semyonovich and Klara Olsufyevna, and he, too, suddenly becoming extremely affable, decided to improvise a modest little dance, regardless of expense; to that end a nimble youth (the one who was more like a state councillor than a youth) was despatched to fetch musicians, and musicians to the number of eleven arrived, and exactly at half-past eight struck up the inviting strains of a French quadrille, followed by various other dances. . . . It is needless to say that my pen is too weak, dull, and spiritless to describe the dance that owed its inspiration to the genial hospitality of the grey-headed host. And how, I ask, can the modest chronicler of Mr. Golyadkin's adventures, extremely interesting as they are in their own way, how can I depict the choice and rare mingling of beauty, brilliance, style, gaiety, polite solidity and solid politeness, sportiveness, joy, all the mirth and playfulness of these wives and daughters of petty officials, more like fairies than ladies—in a complimentary sense—with their lily shoulders and their rosy faces, their ethereal figures, their playfully agile homeopathic—to use the exalted language appropriate—little feet? How can I describe to you, finally, the gallant officials, their partners—gay and solid youths, steady, gleeful, decorously vague, smoking a pipe in the intervals between the dancing in a little green room apart, or not smoking a pipe in the intervals between the dances, every one of them with a highly respectable surname and rank in the service—all steeped in a sense of the elegant and a sense of their own dignity; almost all speaking French to their partners, or if Russian, using only the most well-bred expressions, compliments and profound observations, and only in the smoking-room permitting themselves some genial lapses from this high tone, some phrases of cordial and friendly brevity, such, for instance, as: " 'Pon my soul, Petka, you rake, you did kick off that polka in style," or, "I say, Vasya, you dog, you did give your partner a time of it." For all this, as I've already had the honour of explaining, oh, my readers! my pen fails me, and therefore I am dumb. Let us rather return to Mr. Golyadkin, the true and only hero of my very truthful tale.

The fact is that he found himself now in a very strange position, to say the least of it. He was here also, gentlemen—that is, not at the dance, but almost at the dance; he was "all right, though; he could take care of himself," yet at this moment he was a little astray; he was standing at that moment, strange to say—on the landing of the back stairs to Olsufy Ivanovich's flat. But it was "all right" his standing there; he was "quite well." He was standing in a corner, huddled in a place which was not very warm, though it was dark, partly hidden by a huge cupboard and an old screen, in the midst of rubbish, litter, and odds and ends of all sorts, concealing himself for the time being and watching the course of proceedings as a disinterested spectator. He was only looking on now, gentlemen; he, too, gentlemen, might go in, of course . . . why should he not go in? He had only to take one step and he would go in, and would go in very adroitly. Just now, though he had been standing nearly three hours between the cupboard and the screen in the midst of the rubbish, litter, and odds and ends of all sorts, he was only quoting, in his own justification, a memorable phrase of the French minister, Villesle.[10] "All things come in time to him who has the strength to wait." Mr. Golyadkin had read this sentence in some book on quite a different subject, but now very aptly recalled it. The phrase, to begin with, was exceedingly appropriate to his present position, and, indeed, why should it not occur to the mind of a man who had been waiting for almost three hours in the cold and the dark in expectation of a happy ending to his adventures. After quoting very appropriately the phrase of the French minister, Villesle, Mr. Golyadkin immediately thought of the Turkish Vizier, Martsimiris, as well as the beautiful Marquess Louisa,[11] whose story he had read also in some book. Then it occurred to his mind that the Jesuits made it their rule that any means were justified if only the end were attained. Fortifying himself somewhat with this historical fact, Mr. Golyadkin said to himself, What were the Jesuits? The Jesuits were every one of them very great fools; that he was better than any of them; that if only the refreshment-room would be empty for one minute (the door of the refreshment-room opened straight into the passage to the back stairs, where Mr. Golyadkin was in hiding now), he would, in spite of all the Jesuits in the world, go straight in, first from the refreshment-room into the tea-room, then into the room where they were now playing cards, and then straight into the hall where they were now dancing the polka, and he would go in, he would certainly go in, in spite of anything he would go in—he would slip through—and that would be all, no one would notice him; and once there he would know what to do.

Well, so this is the position in which we find the hero of our perfectly true story, though, indeed, it is difficult to explain what was passing in him at that moment. The fact is that he had made his way to the back stairs, and to the passage, on the ground that, as he said, "Why shouldn't he? And everyone did go that way"; but he had not ventured to penetrate further, evidently he did not dare to do so . . . "not because there was anything he did not dare, but just because he did not care to, because he preferred to be in hiding"; so here he was, waiting now for a chance to slip in, and he had been waiting for it two hours and a half. "Why not wait? Villesle himself had waited. But what had Villesle to do with it?" thought Mr. Golyadkin: "How does Villesle come in? But how am I to . . . to go and walk in? . . . Ech, you dummy!" said Mr. Golyadkin, pinching his benumbed cheek with his benumbed fingers; "what a little fool you are, what a nonentity (Golyadka)—that's the kind of last name you have! . . ."

But these compliments paid to himself were only by the way and without any apparent aim. Now he was on the point of pushing forward and slipping in; the refreshment-room was empty and no one was in sight. Mr. Golyadkin saw all this through the little window; in two steps he was at the door and had already opened it. "Should he go in or not? Come, should he or not? I'll go in . . . why not? to the bold all ways lie open!" Reassuring himself in this way, our hero suddenly and quite unexpectedly retreated behind the screen. "No," he thought. "Ah, now, somebody's coming in? Yes, they've come in; why did I dawdle when there were no people about? Even so, shall I go and slip in? . . . No, how slip in when a man has such a temperament! Fie, what a low tendency! I'm as scared as a hen! Being scared is our special line, that's the fact of the matter! To be abject on every occasion is our line: no need to ask us about that. Just stand here like a post and that's all! At home I should be having a cup of tea now. . . . It would be pleasant, too, to have a cup of tea. If I come in later Petrushka'll grumble, maybe. Shall I go home? Damnation take all this! I'll go and that'll be the end of it!" Reflecting on his position in this way, Mr. Golyadkin dashed forward as though some one had touched a spring in him; in two steps he found himself in the refreshment-room, flung off his overcoat, took off his hat, hurriedly thrust these things into a corner, straightened himself and smoothed himself down; then . . . then he moved on to the tea-room, and from the tea-room darted into the next room, slipped almost unnoticed between the card-players, who were at the tip-top of excitement, then . . . Mr. Golyadkin forgot everything that was going on about him, and went straight as an arrow into the drawing-room.

As luck would have it they were not dancing. The ladies were promenading up and down the room in picturesque groups. The gentlemen were standing about in twos and threes or flitting about the room engaging partners. Mr. Golyadkin noticed nothing of this. He saw only Klara Olsufyevna, near her Andrey Filippovich, then Vladimir Semyonovich, two or three officers, and, finally, two or three other young men who were also very interesting and, as any one could see at once, were either very promising or had actually done something. . . . He saw some one else too. Or, rather, he saw nobody and looked at nobody . . . but, moved by the same spring which had sent him dashing into the midst of a ball to which he had not been invited, he moved forward, and then forwarder and forwarder. On the way he jostled against a councillor and trod on his foot, and incidentally stepped on a very venerable old lady's dress and tore it a little, pushed against a servant with a tray and then ran against somebody else, and, not noticing all this, or rather noticing it but at the same time looking at no one, pressing further and further forward, he suddenly found himself facing Klara Olsufyevna. There is no doubt whatever that he would, with the utmost delight, without winking an eyelid, have sunk through the earth at that moment; but what has once been done cannot be recalled . . . can never be recalled. What was he to do? "If I fail I don't lose heart, if I succeed I persevere."

Mr. Golyadkin was, of course, not "one to intrigue," and "not accomplished in the art of polishing the floor with his boots." . . . And so, indeed, it proved. Besides, the Jesuits had some hand in it too . . . though Mr. Golyadkin had no thoughts to spare for them now! All the moving, noisy, talking, laughing groups were suddenly hushed as though at a signal and, little by little, crowded round Mr. Golyadkin. He, however, seemed to hear nothing, to see nothing, he could not look . . . he could not possibly look at anything; he kept his eyes on the floor and so stood, giving himself his word of honour, in passing, to shoot himself one way or another that night. Making this vow, Mr. Golyadkin inwardly said to himself, "Here goes!" and to his own great astonishment began unexpectedly to speak.

He began with congratulations and polite wishes. The congratulations went off well, but over the good wishes our hero stammered. He felt that if he stammered all would be lost at once. And so it turned out—he stammered and floundered . . . floundering, he blushed crimson; blushing, he was overcome with confusion. In his confusion he raised his eyes; raising his eyes he looked about him; looking about him—he almost swooned. . . . Every one stood still, every one was silent, every one was waiting; a little way off there was whispering; a little nearer there was laughter. Mr. Golyadkin fastened a humble, imploring look on Andrey Filippovich. Andrey Filippovich responded with such a look that if our hero had not been utterly crushed already he certainly would have been crushed a second time—that is, if that were possible. The silence lasted long.

"This is rather concerned with my domestic circumstances and my private life, Andrey Filippovich," our hero, half-dead, articulated in a scarcely audible voice; "it is not an official incident, Andrey Filippovich. . . ."

"For shame, sir, for shame!" Andrey Filippovich pronounced in a half-whisper, with an indescribable air of indignation; he pronounced these words and, giving Klara Olsufyevna his arm, he turned away from Mr. Golyadkin.

"I've nothing to be ashamed of, Andrey Filippovich," answered Mr. Golyadkin, also in a whisper, turning his miserable eyes about him, trying helplessly to discover in the amazed crowd something on which he could gain a footing and retrieve his social position.

"Why, it's all right, it's nothing, gentlemen! Why, what's the matter? Why, it might happen to any one," whispered Mr. Golyadkin, moving a little away and trying to escape from the crowd surrounding him.

They made way for him. Our hero passed through two rows of inquisitive and wondering spectators. Fate drew him on. He felt that himself, that fate was leading him on. He would have given a great deal, of course, for a chance to be back in the passage by the back stairs, without having committed a breach of propriety; but as that was utterly impossible he began trying to creep away into a corner and to stand there—modestly, decorously, apart, without interfering with any one, without attracting especial attention, but at the same time to win the favourable notice of his host and the company. At the same time Mr. Golyadkin felt as though the ground were giving way under him, as though he were staggering, falling. At last he made his way to a corner and stood in it, like an unconcerned, rather indifferent spectator, leaning his arms on the backs of two chairs, taking complete possession of them in that way, and trying, as far as he could, to glance confidently at Olsufy Ivanovich's guests, grouped about him. Standing nearest him was an officer, a tall and handsome fellow, beside whom Golyadkin felt himself an insect.

"These two chairs, Lieutenant, are intended, one for Klara Olsufyevna, and the other for Princess Chevchekhanova; I'm taking care of them for them," said Mr. Golyadkin breathlessly, turning his imploring eyes on the officer. The lieutenant said nothing, but turned away with a murderous smile. Checked in this direction, our hero was about to try his luck in another quarter, and directly addressed an important councillor with a cross of great distinction on his breast. But the councillor looked him up and down with such a frigid stare that Mr. Golyadkin felt distinctly as though a whole bucketful of cold water had been thrown over him. He subsided into silence. He made up his mind that it was better to keep quiet, not to open his lips, and to show that he was "all right," that he was "like every one else," and that his position, as far as he could see, was quite a proper one. With this object he riveted his gaze on the lining of his coat, then raised his eyes and fixed them upon a very respectable-looking gentleman. "That gentleman has a wig on," thought Mr. Golyadkin; "and if he takes off that wig he will be bald, his head will be as bare as the palm of my hand." Having made this important discovery, Mr. Golyadkin thought of the Arab Emirs, whose heads are left bare and shaven if they take off the green turbans they wear as a sign of their descent from the prophet Muhammad. Then, probably from some special connection of ideas with the Turks, he thought of Turkish slippers and at once, apropos of that, recalled the fact that Andrey Filippovich was wearing boots, and that his boots were more like slippers than boots. It was evident that Mr. Golyadkin had become to some extent reconciled to his position. "What if that chandelier," flashed through Mr. Golyadkin's mind, "were to come down from the ceiling and fall upon the company. I should rush at once to save Klara Olsufyevna. 'Save her!' I should cry. 'Don't be alarmed, madam, it's of no consequence, I will rescue you, I.' Then . . ." At that moment Mr. Golyadkin looked about in search of Klara Olsufyevna, and saw Gerasimich, Olsufy

Ivanovich's old butler. Gerasimich, with a most anxious and solemnly official air, was making straight for him. Mr. Golyadkin started and frowned from an unaccountable but most disagreeable sensation; he looked about him mechanically; it occurred to his mind if only he could somehow creep off somewhere, unobserved, on the sly—simply disappear, that is, behave as though he had done nothing at all, as though the matter did not concern him in the least! . . . But before our hero could make up his mind to do anything, Gerasimich was standing before him.

"Do you see, Gerasimich," said our hero, with a little smile, addressing Gerasimich; "you go and tell them—do you see the candle there in the chandelier, Gerasimich—it will be falling down directly: so, you know, you must tell them to see to it; it really will fall down, Gerasimich. . . ."

"The candle? No, the candle's standing straight; but somebody is asking for you, sir."

"Who is asking for me, Gerasimich?"

"I really can't say, sir, who it is. A man with a message. 'Is Yakov Petrovich Golyadkin here?' says he. 'Then call him out,' says he, 'on very urgent and important business . . .' you see."

"No, Gerasimich, you are making a mistake; in that you are making a mistake, Gerasimich."

"I doubt it, sir."

"No, Gerasimich, it isn't doubtful; there's nothing doubtful about it, Gerasimich. Nobody's asking for me, but I'm quite at home here—that is, in my right place, Gerasimich."

Mr. Golyadkin took breath and looked about him. Yes! every one in the room, all had their eyes fixed upon him, and were listening in a sort of solemn expectation. The men had crowded a little nearer and were all attention. A little further away the ladies were whispering together. The master of the house made his appearance at no great distance from Mr. Golyadkin, and though it was impossible to detect from his expression that he, too, was taking a close and direct interest in Mr. Golyadkin's position, for everything was being done with delicacy, yet, nevertheless, it all made our hero feel that the decisive moment had

come for him. Mr. Golyadkin saw clearly that the time had
come for a bold stroke, the chance of putting his enemies to
shame. Mr. Golyadkin was in great agitation. He was aware of a
sort of inspiration and, in a quivering and impressive voice, he
began again, addressing the waiting butler—

"No, my dear fellow, no one's calling for me. You are mistaken. I will say more: you were mistaken this morning, too,
when you assured me . . . dared to assure me, I say (he raised
his voice), "that Olsufy Ivanovich, who has been my benefactor as long as I can remember and has, in a sense, been a father
to me, was shutting his door upon me at the moment of
solemn family rejoicing for his paternal heart." (Mr. Golyadkin
looked about him complacently, but with deep feeling. A tear
glittered on his eyelash.). "I repeat, my friend," our hero concluded, "you were mistaken, you were cruelly and unpardonably mistaken. . . ."

The moment was a solemn one. Mr. Golyadkin felt that the
effect was quite certain. He stood with modestly downcast eyes,
expecting Olsufy Ivanovich to embrace him. Excitement and
perplexity were apparent in the guests, even the inflexible and
terrible Gerasimich faltered over the words "I doubt it . . ."
when suddenly the ruthless orchestra, apropos of nothing,
struck up a polka. All was lost, all was scattered to the winds.
Mr. Golyadkin started; Gerasimich stepped back; everything in
the room began undulating like the sea; and Vladimir Semyonovich led the dance with Klara Olsufyevna, while the
handsome lieutenant followed with Princess Chevchekhanova.
Onlookers, curious and delighted, squeezed in to watch them
dancing the polka—an interesting, fashionable new dance
which every one was crazy over. Mr. Golyadkin was, for the
time, forgotten. But suddenly all were thrown into excitement,
confusion and bustle; the music ceased . . . a strange incident
had occurred. Tired out with the dance, and almost breathless
with fatigue, Klara Olsufyevna, with glowing cheeks and heaving bosom, sank into an armchair, completely exhausted. . . .
All hearts turned to the fascinating creature, all vied with one
another in complimenting her and thanking her for the plea-

sure conferred on them,—all at once there stood before her Mr.
Golyadkin. He was pale, extremely perturbed; he, too, seemed
completely exhausted, he could scarcely move. He was smiling
for some reason, he stretched out his hand imploringly. Klara
Olsufyevna was so taken aback that she had not time to withdraw hers and mechanically got up at his invitation. Mr.
Golyadkin lurched forward, first once, then a second time, then
lifted his leg, then made a scrape, then gave a sort of stamp,
then stumbled . . . he, too, wanted to dance with Klara Olsufyevna. Klara Olsufyevna uttered a shriek; every one rushed to
release her hand from Mr. Golyadkin's, and in a moment our
hero was carried almost ten paces away by the rush of the
crowd. A circle formed round him too. Two old ladies, whom
he had almost knocked down in his retreat, raised a great
shrieking and outcry. The confusion was awful; all were asking
questions, every one was shouting, every one was finding fault.
The orchestra was silent. Our hero whirled round in his circle
and mechanically, with a semblance of a smile, muttered something to himself, such as, "Why not?" and "that the polka, so
far, at least, as he could see, was a new and very interesting
dance, invented for the diversion of the ladies . . . but that since
things had taken this turn, he was ready to consent." But Mr.
Golyadkin's consent no one apparently thought of asking. Our
hero was suddenly aware that some one's hand was laid on his
arm, that another hand was pressed against his back, that he
was with peculiar solicitude being guided in a certain direction. At last he noticed that he was going straight to the door.
Mr. Golyadkin wanted to say something, to do something. . . .
But no, he no longer wanted to do anything. He only mechanically kept laughing in answer. At last he was aware that they
were putting on his greatcoat, that his hat was thrust over his
eyes; finally he felt that he was in the entry on the stairs in the
dark and cold. At last he stumbled, he felt that he was falling
down a precipice; he tried to cry out—and suddenly found
himself in the courtyard. The air blew fresh on him, he stood
still for a minute; at that very instant, the strains reached him of
the orchestra striking up again. Mr. Golyadkin suddenly recalled

it all; it seemed to him that all his flagging energies came back to him again. He had been standing as though riveted to the spot, but now he started off and rushed away headlong, anywhere, into the air, into freedom, wherever chance might take him.

CHAPTER V

It was striking midnight from all the clock towers in Petersburg when Mr. Golyadkin, beside himself, ran out on the Fontanka Embankment, close to the Izmailovsky Bridge, fleeing from his foes, from persecution, from a hailstorm of nips and pinches aimed at him, from the shrieks of excited old ladies, from the Ohs and Ahs of women and from the murderous eyes of Andrey Filippovich. Mr. Golyadkin was killed— killed entirely, in the full sense of the word, and if he still preserved the power of running, it was simply through some sort of miracle, a miracle in which at last he refused himself to believe. It was an awful November night—wet, foggy, rainy, snowy, teeming with colds in the head, fevers, swollen faces, quinseys, inflammations of all kinds and descriptions—teeming, in fact, with all the gifts of a Petersburg November. The wind howled in the deserted streets, lifting up the black water of the canal above the rings on the bank, and irritably brushing against the lean lamp-posts which chimed in with its howling in a thin, shrill creak, keeping up the endless squeaky, jangling concert with which every inhabitant of Petersburg is so familiar. Snow and rain were falling both at once. Lashed by the wind, the streams of rainwater spurted almost horizontally, as though from a fireman's hose, pricking and stinging the face of the luckless Mr. Golyadkin like a thousand pins and needles. In the stillness of the night, broken only by the distant rumbling of carriages, the howl of the wind and the creaking of the lamp-posts, there was the dismal sound of the splash and gurgle of water, rushing from every roof, every porch, every pipe and every cornice, on to the granite of the pavement. There was not a soul, near or far, and, indeed, it seemed there could not be at such an hour and in such weather. And so only Mr. Golyadkin, alone with his despair, was fleeing in terror along the pavement of Fontanka, with his usual rapid little step, in haste to get home as soon as possible to his flat on the fourth storey in Shestilavochny Street.

Though the snow, the rain, and all the nameless horrors of a raging snowstorm and fog, under a Petersburg November sky, were attacking Mr. Golyadkin, already shattered by misfortunes, were showing him no mercy, giving him no rest, drenching him to the bone, glueing up his eyelids, blowing right through him from all sides, baffling and perplexing him—though all this was hurled upon Mr. Golyadkin at once, as though conspiring and combining with all his enemies to make a grand day, evening, and night for him, in spite of all this Mr. Golyadkin was almost insensible to this final proof of the persecution of destiny: so violent had been the shock and the impression made upon him a few minutes before at the state councillor Berendeyev's! If any disinterested spectator could have glanced casually at Mr. Golyadkin's painful progress, he would instantly have grasped the awful horror of his pitiful plight and would certainly have said that Mr. Golyadkin looked as though he wanted to hide from himself, as though he were trying to run away from himself! Yes! It was really so. One may say more: Mr. Golyadkin did not want only to run away from himself, but to be obliterated, to cease to be, to return to dust. At the moment he took in nothing surrounding him, understood nothing of what was going on about him, and looked as though the miseries of the stormy night, of the long tramp, the rain, the snow, the wind, all the cruelty of the weather, did not exist for him. The golosh slipping off the boot on Mr. Golyadkin's right foot was left behind in the snow and slush on the pavement of Fontanka, and Mr. Golyadkin did not think of turning back to get it, did not, in fact, notice that he had lost it. He was so perplexed that, in spite of everything surrounding him, he stood several times stockstill in the middle of the pavement, completely possessed by the thought of his recent horrible humiliation; at that instant he was dying, disappearing; then he suddenly set off again like mad and ran and ran without looking back, as though he were pursued, as though he were fleeing from some still more awful calamity. . . . The position was truly awful! . . . At last Mr. Golyadkin halted in exhaustion, leaned on the railing in the attitude of a man whose nose has suddenly begun to bleed, and began looking intently at the black and troubled waters of the canal. There is no knowing what length of time he spent like this. All that is known is that at that instant Mr. Golyadkin reached such a pitch of despair, was so harassed, so tortured, so exhausted, and so weakened in what feeble faculties were left him that he forgot everything, forgot the Izmailovsky Bridge, forgot Shestilavochny Street, forgot his present plight. . . . After all, what did it matter to him? The thing was done. The decision was affirmed and ratified; what could he do! All at once . . . all at once he started and involuntarily skipped a couple of paces aside. With unaccountable uneasiness he began gazing about him; but no one was there, nothing special had happened, and yet . . . and yet he fancied that just now, that very minute, some one was standing near him, beside him, also leaning on the railing, and—marvellous to relate!—had even said something to him, said something quickly, abruptly, not quite intelligibly, but something quite private, something concerning himself.

"Why, was it my fancy?" said Mr. Golyadkin, looking round once more. "But where am I standing? . . . Ech, ech," he thought finally, shaking his head, though he began gazing with an uneasy, miserable feeling into the damp, murky distance, straining his sight and doing his utmost to pierce with his short-sighted eyes the wet darkness that stretched all round him. There was nothing new, however, nothing special caught the eye of Mr. Golyadkin. Everything seemed to be all right, as it should be, that is, the snow was falling more violently, more thickly and in larger flakes, nothing could be seen twenty paces away, the lamp-posts creaked more shrilly than ever and the wind seemed to intone its melancholy song even more tearfully, more piteously, like an importunate beggar whining for a copper to get a crust of bread. At the same time a new sensation took possession of Mr. Golyadkin's whole being: agony upon agony, terror upon terror . . . a feverish tremor ran through his veins. The moment was insufferably unpleasant! "Well, it's no matter," he said, to encourage himself. "Well, no matter; perhaps it's no matter at all, and there's no stain on any one's honour. Perhaps it's as it should be," he went on, without understanding what he was saying. "Perhaps it will all be for the best in the end, and there will be nothing to complain of, and every one will be justified."

Talking like this and comforting himself with words, Mr. Golyadkin shook himself a little, shook off the snow which had drifted in thick layers on his hat, his collar, his overcoat, his tie, his boots and everything—but his strange feeling, his strange, obscure misery he could not get rid of, could not shake off. Somewhere in the distance there was the boom of a cannon shot.[12] "Ach, what weather!" thought our hero. "Choo! isn't there going to be a flood? It seems as though the water has risen so violently."

Mr. Golyadkin had hardly said or thought this when he saw a person coming towards him, belated, no doubt, like him, through some accident. An unimportant, casual incident, one might suppose, but for some unknown reason Mr. Golyadkin was troubled, even scared, and rather flurried. It was not that he was exactly afraid of some ill-intentioned man, but just that "perhaps . . . after all, who knows, this belated individual," flashed through Mr. Golyadkin's mind, "maybe he's that very thing, maybe he's the very principal thing in it, and isn't here for nothing, but is here with an object, crossing my path and provoking me." Possibly, however he did not think this precisely, but only had a passing feeling of something like it—and very unpleasant. There was no time, however, for thinking and feeling. The stranger was already within two paces. Mr. Golyadkin, as he invariably did, hastened to assume a quite peculiar air, an air that expressed clearly that he, Golyadkin, kept himself to himself, that he was "all right," that the road was wide enough for all, and that he, Golyadkin, was not interfering with any one. Suddenly he stopped short as though petrified, as though struck by lightning, and quickly turned round after the figure which had only just passed him—turned as though some one had given him a tug from behind, as though the wind had turned him like a weathercock. The passer-by vanished quickly in the snowstorm. He, too, walked quickly; he was dressed like Mr. Golyadkin and, like him, too, wrapped up from head to foot, and he, too, tripped and trotted along the pavement of Fontanka with rapid little steps that suggested that he was a little scared.

"What—what is it?" whispered Mr. Golyadkin, smiling mistrustfully, though he trembled all over. An icy shiver ran down his back. Meanwhile, the stranger had vanished completely; there was no sound of his step, while Mr. Golyadkin still stood and gazed after him. At last, however, he gradually came to himself.

"Why, what's the meaning of it?" he thought with vexation. "Why, have I really gone out of my mind, or what?" He turned and went on his way, making his footsteps more rapid and frequent, and doing his best not to think of anything at all. He even closed his eyes at last with the same object. Suddenly, through the howling of the wind and the uproar of the storm, the sound of steps very close at hand reached his ears again. He started and opened his eyes. Again a rapidly approaching figure stood out black before him, some twenty paces away. This little figure was hastening, tripping along, hurrying nervously; the distance between them grew rapidly less. Mr. Golyadkin could by now get a full view of this second belated companion. He looked full at him and cried out with amazement and horror; his legs gave way under him. It was the same individual who had passed him ten minutes before, and who now quite unexpectedly turned up facing him again. But this was not the only marvel that struck Mr. Golyadkin. He was so amazed that he stood still, cried out, tried to say something, and rushed to overtake the stranger, even shouted something to him, probably anxious to stop him as quickly as possible. The stranger did, in fact, stop ten paces from Mr. Golyadkin, so that the light from the lamp-post that stood near fell full upon his whole figure— stood still, turned to Mr. Golyadkin, and with impatient and anxious face waited to hear what he would say.

"Excuse me, possibly I'm mistaken," our hero brought out in a quavering voice.

The stranger in silence, and with an air of annoyance, turned and rapidly went on his way, as though in haste to make up for the two seconds he had wasted on Mr. Golyadkin. As for the latter, he was quivering in every nerve, his knees shook and gave way under him, and with a moan he squatted on a stone at the edge of the pavement. There really was reason, however, for his being so overwhelmed. The fact is that this stranger seemed to him now somehow familiar. That would have been nothing, though. But he recognized, almost certainly recognized this man. He had often seen him, that man, had seen him some time, and very lately too; where could it have been? Surely not yesterday? But, again, that was not the chief thing that Mr. Golyadkin had often seen him before; there was hardly anything special about the man; the man at first sight would not have aroused any special attention. He was just a man like any one else, a gentleman like all other gentlemen, of course, and perhaps he had some good qualities and very valuable ones too—in fact, he was a man who was quite himself. Mr. Golyadkin cherished no sort of hatred or enmity, not even the slightest hostility towards this man—quite the contrary, it would seem, indeed—and yet (and this was the real point) he would not for any treasure on earth have been willing to meet that man, and especially to meet him as he had done now, for instance. We may say more: Mr. Golyadkin knew that man perfectly well: he even knew what he was called, what his name was; and yet nothing would have induced him, and again, for no treasure on earth would he have consented to name him, to consent to acknowledge that he was called so-and-so, that his father's name was this and his surname was that. Whether Mr.

Golyadkin's stupefaction lasted a short time or a long time, whether he was sitting for a long time on the stone of the pavement I cannot say; but, recovering himself a little at last, he suddenly fell to running, without looking round, as fast as his legs could carry him; his mind was preoccupied, twice he stumbled and almost fell—and through this circumstance his other boot was also bereaved of its golosh. At last Mr. Golyadkin slackened his pace a little to get breath, looked hurriedly round and saw that he had already, without being aware of it, run right across Fontanka, had crossed the Anichkov Bridge, had passed part of Nevsky Prospect and was now standing at the turning into Liteyny Street. Mr. Golyadkin turned into Liteyny Street. His position at that instant was like that of a man standing at the edge of a fearful precipice, while the earth is bursting open under him, is already shaking, moving, rocking for the last time, falling, drawing him into the abyss, and yet the luckless wretch has not the strength, nor the resolution, to leap back, to avert his eyes from the yawning gulf below; the abyss draws him and at last he leaps into it of himself, himself hastening the moment of his destruction. Mr. Golyadkin knew, felt and was firmly convinced that some other evil would certainly befall him on the way, that some unpleasantness would overtake him, that he would, for instance, meet his stranger once more: but—strange to say, he positively desired this meeting, considered it inevitable, and all he asked was that it might all be quickly over, that he should be relieved from his position in one way or another, but as soon as possible. And meanwhile he ran on and on, as though moved by some external force, for he felt a weakness and numbness in his whole being: he could not think of anything, though his thoughts caught at everything like brambles. A little lost dog, soaked and shivering, attached itself to Mr. Golyadkin, and ran beside him, scurrying along with tail and ears drooping, looking at him from time to time with timid comprehension. Some remote, long-forgotten idea—some memory of something that had happened long ago—came back into his mind now, kept knocking at his brain as with a hammer, vexing him and refusing to be shaken off.

"Ech, that horrid little cur!" whispered Mr. Golyadkin, not understanding himself.

At last he saw his stranger at the turning into Italyansky Street. But this time the stranger was not coming to meet him, but was going in the same direction as he was, and he, too, was running, a few steps in front. At last they turned into Shestila-vochny Street.

Mr. Golyadkin caught his breath. The stranger stopped exactly before the house in which Mr. Golyadkin lodged. He heard a ring at the bell and almost at the same time the grating of the iron bolt. The gate opened, the stranger stooped, darted in and disappeared. Almost at the same instant Mr. Golyadkin reached the spot and like an arrow flew in at the gate. Heedless of the grumbling porter, he ran, gasping for breath, into the yard, and immediately saw his interesting companion, whom he had lost sight of for a moment.

The stranger darted towards the staircase which led to Mr. Golyadkin's flat. Mr. Golyadkin rushed after him. The stairs were dark, damp and dirty. At every turning there were heaped-up masses of refuse from the flats, so that any unaccustomed stranger who found himself on the stairs in the dark was forced to travel to and fro for half an hour in danger of breaking his legs, cursing the stairs as well as the friends who lived in such an inconvenient place. But Mr. Golyadkin's companion seemed as though familiar with it, as though at home; he ran up lightly, without difficulty, showing a perfect knowledge of his surroundings. Mr. Golyadkin had almost caught him up; in fact, once or twice the stranger's coat flicked him on the nose. His heart stood still. The stranger stopped before the door of Mr. Golyadkin's flat, knocked on it, and (which would, however, have surprised Mr. Golyadkin at any other time) Petrushka, as though he had been sitting up in expectation, opened the door at once and, with a candle in his hand, followed the stranger as the latter went in. The hero of our story dashed into his lodging beside himself; without taking off his hat or coat he crossed the little passage and stood still in the doorway of his room, as though thunderstruck. All his presentiments had come true. All that he had dreaded and surmised was coming to pass in reality. His breath failed him, his head was in a whirl. The stranger, also in his coat and hat, was sitting before him on his bed, and with a faint smile, screwing up his eyes, nodded to him in a friendly way. Mr. Golyadkin wanted to scream, but could not— to protest in some way, but his strength failed him. His hair stood on end, and he almost fell down with horror. And, indeed, there was good reason. He recognized his nocturnal visitor. The nocturnal visitor was no other than himself—Mr. Golyadkin himself, another Mr. Golyadkin, but absolutely the same as himself—in fact, what is called a double in every respect. . . .

CHAPTER VI

At eight o'clock next morning Mr. Golyadkin woke up in his bed. At once all the extraordinary incidents of the previous day and the wild, incredible night, with all its almost impossible adventures, presented themselves to his imagination and memory with terrifying vividness. Such intense, diabolical malice on the part of his enemies, and, above all, the final proof of that malice, froze Mr. Golyadkin's heart. But at the same time it was all so strange, incomprehensible, wild, it seemed so impossible, that it was really hard to credit the whole business; Mr. Golyadkin was, indeed, ready to admit himself that it was all an incredible delusion, a passing aberration of the fancy, a darkening of the mind, if he had not fortunately known by bitter experience to what lengths spite will sometimes carry any one, what a pitch of ferocity an enemy may reach when he is bent on revenging his honour and prestige. Besides, Mr. Golyadkin's exhausted limbs, his heavy head, his aching back, and the malignant cold in his head bore vivid witness to the probability of his expedition of the previous night and upheld the reality of it, and to some extent of all that had happened during that expedition. And, indeed, Mr. Golyadkin had known long, long before that something was being got up among them, that there was some one else with them. But after all, thinking it over thoroughly, he made up his mind to keep quiet, to submit and not to protest for the time.

"They are simply plotting to frighten me, perhaps, and when they see that I don't mind, that I make no protest, but keep perfectly quiet and put up with it meekly, they'll give it up, they'll give it up of themselves, give it up of their own accord."

Such, then, were the thoughts in the mind of Mr. Golyadkin as, stretching in his bed, trying to nest his exhausted limbs, he waited for Petrushka to come into his room as usual. . . . He waited for a full quarter of an hour. He heard the lazy scamp fiddling about with the samovar behind the screen, and yet he could not bring himself to call him. We may say more: Mr. Golyadkin was a little afraid of confronting Petrushka.

"Why, goodness knows," he thought, "goodness knows how that rascal looks at it all. He keeps on saying nothing, but he has his own ideas."

At last the door creaked and Petrushka came in with a tray in his hands. Mr. Golyadkin stole a timid glance at him, impatiently waiting to see what would happen, waiting to see whether he would not say something about a certain circumstance. But Petrushka said nothing; he was, on the contrary, more silent, more glum and ill-humoured than usual; he looked askance from under his brows at everything; altogether it was evident that he was very much put out about something; he did not even once glance at his master, which, by the way, rather piqued the latter. Setting all he had brought on the table, he turned and went out of the room without a word.

"He knows, he knows, he knows all about it, the scoundrel!" Mr. Golyadkin grumbled to himself as he took his tea. Yet our hero did not address a single question to his servant, though Petrushka came into his room several times afterwards on various errands. Mr. Golyadkin was in great trepidation of spirit. He dreaded going to the office. He had a strong presentiment that there he would find something that would not be "just so."

"You may be sure," he thought, "that as soon as you go you will light upon something! Isn't it better to endure in patience? Isn't it better to wait a bit now? Let them do what they like there; but I'd better stay here a bit to-day, recover my strength, get better, and think over the whole affair more thoroughly, then afterwards I could seize the right moment, fall upon them like snow from the sky, and get off scot free myself."

Reasoning like this, Mr. Golyadkin smoked pipe after pipe; time was flying. It was already nearly half-past nine.

"Why, it's half-past nine already," thought Mr. Golyadkin; "it's late for me to make my appearance. Besides, I'm ill, of course I'm ill, I'm certainly ill; who denies it? What's the matter with me? If they send to make inquiries, let the executive clerk come; and, indeed, what is the matter with me really? My back aches, I have a cough, and a cold in my head; and, in fact, it's out of the question for me to go out, utterly out of the question in such weather. I might be taken ill and, very likely, die; nowadays especially the death-rate is so high. . . ."

With such reasoning Mr. Golyadkin succeeded at last in setting his conscience at rest, and defended himself against the reprimands he expected from Andrey Filippovich for neglect of his duty. As a rule in such cases our hero was particularly fond of justifying himself in his own eyes with all sorts of irrefutable arguments, and so completely setting his conscience at rest. And so now, having completely soothed his conscience, he took up his pipe, filled it, and had no sooner settled down comfortably to smoke, when he jumped up quickly from the sofa, flung away the pipe, briskly washed, shaved, and brushed his hair, got into his uniform and so on, snatched up some papers, and flew off to the office.

Mr. Golyadkin went into his department timidly, in quivering expectation of something unpleasant—an expectation which was none the less disagreeable for being vague and unconscious; he sat timidly down in his invariable place next the head clerk, Anton Antonovich Setochkin. Without looking at anything or allowing his attention to be distracted, he plunged into the contents of the papers that lay before him. He made up his mind and vowed to himself to avoid, as far as possible, anything provocative, anything that might compromise him, such as indiscreet questions, jests, or unseemly allusions to any incidents of the previous evening; he made up his mind also to abstain from the usual interchange of civilities with his colleagues, such as inquiries after health and such like. But evidently it was impossible, out of the question, to keep to this. Anxiety and uneasiness in regard to anything near him that was annoying always worried him far more than the annoyance itself. And that was why, in spite of his inward vows to refrain from entering into anything, whatever happened, and to keep aloof from everything, Mr. Golyadkin from time to time, on the sly, very, very quietly, raised his head and stealthily looked about him to right and to left, peeped at the countenances of his colleagues, and tried to gather whether there were not something new and particular in them referring to himself and with sinister motives concealed from him. He assumed that there must be a connection between all that had happened yesterday and all that surrounded him now. At last, in his misery, he began to long for something—goodness knows what—to happen to put an end to it—even some calamity—he did not care. At this point destiny caught Mr. Golyadkin: he had hardly felt this desire when his doubts were solved in the strangest and most unexpected manner.

The door leading from the next room suddenly gave a soft and timid creak, as though to indicate that the person about to enter was a very unimportant one, and a figure, very familiar to Mr. Golyadkin, stood shyly before the very table at which our hero was seated. The latter did not raise his head—no, he only stole a glance at him, the tiniest glance; but he knew all, he understood all, to every detail. He grew hot with shame, and buried his devoted head in his papers with precisely the same object with which the ostrich, pursued by hunters, hides his head in the burning sand. The new arrival bowed to Andrey Filippovich, and thereupon he heard a voice speaking in the regulation tone of condescending politeness with which all persons in authority address their subordinates in public offices.

"Take a seat here," said Andrey Filippovich, motioning the newcomer to Anton Antonovich's table. "Here, opposite Mr. Golyadkin, and we'll soon give you something to do."

Andrey Filippovich ended by making a rapid gesture that decorously admonished the newcomer of his duty, and then he immediately became engrossed in the study of the papers that lay in a heap before him.

Mr. Golyadkin lifted his eyes at last, and that he did not fall into a swoon was simply because he had foreseen it all from the first, that he had been forewarned from the first, guessing in his soul who the stranger was. Mr. Golyadkin's first movement was to look quickly about him, to see whether there were any whispering, any office joke being cracked on the subject, whether any one's face was agape with wonder, whether, indeed, some one had not fallen under the table from terror. But to his intense astonishment there was no sign of anything of the sort. The behaviour of his colleagues and companions surprised him. It seemed contrary to the dictates of common sense. Mr. Golyadkin was positively scared at this extraordinary reticence. The fact spoke for itself; it was a strange, horrible, uncanny thing. It was enough to rouse any one. All this, of course, only passed rapidly through Mr. Golyadkin's mind. He felt as though he were burning in a slow fire. And, indeed, there was enough to make him. The figure that was sitting opposite Mr. Golyadkin now was his terror, was his shame, was his nightmare of the evening before; in short, was Mr. Golyadkin himself, not the Mr. Golyadkin who was sitting now in his chair with his mouth wide open and his pen petrified in his hand, not the one who acted as assistant to his chief, not the one who liked to efface himself and slink away in the crowd, not the one whose deportment plainly said, "Don't touch me and I won't touch you," or, "Don't interfere with me, you see I'm not touching you"; no, this was another Mr. Golyadkin, quite different, yet, at the same time, exactly like the first—the same height, the same figure, the same clothes, the same baldness; in fact, nothing, absolutely nothing, was lacking to complete the likeness, so that if one were to set them side by side, nobody, absolutely nobody, could have undertaken to distinguish which was the real Golyadkin and which was the counterfeit, which was the old one and which was the new one, which was the original and which was the copy.

Our hero was—if the comparison can be made—in the position of a man upon whom some practical joker has stealthily, by way of jest, turned a burning-glass.

"What does it mean? Is it a dream?" he wondered. "Is it reality or the continuation of what happened yesterday? And besides, by what right is this all being done? Who sanctioned such a clerk, who authorized this? Am I asleep, am I in a waking dream?"

Mr. Golyadkin tried pinching himself, even tried to screw up his courage to pinch some one else. . . . No, it was not a dream, and that was all about it. Mr. Golyadkin felt that the sweat was trickling down him in big drops; he felt that what was happening to him was something incredible, unheard of, and for that very reason was, to complete his misery, utterly unseemly, for Mr. Golyadkin realized and felt how disadvantageous it was to be the first example of such a burlesque adventure. He even began to doubt his own existence, and though he was prepared for anything and had been longing for his doubts to be settled in any way whatever, yet the actual reality was startling in its unexpectedness. His misery was poignant and overwhelming. At times he lost all power of thought and memory. Coming to himself after such a moment, he noticed that he was mechanically and unconsciously moving the pen over the paper. Mistrustful of himself, he began going over what he had written—and could make nothing of it. At last the other Mr. Golyadkin, who had been sitting discreetly and decorously at the table, got up and disappeared through the door into the other room. Mr. Golyadkin looked round—everything was quiet; he heard nothing but the scratching of pens, the rustle of turning over pages, and conversation in the corners furthest from Andrey Filippovich's seat. Mr. Golyadkin looked at Anton

Antonovich, and as, in all probability, our hero's countenance fully reflected his real condition and harmonized with the whole position, and was consequently, from one point of view, very remarkable, good-natured Anton Antonovich, laying aside his pen, inquired after his health with marked sympathy.

"I'm very well, thank God, Anton Antonovich," said Mr. Golyadkin, stammering. "I am perfectly well, Anton Antonovich. I am all right now, Anton Antonovich," he added uncertainly, not yet fully trusting Anton Antonovich, whose name he had mentioned so often.

"I fancied you were not quite well: though that's not to be wondered at; no, indeed! Nowadays especially there's such a lot of illness going about. Do you know . . ."

"Yes, Anton Antonovich, I know there is such a lot of illness . . . I did not mean that, Anton Antonovich," Mr. Golyadkin went on, looking intently at Anton Antonovich. "You see, Anton Antonovich, I don't even know how you, that is, I mean to say, how to approach this matter, Anton Antonovich. . . ."

"How so? I really . . . do you know . . . I must confess I don't quite understand; you must . . . you must explain, you know, in what way you are in difficulties," said Anton Antonovich, beginning to be in difficulties himself, seeing that there were actually tears in Mr. Golyadkin's eyes.

"Really, Anton Antonovich . . . I . . . here . . . there's a clerk here, Anton Antonovich . . ."

"Well! I don't understand now."

"I mean to say, Anton Antonovich, there's a new clerk here."

"Yes, there is; a namesake of yours."

"What?" cried Mr. Golyadkin.

"I say a namesake of yours; his name's Golyadkin too. Isn't he a brother of yours?"

"No, Anton Antonovich, I . . ."

"H'm! you don't say so! Why, I thought he must be a relation of yours. Do you know, there's a sort of family likeness."

Mr. Golyadkin was petrified with astonishment, and for the moment he could not speak. To treat so lightly such a horrible, unheard-of thing, a thing undeniably rare and curious in its way, a thing which would have amazed even an unconcerned spectator, to talk of a family resemblance when he could see himself as in a looking-glass!

"Do you know, Yakov Petrovich, what I advise you to do?" Anton Antonovich went on. "Go and consult a doctor. Do you know, you look somehow quite unwell. Your eyes look peculiar . . . you know, there's a peculiar expression in them."

"No, Anton Antonovich, I feel, of course . . . that is, I keep wanting to ask about this clerk."

"Well?"

"That is, have not you noticed, Anton Antonovich, something peculiar about him, something very marked?"

"That is . . . ?"

"That is, I mean, Anton Antonovich, a striking likeness with somebody, for instance; with me, for instance? You spoke just now, you see, Anton Antonovich, of a family likeness. You let slip the remark. . . . You know there really are sometimes twins exactly alike, like two drops of water, so that they can't be told apart. Well, it's that that I mean."

"To be sure," said Anton Antonovich, after a moment's thought, speaking as though he were struck by the fact for the first time: "yes, indeed! You are right, there is a striking likeness, and you are quite right in what you say. You really might be mistaken for one another," he went on, opening his eyes wider and wider; "and, do you know, Yakov Petrovich, it's positively a marvellous likeness, fantastic, in fact, as the saying is; that is, just as you . . . Have you observed, Yakov Petrovich? I wanted to ask you to explain it; yes, I must confess I didn't take particular notice at first. It's wonderful, it's really wonderful! And, you know, you are not a native of these parts, are you, Yakov Petrovich?"

"No."

"He is not from these parts, you know, either. Perhaps he comes from the same part of the country as you do. Where, may I make bold to inquire, did your mother live for the most part?"

"You said . . . you say, Anton Antonovich, that he is not a native of these parts?"

"No, he is not. And, indeed, how strange it is!" continued the talkative Anton Antonovich, for whom it was a genuine treat to gossip. "It may well arouse curiosity; and yet, you know, you might often pass him by, brush against him, without noticing anything. But you mustn't be upset about it. It's a thing that does happen. Do you know, the same thing, I must tell you, happened to my aunt on my mother's side; she saw her own double before her death . . ."

"No, I—excuse my interrupting you, Anton Antonovich—I wanted to find out, Anton Antonovich, how that clerk . . . that is, on what footing is he here?"

"In place of Semyon Ivanovich, to fill the vacancy left by his death; the post was vacant, so he was appointed. Do you know, I'm told poor dear Semyon Ivanovich left three children, all tiny dots. The widow fell at the feet of his Excellency. They do say she's hiding something; she's got a bit of money, but she's hiding it."

"No, Anton Antonovich, I was still referring to that circumstance."

"You mean . . . ? To be sure! But why are you so interested in that? I tell you not to upset yourself. All this is temporary to some extent. Why, after all, you know, you have nothing to do with it. So it has been ordained by God Almighty, it's His will, and it is sinful repining. His wisdom is apparent in it. And as far as I can make out, Yakov Petrovich, you are not to blame in any way. There are all sorts of strange things in the world! Mother Nature is liberal with her gifts, and you are not called upon to answer for it, you won't be responsible. Here, for instance, you have heard, I expect, of those—what's their name?—oh, the Siamese twins who are joined together at the back, live and eat and sleep together. I'm told they get a lot of money."

"Allow me, Anton Antonovich . . ."

"I understand, I understand! Yes! But what of it? It's no matter, I tell you, as far as I can see there's nothing for you to upset yourself about. After all, he's a clerk—as a clerk he seems to be a capable man. He says his name is Golyadkin, that he's not a native of this district, and that he's a titular councillor. He had a personal interview with his Excellency."

"And how did his Excellency . . . ?"

"It was all right; I am told he gave a satisfactory account of himself, gave his reasons, said, 'It's like this, your Excellency,' and that he was without means and anxious to enter the service, and would be particularly flattered to be serving under his Excellency . . . all that was proper, you know; he expressed himself neatly. He must be a sensible man. But of course he came with a recommendation; he couldn't have got in without that. . . ."

"Oh, from whom . . . that is, I mean, who is it has had a hand in this shameful business?"

"Yes, a good recommendation, I'm told; his Excellency, I'm told, laughed with Andrey Filippovich."

"Laughed with Andrey Filippovich?"

"Yes, he only just smiled and said that it was all right, and that he had nothing against it, so long as he did his duty. . . ."

"Well, and what more? You relieve me to some extent, Anton Antonovich; go on, I entreat you."

"Excuse me, I must tell you again. . . . Well, then, come, it's nothing, it's a very simple matter; you mustn't upset yourself, I tell you, and there's nothing suspicious about it. . . ."

"No. I . . . that is, Anton Antonovich, I want to ask you, didn't his Excellency say anything more . . . about me, for instance?"

"Well! To be sure! No, nothing of the sort; you can set your mind quite at rest. You know it is, of course, a rather striking circumstance, and at first . . . why, here, I, for instance, I scarcely noticed it. I really don't know why I didn't notice it till you mentioned it. But you can set your mind at rest entirely. He said nothing particular, absolutely nothing," added good-natured Anton Antonovich, getting up from his chair.

"So then, Anton Antonovich, I . . ."

"Oh, you must excuse me. Here I've been gossiping about these trivial matters, and I've business that is important and urgent. I must inquire about it."

"Anton Antonovich!" Andrey Filippovich's voice sounded, summoning him politely, "his Excellency has been asking for you."

"This minute, I'm coming this minute, Andrey Filippovich." And Anton Antonovich, taking a pile of papers, flew off first to Andrey Filippovich and then into his Excellency's room.

"Then what is the meaning of it?" thought Mr. Golyadkin. "Is there some sort of game going on? So the wind's in that quarter now. . . . That's just as well; so things have taken a much pleasanter turn," our hero said to himself, rubbing his hands, and so delighted that he scarcely knew where he was. "So our position is an ordinary thing. So it turns out to be all nonsense, it comes to nothing at all. No one has done anything really, and they are not budging, the rascals, they are sitting busy over their work; that's splendid, splendid! I like the good-natured fellow, I've always liked him, and I'm always ready to respect him . . . though it must be said one doesn't know what to think; this Anton Antonovich . . . I'm afraid to trust him; his hair's very grey, and he's so old he's getting shaky. It's an immense and glorious thing that his Excellency said nothing, and let it pass! It's a good thing! I approve! Only why does Andrey Filippovich interfere with his grins? What's he got to do with it? The old rogue. Always on my track, always, like a black cat, on the watch to run across a man's path, always thwarting and annoying a man, always annoying and thwarting a man. . . ."

Mr. Golyadkin looked around him again, and again his hopes revived. Yet he felt that he was troubled by one remote idea, an unpleasant idea. It even occurred to him that he might try somehow to make up to the clerks, to be the first in the field even (perhaps when leaving the office or going up to them as though about his work), to drop a hint in the course of conversation, saying, "This is how it is, what a striking likeness, gentlemen, a strange circumstance, a burlesque farce!"—that is, treat it all lightly, and in this way sound the depth of the danger. "Devils breed in still waters," our hero concluded inwardly.

Mr. Golyadkin, however, only contemplated this; he thought better of it in time. He realized that this would be going too far.

"That's your temperament," he said to himself, tapping himself lightly on the forehead; "as soon as you gain anything you are delighted! You're a simple soul! No, you and I had better be patient, Yakov Petrovich; let us wait and be patient!"

Nevertheless, as we have mentioned already, Mr. Golyadkin was buoyed up with the most confident hopes, feeling as though he had risen from the dead.

"No matter," he thought, "it's as though a hundred tons had been lifted off my chest! Here is a circumstance, to be sure! The box has been opened by lifting the lid. Krylov is right, a clever chap, a rogue, that Krylov, and a great fable-writer![13] And as for him, let him work in the office, and good luck to him so long as he doesn't meddle or interfere with any one; let him work in the office—I consent and approve!"

Meanwhile the hours were passing, flying by, and before he noticed the time it struck four. The office was closed. Andrey Filippovich took his hat, and all followed his example in due course. Mr. Golyadkin dawdled a little on purpose, long enough to be the last to go out when all the others had gone their several ways. Going out from the street he felt as though he were in Paradise, so that he even felt inclined to go a longer way round, and to walk along Nevsky Prospect.

"To be sure this is destiny," thought our hero, "this unexpected turn in affairs. And the weather's more cheerful, and the frost and the little sledges. And the frost suits the Russian, the Russian gets on capitally with the frost. I like the Russian. And the dear little snow, and the first few flakes in autumn; the sportsman would say, 'It would be nice to go shooting hares in the first snow.' Well, there, it doesn't matter."

This was how Mr. Golyadkin's enthusiasm found expression. Yet something was fretting in his brain, not exactly melancholy, but at times he had such a gnawing at his heart that he did not know how to find relief.

"Let us wait for the day, though, and then we shall rejoice. And, after all, you know, what does it matter? Come, let us think it over, let us look at it. Come, let us consider it, my young friend, let us consider it. Why, a man's exactly like you in the first place, absolutely the same. Well, what is there in that? If there is such a man, why should I weep over it? What is it to me? I stand aside, I whistle to myself, and that's all! That's what I laid myself open to, and that's all about it! Let him work in the office! Well, it's strange and marvellous, they say, that the Siamese twins . . . But why bring in the Siamese twins? They are twins, of course, but even great men, you know, sometimes look queer creatures. In fact, we know from history that the famous Suvorov used to crow like a cock. . . . But there, he did all that with political motives; and he was a great general . . . but what are generals, after all? But I keep myself to myself, that's all, and I don't care about any one else, and, secure in my innocence, I scorn my enemies. I am not one to intrigue, and I'm proud of it. Genuine, straightforward, neat and nice, meek and mild."

All at once Mr. Golyadkin broke off, his tongue failed him and he began trembling like a leaf; he even closed his eyes for a minute. Hoping, however, that the object of his terror was only an illusion, he opened his eyes at last and stole a timid glance to the right. No, it was not an illusion! . . . His acquaintance of that morning was tripping along by his side, smiling, peeping into his face, and apparently seeking an opportunity to begin a conversation with him. The conversation was not begun, however. They both walked like this for about fifty paces. All Mr. Golyadkin's efforts were concentrated on muffling himself up, hiding himself in his coat and pulling his hat down as far as possible over his eyes. To complete his mortification, his companion's coat and hat looked as though they had been taken off Mr. Golyadkin himself.

"Sir," our hero articulated at last, trying to speak almost in a whisper, and not looking at his companion, "we are going different ways, I believe. . . . I am convinced of it, in fact," he said, after a brief pause. "I am convinced, indeed, that you quite understand me," he added, rather severely, in conclusion.

"I could have wished . . ." his companion pronounced at last, "I could have wished . . . no doubt you will be magnanimous and pardon me . . . I don't know to whom to address myself here . . . my circumstances . . . I trust you will pardon my intrusiveness. I fancied, indeed, that, moved by compassion, you showed some interest in me this morning. On my side, I felt drawn to you from the first moment. I . . ."

At this point Mr. Golyadkin inwardly wished that his companion might sink into the earth.

"If I might venture to hope that you would accord me an indulgent hearing, Yakov Petrovich . . ."

"We—here, we—we . . . you had better come home with me," answered Mr. Golyadkin. "We will cross now to the other side of Nevsky Prospect, it will be more convenient for us there, and then by the little back street . . . we'd better go by the back street."

"Very well, by all means let us go by the back street," our hero's meek companion responded timidly, suggesting by the tone of his reply that it was not for him to choose, and that in his position he was quite prepared to accept the back street. As for Mr. Golyadkin, he was utterly unable to grasp what was happening to him. He could not believe in himself. He could not get over his amazement.

CHAPTER VII

He recovered himself a little on the staircase as he went up to his flat.

"Oh, I'm a sheep's head," he railed at himself inwardly. "Where am I taking him? I am thrusting my head into the noose. What will Petrushka think, seeing us together? What will the scoundrel dare to imagine now? He's suspicious. . . ."

But it was too late to regret it. Mr. Golyadkin knocked at the door; it was opened, and Petrushka began taking off the visitor's coat as well as his master's. Mr. Golyadkin looked askance, just stealing a glance at Petrushka, trying to read his counte-

nance and divine what he was thinking. But to his intense astonishment he saw that his servant showed no trace of surprise,
but seemed, on the contrary, to be expecting something of the
sort. Of course he did look morose, as it was; he kept his eyes
turned away and looked as though he would like to fall upon
somebody.

"Hasn't somebody bewitched them all to-day?" thought our
hero. "Some devil must have got round them. There certainly
must be something peculiar in the whole lot of them to-day.
Damn it all, what a worry it is!"

Such were Mr. Golyadkin's thoughts and reflections as he led
his visitor into his room and politely asked him to sit down. The
visitor appeared to be greatly embarrassed, he was very shy, and
humbly watched every movement his host made, caught his
glance, and seemed trying to divine his thoughts from them.
There was a downtrodden, crushed, scared look about all his
gestures, so that—if the comparison may be allowed—he was
at that moment rather like the man who, having lost his clothes,
is dressed up in somebody else's: the sleeves work up to the elbows, the waist is almost up to his neck, and he keeps every
minute pulling down the short waistcoat; he wriggles sideways
and turns away, tries to hide himself, or peeps into every face,
and listens whether people are talking of his position, laughing
at him or putting him to shame—and he is crimson with
shame and overwhelmed with confusion and wounded vanity. . . . Mr. Golyadkin put down his hat in the window, and
carelessly sent it flying to the floor. The visitor darted at once to
pick it up, brushed off the dust, and carefully put it back, while
he laid his own on the floor near a chair, on the edge of which
he meekly seated himself. This little circumstance did something to open Mr. Golyadkin's eyes; he realized that the man
was in great straits, and so did not put himself out for his visitor as he had done at first, very properly leaving all that to the
man himself. The visitor, for his part, did nothing either;
whether he was shy, a little ashamed, or from politeness was
waiting for his host to begin is not certain and would be difficult to determine. At that moment Petrushka came in; he stood

still in the doorway, and fixed his eyes in the direction furthest from where the visitor and his master were seated.

"Shall I bring in dinner for two?" he said carelessly, in a husky voice.

"I—I don't know . . . you . . . yes, bring dinner for two, my boy."

Petrushka went out. Mr. Golyadkin glanced at his visitor. The latter crimsoned to his ears. Mr. Golyadkin was a kind-hearted man, and so in the kindness of his heart he at once elaborated a theory.

"The fellow's hard up," he thought. "Yes, and in his situation only one day. Most likely he's suffered in his time. Maybe his good clothes are all that he has, and nothing to get him a dinner. Ah, poor fellow, how crushed he seems! But no matter; in a way it's better so. . . . Excuse me," began Mr. Golyadkin, "allow me to ask what I may call you."

"I . . . I . . . I'm Yakov Petrovich," his visitor almost whispered, as though conscience-stricken and ashamed, as though apologizing for being called Yakov Petrovich too.

"Yakov Petrovich!" repeated our hero, unable to conceal his confusion.

"Yes, just so. . . . The same name as yours," responded the meek visitor, venturing to smile and speak a little jocosely. But at once he drew back, assuming a very serious air, though a little disconcerted, noticing that his host was in no joking mood.

"You . . . allow me to ask you, to what am I indebted for the honour . . . ?"

"Knowing your generosity and your benevolence," interposed the visitor in a rapid but timid voice, half rising from his seat, "I have ventured to appeal to you and to beg for your . . . acquaintance and protection . . ." he concluded, choosing his phrases with difficulty and trying to select words not too flattering or servile, that he might not compromise his dignity and not so bold as to suggest an unseemly equality. In fact, one may say the visitor behaved like a gentlemanly beggar with a darned waistcoat, with an honourable passport in his pocket, who has not yet learnt by practice to hold out his hand properly for alms.

"You perplex me," answered Mr. Golyadkin, gazing round at himself, his walls and his visitor. "In what could I . . . that is, I mean, in what way could I be of service to you?"

"I felt drawn to you, Yakov Petrovich, at first sight, and, graciously forgive me, I built my hopes on you—I made bold to build my hopes on you, Yakov Petrovich. I . . . I'm in a desperate plight here, Yakov Petrovich; I'm poor, I've had a great deal of trouble, Yakov Petrovich, and have only recently come here. Learning that you, with your innate goodness and excellence of heart, are of the same name . . ."

Mr. Golyadkin frowned.

"Of the same name as myself and a native of the same district, I made up my mind to appeal to you, and to make known to you my difficult position."

"Very good, very good; I really don't know what to say," Mr. Golyadkin responded in an embarrassed voice. "We'll have a talk after dinner. . . ."

The visitor bowed; dinner was brought in. Petrushka laid the table, and Mr. Golyadkin and his visitor proceeded to partake of it. The dinner did not last long, for they were both in a hurry, the host because he felt ill at ease, and was, besides, ashamed that the dinner was a poor one—he was partly ashamed because he wanted to give the visitor a good meal, and partly because he wanted to show him he did not live like a beggar. The visitor, on his side too, was in terrible confusion and extremely embarrassed. When he had finished the piece of bread he had taken, he was afraid to put out his hand to take another piece, was ashamed to help himself to the best morsels, and was continually assuring his host that he was not at all hungry, that the dinner was excellent, that he was absolutely satisfied with it, and should not forget it to his dying day. When the meal was over Mr. Golyadkin lighted his pipe, and offered a second, which was brought in, to the visitor. They sat facing each other, and the visitor began telling his adventures.

Mr. Golyadkin junior's story lasted for three or four hours.

His history was, however, composed of the most trivial and wretched, if one may say so, incidents. It dealt with details of service in some lawcourt in the provinces, of prosecutors and presidents, of some department intrigues, of the depravity of some registration clerks, of an inspector, of the sudden appointment of a new chief in the department, of how the second Mr. Golyadkin had suffered, quite without any fault on his part; of his aged aunt, Pelagea Semyonovna; of how, through various intrigues on the part of his enemies, he had lost his situation, and had come to Petersburg on foot; of the harassing and wretched time he had spent here in Petersburg, how for a long time he had tried in vain to get a job, had spent all his money, had nothing left, had been living almost in the street, lived on a crust of bread and washed it down with his tears, slept on the bare floor, and finally how some good Christian had exerted himself on his behalf, had given him an introduction, and had nobly got him into a new berth. Mr. Golyadkin's visitor shed tears as he told his story, and wiped his eyes with a blue-check handkerchief that looked like oilcloth. He ended by making a clean breast of it to Mr. Golyadkin, and confessing that he was not only for the time without means of subsistence and money for a decent lodging, but had not even the wherewithal to fit himself out properly, so that he had not, he said in conclusion, been able to get together enough for a pair of wretched boots, and that he had had to hire a uniform for the time.

Mr. Golyadkin was melted; he was genuinely touched. Even though his visitor's story was the paltriest story, every word of it was like heavenly manna to his heart. The fact was that Mr. Golyadkin was beginning to forget his last misgivings, to surrender his soul to freedom and rejoicing, and at last mentally dubbed himself a fool. It was all so natural! And what a thing to break his heart over, what a thing to be so distressed about! To be sure there was, there really was, one ticklish circumstance— but, after all, it was not a misfortune; it could be no disgrace to a man, it could not cast a slur on his honour or ruin his career, if he were innocent, since nature herself was mixed up in it. Moreover, the visitor begged for protection, wept, railed at des-

tiny, seemed such an artless, pitiful, insignificant person, with
no craft or malice about him, and he seemed now to be
ashamed himself, though perhaps on different grounds, of the
strange resemblance of his countenance with that of Mr.
Golyadkin's. His behaviour was absolutely unimpeachable; his
one desire was to please his host, and he looked as a man looks
who feels conscience-stricken and to blame in regard to some
one else. If any doubtful point were touched upon, for instance,
the visitor at once agreed with Mr. Golyadkin's opinion. If by
mistake he advanced an opinion in opposition to Mr. Golyadkin's, and afterwards noticed that he had made a slip, he immediately corrected his mistake, explained himself and made it
clear that he meant the same thing as his host, that he thought
as he did and took the same view of everything as he did. In
fact, the visitor made every possible effort to "make up to" Mr.
Golyadkin, so that the latter made up his mind at last that his
visitor must be a very amiable person in every way. Meanwhile,
tea was brought in; it was nearly nine o'clock. Mr. Golyadkin
felt in a very good humour, grew lively and skittish, let himself
go a little, and finally plunged into a most animated and interesting conversation with his visitor. In his festive moments Mr.
Golyadkin was fond of telling interesting anecdotes. So now he
told the visitor a great deal about Petersburg, about its entertainments and attractions, about the theatre, the clubs, about
Brullov's picture,[14] and about the two Englishmen who came
from England to Petersburg on purpose to look at the iron railing of the Summer Garden, and returned at once when they had
seen it; about the office; about Olsufy Ivanovich and Andrey
Filippovich; about the way that Russia was progressing, was
hour by hour progressing towards a state of perfection, so that

"Arts and letters flourish here to-day";

about an anecdote he had lately read in the Northern Bee concerning a boa-constrictor in India of immense strength; about
Baron Brambeus,[15] and so on. In short, Mr. Golyadkin was quite
happy, first, because his mind was at rest; secondly, because, so

far from being afraid of his enemies, he was quite prepared now to challenge them all to mortal combat; thirdly, because he was now in the role of patron and was doing a good deed. Yet he was conscious at the bottom of his heart that he was not perfectly happy, that there was still a hidden worm gnawing at his heart, though it was only a tiny one. He was extremely worried by the thought of the previous evening at Olsufy Ivanovich's. He would have given a great deal now for nothing to have happened of what took place then.

"It's no matter, though!" our hero decided at last, and he firmly resolved in his heart to behave well in future and never to be guilty of such pranks again. As Mr. Golyadkin was now completely worked up, and had suddenly become almost blissful, the fancy took him to have a jovial time. Rum was brought in by Petrushka, and punch was prepared. The visitor and his host drained a glass each, and then a second. The visitor appeared even more amiable than before, and gave more than one proof of his frankness and charming character; he entered keenly into Mr. Golyadkin's joy, seemed only to rejoice in his rejoicing, and to look upon him as his one and only benefactor. Taking up a pen and a sheet of paper, he asked Mr. Golyadkin not to look at what he was going to write, but afterwards showed his host what he had written. It turned out to be a verse of four lines, written with a good deal of feeling, in excellent language and handwriting, and evidently was the composition of the amiable visitor himself. The lines were as follows—

> "If thou forget me,
> I shall not forget thee;
> Though all things may be,
> Do not thou forget me."[16]

With tears in his eyes Mr. Golyadkin embraced his companion, and, completely overcome by his feelings, he began to initiate his friend into some of his own secrets and private affairs, Andrey Filippovich and Klara Olsufyevna being prominent in his remarks.

"Well, you may be sure we shall get on together, Yakov Petrovich," said our hero to his visitor. "You and I will take to each other like fish to the water, Yakov Petrovich; we shall be like brothers; we'll be cunning, my dear fellow, we'll work together; we'll get up an intrigue, too, to pay them out. To pay them out we'll get up an intrigue too. And don't you trust any of them. I know you, Yakov Petrovich, and I understand your character; you'll tell them everything straight out, you know, you're a guileless soul! You must hold aloof from them all, my boy."

His companion entirely agreed with him, thanked Mr. Golyadkin, and he, too, grew tearful at last.

"Do you know, Yasha," Mr. Golyadkin went on in a shaking voice, weak with emotion, "you must stay with me for a time, or stay with me for ever. We shall get on together. What do you say, brother, eh? And don't you worry or repine because there's such a strange circumstance about us now; it's a sin to repine, brother; it's nature! And Mother Nature is liberal with her gifts, so there, brother Yasha! It's from love for you that I speak, from brotherly love. But we'll be cunning, Yasha; we'll lay a mine, too, and we'll make them laugh the other side of their mouths."

They reached their third and fourth glasses of punch at last, and then Mr. Golyadkin began to be aware of two sensations: the one that he was extraordinarily happy, and the other that he could not stand upon his legs. The guest was, of course, invited to stay the night. A bed was somehow made up on two chairs. Mr. Golyadkin junior declared that under a friend's roof the bare floor would be a soft bed, that for his part he could sleep anywhere, humbly and gratefully; that he was in paradise now, that he had been through a great deal of trouble and grief in his time; he had seen ups and downs, had all sorts of things to put up with, and—who could tell what the future would be?— maybe he would have still more to put up with. Mr. Golyadkin senior protested against this, and began to maintain that one must put one's faith in God. His guest entirely agreed, observing that there was, of course, no one like God. At this point Mr.

Golyadkin senior observed that in certain respects the Turks were right in calling upon God even in their sleep. Then, though disagreeing with certain learned professors in the slanders they had promulgated against the Turkish prophet Muhammad[17] and recognizing him as a great politician in his own line, Mr. Golyadkin passed to a very interesting description of an Algerian barber's shop which he had read in a book of miscellanies. The friends laughed heartily at the simplicity of the Turks, but paid due tribute to their fanaticism, which they ascribed to opium. . . . At last the guest began undressing, and thinking in the kindness of his heart that very likely he hadn't even a decent shirt, Mr. Golyadkin went behind the screen to avoid embarrassing a man who had suffered enough, and partly to reassure himself as far as possible about Petrushka, to sound him, to cheer him up if he could, to be kind to the fellow so that every one might be happy and that everything might be pleasant all round. It must be remarked that Petrushka still rather bothered Mr. Golyadkin.

"You go to bed now, Pyotr," Mr. Golyadkin said blandly, going into his servant's domain; "you go to bed now and wake me up at eight o'clock. Do you understand, Petrushka?"

Mr. Golyadkin spoke with exceptional softness and friendliness. But Petrushka remained mute. He was busy making his bed, and did not even turn round to face his master, which he ought to have done out of simple respect.

"Did you hear what I said, Pyotr?" Mr. Golyadkin went on. "You go to bed now and wake me to-morrow at eight o'clock; do you understand?"

"Why, I know that; what's the use of telling me?" Petrushka grumbled to himself.

"Well, that's right, Petrushka; I only mentioned it that you might be happy and at rest. Now we are all happy, so I want you, too, to be happy and satisfied. And now I wish you good-night. Sleep, Petrushka, sleep; we all have to work. . . . Don't think anything amiss, my man . . ." Mr. Golyadkin began, but stopped short. "Isn't this too much?" he thought. "Haven't I gone too far? That's how it always is; I always overdo things."

Our hero felt much dissatisfied with himself as he left Petrushka. He was, besides, rather wounded by Petrushka's grumpiness and rudeness. "One jests with the rascal, his master does him too much honour, and the rascal does not feel it," thought Mr. Golyadkin. "But there, that's the nasty way of all that sort of people!"

Somewhat shaken, he went back to his room, and, seeing that his guest had settled himself for the night, he sat down on the edge of his bed for a minute.

"Come, you must own, Yasha," he began in a whisper, wagging his head, "you're a rascal, you know; what a way you've treated me! You see, you've got my name, do you know that?" he went on, jesting in a rather familiar way with his visitor. At last, saying a friendly good-night to him, Mr. Golyadkin began preparing for the night. The visitor meanwhile began snoring. Mr. Golyadkin in his turn got into bed, laughing and whispering to himself: "You are drunk to-day, my dear fellow, Yakov Petrovich, you rascal, you old Golyadkin—what a surname to have! Why, what are you so pleased about? You'll be crying to-morrow, you know, you sniveller; what am I to do with you?"

At this point a rather strange sensation pervaded Mr. Golyadkin's whole being, something like doubt or remorse.

"I've been over-excited and let myself go," he thought; "now I've a noise in my head and I'm drunk; I couldn't restrain myself, ass that I am! and I've been babbling bushels of nonsense, and, like a rascal, I was planning to be so sly. Of course, to forgive and forget injuries is the height of virtue; but it's a bad thing, nevertheless! Yes, that's so!"

At this point Mr. Golyadkin got up, took a candle and went on tiptoe to look once more at his sleeping guest. He stood over him for a long time, meditating deeply.

"An unpleasant picture! A burlesque, a regular burlesque, and that's the fact of the matter!"

At last Mr. Golyadkin settled down finally. There was a humming, a buzzing, a ringing in his head. He grew more and more drowsy . . . tried to think about something, to remember something very interesting, to decide something very important, some delicate question—but could not. Sleep descended upon his devoted head, and he slept as people generally do sleep who are not used to drinking and have consumed five glasses of punch at some festive gathering.

CHAPTER VIII

Mr. Golyadkin woke up next morning at eight o'clock as usual; as soon as he was awake he recalled all the adventures of the previous evening—and frowned as he recalled them. "Ugh, I did play the fool last night!" he thought, sitting up and glancing at his visitor's bed. But what was his amazement when he saw in the room no trace, not only of his visitor, but even of the bed on which his visitor had slept!

"What does it mean?" Mr. Golyadkin almost shrieked. "What can it be? What does this new circumstance portend?"

While Mr. Golyadkin was gazing in open-mouthed bewilderment at the empty spot, the door creaked and Petrushka came in with the tea-tray.

"Where, where?" our hero said in a voice hardly audible, pointing to the place which had been occupied by his visitor the night before.

At first Petrushka made no answer and did not look at his master, but fixed his eyes upon the corner to the right till Mr. Golyadkin felt compelled to look into that corner too. After a brief silence, however, Petrushka in a rude and husky voice answered that his master was not at home.

"You idiot; why I'm your master, Petrushka!" said Mr. Golyadkin in a breaking voice, looking open-eyed at his servant.

Petrushka made no reply, but he gave Mr. Golyadkin such a look that the latter crimsoned to his ears—looked at him with an insulting reproachfulness almost equivalent to open abuse.

Mr. Golyadkin was utterly flabbergasted, as the saying is. At last Petrushka explained that the *other one* had gone away an hour and a half ago, and would not wait. His answer, of course, sounded truthful and probable; it was evident that Petrushka was not lying; that his insulting look and the phrase the *other one* employed by him were only the result of the disgusting circumstance with which he was already familiar, but still he understood, though dimly, that something was wrong, and that destiny had some other surprise, not altogether a pleasant one, in store for him.

"All right, we shall see," he thought to himself. "We shall see in due time; we'll get to the bottom of all this. . . . Oh, Lord, have mercy upon us!" he moaned in conclusion, in quite a different voice. "And why did I invite him, to what end did I do all that? Why, I am thrusting my head into their thievish noose myself; I am tying the noose with my own hands. Ach, you fool, you fool! You can't resist babbling like some silly boy, some chancery clerk, some wretched creature of no class at all, some rag, some rotten dishclout; you're a gossip, an old woman! . . . Oh, all ye saints! And he wrote verses, the rogue, and expressed his love for me! How could . . . How can I show him the door in a polite way if he turns up again, the rogue? Of course, there are all sorts of ways and means. I can say this is how it is, my salary being so limited. . . . Or scare him off in some way saying that, taking this and that into consideration, I am forced to make clear . . . that he would have to pay an equal share of the cost of board and lodging, and pay the money in advance. H'm! No, damn it all, no! That would be degrading to me. It's not quite delicate! Couldn't I do something like this: suggest to Petrushka that he should annoy him in some way, should be disrespectful, be rude, and get rid of him in that way. Set them at each other in some way. . . . No, damn it all, no! It's dangerous and again, if one looks at it from that point of view—it's not the right thing at all! Not the right thing at all! But there, even if he doesn't come, it will be a bad look-out, too! I babbled to him last night! . . . Ach, it's a bad look-out, a bad look-out! Ach, we're in a bad way! Oh, I'm a cursed fool, a

cursed fool! You can't train yourself to behave as you ought, you
can't conduct yourself reasonably. Well, what if he comes, and
refuses. And God grant he may come! I should be very glad if
he did come. . . ."

Such were Mr. Golyadkin's reflections as he swallowed his
tea and glanced continually at the clock on the wall.

"It's a quarter to nine; it's time to go. And something will
happen! What will there be there? I should like to know what
exactly lies hidden in this—that is, the object, the aim, and the
various intrigues. It would be a good thing to find out what all
these people are plotting, and what will be their first step. . . ."

Mr. Golyadkin could endure it no longer. He threw down his
unfinished pipe, dressed and set off for the office, anxious to
ward off the danger if possible and to reassure himself about
everything by his presence in person. There was danger: he
knew himself that there was danger.

"We . . . will get to the bottom of it," said Mr. Golyadkin,
taking off his coat and goloshes in the entry. "We'll go into all
these matters immediately."

Making up his mind to act in this way, our hero put himself
to rights, assumed a correct and official air, and was just about to
pass into the adjoining room, when suddenly, in the very doorway, he jostled against his acquaintance of the day before, his
friend and companion. Mr. Golyadkin junior seemed not to notice Mr. Golyadkin senior, though they met almost nose to nose.
Mr. Golyadkin junior seemed to be busy, to be hastening somewhere, was breathless; he had such an official, such a businesslike air that it seemed as though any one could read in his face:
'Entrusted with a special commission.' . . .

"Oh, it's you, Yakov Petrovich!" said our hero, clutching the
hand of his last night's visitor.

"Presently, presently, excuse me, tell me about it afterwards,"
cried Mr. Golyadkin junior, dashing on.

"But, excuse me; I believe, Yakov Petrovich, you wanted . . ."

"What is it? Make haste and explain."

At this point his visitor of the previous night halted as

though reluctantly and against his will, and put his ear almost to Mr. Golyadkin's nose.

"I must tell you, Yakov Petrovich, that I am surprised at behaviour . . . behaviour which seemingly I could not have expected at all."

"There's a proper form for everything. Go to his Excellency's secretary and then appeal in the proper way to the directors of the office. Have you got your petition?"

"You . . . I really don't know, Yakov Petrovich! You simply amaze me, Yakov Petrovich! You certainly don't recognize me or, with your characteristic gaiety, you are joking."

"Oh, it's you," said Mr. Golyadkin junior, seeming only now to recognize Mr. Golyadkin senior. "So it's you? Well, have you had a good night?"

Then, smiling a little—a formal and conventional smile, by no means the sort of smile that was befitting (for, after all, he owed a debt of gratitude to Mr. Golyadkin senior)—smiling this formal and conventional smile, Mr. Golyadkin junior added that he was very glad Mr. Golyadkin senior had had a good night; then he made a slight bow and shuffling a little with his feet, looked to the right, and to the left, then dropped his eyes to the floor, made for the side door and muttering in a hurried whisper that he had a special commission, dashed into the next room. He vanished like an apparition.

"Well, this is queer!" muttered our hero, petrified for a moment; "this is queer! This is a strange circumstance."

At this point Mr. Golyadkin felt as though he had pins and needles all over him.

"However," he went on to himself, as he made his way to his department, "however, I spoke long ago of such a circumstance: I had a presentiment long ago that he had a special commission. Why, I said yesterday that the man must certainly be employed on some special commission."

"Have you finished copying out the document you had yesterday, Yakov Petrovich," Anton Antonovich Setochkin asked Mr. Golyadkin, when the latter was seated beside him. "Have you got it here?"

"Yes," murmured Mr. Golyadkin, looking at the head clerk with a rather helpless glance.

"That's right! I mention it because Andrey Filippovich has asked for it twice. I'll be bound his Excellency wants it. . . ."

"Yes, it's finished. . . ."

"Well, that's all right then."

"I believe, Anton Antonovich, I have always performed my duties properly. I'm always scrupulous over the work entrusted to me by my superiors, and I attend to it conscientiously."

"Yes. Why, what do you mean by that?"

"I mean nothing, Anton Antonovich. I only want to explain, Anton Antonovich, that I . . . that is, I meant to express that spite and malice sometimes spare no person whatever in their search for their daily and revolting food. . . ."

"Excuse me, I don't quite understand you. What person are you alluding to?"

"I only meant to say, Anton Antonovich, that I'm seeking the straight path and I scorn going to work in a roundabout way. That I am not one to intrigue, and that, if I may be allowed to say so, I may very justly be proud of it. . . ."

"Yes. That's quite so, and to the best of my comprehension I thoroughly endorse your remarks; but allow me to tell you, Yakov Petrovich, that personalities are not quite permissible in good society, that I, for instance, am ready to put up with anything behind my back—for every one's abused behind his back—but to my face, if you please, my good sir, I don't allow any one to be impudent. I've grown grey in the government service, sir, and I don't allow any one to be impudent to me in my old age. . . ."

"No, Anton Antonovich . . . you see, Anton Antonovich . . . you haven't quite caught my meaning. To be sure, Anton Antonovich, I for my part could only think it an honour. . . ."

"Well, then, I ask your pardon too. We've been brought up in the old school. And it's too late for us to learn your new-fangled ways. I believe we've had understanding enough for the service of our country up to now. As you are aware, sir, I have an order of merit for twenty-five years' irreproachable service. . . ."

"I feel it, Anton Antonovich, on my side, too, I quite feel all that. But I didn't mean that, I am speaking of a mask, Anton Antonovich. . . ."

"A mask?"

"Again you . . . I am apprehensive that you are taking this, too, in a wrong sense, that is the sense of my remarks, as you say yourself, Anton Antonovich. I am simply enunciating a theory, that is, I am advancing the idea, Anton Antonovich, that persons who wear a mask have become far from uncommon, and that nowadays it is hard to recognize the man beneath the mask. . . ."

"Well, do you know, it's not altogether so hard. Sometimes it's fairly easy. Sometimes one need not go far to look for it."

"No, you know, Anton Antonovich, I say, I say of myself that I, for instance, do not put on a mask except when there is need of it; that is simply at carnival time or at some festive gathering, speaking in the literal sense; but that I do not wear a mask before people in daily life, speaking in another less obvious sense. That's what I meant to say, Anton Antonovich."

"Oh, well, but we must drop all this, for now I've no time to spare," said Anton Antonovich, getting up from his seat and collecting some papers in order to report upon them to his Excellency. "Your business, as I imagine, will be explained in due course without delay. You will see for yourself whom you should censure and whom you should blame, and thereupon I humbly beg you to spare me from further private explanations and arguments which interfere with my work. . . ."

"No, Anton Antonovich," Mr. Golyadkin, turning a little pale, began to the retreating figure of Anton Antonovich; "I had no thought of the kind."

"What does it mean?" our hero went on to himself, when he was left alone; "what quarter is the wind in now, and what is one to make of this new turn?"

At the very time when our bewildered and half-crushed hero was setting himself to solve this new question, there was a sound of movement and bustle in the next room, the door opened and Andrey Filippovich, who had been on some business in his Excellency's study, appeared breathless in the doorway, and called to Mr. Golyadkin. Knowing what was wanted and anxious not to keep Andrey Filippovich waiting, Mr. Golyadkin leapt up from his seat, and as was fitting immediately bustled for all he was worth getting the manuscript that was required finally neat and ready and preparing to follow the manuscript and Andrey Filippovich into his Excellency's study. Suddenly, almost slipping under the arm of Andrey Filippovich, who was standing right in the doorway, Mr. Golyadkin junior darted into the room in breathless haste and bustle, with a solemn and resolutely official air; he bounded straight up to Mr. Golyadkin senior, who was expecting nothing less than such a visitation.

"The papers, Yakov Petrovich, the papers . . . his Excellency has been pleased to ask for them; have you got them ready?" Mr. Golyadkin senior's friend whispered in a hurried undertone. "Andrey Filippovich is waiting for you. . . ."

"I know he is waiting without your telling me," said Mr. Golyadkin senior, also in a hurried whisper.

"No, Yakov Petrovich, I did not mean that; I did not mean that at all, Yakov Petrovich, not that at all; I sympathize with you, Yakov Petrovich, and am moved by genuine interest."

"Which I most humbly beg you to spare me. Allow me, allow me . . ."

"You'll put it in an envelope, of course, Yakov Petrovich, and you'll put a mark in the third page; allow me, Yakov Petrovich. . . ."

"You allow me, if you please. . . ."

"But, I say, there's a blot here, Yakov Petrovich; did you know there was a blot here? . . ."

At this point Andrey Filippovich called Yakov Petrovich a second time.

"One moment, Andrey Filippovich, I'm only just . . . Do you understand Russian, sir?"

"It would be best to take it out with a penknife, Yakov Petro-

vich. You had better rely upon me; you had better not touch it
yourself, Yakov Petrovich, rely upon me—I'll do it with a
penknife. . . ."

Andrey Filippovich called Mr. Golyadkin a third time.

"But, allow me, where's the blot? I don't think there's a blot
at all."

"It's a huge blot. Here it is! Here, allow me, I saw it here . . .
you just let me, Yakov Petrovich, I'll just touch it with the
penknife, I'll scratch it out with the penknife from true-hearted
sympathy. There, like this; see, it's done."

At this point, and quite unexpectedly, Mr. Golyadkin junior
overpowered Mr. Golyadkin senior in the momentary struggle
that had arisen between them, and so, entirely against the latter's will, suddenly, without rhyme or reason, took possession
of the document required by the authorities, and instead of
scratching it out with the penknife in true-hearted sympathy as
he had perfidiously promised Mr. Golyadkin senior, hurriedly
rolled it up, put it under his arm, in two bounds was beside Andrey Filippovich, who noticed none of his manœuvres, and
flew with the latter into the Director's room. Mr. Golyadkin remained as though riveted to the spot, holding the penknife in
his hand and apparently on the point of scratching something
out with it. . . .

Our hero could not yet grasp his new position. He could not
at once recover himself. He felt the blow, but thought that it was
somehow all right. In terrible, indescribable misery he tore
himself at last from his seat, rushed straight to the Director's
room, imploring heaven on the way that it might somehow all
be arranged satisfactorily and so would be all right. . . . In the
furthermost room, which adjoined the Director's private room,
he ran straight upon Andrey Filippovich in company with his
namesake. Both of them were coming back; Mr. Golyadkin
moved aside. Andrey Filippovich was talking with a good-
humoured smile, Mr. Golyadkin senior's namesake was smiling,
too, fawning upon Andrey Filippovich and tripping about at a
respectful distance from him, and was whispering something
in his ear with a delighted air, to which Andrey Filippovich as-

sented with a gracious nod. In a flash our hero grasped the whole position. The fact was that the work had surpassed his Excellency's expectations (as he learnt afterwards) and was finished punctually by the time it was needed. His Excellency was extremely pleased with it. It was even said that his Excellency had said "Thank you" to Mr. Golyadkin junior, had thanked him warmly, had said that he would remember it on occasion and would never forget it. . . . Of course, the first thing Mr. Golyadkin did was to protest, to protest with the utmost vigour of which he was capable. Pale as death, and hardly knowing what he was doing, he rushed up to Andrey Filippovich. But the latter, hearing that Mr. Golyadkin's business was a private matter, refused to listen, observing firmly that he had not a minute to spare even for his own affairs.

The curtness of his tone and his refusal struck Mr. Golyadkin.

"I had better, perhaps, try in another quarter. . . . I had better appeal to Anton Antonovich."

But to his disappointment Anton Antonovich was not available either: he, too, was busy over something somewhere!

"Ah, it was not without design that he asked me to spare him explanation and discussion!" thought our hero. "This was what the old rogue had in his mind! In that case I shall simply make bold to approach his Excellency."

Still pale and feeling that his brain was in a complete ferment, greatly perplexed as to what he ought to decide to do, Mr. Golyadkin sat down on the edge of the chair. "It would have been a great deal better if it had all been just nothing," he kept incessantly thinking to himself. "Indeed, such a mysterious business was utterly improbable. In the first place, it was nonsense, and secondly it could not happen. Most likely it was imagination, or something else happened, and not what really did happen; or perhaps I went myself . . . and somehow mistook myself for some one else . . . in short, it's an utterly impossible thing."

Mr. Golyadkin had no sooner made up his mind that it was an utterly impossible thing than Mr. Golyadkin junior flew into

the room with papers in both hands as well as under his arm.
Saying two or three words about business to Andrey Filippovich
as he passed, exchanging remarks with one, polite greetings
with another, and familiarities with a third, Mr. Golyadkin junior, having apparently no time to waste, seemed on the point
of leaving the room, but luckily for Mr. Golyadkin senior he
stopped near the door to say a few words as he passed two or
three clerks who were at work there. Mr. Golyadkin senior
rushed straight at him. As soon as Mr. Golyadkin junior saw Mr.
Golyadkin senior's movement he began immediately, with great
uneasiness, looking about him to make his escape. But our hero
already held his last night's guest by the sleeve. The clerks surrounding the two titular councillors stepped back and waited
with curiosity to see what would happen. The senior titular
councillor realized that public opinion was not on his side, he
realized that they were intriguing against him: which made it
all the more necessary to hold his own now. The moment was
a decisive one.

"Well!" said Mr. Golyadkin junior, looking rather impatiently at Mr. Golyadkin senior.

The latter could hardly breathe.

"I don't know," he began, "in what way to make plain to
you the strangeness of your behaviour, sir."

"Well. Go on." At this point Mr. Golyadkin junior turned
round and winked to the clerks standing round, as though to
give them to understand that a comedy was beginning.

"The impudence and shamelessness of your manners with
me, sir, in the present case, unmasks your true character . . .
better than any words of mine could do. Don't rely on your
trickery: it is worthless. . . ."

"Come, Yakov Petrovich, tell me now, how did you spend the
night?" answered Mr. Golyadkin junior, looking Mr. Golyadkin
senior straight in the eye.

"You forget yourself, sir," said the titular councillor, completely flabbergasted, hardly able to feel the floor under his feet.
"I trust that you will take a different tone. . . ."

"My darling!" exclaimed Mr. Golyadkin junior, making a

rather unseemly grimace at Mr. Golyadkin senior, and suddenly, quite unexpectedly, under the pretence of caressing him, he pinched his chubby cheek with two fingers.

Our hero grew as hot as fire. . . . As soon as Mr. Golyadkin junior noticed that his opponent, quivering in every limb, speechless with rage, as red as a lobster, and exasperated beyond all endurance, might actually be driven to attack him, he promptly and in the most shameless way hastened to be before-hand with his victim. Patting him two or three times on the cheek, tickling him two or three times, playing with him for a few seconds in this way while his victim stood rigid and beside himself with fury to the no little diversion of the young men standing round, Mr. Golyadkin junior ended with a most re-volting shamelessness by giving Mr. Golyadkin senior a poke in his rather prominent stomach, and with a most venomous and suggestive smile said to him: "You're mischievous, brother Yakov, you are mischievous! We'll be sly, you and I, Yakov Petro-vich, we'll be sly."

Then, and before our hero could gradually come to himself after the last attack, Mr. Golyadkin junior (with a little smile be-forehand to the spectators standing round) suddenly assumed a most businesslike, busy and official air, dropped his eyes to the floor and, drawing himself in, shrinking together, and pro-nouncing rapidly "on a special commission" he cut a caper with his short leg, and darted away into the next room. Our hero could not believe his eyes and was still unable to pull him-self together. . . .

At last he roused himself. Recognizing in a flash that he was ruined, in a sense annihilated, that he had disgraced himself and sullied his reputation, that he had been turned into ridicule and treated with contempt in the presence of spectators, that he had been treacherously insulted, by one whom he had looked on only the day before as his greatest and most trustworthy friend, that he had been put to utter confusion, Mr. Golyadkin senior rushed in pursuit of his enemy. At the moment he would not even think of the witnesses of his ignominy.

"They're all in a conspiracy together," he said to himself;

"they stand by each other and set each other on to attack me."
After taking a dozen steps, however, our hero perceived clearly
that all pursuit would be vain and useless, and so he turned
back. "You won't get away," he thought, "you will get caught
one day; the wolf will have to pay for the sheep's tears."

With ferocious composure and the most resolute determination Mr. Golyadkin went up to his chair and sat down upon
it. "You won't escape," he said again.

Now it was not a question of passive resistance: there was
determination and pugnacity in the air, and any one who had
seen how Mr. Golyadkin at that moment, flushed and scarcely
able to restrain his excitement, stabbed his pen into the inkstand and with what fury he began scribbling on the paper,
could be certain beforehand that the matter would not pass off
like this, and could not end in a simple, womanish way. In the
depth of his soul he formed a resolution, and in the depth of
his heart swore to carry it out. To tell the truth he still did not
quite know how to act, or rather did not know at all, but never
mind, that did not matter!

"Imposture and shamelessness do not pay nowadays, sir. Imposture and shamelessness, sir, lead to no good, but lead to the
halter. Grishka Otrepyov was the only one, sir, who gained by
imposture,[18] deceiving the blind people and even that not for
long."

In spite of this last circumstance Mr. Golyadkin proposed to
wait till such time as the mask should fall from certain persons
and something should be made manifest. For this it was necessary, in the first place, that office hours should be over as soon
as possible, and till then our hero proposed to take no step.
Then, when office hours were over, he would take one step. He
knew then how he must act after taking that step, how to
arrange his whole plan of action, to abase the horn of arrogance
and crush the snake gnawing the dust in contemptible impotence.[19] To allow himself to be treated like a rag used for wiping dirty boots, Mr. Golyadkin could not. He could not consent
to that, especially in the present case. Had it not been for that
last insult, our hero might have, perhaps, brought himself to

control his anger; he might, perhaps, have been silent, have submitted and not have protested too obstinately; he would just have disputed a little, have made a slight complaint, have proved that he was in the right, then he would have given way a little, then, perhaps, he would have given way a little more, then he would have come round altogether, then, especially when the opposing party solemnly admitted that he was right, perhaps, he would have overlooked it completely, would even have been a little touched, there might even, perhaps—who could tell—spring up a new, close, warm friendship, on an even broader basis than the friendship of last night, so that this friendship might, in the end, completely eclipse the unpleasantness of the rather unseemly resemblance of the two individuals, so that both the titular councillors might be highly delighted, and might go on living till they were a hundred, and so on. To tell the whole truth, Mr. Golyadkin began to regret a little that he had stood up for himself and his rights, and had at once come in for unpleasantness in consequence.

"Should he give in," thought Mr. Golyadkin, "say he was joking, I would forgive him. I would forgive him even more if he would acknowledge it aloud. But I won't let myself be treated like a rag. And I have not allowed even persons very different from him to treat me so, still less will I permit a depraved person to attempt it. I am not a rag. I am not a rag, sir!"

In short, our hero made up his mind. "You're in fault yourself, sir!" he thought. He made up his mind to protest, and to protest with all his might to the very last. That was the sort of man he was! He could not consent to allow himself to be insulted, still less to allow himself to be treated as a rag, and, above all, to allow a thoroughly vicious man to treat him so. No quarrelling, however, no quarrelling! Possibly if some one wanted, if some one, for instance, actually insisted on turning Mr. Golyadkin into a rag, he might have done so, might have done so without opposition or punishment (Mr. Golyadkin was himself conscious of this at times), and he would have been a rag and not Golyadkin—yes, a nasty, filthy rag; but that rag would not have been a simple rag, it would have been a rag possessed of dignity, it would have been a rag possessed of feelings and sentiments, even though dignity was defenceless and feelings could not assert themselves, and lay hidden deep down in the filthy folds of the rag, still the feelings were there . . .

The hours dragged on incredibly slowly; at last it struck four. Soon after, all got up and, following the head of the department, moved each on his homeward way. Mr. Golyadkin mingled with the crowd; he kept a vigilant look out, and did not lose sight of the man he wanted. At last our hero saw that his friend ran up to the office attendants who handed the clerks their overcoats, and hung about near them waiting for his in his usual nasty way. The minute was a decisive one. Mr. Golyadkin forced his way somehow through the crowd and, anxious not to be left behind, he, too, began fussing about his overcoat. But Mr. Golyadkin's friend and companion was given his overcoat first because on this occasion, too, he had succeeded, as he always did, in making up to them, whispering something to them, cringing upon them and getting round them.

After putting on his overcoat, Mr. Golyadkin junior glanced ironically at Mr. Golyadkin senior, acting in this way openly and defiantly, looked about him with his characteristic insolence, finally he tripped to and fro among the other clerks—no doubt in order to leave a good impression on them—said a word to one, whispered something to another, respectfully accosted a third, directed a smile at a fourth, gave his hand to a fifth, and gaily darted downstairs. Mr. Golyadkin senior flew after him, and to his inexpressible delight overtook him on the last step, and seized him by the collar of his overcoat. It seemed as though Mr. Golyadkin junior was a little disconcerted, and he looked about him with a helpless air.

"What do you mean by this?" he whispered to Mr. Golyadkin at last, in a weak voice.

"Sir, if you are a gentleman, I trust that you remember our friendly relations yesterday," said our hero.

"Ah, yes! Well? Did you sleep well?"

Fury rendered Mr. Golyadkin senior speechless for a moment.

"I slept well, sir . . . but allow me to tell you, sir, that you are playing a very complicated game. . . ."

"Who says so? My enemies say that," answered abruptly the man who called himself Mr. Golyadkin, and saying this, he unexpectedly freed himself from the feeble hand of the real Mr. Golyadkin. As soon as he was free he rushed away from the stairs, looked around him, saw a cab, ran up to it, got in, and in one moment vanished from Mr. Golyadkin senior's sight. The despairing titular councillor, abandoned by all, gazed about him, but there was no other cab. He tried to run, but his legs gave way under him. With a look of open-mouthed astonishment on his countenance, feeling crushed and shrivelled up, he leaned helplessly against a lamp post, and remained so for some minutes in the middle of the pavement. It seemed as though all were over for Mr. Golyadkin.

CHAPTER IX

Everything, apparently, and even nature itself, seemed up in arms against Mr. Golyadkin; but he was still on his legs and unconquered; he felt that he was unconquered. He was ready to struggle. He rubbed his hands with such feeling and such energy when he recovered from his first amazement that it could be deduced from his very air that he would not give in. Yet the danger was imminent; it was evident; Mr. Golyadkin felt it; but how to grapple with it, with this danger?—that was the question. The thought even flashed through Mr. Golyadkin's mind for a moment, "After all, why not leave it so, simply give it up? Why, what is it? Why, it's nothing. I'll keep apart as though it were not I," thought Mr. Golyadkin. "I'll let it all pass; it's not I, and that's all about it; he's separate too, maybe he'll give it up too; he'll hang about, the rascal, he'll hang about. He'll come back and give it up again. That's how it will be! I'll take it meekly. And, indeed, where is the danger? Come, what danger is there? I should like any one to tell me where the danger lies in this business. It is a trivial affair. An everyday affair. . . ."

At this point Mr. Golyadkin's tongue failed; the words died away on his lips; he even swore at himself for this thought; he convicted himself on the spot of abjectness, of cowardice for having this thought; things were no forwarder, however. He felt that to make up his mind to some course of action was absolutely necessary for him at the moment; he even felt that he would have given a great deal to any one who could have told him what he must decide to do. Yes, but how could he guess what? Though, indeed, he had no time to guess. In any case, that he might lose no time he took a cab and dashed home.

"Well? What are you feeling now?" he wondered; "what are you graciously pleased to be thinking of, Yakov Petrovich? What are you doing? What are you doing now, you rogue, you rascal? You've brought yourself to this plight, and now you are weeping and whimpering!"

So Mr. Golyadkin taunted himself as he jolted along in the vehicle. To taunt himself and so to irritate his wounds was, at this time, a great satisfaction to Mr. Golyadkin, almost a voluptuous enjoyment.

"Well," he thought, "if some magician were to turn up now, or if it could come to pass in some official way and I were told: 'Give a finger of your right hand, Golyadkin—and it's a bargain with you; there shall not be the other Golyadkin, and you will be happy, only you won't have your finger'—yes, I would sacrifice my finger, I would certainly sacrifice it, I would sacrifice it without winking. . . . The devil take it all!" the despairing titular councillor cried at last. "Why, what is it all for? Well, it all had to be; yes, it absolutely had to; yes, just this had to be, as though nothing else were possible! And it was all right at first. Every one was pleased and happy. But there, it had to be! There's nothing to be gained by talking, though; you must act."

And so, almost resolved upon some action, Mr. Golyadkin reached home, and without a moment's delay snatched up his pipe and, sucking at it with all his might and puffing out clouds of smoke to right and to left, he began pacing up and down the room in a state of violent excitement. Meanwhile, Petrushka began laying the table. At last Mr. Golyadkin made up his mind completely, flung aside his pipe, put on his overcoat, said he would not dine at home and ran out of the flat. Petrushka, panting, overtook him on the stairs, bringing the hat he had forgotten. Mr. Golyadkin took his hat, wanted to say something incidentally to justify himself in Petrushka's eyes that the latter might not think anything particular, such as, "What a queer circumstance! here he forgot his hat—and so on," but as Petrushka walked away at once and would not even look at him, Mr. Golyadkin put on his hat without further explanation, ran downstairs, and repeating to himself that perhaps everything might be for the best, and that affairs would somehow be arranged, though he was conscious among other things of a cold chill right down to his heels, he went out into the street, took a cab and hastened to Andrey Filippovich's.

"Would it not be better to-morrow, though?" thought Mr. Golyadkin, as he took hold of the bell-rope of Andrey Filippovich's flat. "And, besides, what can I say in particular? There is nothing particular in it. It's such a wretched affair, yes, it really is wretched, paltry, yes, that is, almost a paltry affair . . . yes, that's what it all is, the incident. . . ." Suddenly Mr. Golyadkin pulled at the bell; the bell rang; footsteps were heard within. . . . Mr. Golyadkin cursed himself on the spot for his hastiness and audacity. His recent unpleasant experiences, which he had almost forgotten over his work, and his encounter with Andrey Filippovich immediately came back into his mind. But by now it was too late to run away: the door opened. Luckily for Mr. Golyadkin he was informed that Andrey Filippovich had not returned from the office and had not dined at home.

"I know where he dines: he dines near the Izmailovsky Bridge," thought our hero; and he was immensely relieved. To the footman's inquiry what message he would leave, he said: "It's all right, my good man, I'll look in later," and he even ran

downstairs with a certain cheerful briskness. Going out into the
street, he decided to dismiss the cab and paid the driver. When
the man asked for something extra, saying he had been waiting
in the street and had not spared his horse for his honour,
he gave him five kopeks extra, and even willingly; and then
walked on.

"It really is such a thing," thought Mr. Golyadkin, "that it
cannot be left like that; though, if one looks at it that way, looks
at it sensibly, why am I hurrying about here, in reality? Well,
yes, though, I will go on discussing why I should take a lot of
trouble; why I should rush about, exert myself, worry myself
and wear myself out. To begin with, the thing's done and there's
no recalling it . . . of course, there's no recalling it! Let us put it
like this: a man turns up with a satisfactory reference, said to be
a capable clerk, of good conduct, only he is a poor man and has
suffered many reverses—all sorts of ups and downs—well,
poverty is not a crime: so I must stand aside. Why, what nonsense it is! Well, he came; he is so made, the man is so made by
nature itself that he is as like another man as though they were
two drops of water, as though he were a perfect copy of another
man; how could they refuse to take him into the department on
that account? If it is fate, if it is only fate, if it is only blind
chance that is to blame—is he to be treated like a rag, is he to
be refused a job in the office? . . . Why, what would become of
justice after that? He is a poor man, hopeless, downcast; it
makes one's heart ache: compassion bids one care for him! Yes!
There's no denying, there would be a fine set of head officials,
if they took the same view as a reprobate like me! What an ad-
dlepate I am! I have foolishness enough for a dozen! Yes, yes!
They did right, and many thanks to them for being good to a
poor, luckless fellow. . . . Why, let us imagine for a moment that
we are twins, that we had been born twin brothers, and nothing else—there it is! Well, what of it? Why, nothing! All the
clerks can get used to it. . . . And an outsider, coming into our
office, would certainly find nothing unseemly or offensive in
the circumstance. In fact, there is really something touching in
it; to think that the divine Providence created two men exactly

alike, and the heads of the department, seeing the divine hand-iwork, provided for two twins. It would, of course," Mr. Golyadkin went on, drawing a breath and dropping his voice, "it would, of course . . . it would, of course, have been better if there had been . . . if there had been nothing of this touching kindness, and if there had been no twins either. . . . The devil take it all! And what need was there for it? And what was the particular necessity that admitted of no delay! My goodness! The devil has made a mess of it! Besides, he has such a charac-ter, too, he's of such a playful, horrid disposition—he's such a scoundrel, he's such a nimble fellow! He's such a toady! Such a lickspittle! He's such a Golyadkin! I daresay he will misconduct himself; yes, he'll disgrace my name, the blackguard! And now I have to look after him and wait upon him! What an infliction! But, after all, what of it? It doesn't matter. Granted, he's a scoundrel, well, let him be a scoundrel, but to make up for it, the other one's honest; so he will be a scoundrel and I'll be honest, and they'll say that this Golyadkin's a rascal, don't take any notice of him, and don't mix him up with the other; but the other one's honest, virtuous, mild, free from malice, always to be relied upon in the service, and worthy of promotion; that's how it is, very good . . . but what if . . . what if they get us mixed up! . . . He is equal to anything! Ah, Lord, have mercy upon us! . . . He will counterfeit a man, he will counterfeit him, the rascal—he will change one man for another as though he were a rag, and not reflect that a man is not a rag. Ach, mercy on us! Ough, what a calamity!" . . .

Reflecting and lamenting in this way, Mr. Golyadkin ran on, regardless of where he was going. He came to his senses in Nevsky Prospect, only owing to the chance that he ran so neatly full-tilt into a passer-by that he saw stars in his eyes. Mr. Golyad-kin muttered his excuses without raising his head, and it was only after the passer-by, muttering something far from flatter-ing, had walked a considerable distance away, that he raised his nose and looked about to see where he was and how he had got there. Noticing when he did so that he was close to the restau-rant in which he had sat for a while before the dinner-party at

Olsufy Ivanovich's, our hero was suddenly conscious of a
pinching and nipping sensation in his stomach; he remembered that he had not dined; he had no prospect of a dinner-
party anywhere. And so, without losing precious time, he ran
upstairs into the restaurant to have a snack of something as
quickly as possible, and to avoid delay by making all the haste
he could. And though everything in the restaurant was rather
dear, that little circumstance did not on this occasion make Mr.
Golyadkin pause, and, indeed, he had no time to pause over
such a trifle. In the brightly lighted room the customers were
standing in rather a crowd round the counter, upon which lay
heaps of all sorts of such edibles as are eaten by well-bred persons at lunch. The waiter scarcely had time to fill glasses, to
serve, to take money and give change. Mr. Golyadkin waited for
his turn and modestly stretched out his hand for a savoury patty.
Retreating into a corner, turning his back on the company and
eating with appetite, he went back to the attendant, put down
his plate and, knowing the price, took out a ten-kopek piece
and laid the coin on the counter, catching the waiter's eye as
though to say, "Look, here's the money, one pie," and so on.

"One ruble ten kopeks is your bill," the waiter filtered
through his teeth.

Mr. Golyadkin was a good deal surprised.

"You are speaking to me? . . . I . . . I took one pie, I believe."

"You've had eleven," the man retorted confidently.

"You . . . so it seems to me . . . I believe you're mistaken. . . .
I really took only one pie, I think."

"I counted them; you took eleven. Since you've had them
you must pay for them; we don't give anything away for nothing."

Mr. Golyadkin was petrified. "What sorcery is this, what is
happening to me?" he wondered. Meanwhile, the man waited
for Mr. Golyadkin to make up his mind; people crowded round
Mr. Golyadkin; he was already feeling in his pocket for a silver
ruble, to pay the full amount at once, to avoid further trouble.
"Well, if it was eleven, it was eleven," he thought, turning as
red as a lobster. "Why, what does it matter if eleven pies have

been eaten? Why, a man's hungry, so he eats eleven pies; well, let him eat, and may it do him good; and there's nothing to wonder at in that, and there's nothing to laugh at. . . ."

At that moment something seemed to stab Mr. Golyadkin. He raised his eyes and—at once he guessed the riddle. He knew what the sorcery was. All his difficulties were solved. . . .

In the doorway of the next room, almost directly behind the waiter and facing Mr. Golyadkin, in the doorway which, till that moment, our hero had taken for a looking-glass, a man was standing—he was standing, Mr. Golyadkin was standing—not the original Mr. Golyadkin, the hero of our story, but the other Mr. Golyadkin, the new Mr. Golyadkin. The second Mr. Golyadkin was apparently in excellent spirits. He smiled to Mr. Golyadkin the first, nodded to him, winked, shuffled his feet a little, and looked as though in another minute he would vanish, would disappear into the next room, and then go out, maybe, by a back way out; and there it would be, and all pursuit would be in vain. In his hand he had the last morsel of the tenth pie, and before Mr. Golyadkin's very eyes he popped it into his mouth and smacked his lips.

"He has impersonated me, the scoundrel!" thought Mr. Golyadkin, flushing hot with shame. "He is not ashamed of the publicity of it! Do they see him? I fancy no one notices him. . . ."

Mr. Golyadkin threw down his ruble as though it burnt his fingers, and without noticing the waiter's insolently significant grin, a smile of triumph and serene power, he extricated himself from the crowd, and rushed away without looking round. "We must be thankful that at least he has not completely compromised any one!" thought Mr. Golyadkin senior. "We must be thankful to him, the brigand, and to fate, that everything was satisfactorily settled. The waiter was rude, that was all. But, after all, he was in the right. One ruble and ten kopeks were owing: so he was in the right. 'We don't give things away for nothing,' he said! Though he might have been more polite, the rascal . . ."

All this Mr. Golyadkin said to himself as he went downstairs to the entrance, but on the last step he stopped suddenly, as though he had been shot, and suddenly flushed till the tears came into his eyes at the insult to his dignity. After standing stockstill for half a minute, he stamped his foot resolutely, at one bound leapt from the step into the street and, without looking round, rushed breathless and unconscious of fatigue back home to his flat in Shestilavochny Street. When he got home, without changing his coat, though it was his habit to change into an old coat at home, without even stopping to take his pipe, he sat down on the sofa, drew the inkstand towards him, took up a pen, got a sheet of notepaper, and with a hand that trembled from inward excitement, began scribbling the following epistle.

"Dear Sir Yakov Petrovich!

"I should not take up my pen if my circumstances, and your own action, sir, had not compelled me to that step. Believe me that nothing but necessity would have induced me to enter upon such a discussion with you and therefore, first of all, I beg you, sir, to look upon this step of mine not as a premeditated design to insult you, but as the inevitable consequence of the circumstance that is a bond between us now."

("I think that's all right, proper, courteous, though not lacking in force and firmness. . . . I don't think there is anything for him to take offence at. Besides, I'm fully within my rights," thought Mr. Golyadkin, reading over what he had written.)

"Your strange and sudden appearance, sir, on a stormy night, after the coarse and unseemly behaviour of my enemies to me, for whom I feel too much contempt even to mention their names, was the starting-point of all the misunderstanding existing between us at the present time. Your obstinate desire to persist in your course of action, sir, and forcibly to enter the circle of my existence and all my relations in practical life, transgresses every limit imposed by the merest politeness and every rule of civilized society. I imagine there is no need, sir, for me to refer to the seizure by you of my papers, and particularly to your taking away my good name, in order to gain the favour of my superiors—favour you have not deserved. There is no need to refer here either to your intentional and insulting refusal of the necessary explanation in regard to us. Finally, to omit nothing, I will not allude here to your last strange, one may even say, your incomprehensible behaviour to me in the coffee-house. I am far from lamenting over the needless—for me—loss of a ruble; but I cannot help expressing my indignation at the recollection of your public outrage upon me, to the detriment of my honour, and what is more, in the presence of several persons of good breeding, though not belonging to my circle of acquaintance."

("Am I not going too far?" thought Mr. Golyadkin. "Isn't it too much; won't it be too insulting—that taunt about good breeding, for instance? . . . But there, it doesn't matter! I must show him the resoluteness of my character. I might, however, to soften him, flatter him, and butter him up at the end. But there, we shall see.")

"But I should not weary you with my letter, sir, if I were not firmly convinced that the nobility of your sentiments and your open, candid character would suggest to you yourself a means for retrieving all lapses and returning everything to its original position.

"With full confidence I venture to rest assured that you will not take my letter in a sense derogatory to yourself, and at the same time that you will not refuse to explain yourself expressly on this occasion by letter, sending the same by my man.

"In expectation of your reply, I have the honour, dear sir, to remain,

"Your humble servant,
"Y. GOLYADKIN."

"Well, that is quite all right. The thing's done, it has come to letter-writing. But who is to blame for that? He is to blame himself: by his own action he reduces a man to the necessity of resorting to epistolary composition. And I am within my rights. . . ."

Reading over his letter for the last time, Mr. Golyadkin folded it up, sealed it and called Petrushka. Petrushka came in looking, as usual, sleepy and cross about something.

"You will take this letter, my boy . . . do you understand?"

Petrushka did not speak.

"You will take it to the department; there you must find the secretary on duty, Vakhrameyev. He is the one on duty to-day. Do you understand that?"

"I understand."

" 'I understand'! He can't even say, 'I understand, sir!' You must ask for the secretary, Vakhrameyev, and tell him that your master desired you to send his regards, and humbly requests him to refer to the address book of our office and find out where the titular councillor, Golyadkin, is living?"

Petrushka remained mute, and, as Mr. Golyadkin fancied, smiled.

"Well, so you see, Pyotr, you have to ask him for the address, and find out where the new clerk, Golyadkin, lives."

"Yes."

"You must ask for the address and then take this letter there. Do you understand?"

"I understand."

"If there . . . where you have to take the letter, that gentleman to whom you have to give the letter, that Golyadkin . . . What are you laughing at, you blockhead?"

"What is there to laugh at? What is it to me! I wasn't doing anything, sir. It's not for the likes of us to laugh. . . ."

"Oh, well . . . if that gentleman should ask, 'How is your master, how is he'; if he . . . well, if he should ask you any-thing—you hold your tongue, and answer, 'My master is all right, and begs you for an answer to his letter.' Do you under-stand?"

"Yes, sir."

"Well, then, say, 'My master is all right and quite well,' say, 'and is just getting ready to pay a call: and he asks you,' say, 'for an answer in writing.' Do you understand?"

"Yes."

"Well, go along, then."

"Why, what a bother I have with this blockhead too! He's laughing, and there's nothing to be done. What's he laughing at? I've lived to see trouble. Here I've lived like this to see trouble. Though perhaps it may all turn out for the best. . . . That rascal will be loitering about for the next two hours now, I expect; he'll go off somewhere else. . . . There's no sending him anywhere. What a misery it is! . . . What misery has come upon me!"

Feeling his troubles to the full, our hero made up his mind to remain passive for two hours till Petrushka returned. For an hour of the time he walked about the room, smoked, then put aside his pipe and sat down to a book, then he lay down on the sofa, then took up his pipe again, then again began running about the room. He tried to think things over but was absolutely unable to think about anything. At last the agony of remaining passive reached the climax and Mr. Golyadkin made up his mind to take a step. "Petrushka will come in another hour," he thought. "I can give the key to the porter, and I myself can, so to speak . . . I can investigate the matter: I shall investigate the matter in my own way."

Without loss of time, in haste to investigate the matter, Mr. Golyadkin took his hat, went out of the room, locked up his flat, went in to the porter, gave him the key, together with ten kopeks—Mr. Golyadkin had become extraordinarily free-handed of late—and rushed off. Mr. Golyadkin went first on foot to the Izmailovsky Bridge. It took him half an hour to get there. When he reached the goal of his journey he went straight into the yard of the house so familiar to him, and glanced up at the windows of the state councillor Berendeyev's flat. Except for three windows hung with red curtains all the rest was dark.

"Olsufy Ivanovich has no visitors to-day," thought Mr. Golyadkin; "they must all be staying at home to-day."

After standing for some time in the yard, our hero tried to

decide on some course of action. But he was apparently not destined to reach a decision. Mr. Golyadkin changed his mind, and with a wave of his hand went back into the street.

"No, there's no need for me to go to-day. What could I do here? . . . No, I'd better, so to speak . . . I'll investigate the matter personally."

Coming to this conclusion, Mr. Golyadkin rushed off to his office. He had a long way to go. It was horribly muddy, besides, and the wet snow lay about in thick drifts. But it seemed as though difficulty did not exist for our hero at the moment. He was drenched through, it is true, and he was a good deal spattered with mud.

"But that's no matter, so long as the object is obtained."

And Mr. Golyadkin certainly was nearing his goal. The dark mass of the huge government building stood up black before his eyes.

"Stay," he thought; "where am I going, and what am I going to do here? Suppose I do find out where he lives? Meanwhile, Petrushka will certainly have come back and brought me the answer. I am only wasting my precious time, I am simply wasting my time. Though shouldn't I, perhaps, go in and see Vakhrameyev? But, no, I'll go later. . . . Ech! There was no need to have gone out at all. But, there, it's my temperament! I've a knack of always seizing a chance of rushing ahead of things, whether there is a need to or not. . . . H'm! . . . what time is it? It must be nine by now. Petrushka might come and not find me at home. It was pure folly on my part to go out . . . Ech, it is really a nuisance!"

Sincerely acknowledging that he had been guilty of an act of folly, our hero ran back to Shestilavochny Street. He arrived there, weary and exhausted. From the porter he learned that Petrushka had not dreamed of turning up yet.

"To be sure! I foresaw it would be so," thought our hero; "and meanwhile it's nine o'clock. Ech, he's such a good-for-nothing chap! He's always drinking somewhere! Mercy on us! What a day has fallen to my miserable lot!"

Reflecting in this way, Mr. Golyadkin unlocked his flat, got a light, took off his outdoor things, lighted his pipe and, tired, worn-out, exhausted and hungry, lay down on the sofa and waited for Petrushka. The candle burnt dimly; the light flickered on the wall. . . . Mr. Golyadkin gazed and gazed, and thought and thought, and fell asleep at last, worn out.

It was late when he woke up. The candle had almost burnt down, was smoking and on the point of going out. Mr. Golyadkin jumped up, shook himself, and remembered it all, absolutely all. Behind the screen he heard Petrushka snoring lustily. Mr. Golyadkin rushed to the window—not a light anywhere. He opened the movable pane—all was still; the city was asleep as though it were dead: so it must have been two or three o'clock; it proved to be, indeed; the clock behind the partition made an effort and struck two. Mr. Golyadkin rushed behind the partition.

He succeeded, somehow, though only after great exertions, in rousing Petrushka, and making him sit up in his bed. At that moment the candle went out completely. About ten minutes passed before Mr. Golyadkin succeeded in finding another candle and lighting it. In the interval Petrushka had fallen asleep again.

"You scoundrel, you worthless fellow!" said Mr. Golyadkin, shaking him up again. "Will you get up, will you wake?" After half an hour of effort Mr. Golyadkin succeeded, however, in rousing his servant thoroughly, and dragging him out from behind the partition. Only then, our hero remarked the fact that Petrushka was what is called dead-drunk and could hardly stand on his legs.

"You good-for-nothing fellow!" cried Mr. Golyadkin; "you ruffian! You'll be the death of me! Good heavens! whatever has he done with the letter? Ach, my God! where is it? . . . And why did I write it? As though there were any need for me to have written it! I went scribbling away out of ambition, like a fool! I've got myself into this fix out of ambition! That is what ambition does for you, you rascal, that is ambition! . . . Come, what have you done with the letter, you ruffian? To whom did you give it?"

"I didn't give any one any letter; and I never had any letter . . . so there!"

Mr. Golyadkin wrung his hands in despair.

"Listen, Pyotr . . . listen to me, listen to me. . . ."

"I am listening. . . ."

"Where have you been?—answer . . ."

"Where have I been. . . . I've been to see good people! What is it to me!"

"Oh, Lord, have mercy on us! Where did you go, to begin with? Did you go to the department? . . . Listen, Pyotr, perhaps you're drunk?"

"Me drunk! If I should be struck on the spot this minute, not a drop, not a drop—so there. . . ."

"No, no, it's no matter you're being drunk. . . . I only asked; it's all right your being drunk; I don't mind, Petrushka, I don't mind. . . . Perhaps it's only that you have forgotten, but you'll remember it all. Come, try to remember—have you been to that clerk's, to Vakhrameyev's; have you been to him or not?"

"I have not been, and there's no such clerk. Not if I were this minute . . ."

"No, no, Pyotr! No, Petrushka, you know I don't mind. Why, you see I don't mind. . . . Come, what happened? To be sure, it's cold and damp in the street, and so a man has a drop, and it's no matter. I am not angry. I've been drinking myself to-day, my boy. . . . Come, think and try and remember, did you go to Vakhrameyev?"

"Well, then, now, this is how it was, it's the truth—I did go, if this very minute . . ."

"Come, that is right, Petrushka, that is quite right that you've been. You see I'm not angry. . . . Come, come," our hero went on, coaxing his servant more and more, patting him on the shoulder and smiling to him, "come, you had a little nip, you scoundrel. . . . You had two-penn'orth of something, I suppose? You're a sly rogue! Well, that's no matter; come, you see that I'm not angry. . . . I'm not angry, my boy, I'm not angry. . . ."

"No, I'm not a sly rogue, say what you like. . . . I only went to see some good friends. I'm not a rogue, and I never have been a rogue. . . ."

"Oh, no, no, Petrushka; listen, Petrushka, you know I'm not scolding when I called you a rogue. I said that in fun, I said it in a good sense. You see, Petrushka, it is sometimes a compliment to a man when you call him a rogue, a cunning fellow, that he's a sharp chap and would not let any one take him in. Some men like it. . . . Come, come, it doesn't matter! Come, tell me, Petrushka, without keeping anything back, openly, as to a friend . . . did you go to Vakhrameyev's, and did he give you the address?"

"He did give me the address, he did give me the address too. He's a nice gentleman! 'Your master,' says he, 'is a nice man,' says he, 'very nice man;' says he, 'I send my regards,' says he, 'to your master, thank him and say that I like him,' says he—'how I do respect your master,' says he. 'Because,' says he, 'your master, Petrushka,' says he, 'is a good man, and you,' says he, 'Petrushka, are a good man too. . . .' "

"Ah, mercy on us! But the address, the address! You Judas!" The last word Mr. Golyadkin uttered almost in a whisper.

"And the address . . . he did give the address too."

"He did? Well, where does Golyadkin, the clerk Golyadkin, the titular councillor, live?"

" 'Why,' says he, 'Golyadkin will be now at Shestilavochny Street. When you get into Shestilavochny Street take the stairs on the right and it's the fourth floor. And there,' says he, 'you'll find Golyadkin. . . .' "

"You scoundrel!" our hero cried, out of patience at last. "You're a ruffian! Why, that's my address; why, you are talking about me. But there's another Golyadkin; I'm talking of the other one, you scoundrel!"

"Well, that's as you please! What is it to me? Have it your own way. . . ."

"And the letter, the letter?" . . .

"What letter? There wasn't any letter, and I didn't see any letter."

"But what have you done with it, you rascal?"

"I delivered the letter, I delivered it. He sent his regards. 'Thank you,' says he, 'your master's a nice man,' says he. 'Give my regards,' says he, 'to your master. . . .'"

"But who said that? Was it Golyadkin said it?"

Petrushka said nothing for a moment, and then, with a broad grin, he stared straight into his master's face. . . .

"Listen, you scoundrel!" began Mr. Golyadkin, breathless, beside himself with fury; "listen, you rascal, what have you done to me? Tell me what you've done to me! You've destroyed me, you villain, you've cut the head off my shoulders, you Judas!"

"Well, have it your own way! I don't care," said Petrushka in a resolute voice, retreating behind the screen.

"Come here, come here, you ruffian. . . ."

"I'm not coming to you now, I'm not coming at all. What do I care, I'm going to good folks. . . . Good folks live honestly, good folks live without falsity, and they never have doubles. . . ."

Mr. Golyadkin's hands and feet went icy cold, his breath failed him. . . .

"Yes," Petrushka went on, "they never have doubles. God doesn't afflict honest folk. . . ."

"You worthless fellow, you are drunk! Go to sleep now, you ruffian! And to-morrow you'll catch it," Mr. Golyadkin added in a voice hardly audible. As for Petrushka, he muttered something more; then he could be heard getting into bed, making the bed creak. After a prolonged yawn, he stretched; and at last began snoring, and slept the sleep of the just, as they say. Mr. Golyadkin was more dead than alive. Petrushka's behaviour, his very strange hints, which were yet so remote that it was useless to be angry at them, especially as they were uttered by a drunken man, and, in short, the sinister turn taken by the affair altogether, all this shook Mr. Golyadkin to the depths of his being.

"And what possessed me to go for him in the middle of the night?" said our hero, trembling all over from a sickly sensation. "What the devil made me have anything to do with a drunken man! What could I expect from a drunken man? Whatever he says is a lie. But what was he hinting at, the ruffian? Lord, have mercy on us! And why did I write all that letter? I'm my own enemy, I'm my own murderer! As if I couldn't hold my tongue? I had to go scribbling nonsense! And what now! You are going to ruin, you are like an old rag, and yet you worry about your pride; you say, 'my honour is wounded,' you must stick up for your honour! My own murderer, that is what I am!"

Thus spoke Mr. Golyadkin and hardly dared to stir for terror. At last his eyes fastened upon an object which excited his interest to the utmost. In terror lest the object that caught his attention should prove to be an illusion, a deception of his fancy, he stretched out his hand to it with hope, with dread, with indescribable curiosity. . . . No, it was not a deception! Not a delusion! It was a letter, really a letter, undoubtedly a letter, and addressed to him. Mr. Golyadkin took the letter from the table. His heart beat terribly.

"No doubt that scoundrel brought it," he thought, "put it there, and then forgot it; no doubt that is how it happened: no doubt that is just how it happened. . . ."

The letter was from Vakhrameyev, a young fellow-clerk who had once been his friend. "I had a presentiment of this, though," thought our hero, "and I had a presentiment of all that there will be in the letter. . . ."

The letter was as follows—

"Dear Sir Yakov Petrovich!

"Your servant is drunk, and there is no getting any sense out of him. For that reason I prefer to reply by letter. I hasten to inform you that the commission you've entrusted to me—that is, to deliver a letter to a certain person you know, I agree to carry out carefully and exactly. That person, who is very well known to you and who has taken the place of a friend to me, whose name I will refrain from mentioning (because I do not wish unnecessarily to blacken the reputation of a perfectly innocent man), lodges with us at Karolina Ivanovna's, in the room in which, when you were among us, the infantry officer from Tambov used to be. That person, however, is always to be found in the company of honest and true-hearted persons, which is more than one can say for some people. I intend from this day to break off all connection with you; it's impossible for us to remain on friendly terms and to keep up the appearance of comradeship congruous with them. And, therefore, I beg you, my dear sir, immediately on the receipt of this candid letter from me, to send me the two rubles you owe me for the razor of foreign make which I sold you seven months ago, if you will kindly remember, when you were still living with us in the lodgings of Karolina Ivanovna, a lady whom I respect from the bottom of my heart. I am acting in this way because you, from the accounts I hear from sensible persons, have lost your dignity and reputation and have become a source of danger to the morals of the innocent and uncontaminated. For some persons are not straightforward, their words are full of falsity and their show of good intentions is suspicious. People can always be found capable of insulting Karolina Ivanovna, who is always irreproachable in her conduct, and an honest woman, and, what's more, a maiden lady, though no longer young—though, on the other hand, of a good foreign family—and this fact I've been asked to mention in this letter by several persons, and I speak also for myself. In any case you will learn all in due time, if you haven't learnt it yet, though you've made yourself notorious from one end of the town to the other, according to the accounts I hear from sensible people, and consequently might well have received intelligence relating to you, my dear sir, in many places. In conclusion, I beg to inform you, my dear sir, that a certain person you know, whose name I will not mention here, for certain honourable reasons, is highly respected by right-thinking people, and is, moreover, of lively and agreeable disposition, and is equally successful in the service and in the society of persons of common sense, is true in word and in friendship, and does not insult behind their back those with whom he is on friendly terms to their face.

"In any case, I remain

"Your obedient servant,
"N. VAKHRAMEYEV."

"P.S. You had better dismiss your man: he is a drunkard and probably gives you a great deal of trouble; you had better engage Yevstafy, who used to be in service here, and is now out of a place. Your present servant is not only a drunkard, but, what's more, he's a thief, for only last week he sold a pound of lump sugar to Karolina Ivanovna at less than cost price, which, in my opinion, he could not have done otherwise than by robbing you in a very sly way, little by little, at different times. I write this to you for your own good, although some people can do nothing but insult and deceive everybody, especially persons of honesty and good nature; what is more, they slander them behind their back and misrepresent them, simply from envy, and because they can't call themselves the same.

"V."

After reading Vakhrameyev's letter our hero remained for a long time sitting motionless on his sofa. A new light seemed breaking through the obscure and baffling fog which had surrounded him for the last two days. Our hero seemed to reach a partial understanding. . . . He tried to get up from the sofa to take a turn about the room, to rouse himself, to collect his scattered ideas, to fix them upon a certain subject and then to set himself to rights a little, to think over his position thoroughly. But as soon as he tried to stand up he fell back again at once, weak and helpless. "Yes, of course, I had a presentiment of all that; how he writes though, and what is the real meaning of his words. Supposing I do understand the meaning; but what is it leading to? He should have said straight out: this and that is wanted, and I would have done it. Things have taken such a turn, things have come to such an unpleasant pass! Oh, if only to-morrow would make haste and come, and I could make haste and get to work! I know now what to do. I shall say this and that, I shall agree with his arguments, I won't sell my honour, but . . . maybe; but he, that person we know of, that disagreeable person, how does he come to be mixed up in it? And why has he turned up here? Oh, if to-morrow would make haste and come! They'll slander me before then, they are in-

triguing, they are working to spite me! The great thing is not to
lose time, and now, for instance, to write a letter, and to say this
and that and that I agree to this and that. And as soon as it is
daylight to-morrow send it off, before he can do anything . . .
and so checkmate them, get in before them, the darlings. . . .
They will ruin me by their slanders, and that's the fact of the
matter!"

Mr. Golyadkin drew the paper to him, took up a pen and
wrote the following missive in answer to the secretary's letter—

"Dear Sir Nestor Ignatyevich!

"With amazement mingled with heartfelt distress I have
perused your insulting letter to me, for I see clearly that you are
referring to me when you speak of certain discreditable persons
and false friends. I see with genuine sorrow how rapidly the
calumny has spread and how deeply it has taken root, to the
detriment of my prosperity, my honour and my good name.
And this is the more distressing and mortifying that even honest people of a genuinely noble way of thinking and, what is
even more important, of straightforward and open dispositions,
abandon the interests of honourable men and with all the qualities of their hearts attach themselves to the pernicious corruption, which in our difficult and immoral age has unhappily
increased and multiplied so greatly and so disloyally. In conclusion, I will say that the debt of two rubles of which you remind
me I regard as a sacred duty to return to you in its entirety.

"As for your hints concerning a certain person of the female sex, concerning the intentions, calculations and various
designs of that person, I can only tell you, sir, that I have but a
very dim and obscure understanding of those insinuations. Permit me, sir, to preserve my honourable way of thinking and my
good name undefiled, in any case. I am ready to stoop to an explanation in person, preferring a personal interview to a written explanation as more secure, and I am, moreover, ready to
enter into conciliatory proposals on mutual terms, of course. To
that end I beg you, my dear sir, to convey to that person my
readiness for a personal arrangement and, what is more, to beg

her to fix the time and place of the interview. It grieved me, sir, to read your hints of my having insulted you, having been treacherous to our original friendship and having spoken ill of you. I ascribe this misunderstanding to the abominable calumny, envy and ill-will of those whom I may justly stigmatize as my bitterest foes. But I suppose they do not know that innocence is strong through its very innocence, that the shamelessness, the insolence and the revolting familiarity of some persons, sooner or later gains the stigma of universal contempt; and that such persons come to ruin through nothing but their own worthlessness and the corruption of their own hearts. In conclusion, I beg you, sir, to convey to those persons that their strange pretensions and their dishonourable and fantastic desire to squeeze others out of the position which those others occupy, by their very existence in this world, and to take their place, are deserving of contempt, amazement, compassion and, what is more, the madhouse; moreover, such efforts are severely prohibited by law, which in my opinion is perfectly just, for every one ought to be satisfied with his own position. Every one has his fixed position, and if this is a joke it is a joke in very bad taste. I will say more: it is utterly immoral, for, I make bold to assure you, sir, my own views which I have expounded above, in regard to keeping *one's own place*, are purely moral.

"In any case I have the honour to remain,

"Your humble servant,

"Y. GOLYADKIN."

CHAPTER X

Altogether, we may say, the adventures of the previous day had thoroughly unnerved Mr. Golyadkin. Our hero passed a very bad night; that is, he did not get thoroughly off to sleep for five minutes: as though some practical joker had scattered bristles in his bed. He spent the whole night in a sort of half-sleeping state, tossing from side to side, from right to left, moaning and groaning, dozing off for a moment, waking up again a minute later, and all was accompanied by a strange misery, vague memories, hideous visions—in fact, everything disagreeable that can be imagined. . . .

At one moment the figure of Andrey Filippovich appeared before him in a strange, mysterious half-light. It was a frigid, wrathful figure, with a cold, harsh eye and with stiffly polite words of blame on its lips . . . and as soon as Mr. Golyadkin began going up to Andrey Filippovich to defend himself in some way and to prove to him that he was not at all such as his enemies represented him, that he was like this and like that, that he even possessed innate virtues of his own, superior to the average—at once a person only too well known for his discreditable behaviour appeared on the scene, and by some most revolting means instantly frustrated poor Mr. Golyadkin's efforts, on the spot, almost before the latter's eyes, blackened his reputation, trampled his dignity in the mud, and then immediately took possession of his place in the service and in society.

At another time Mr. Golyadkin's head felt sore from some sort of slight blow of late conferred and humbly accepted, received either in the course of daily life or somehow in the performance of his duty, against which blow it was difficult to protest. . . . And while Mr. Golyadkin was racking his brains over the question why it was so difficult to protest even against such a blow, this idea of a blow gradually melted away into a different form—into the form of some familiar, trifling, or rather important piece of nastiness which he had seen, heard, or even himself committed—and frequently committed, indeed, and not on nasty grounds, not from any nasty impulse, even, but just because it happened—sometimes, for instance, out of delicacy, another time owing to his absolute defencelessness—in fact, because . . . because, in fact, Mr. Golyadkin knew perfectly well *because of what!* At this point Mr. Golyadkin blushed in his sleep, and, smothering his blushes, muttered to himself that in this case he ought to be able to show the strength of his character, he ought to be able to show in this case the remarkable strength of his character, and then wound up by asking himself, "What, after all, is strength of character? Why understand it now?" . . .

But what irritated and enraged Mr. Golyadkin most of all was that invariably, at such a moment, a person well known for his undignified burlesque behaviour turned up uninvited, and, regardless of the fact that the matter was apparently settled, he, too, would begin muttering, with an unseemly little smile, "What's the use of strength of character! How could you and I, Yakov Petrovich, have strength of character? . . ."

Then Mr. Golyadkin would dream that he was in the company of a number of persons distinguished for their wit and good breeding; that he, Mr. Golyadkin, too, was conspicuous for his wit and politeness, that everybody liked him, even some of his enemies who were present began to like him, which was very agreeable to Mr. Golyadkin; that every one gave him precedence, and that at last Mr. Golyadkin himself, with gratification, overheard the host, drawing one of the guests aside, speak in his, Mr. Golyadkin's, praise . . . and all of a sudden, apropos of nothing, there appeared again a person, notorious for his treachery and brutal impulses, in the form of Mr. Golyadkin junior, and on the spot, at once, by his very appearance on the scene, Mr. Golyadkin junior destroyed the whole triumph and glory of Mr. Golyadkin senior, eclipsed Mr. Golyadkin senior, trampled him in the mud, and, at last, proved clearly that Golyadkin senior—that is, the genuine one—was not the genuine one at all but the sham, and that he, Golyadkin junior, was the real one; that, in fact, Mr. Golyadkin senior was not at all what he appeared to be, but something very disgraceful, and that consequently he had no right to mix in the society of honourable and well-bred people. And all this was done so quickly that Mr. Golyadkin had not time to open his mouth before all of them were subjugated, body and soul, by the wicked, sham Mr. Golyadkin, and with profound contempt rejected him, the real and innocent Mr. Golyadkin. There was not one person left whose opinion the infamous Mr. Golyadkin would not have

changed round. There was not left one person, even the most
insignificant of the company, to whom the false and worthless
Mr. Golyadkin would not make up in his blandest manner, upon
whom he would not fawn in his own way, before whom he
would not burn sweet and agreeable incense, so that the flattered person simply sniffed and sneezed till the tears came, in
token of the intensest pleasure. And the worst of it was that all
this was done in a flash: the swiftness of movement of the false
and worthless Mr. Golyadkin was marvellous! He scarcely had
time, for instance, to make up to one person and win his good
graces—and before one could wink an eye he was at another.
He stealthily fawns on another, drops a smile of benevolence,
twirls on his short, round, though rather wooden-looking leg,
and already he's at a third, and is cringing upon a third, he's
making up to him in a friendly way; before one has time to
open one's mouth, before one has time to feel surprised he's at
a fourth, at the same manœuvres with him—it was horrible:
sorcery and nothing else! And every one was pleased with him
and everybody liked him, and every one was exalting him, and
all were proclaiming in chorus that his politeness and sarcastic
wit were infinitely superior to the politeness and sarcastic wit
of the real Mr. Golyadkin and putting the real and innocent Mr.
Golyadkin to shame thereby and rejecting the veritable Mr.
Golyadkin, and shoving and pushing out the loyal Mr. Golyadkin, and showering blows on the man so well known for his
love towards his fellow creatures! . . .

In misery, in terror and in fury, the cruelly treated Mr.
Golyadkin ran out into the street and began trying to take a cab
in order to drive straight to his Excellency's, or, at any rate, to
Andrey Filippovich's, but—horror! the cabman absolutely refused to take Mr. Golyadkin, saying, "We cannot drive two gentlemen exactly alike, sir; a good man tries to live honestly, your
honour, and never has a double." Overcome with shame, the
unimpeachable, honest Mr. Golyadkin looked round and did, in
fact, assure himself with his own eyes that the cabman and
Petrushka, who had joined them, were all quite right, for the
depraved Mr. Golyadkin was actually on the spot, beside him,

close at hand, and with his characteristic nastiness was again, at this critical moment, certainly preparing to do something very unseemly, and quite out of keeping with that gentlemanliness of character which is usually acquired by good breeding—that gentlemanliness of which the loathsome Mr. Golyadkin the second was always boasting on every opportunity. Beside himself with shame and despair, the utterly ruined though perfectly just Mr. Golyadkin dashed headlong away, wherever fate might lead him; but with every step he took, with every thud of his foot on the granite of the pavement, there leapt up as though out of the earth a Mr. Golyadkin precisely the same, perfectly alike, and of a revolting depravity of heart. And all these precisely similar Golyadkins set to running after one another as soon as they appeared, and stretched in a long chain like a file of geese, hobbling after the real Mr. Golyadkin, so there was nowhere to escape from these duplicates—so that Mr. Golyadkin, who was in every way deserving of compassion, was breathless with terror; so that at last a terrible multitude of duplicates had sprung into being; so that the whole town was obstructed at last by duplicate Golyadkins, and the police officer, seeing such a breach of decorum, was obliged to seize all these duplicates by the collar and to put them into the watch-house, which happened to be beside him. . . . Numb and chill with horror, our hero woke up, and numb and chill with horror felt that his waking state was hardly more cheerful. . . . It was oppressive and harrowing. . . . He was overcome by such anguish that it seemed as though some one were gnawing at his heart.

At last Mr. Golyadkin could endure it no longer. "This shall not be!" he cried, resolutely sitting up in bed, and after this exclamation he felt fully awake.

It seemed as though it were rather late in the day. It was unusually light in the room. The sunshine filtered through the frozen panes and flooded the room with light, which surprised Mr. Golyadkin not a little and, so far as Mr. Golyadkin could remember, at least, there had scarcely ever been such exceptions in the course of the heavenly luminary before. Our hero had hardly time to wonder at this when he heard the clock buzzing behind the partition as though it was just on the point of striking. "Now," thought Mr. Golyadkin, and he prepared to listen with painful suspense. . . .

But to complete Mr. Golyadkin's astonishment, the clock whirred and only struck once.

"What does this mean?" cried our hero, finally leaping out of bed. And, unable to believe his ears, he rushed behind the screen just as he was. It actually was one o'clock. Mr. Golyadkin glanced at Petrushka's bed; but the room did not even smell of Petrushka: his bed had long been made and left, his boots were nowhere to be seen either—an unmistakable sign that Petrushka was not in the house. Mr. Golyadkin rushed to the door: the door was locked. "But where is he, where is Petrushka?" he went on in a whisper, conscious of intense excitement and feeling a perceptible tremor run all over him . . . Suddenly a thought floated into his mind . . . Mr. Golyadkin rushed to the table, looked all over it, felt all round—yes, it was true, his letter of the night before to Vakhrameyev was not there. Petrushka was nowhere behind the screen either, the clock had just struck one, and some new points were evident to him in Vakhrameyev's letter, points that were obscure at first sight though now they were fully explained. Petrushka had evidently been bribed at last! "Yes, yes, that was so!"

"So this was how the chief plot was hatched!" cried Mr. Golyadkin, slapping himself on the forehead, opening his eyes wider and wider; "so in that filthy German woman's den the whole power of evil lies hidden now! So she was only making a strategic diversion in directing me to the Izmailovsky Bridge—she was putting me off the scent, confusing me (the worthless witch), and in that way laying her mines! Yes, that is so! If one only looks at the thing from that point of view, all of this is bound to be so, and the scoundrel's appearance on the scene is fully explained: it's all part and parcel of the same thing. They've kept him in reserve a long while, they had him in readiness for the evil day. This is how it has all turned out! This is what it has come to. But there, never mind. No time has been lost so far."

At this point Mr. Golyadkin recollected with horror that it was past one in the afternoon. "What if they have succeeded by now? . . ." He uttered a moan. . . . "But, no, they are lying; they've not had time—we shall see. . . ."

He dressed after a fashion, seized paper and a pen, and scribbled the following missive—

"Dear Sir Yakov Petrovich!
  "Either you or I, but both together is out of the question! And so I must inform you that your strange, absurd, and at the same time impossible desire to appear to be my twin and to give yourself out as such serves no other purpose than to bring about your complete disgrace and discomfiture. And so I beg you, for the sake of your own advantage, to step aside and make way for really honourable men of loyal aims. In the opposite case I am ready to determine upon extreme measures. I lay down my pen and await . . . However, I remain ready to oblige or to meet you with pistols.

                                        "Y. GOLYADKIN."

Our hero rubbed his hands energetically when he had finished the letter. Then, pulling on his greatcoat and putting on his hat, he unlocked his flat with a spare key and set off for the department. He reached the office but could not make up his mind to go in—it was by now too late. It was half-past two by Mr. Golyadkin's watch. All at once a circumstance of apparently little importance settled some doubts in Mr. Golyadkin's mind: a flushed and breathless figure suddenly made its appearance from behind the screen of the department building and with a stealthy movement like a rat he darted up the steps and into the entry. It was a copying clerk called Ostafyev, a man Mr. Golyadkin knew very well, who was rather useful and ready to do anything for a trifle. Knowing Ostafyev's weak spot and surmising that after his brief, unavoidable absence he would probably be greedier than ever for tips, our hero made up his mind not to be sparing of them, and immediately darted up the steps, and then into the entry after him, called to him and, with a myste-

rious air, drew him aside into a convenient corner behind a
huge iron stove. And having led him there, our hero began
questioning him.

"Well, my dear fellow, how are things going in there . . .
you understand me?" . . .

"Yes, your honour, I wish you good health, your honour."

"All right, my good man, all right; but I'll reward you, my
good fellow. Well, you see, how are things?"

"What is your honour asking?" At this point Ostafyev held
his hand as though by accident before his open mouth.

"You see, my dear fellow, this is how it is . . . but don't you
imagine . . . Come, is Andrey Filippovich here?" . . .

"Yes, he is here."

"And are the clerks here?"

"Yes, sir, they are here as usual."

"And his Excellency too?"

"And his Excellency too." Here the man held his hand before his open mouth again, and looked rather curiously and
strangely at Mr. Golyadkin, so at least our hero fancied.

"And there's nothing special there, my good man?"

"No, sir, certainly not, sir."

"So there's nothing concerning me, my friend. Is there
nothing going on there—that is, nothing more than . . . eh?
nothing more, you understand, my friend?"

"No, sir, I've heard nothing so far, sir." Again the man put his
hand before his mouth and again looked rather strangely at Mr.
Golyadkin. The fact was, Mr. Golyadkin was trying to read
Ostafyev's countenance, trying to discover whether there was
not something hidden in it. And, in fact, he did look as though
he were hiding something: Ostafyev seemed to grow colder
and more churlish, and did not enter into Mr. Golyadkin's interests with the same sympathy as at the beginning of the conversation. "He is to some extent justified," thought Mr.
Golyadkin. "After all, what am I to him? Perhaps he has already
been bribed by the other side, and that's why he has just been
absent. But, here, I'll try him. . . ." Mr. Golyadkin realized that
the moment for kopeks had arrived.

"Here, my dear fellow . . ."

"I'm feelingly grateful for your honour's kindness."

"I'll give you more than that."

"Yes, your honour."

"I'll give you some more directly, and when the business is over I'll give you as much again. Do you understand?"

The clerk did not speak. He stood at attention and stared fixedly at Mr. Golyadkin.

"Come, tell me now: have you heard nothing about me? . . ."

"I think, so far, I have not . . . so to say . . . nothing so far." Ostafyev, like Mr. Golyadkin, spoke deliberately and preserved a mysterious air, moving his eyebrows a little, looking at the ground, trying to fall into the suitable tone, and, in fact, doing his very utmost to earn what had been promised him, for what he had received already he reckoned as already earned.

"And you know nothing?"

"So far, nothing, sir."

"Listen . . . you know . . . maybe you will know . . ."

"Later on, of course, maybe I shall know."

"It's a poor look out," thought our hero. "Listen: here's something more, my dear fellow."

"I am truly grateful to your honour."

"Was Vakhrameyev here yesterday? . . ."

"Yes, sir."

"And . . . somebody else? . . . Was he? . . . Try and remember, brother."

The man ransacked his memory for a moment, and could think of nothing appropriate.

"No, sir, there wasn't anybody else."

"H'm!" a silence followed.

"Listen, brother, here's some more; tell me all, every detail."

"Yes, sir," Ostafyev had by now become as soft as silk; which was just what Mr. Golyadkin needed.

"Explain to me now, my good man, what footing is he on?"

"All right, sir, a good one, sir," answered the man, gazing open-eyed at Mr. Golyadkin.

"How do you mean, all right?"

"Well, it's just like that, sir." Here Ostafyev twitched his eyebrows significantly. But he was utterly nonplussed and didn't know what more to say.

"It's a poor look out," thought Mr. Golyadkin.

"And hasn't anything more happened . . . in there . . . about Vakhrameyev?"

"But everything is just as usual."

"Think a little."

"There is, they say . . ."

"Come, what?"

Ostafyev put his hand in front of his mouth.

"Wasn't there a letter . . . from here . . . to me?"

"Mikheyev the attendant went to Vakhrameyev's lodging, to their German landlady, so I'll go and ask him, if you like."

"Do me the favour, brother, for goodness' sake! . . . I only mean . . . you mustn't imagine anything, brother, I only mean . . . Yes, you question him, brother, find out whether they are not getting up something concerning me. Find out how he is acting. That is what I want; that is what you must find out, my dear fellow, and then I'll reward you, my good man. . . ."

"I will, your honour, and Ivan Semyonovich sat in your place to-day, sir."

"Ivan Semyonovich? Oh! really, you don't say so."

"Andrey Filippovich told him to sit there."

"Re-al-ly! How did that happen? You must find out, brother; for God's sake find out, brother; find it all out—and I'll reward you, my dear fellow; that's what I want to know . . . and don't you imagine anything, brother. . . ."

"Just so, sir, just so; I'll go at once. And aren't you going in to-day, sir?"

"No, my friend; I only looked round, I only looked round, you know. I only came to have a look round, my friend, and I'll reward you afterwards, my friend."

"Yes, sir." The man ran rapidly and eagerly up the stairs and Mr. Golyadkin was left alone.

"It's a poor look out!" he thought. "Ech, it's a bad business, a bad business! Ech! things are in a bad way with us now! What does it all mean? What did that drunkard's insinuations mean, for instance, and whose trickery was it? Ah! I know now whose it was. And what a thing this is. No doubt they found out and made him sit there. . . . But, after all, did they sit him there? It was Andrey Filippovich sat him there, he sat Ivan Semyonovich there himself; why did he make him sit there and with what object? Probably they found out. . . . That is Vakhrameyev's work—that is, not Vakhrameyev, he is as stupid as an ashen poet, Vakhrameyev is, and they are all at work on his behalf, and they egged that scoundrel on to come here for the same purpose, and the German woman brought up her grievance, the one-eyed hussy. I always suspected that this intrigue was not without an object and that in all this old-womanish gossip there must be something, and I said as much to Krestyan Ivanovich, telling him they'd sworn to cut a man's throat—in a moral sense, of course—and they pounced upon Karolina Ivanovna. Yes, there are master hands at work in this, one can see! Yes, sir, there are master hands at work here, and not Vakhrameyev's. I've said already that Vakhrameyev is stupid, but . . . I know who it is behind it all, it's that rascal, that impostor! It's only that he relies upon, which is partly proved by his successes in the best society. And it would certainly be desirable to know on what footing he stands now. What is he now among them? Only, why have they taken Ivan Semyonovich? What the devil do they want with Ivan Semyonovich? Could not they have found any one else? Though it would come to the same thing whoever it had been, and the only thing I know is that I have suspected Ivan Semyonovich for a long time past. I noticed long ago what a nasty, horried old man he was—they say he lends money and takes interest like any Jew. To be sure, the bear's the leading spirit in the whole affair. One can detect the bear in the whole affair. It began in this way. It began at the Izmailovsky Bridge; that's how it began . . ."

At this point Mr. Golyadkin frowned, as though he had taken a bite out of a lemon, probably remembering something very unpleasant.

"But, there, it doesn't matter," he thought. "I keep harping on my own troubles. What will Ostafyev find out? Most likely he is staying on or has been delayed somehow. It is a good thing, in a sense, that I am intriguing like this, and am laying mines on my side too. I've only to give Ostafyev ten kopeks and he's . . . so to speak, on my side. Only the point is, is he really on my side? Perhaps they've got him on their side too . . . and they are carrying on an intrigue by means of him on their side too. He looks a ruffian, the rascal, a regular ruffian; he's hiding something, the rogue. 'No, nothing,' says he, 'and I am deeply grateful to your honour,' says he. You ruffian, you!"

He heard a noise . . . Mr. Golyadkin shrank up and skipped behind the stove. Some one came down stairs and went out into the street. "Who could that be going away now?" our hero thought to himself. A minute later footsteps were audible again. . . . At this point Mr. Golyadkin could not resist poking the very tip of his nose out beyond his corner—he poked it out and instantly withdrew it again, as though some one had pricked it with a pin. This time some one he knew well was coming—that is the scoundrel, the intriguer and the reprobate—he was approaching with his usual mean, tripping little step, prancing and shuffling with his feet as though he were going to kick some one.

"The rascal," said our hero to himself.

Mr. Golyadkin could not, however, help observing that the rascal had under his arm a huge green portfolio belonging to his Excellency.

"He's on a special commission again," thought Mr. Golyadkin, flushing crimson and shrinking into himself more than ever from vexation.

As soon as Mr. Golyadkin junior had slipped past Mr. Golyadkin senior without observing him in the least, footsteps were heard for the third time, and this time Mr. Golyadkin guessed that these were Ostafyev's. It was, in fact, the sleek figure of a copying clerk, Pisarenko by name. This surprised Mr. Golyadkin. Why had he mixed up other people in their secret? our hero wondered. What barbarians! nothing is sacred to them! "Well, my friend?" he brought out, addressing Pisarenko: "who sent you, my friend? . . ."

"I've come about your business. There's no news so far from any one. But should there be any we'll let you know."

"And Ostafyev?"

"It was quite impossible for him to come, your honour. His Excellency has walked through the room twice, and I've no time to stay."

"Thank you, my good man, thank you . . . only, tell me . . ."

"Upon my word, sir, I can't stay. . . . They are asking for us every minute . . . but if your honour will stay here, we'll let you know if anything happens concerning your little affair."

"No, my friend, you just tell me . . ."

"Excuse me, I've no time to stay, sir," said Pisarenko, tearing himself away from Mr. Golyadkin, who had clutched him by the lapel of his coat. "I really can't. If your honour will stay here we'll let you know."

"In a minute, my good man, in a minute! In a minute, my good fellow! I tell you what, here's a letter; and I'll reward you, my good man."

"Yes, sir."

"Try and give it to Mr. Golyadkin my dear fellow."

"Golyadkin?"

"Yes, my man, to Mr. Golyadkin."

"Very good, sir; as soon as I get off I'll take it, and you stay here, meanwhile; no one will see you here. . . ."

"No, my good man, don't imagine . . . I'm not standing here to avoid being seen. But I'm not going to stay here now, my friend. . . . I'll be close here in the side street. There's a coffee-house near here; so I'll wait there, and if anything happens, you let me know about anything, you understand?"

"Very good, sir. Only let me go; I understand."

"And I'll reward you," Mr. Golyadkin called after Pisarenko, when he had at last released him. . . ."

"The rogue seemed to be getting rather rude," our hero reflected as he stealthily emerged from behind the stove. "There's some other dodge here. That's clear. . . . At first it was one thing and another . . . he really was in a hurry, though; perhaps there's a great deal to do in the office. And his Excellency had been through the room twice. . . . How did that happen? . . . Ough! never mind! It may mean nothing, perhaps; but now we shall see. . . ."

At this point Mr. Golyadkin was about to open the door, intending to go out into the street, when suddenly, at that very instant, his Excellency's carriage dashed up to the door. Before Mr. Golyadkin had time to recover from the shock, the door of the carriage was opened from within and a gentleman jumped out. This gentleman was no other than Mr. Golyadkin junior, who had only gone out ten minutes before. Mr. Golyadkin senior remembered that the Director's flat was only a couple of paces away.

"He has been out on a special commission," our hero thought to himself.

Meanwhile, Mr. Golyadkin junior took out of the carriage a thick green portfolio and other papers. Finally, giving some orders to the coachman, he opened the door, almost ran up against Mr. Golyadkin senior, purposely avoided noticing him, acting in this way expressly to annoy him, and mounted the office staircase at a rapid canter.

"It's a bad look out," thought Mr. Golyadkin. "This is what it has come to now! Oh, good Lord! look at him."

For half a minute our hero remained motionless. At last he made up his mind. Without pausing to think, though he was aware of a violent palpitation of the heart and a tremor in all his limbs, he ran up the stairs after his enemy.

"Here goes; what does it matter to me! I have nothing to do with the case," he thought, taking off his hat, his greatcoat and his goloshes in the entry.

When Mr. Golyadkin walked into his office, it was already getting dusk. Neither Andrey Filippovich nor Anton Antonovich were in the room. Both of them were in the Director's room, handing in reports. The Director, so it was rumoured, was in haste to report to a still higher Excellency. In consequence of this, and also because twilight was coming on, and the office hours were almost over, several of the clerks, especially the younger ones, were, at the moment when our hero entered, enjoying a period of inactivity; gathered together in groups, they were talking, arguing, and laughing, and some of the most youthful—that is, belonging to the lowest grades in the service, had got up a game of pitch-farthing in a corner, by a window. Knowing what was proper, and feeling at the moment a special need to conciliate and get on with them, Mr. Golyadkin immediately approached those with whom he used to get on best, in order to wish them good day, and so on. But his colleagues answered his greetings rather strangely. He was unpleasantly impressed by a certain coldness, even curtness, one might almost say severity in their manner. No one shook hands with him. Some simply said, "Good day" and walked away; others barely nodded; one simply turned away and pretended not to notice him; at last some of them—and what mortified Mr. Golyadkin most of all, some of the youngsters of the lowest grades, mere lads who, as Mr. Golyadkin justly observed about them, were capable of nothing but hanging about and playing pitch-farthing at every opportunity—little by little collected round Mr. Golyadkin, formed a group round him and almost barred his way. They all looked at him with a sort of insulting curiosity.

It was a bad sign. Mr. Golyadkin felt this, and very judiciously decided not to notice it. Suddenly a quite unexpected event completely finished him off, as they say, and utterly crushed him.

At the moment most trying to Mr. Golyadkin senior, suddenly, as though by design, there appeared in the group of fellow clerks surrounding him the figure of Mr. Golyadkin junior, gay as ever, smiling a little smile as ever, nimble, too, as ever; in short, mischievous, skipping and tripping, chuckling and fawning, with sprightly tongue and sprightly toe, as always, precisely as he had been the day before at a very unpleasant moment for Mr. Golyadkin senior, for instance.

Grinning, tripping and turning with a smile that seemed to say "good evening," to every one, he squeezed his way into the group of clerks, shaking hands with one, slapping another on

the shoulder, putting his arm round another, explaining to a
fourth how he had come to be employed by his Excellency,
where he had been, what he had done, what he had brought
with him; to the fifth, probably his most intimate friend, he
gave a resounding kiss—in fact, everything happened as it had
in Mr. Golyadkin's dream. When he had skipped about to his
heart's content, polished them all off in his usual way, disposed
them all in his favour, whether he needed them or not, when
he had lavished his blandishments to the delectation of all the
clerks, Mr. Golyadkin junior suddenly, and most likely by mistake, for he had not yet had time to notice his senior, held out
his hand to Mr. Golyadkin senior also. Probably also by mistake—though he had had time to observe the dishonourable
Mr. Golyadkin junior thoroughly, our hero at once eagerly
seized the hand so unexpectedly held out to him and pressed it
in the warmest and friendliest way, pressed it with a strange,
quite unexpected, inner feeling, with a tearful emotion.
Whether our hero was misled by the first movement of his
worthless foe, or was taken unawares, or, without recognizing
it, felt at the bottom of his heart how defenceless he was—it is
difficult to say. The fact remains that Mr. Golyadkin senior, apparently knowing what he was doing, of his own free will, before witnesses, solemnly shook hands with him whom he
called his mortal foe. But what was the amazement, the stupefaction and fury, what was the horror and the shame of Mr.
Golyadkin senior, when his enemy and mortal foe, the dishonourable Mr. Golyadkin junior, noticing the mistake of that per-
secuted, innocent, perfidiously deceived man, without a trace
of shame, of feeling, of compassion or of conscience, pulled his
hand away with insufferable rudeness and insolence. What was
worse, he shook the hand as though it had been polluted with
something horrid; what is more, he spat aside with disgust, accompanying this with a most insulting gesture; worse still, he
drew out his handkerchief and, in the most unseemly way,
wiped all the fingers that had rested for one moment in the
hand of Mr. Golyadkin senior. While he did this Mr. Golyadkin
junior looked about him in his characteristic horrid way, took

care that every one should see what he was doing, glanced into people's eyes and evidently tried to insinuate to every one everything that was most unpleasant in regard to Mr. Golyadkin senior. Mr. Golyadkin junior's revolting behaviour seemed to arouse general indignation among the clerks that surrounded them; even the frivolous youngsters showed their displeasure. A murmur of protest rose on all sides. Mr. Golyadkin could not but discern the general feeling; but suddenly—an appropriate witticism that bubbled from the lips of Mr. Golyadkin junior shattered, annihilated our hero's last hopes, and inclined the balance again in favour of his deadly and undeserving foe.

"He's our Russian Faublas,[20] gentlemen; allow me to introduce the youthful Faublas," piped Mr. Golyadkin junior, with his characteristic insolence, pirouetting and threading his way among the clerks, and directing their attention to the petrified though genuine Mr. Golyadkin. "Let us kiss each other, darling," he went on with insufferable familiarity, addressing the man he had so treacherously insulted. Mr. Golyadkin junior's unworthy jest seemed to touch a responsive chord, for it contained an artful allusion to an incident with which all were apparently familiar. Our hero was painfully conscious of the hand of his enemies. But he had made up his mind by now. With glowing eyes, with pale face, with a fixed smile he tore himself somehow out of the crowd and with uneven, hurried steps made straight for his Excellency's private room. In the room next to the last he was met by Andrey Filippovich, who had only just come out from seeing his Excellency, and although there were present in this room at the moment a good number of persons of whom Mr. Golyadkin knew nothing, yet our hero did not care to take such a fact into consideration. Boldly, resolutely, directly, almost wondering at himself and inwardly admiring his own courage, without loss of time he accosted Andrey Filippovich, who was a good deal surprised by this unexpected attack.

"Ah! . . . What is it . . . what do you want?" asked the head of the division, not hearing Mr. Golyadkin's hesitating words.

"Andrey Filippovich, may . . . might I, Andrey Filippovich,

may I have a conversation with his Excellency at once and in private?" our hero said resolutely and distinctly, fixing the most determined glance on Andrey Filippovich.

"What next! of course not." Andrey Filippovich scanned Mr. Golyadkin from head to foot.

"I say all this, Andrey Filippovich, because I am surprised that no one here unmasks the impostor and scoundrel."

"Wha-a-at!"

"Scoundrel, Andrey Filippovich!"

"Of whom are you pleased to speak in those terms?"

"Of a certain person, Andrey Filippovich; I'm alluding, Andrey Filippovich, to a certain person; I have the right . . . I imagine, Andrey Filippovich, that the authorities would surely encourage such action," added Mr. Golyadkin, evidently hardly knowing what he was saying. "Andrey Filippovich . . . but no doubt you see yourself, Andrey Filippovich, that this honourable action is a mark of my loyalty in every way—of my looking upon my superior as a father, Andrey Filippovich; I as much as to say look upon my benevolent superior as a father and blindly trust my fate to him. It's as much as to say . . . you see . . ." At this point Mr. Golyadkin's voice trembled and two tears ran down his eyelashes.

As Andrey Filippovich listened to Mr. Golyadkin he was so astonished that he could not help stepping back a couple of paces. Then he looked about him uneasily . . . It is difficult to say how the matter would have ended. But suddenly the door of his Excellency's room was opened, and he himself came out, accompanied by several officials. All the persons in his room followed in a string. His Excellency called Andrey Filippovich and walked beside him, beginning to discuss some business details. When all had set off and gone out of the room, Mr. Golyadkin woke up. Growing calmer, he took refuge under the wing of Anton Antonovich, who came last in the procession and who, Mr. Golyadkin fancied, looked stern and anxious. "I've been talking nonsense, I've been making a mess of it again, but there, never mind," he thought.

"I hope, at least, that you, Anton Antonovich, will consent to listen to me and to enter into my position," he said quietly, in a voice that still trembled a little. "Rejected by all, I appeal to you. I am still at a loss to understand what Andrey Filippovich's words mean, Anton Antonovich. Explain them to me if you can. . . ."

"Everything will be explained in due time," Anton Antonovich replied sternly and emphatically, and as Mr. Golyadkin fancied with an air that gave him plainly to understand that Anton Antonovich did not wish to continue the conversation. "You will soon know all about it. You will be officially informed about everything to-day."

"What do you mean by officially informed, Anton Antonovich? Why officially?" our hero asked timidly.

"It is not for you and me to discuss what our superiors decide upon, Yakov Petrovich."

"Why our superiors, Anton Antonovich?" said our hero, still more intimidated; "why our superiors? I don't see what reason there is to trouble our superiors in the matter, Anton Antonovich . . . Perhaps you mean to say something about yesterday's doings, Anton Antonovich?"

"Oh no, nothing to do with yesterday; there's something else amiss with you."

"What is there amiss, Anton Antonovich? I believe, Anton Antonovich, that I have done nothing amiss."

"Why, you were meaning to be sly with some one," Anton Antonovich cut in sharply, completely flabbergasting Mr. Golyadkin.

Mr. Golyadkin started, and turned as white as a pocket-handkerchief.

"Of course, Anton Antonovich," he said, in a voice hardly audible, "if one listens to the voice of calumny and hears one's enemies' tales, without heeding what the other side has to say in its defence, then, of course . . . then, of course, Anton Antonovich, one must suffer innocently and for nothing."

"To be sure; but your unseemly conduct, in injuring the reputation of a virtuous young lady belonging to that benevo-

lent, highly distinguished and well-known family who had be-
friended you . . .

"What conduct do you mean, Anton Antonovich?"

"What I say. Do you know anything about your praiseworthy conduct in regard to that other young lady who, though
poor, is of honourable foreign extraction?"

"Allow me, Anton Antonovich . . . if you would kindly listen
to me, Anton Antonovich . . ."

"And your treacherous behaviour and slander of another
person, your charging another person with your own sins. Ah,
what do you call that?"

"I did not send him away, Anton Antonovich," said our hero,
with a tremor; "and I've never instructed Petrushka, my man, to
do anything of the sort . . . He has eaten my bread, Anton
Antonovich, he has taken advantage of my hospitality," our hero
added expressively and with deep emotion, so much so that his
chin twitched a little and tears were ready to start again.

"That is only your talk, that he has eaten your bread," answered Anton Antonovich, somewhat offended, and there was a
perfidious note in his voice which sent a pang to Mr. Golyadkin's heart.

"Allow me most humbly to ask you again, Anton
Antonovich, is his Excellency aware of all this business?"

"Upon my word, you must let me go now, though. I've no
time for you now. . . . You'll know everything you need to
know to-day."

"Allow me, for God's sake, one minute, Anton Antonovich."

"Tell me afterwards. . . ."

"No, Anton Antonovich; I . . . you see, Anton Antonovich . . .
only listen . . . I am not one for freethinking, Anton Antonovich;
I shun freethinking; I am quite ready for my part . . . and, indeed, I've given up that idea. . . ."

"Very good, very good. I've heard that already."

"No, you have not heard it, Anton Antonovich. It is something else, Anton Antonovich: it's a good thing, really, a good
thing and pleasant to hear. . . . As I've explained to you, Anton
Antonovich, I admit that idea, that divine Providence has cre-

ated two men exactly alike, and that a benevolent government, seeing the hand of Providence, provided a berth for two twins. That is a good thing, Anton Antonovich. You see that it is a very good thing, Anton Antonovich, and that I am very far from free-thinking. I look upon my benevolent government as a father; I say 'yes,' by all means; you are benevolent authorities, and you, of course. . . . A young man must be in the service. . . . Stand up for me, Anton Antonovich, take my part, Anton Antonovich. . . . I am all right . . . Anton Antonovich, for God's sake, one little word more . . . Anton Antonovich. . . ."

But by now Anton Antonovich was far away from Mr. Golyadkin. . . . Our hero was so bewildered and overcome by all that had happened and all that he had heard that he did not know where he was standing, what he had heard, what he had done, what was being done to him, and what was going to be done to him.

With imploring eyes he sought for Anton Antonovich in the crowd of clerks, that he might justify himself further in his eyes and say something to him extremely high toned and very agreeable, and creditable to himself. . . . By degrees, however, a new light began to break upon our hero's bewildered mind, a new and awful light that revealed at once a whole perspective of hitherto unknown and utterly unsuspected circumstances. . . . At that moment somebody gave our bewildered hero a poke in the ribs. He looked around. Pisarenko was standing before him.

"A letter, your honour."

"Ah, you've been out already, then, my good man!"

"No, it was brought at ten o'clock this morning. Sergey Mikheyev, the attendant, brought it from Mr. Vakhrameyev's lodging."

"Very good, very good, and I'll reward you now, my dear fellow."

Saying this, Mr. Golyadkin thrust the letter in the side pocket of his uniform and buttoned up every button of it; then he looked round him, and to his surprise, found that he was by now in the hall of the department, in a group of clerks crowding at the outer door, for office hours were over. Mr. Golyadkin had not only failed till that moment to observe this circumstance, but had no notion how he suddenly came to be wearing his greatcoat and goloshes and to be holding his hat in his hand. All the clerks were standing motionless, in reverential expectation. The fact was that his Excellency was standing at the bottom of the stairs waiting for his carriage, which was for some reason late in arriving, and was carrying on a very interesting conversation with Andrey Filippovich and two councillors. At a little distance from Andrey Filippovich stood Anton Antonovich and several other clerks, who were all smiles, seeing that his Excellency was graciously making a joke. The clerks who were crowded at the top of the stairs were smiling too, in expectation of his Excellency's laughing again. The only one who was not smiling was Fedosyevich, the corpulent hall-porter, who stood stiffly at attention, holding the handle of the door, waiting impatiently for the daily gratification that fell to his share—that is, the task of flinging one half of the door wide open with a swing of his arm, and then, with a low bow, reverentially making way for his Excellency to pass. But the one who seemed to be more delighted than any and to feel the most satisfaction of all was the worthless and ungentlemanly enemy of Mr. Golyadkin. At that instant he positively forgot all the clerks, and even gave up tripping and pirouetting in his usual odious way; he even forgot to make up to anybody. He was all eyes and ears, he even doubled himself up strangely, no doubt in the strained effort to hear, and never took his eyes off his Excellency, and only from time to time his arms, legs and head twitched with faintly perceptible tremors that betrayed the secret emotions of his soul.

"Ah, isn't he in a state!" thought our hero; "he looks like a favourite, the rascal! I should like to know how it is that he deceives society of every class. He has neither brains nor character, neither education nor feeling; he's a lucky rogue! Mercy on us! How can a man, when you think of it, come and make friends with every one so quickly! And he'll get on, I swear the fellow will get on, the rogue will make his way—he's a lucky rascal! I should like to know, too, what he keeps whispering to every one—what plots he is hatching with all these people, and what secrets they are talking about? Lord, have mercy on us! If only I could . . . get on with them a little too . . . say this and that and the other. Hadn't I better ask him . . . tell him I won't do it again; say 'I'm in fault, and a young man must serve nowadays, your Excellency'? I am not in the least abashed by my obscure position—so there! I am not going to protest in any way, either; I shall bear it all with meekness and patience, so there! Is that the way to behave? . . . Though you'll never see through him, though, the rascal; you can't reach him with anything you say; you can't hammer reason into his head. . . . We'll make an effort, though. I may happen to hit on a good moment, so I'll make an effort. . . ."

Feeling in his uneasiness, his misery and his bewilderment that he couldn't leave things like this, that the critical moment had come, that he must explain himself to some one, our hero began to move a little towards the place where his worthless and undeserving enemy stood: but at that very moment his Excellency's long-expected carriage rolled up into the entrance, Fedosyevich flung open the door and, bending double, let his Excellency pass out. All the waiting clerks streamed out towards the door, and for a moment separated Mr. Golyadkin senior from Mr. Golyadkin junior.

"You shan't get away!" said our hero, forcing his way through the crowd while he kept his eyes fixed on the man he wanted. At last the crowd dispersed. Our hero felt he was free and flew in pursuit of his enemy.

CHAPTER XI

Mr. Golyadkin's breath failed him; he flew as though on wings after his rapidly retreating enemy. He was conscious of immense energy. Yet in spite of this terrible energy he might confidently have said that at that moment a humble gnat—had a gnat been able to exist in Petersburg at that time of the year—could very easily have knocked him down. He felt, too, that he was utterly weak again, that he was carried along by a peculiar outside force, that it was not he himself who was running, but, on the contrary, that his legs were giving way under him, and refused to obey him. This all might turn out for the best, however.

"Whether it is for the best or not for the best," thought Mr. Golyadkin, almost breathless from running so quickly, "but that the game is lost there cannot be the slightest doubt now; that I am utterly done for is certain, definite, signed and ratified."

In spite of all this our hero felt as though he had risen from the dead, as though he had withstood a battalion, as though he had won a victory when he succeeded in clutching the overcoat of his enemy, who had already raised one foot to get into the cab he had engaged.

"My dear sir! My dear sir!" he shouted to the infamous Mr. Golyadkin junior, holding him by the button. "My dear sir, I hope that you . . ."

"No, please do not hope for anything," Mr. Golyadkin's heartless enemy answered evasively, standing with one foot on the step of the cab and vainly waving the other leg in the air, in his efforts to get in, trying to preserve his equilibrium, and at the same time trying with all his might to wrench his coat away from Mr. Golyadkin senior, while the latter held on to it with all the strength that had been vouchsafed to him by nature.

"Yakov Petrovich, only ten minutes . . ."

"Excuse me, I've no time . . ."

"You must admit, Yakov Petrovich . . . please, Yakov Petrovich. . . . For God's sake, Yakov Petrovich . . . let us have it out—in a straightforward way . . . one little second, Yakov Petrovich . . ."

"My dear fellow, I can't stay," answered Mr. Golyadkin's dishonourable enemy, with uncivil familiarity, disguised as good-natured heartiness; "another time, believe me, with my whole soul and all my heart; but now I really can't . . ."

"Scoundrel!" thought our hero. "Yakov Petrovich," he cried miserably. "I have never been your enemy. Spiteful people have described me unjustly. . . . I am ready, on my side . . . Yakov Petrovich, shall we go in here together, at once, Yakov Petrovich? And with all my heart, as you have so justly expressed it just now, and in straightforward, honourable language, as you have expressed it just now—here into this coffee-house; there the facts will explain themselves: they will really, Yakov Petrovich. Then everything will certainly explain itself. . . ."

"Into the coffee-house? Very good. I am not against it. Let us go into the coffee-house on one condition only, my dear, on one condition—that these things shall be cleared up. We will have it all out, darling," said Mr. Golyadkin junior, getting out of the cab and shamelessly slapping our hero on the shoulder; "You friend of my heart, for your sake, Yakov Petrovich, I am ready to go by the back street (as you were pleased to observe so aptly on one occasion, Yakov Petrovich). Why, what a rogue he is! Upon my word, he does just what he likes with one!" Mr. Golyadkin's false friend went on, fawning upon him and cajoling him with a little smile. The coffee-house which the two Mr. Golyadkins entered stood some distance away from the main street and was at the moment quite empty. A rather stout German woman made her appearance behind the counter. Mr. Golyadkin and his unworthy enemy went into the second room, where a puffy-looking boy with a closely shaven head was busy with a bundle of chips at the stove, trying to revive the smouldering fire. At Mr. Golyadkin junior's request chocolate was served.

"And a sweet little lady-tart," said Mr. Golyadkin junior, with a sly wink at Mr. Golyadkin senior.

Our hero blushed and was silent.

"Oh, yes, I forgot, I beg your pardon. I know your taste. We are sweet on charming little Germans, sir; you and I are sweet on charming and agreeable little Germans, aren't we, you upright soul? We take their lodgings, we seduce their morals, they win our hearts with their beersoup and their milksoup, and we give them notes of different sorts, that's what we do, you

Faublas, you deceiver!" All this Mr. Golyadkin junior said, making an unworthy though villainously artful allusion to a certain personage of the female sex, while he fawned upon our hero, smiled at him with an amiable air, with a deceitful show of being delighted with him and pleased to have met him. Seeing that Mr. Golyadkin senior was by no means so stupid and deficient in breeding and the manners of good society as to believe in him, the infamous man resolved to change his tactics and to make a more open attack upon him. After uttering his disgusting speech, the false Mr. Golyadkin ended by slapping the real and substantial Mr. Golyadkin on the shoulder, with a revolting effrontery and familiarity. Not content with that, he began playing pranks utterly unfit for well-bred society; he took it into his head to repeat his old, nauseous trick—that is, regardless of the resistance and faint cries of the indignant Mr. Golyadkin senior, he pinched the latter on the cheek. At the spectacle of such depravity our hero boiled within, but was silent . . . only for the time, however.

"That is the talk of my enemies," he answered at last, in a trembling voice, prudently restraining himself. At the same time our hero looked round uneasily towards the door. The fact was that Mr. Golyadkin junior seemed in excellent spirits, and ready for all sorts of little jokes, unseemly in a public place, and, speaking generally, not permissible by the laws of good manners, especially in well-bred society.

"Oh, well, in that case, as you please," Mr. Golyadkin junior gravely responded to our hero's thought, setting down upon the table the empty cup which he had gulped down with unseemly greed. "Well, there's no need for me to stay long with you, however. . . . Well, how are you getting on now, Yakov Petrovich?"

"There's only one thing I can tell you, Yakov Petrovich," our hero answered, with sangfroid and dignity; "I've never been your enemy."

"H'm. . . . Oh, what about Petrushka? Petrushka is his name, I fancy? Yes, it is Petrushka! Well, how is he? Well? The same as ever?"

"He's the same as ever, too, Yakov Petrovich," answered Mr. Golyadkin senior, somewhat amazed. "I don't know, Yakov Petrovich . . . from my standpoint . . . from a candid, honourable standpoint, Yakov Petrovich, you must admit, Yakov Petrovich. . . ."

"Yes, but you know yourself, Yakov Petrovich," Mr. Golyadkin junior answered in a soft and expressive voice, so posing falsely as a sorrowful man overcome with remorse and deserving compassion. "You know yourself we live in difficult times. . . . I appeal to you, Yakov Petrovich; you are an intelligent man and your reflections are just," Mr. Golyadkin junior said in conclusion, flattering Mr. Golyadkin senior in an abject way. "Life is not a game, you know yourself, Yakov Petrovich," Mr. Golyadkin junior added, with vast significance, assuming the character of a clever and learned man, who is capable of passing judgments on lofty subjects.

"For my part, Yakov Petrovich," our hero answered warmly, "for my part, scorning to be roundabout and speaking boldly and openly, using straightforward, honourable language and putting the whole matter on an honourable basis, I tell you I can openly and honourably assert, Yakov Petrovich, that I am absolutely pure, and that, you know it yourself, Yakov Petrovich, the error is mutual—it may all be the world's judgment, the opinion of the slavish crowd. . . . I speak openly, Yakov Petrovich, everything is possible. I will say, too, Yakov Petrovich, if you judge it in this way, if you look at the matter from a lofty, noble point of view, then I will boldly say, without false shame I will say, Yakov Petrovich, it will positively be a pleasure to me to discover that I have been in error, it will positively be a pleasure to me to recognize it. You know yourself you are an intelligent man and, what is more, you are a gentleman. Without shame, without false shame, I am ready to recognize it," he wound up with dignity and nobility.

"It is the decree of destiny, Yakov Petrovich . . . but let us drop all this," said Mr. Golyadkin junior. "Let us rather use the brief moment of our meeting for a more pleasant and profitable conversation, as is only suitable between two colleagues in the service. . . . Really, I have not succeeded in saying two words to you all this time. . . . I am not to blame for that, Yakov Petrovich. . . ."

"Nor I," answered our hero warmly, "nor I, either! My heart tells me, Yakov Petrovich, that I'm not to blame in all this matter. Let us blame fate for all this, Yakov Petrovich," added Mr. Golyadkin senior, in a quick, conciliatory tone of voice. His voice began little by little to soften and to quaver.

"Well! How are you in health?" said the sinner in a sweet voice.

"I have a little cough," answered our hero, even more sweetly.

"Take care of yourself. There is so much illness going about, you may easily get quinsy; for my part I confess I've begun to wrap myself up in flannel."

"One may, indeed, Yakov Petrovich, very easily get quinsy," our hero pronounced after a brief silence; "Yakov Petrovich, I see that I have made a mistake, I remember with softened feelings those happy moments which we were so fortunate as to spend together, under my poor, though I venture to say, hospitable roof . . ."

"In your letter, however, you wrote something very different," said Mr. Golyadkin junior reproachfully, speaking on this occasion—though only on this occasion—quite justly.

"Yakov Petrovich, I was in error. . . . I see clearly now that I was in error in my unhappy letter too. Yakov Petrovich, I am ashamed to look at you, Yakov Petrovich, you wouldn't believe. . . . Give me that letter that I may tear it to pieces before your eyes, Yakov Petrovich, and if that is utterly impossible I entreat you to read it the other way before—precisely the other way before—that is, expressly with a friendly intention, giving the opposite sense to the whole letter. I was in error. Forgive me, Yakov Petrovich, I was quite . . . I was grievously in error, Yakov Petrovich."

"You say so?" Mr. Golyadkin's perfidious friend inquired, rather casually and indifferently.

"I say that I was quite in error, Yakov Petrovich, and that for my part, quite without false shame, I am . . ."

"Ah, well, that's all right! That's a nice thing your being in error," answered Mr. Golyadkin junior.

"I even had an idea, Yakov Petrovich," our candid hero answered in a gentlemanly way, completely failing to observe the horrible perfidy of his deceitful enemy; "I even had an idea that here were two people created exactly alike. . . ."

"Ah, is that your idea?"

At this point the notoriously worthless Mr. Golyadkin took up his hat. Still failing to observe his treachery, Mr. Golyadkin senior, too, got up and with a noble, simple-hearted smile to his false friend, tried in his innocence to be friendly to him, to encourage him, and in that way to form a new friendship with him.

"Good-bye, your Excellency," Mr. Golyadkin junior called out suddenly. Our hero started, noticing in his enemy's face something positively Bacchanalian, and, solely to get rid of him put two fingers into the unprincipled man's outstretched hand but then . . . then his enemy's shamelessness passed all bounds. Seizing the two fingers of Mr. Golyadkin's hand and at first pressing them, the worthless fellow on the spot, before Mr. Golyadkin's eyes, had the effrontery to repeat the shameful joke of the morning. The limit of human patience was exhausted.

He had just hidden in his pocket the handkerchief with which he had wiped his fingers when Mr. Golyadkin senior recovered from the shock and dashed after him into the next room, into which his irreconcilable foe had in his usual hasty way hastened to decamp. As though perfectly innocent, he was standing at the counter eating pies, and with perfect composure, like a virtuous man, was making polite remarks to the German woman behind the counter.

"I can't go into it before ladies," thought our hero, and he, too, went up to the counter, so agitated that he hardly knew what he was doing.

"The tart is certainly not bad! What do you think?" Mr. Golyadkin junior began upon his unseemly sallies again, reck-

oning, no doubt, upon Mr. Golyadkin's infinite patience. The
stout German, for her part, looked at both her visitors with
pewtery, vacant-looking eyes, smiling affably and evidently not
understanding Russian. Our hero flushed red as fire at the
words of the unabashed Mr. Golyadkin junior, and, unable to
control himself, rushed at him with the evident intention of
tearing him to pieces and finishing him off completely, but Mr.
Golyadkin junior, in his usual mean way, was already far off; he
took flight, he was already on the steps. It need hardly be said
that, after the first moment of stupefaction with which Mr.
Golyadkin senior was naturally overcome, he recovered himself
and went at full speed after his insulting enemy, who had already got into a cab, whose driver was obviously in collusion
with him. But at that very instant the stout German, seeing both
her customers make off, shrieked and rang her bell with all her
might. Our hero was on the point of flight, but he turned back,
and, without asking for change, flung her money for himself
and for the shameless man who had left without paying, and although thus delayed he succeeded in catching up his enemy.
Hanging on to the side of the cab with all the force bestowed
on him by nature, our hero was carried for some time along the
street, clambering upon the vehicle, while Mr. Golyadkin junior
did his utmost to dislodge him. Meanwhile the cabman, with
whip, with reins, with kicks and with shouts urged on his exhausted nag, who quite unexpectedly dropped into a gallop,
biting at the bit, and kicking with his hind legs in a horrid way.
At last our hero succeeded in climbing into the cab, facing his
enemy and with his back to the driver, his knees touching the
knees and his right hand clutching the very shabby fur collar of
his depraved and exasperated foe.

The enemies were borne along for some time in silence. Our
hero could scarcely breathe. It was a bad road and he was jolted
at every step and in peril of breaking his neck. Moreover, his exasperated foe still refused to acknowledge himself vanquished
and was trying to shove him off into the mud. To complete the
unpleasantness of his position the weather was detestable. The
snow was falling in heavy flakes and doing its utmost to creep

under the unfastened overcoat of the genuine Mr. Golyadkin. It
was foggy and nothing could be seen. It was difficult to tell
through what street and in what direction they were being
taken. . . . It seemed to Mr. Golyadkin that what was happening
to him was somehow familiar. One instant he tried to remember whether he had had a presentiment of it the day before, in
a dream, for instance. . . .

At last his wretchedness reached the utmost pitch of agony.
Leaning upon his merciless opponent, he was beginning to cry
out. But his cries died away upon his lips. . . . There was a moment when Mr. Golyadkin forgot everything, and made up his
mind that all this was of no consequence and that it was all
nothing, that it was happening in some inexplicable manner,
and that, therefore, to protest was effort thrown away. . . . But
suddenly and almost at the same instant that our hero was
drawing this conclusion, an unexpected jolt gave quite a new
turn to the affair. Mr. Golyadkin fell off the cab like a sack of
flour and rolled on the ground, quite correctly recognizing, at
the moment of his fall, that his excitement had been very inappropriate. Jumping up at last, he saw that they had arrived
somewhere; the cab was standing in the middle of some courtyard, and from the first glance our hero noticed that it was the
courtyard of the house in which was Olsufy Ivanovich's flat. At
the same instant he noticed that his enemy was mounting the
steps, probably on his way to Olsufy Ivanovich's. In indescribable misery he was about to pursue his enemy, but, fortunately
for himself, prudently thought better of it. Not forgetting to pay
the cabman, Mr. Golyadkin ran with all his might along the
street, regardless of where he was going. The snow was falling
heavily as before; as before it was muggy, wet, and dark. Our
hero did not walk, but flew, coming into collision with every
one on the way—men, women and children, and himself re-
bounding from every one—men, women and children. About
him and after him he heard frightened voices, squeals,
screams. . . . But Mr. Golyadkin seemed unconscious and would
pay no heed to anything. . . . He came to himself, however, on
Semyonovsky Bridge, and then only through succeeding in

tripping against and upsetting two peasant women and the wares they were selling, and tumbling over them.

"That's no matter," thought Mr. Golyadkin, "that can easily be set right," and he felt in his pocket at once, intending to make up for the cakes, apples, nuts and various trifles he had scattered, with a ruble. Suddenly a new light dawned upon Mr. Golyadkin; in his pocket he felt the letter given him in the morning by the clerk. Remembering that there was a tavern he knew close by, he ran to it without a moment's delay, settled himself at a little table lighted up by a tallow candle, and, taking no notice of anything, regardless of the waiter who came to ask for his orders, broke the seal and began reading the following letter, which completely astounded him—

"You noble man, who are suffering for my sake, and will be dear to my heart for ever!

"I am suffering, I am perishing—save me! The slanderer, the intriguer, notorious for the immorality of his tendencies, has entangled me in his snares and I am undone! I am lost! But he is abhorrent to me, while you! . . . They have separated us, they have intercepted my letters to you—and all this has been the work of the vicious man who has taken advantage of his one good quality—his likeness to you. A man can always be plain in appearance, yet fascinate by his intelligence, his strong feelings and his agreeable manners. . . . I am ruined! I am being married against my will, and the chief part in this intrigue is taken by my parent, benefactor and civil councillor, Olsufy Ivanovich, no doubt desirous of securing me a place and relations in well-bred society. . . . But I have made up my mind and I protest by all the powers bestowed on me by nature. Be waiting for me with a carriage at nine o'clock this evening at the window of Olsufy Ivanovich's flat. We are having another ball and a handsome lieutenant is coming. I will come out and we will fly. Moreover, there are other government offices in which one can be of service to one's country. In any case, remember, my friend, that innocence is strong in its very innocence. Farewell. Wait with the carriage at the entrance. I shall throw myself into the protection of your arms at two o'clock in the night.

"Yours till death,
"KLARA OLSUFYEVNA."

After reading the letter our hero remained for some minutes as though petrified. In terrible anxiety, in terrible agitation, white as a sheet, with the letter in his hand, he walked several times up and down the room; to complete the unpleasantness of his position, though our hero failed to observe it, he was at that moment the object of the exclusive attention of every one in the room. Probably the disorder of his attire, his unrestrained excitement, his walking, or rather running about the room, his gesticulating with both hands, perhaps some enigmatic words unconsciously addressed to the air, probably all this prejudiced Mr. Golyadkin in the opinion of the customers, and even the waiter began to look at him suspiciously. Coming to himself, Mr. Golyadkin noticed that he was standing in the middle of the room and was in an almost unseemly, discourteous manner staring at an old man of very respectable appearance who, having dined and said grace before the ikon, had sat down again and fixed his eyes upon Mr. Golyadkin. Our hero looked vaguely about him and noticed that every one, actually every one, was looking at him with a hostile and suspicious air. All at once a retired military man in a red collar asked loudly for the *Police News*. Mr. Golyadkin started and turned crimson: he happened to look down and saw that he was in such disorderly attire as he would not have worn even at home, much less in a public place. His boots, his trousers and the whole of his left side were covered with mud; the trouser-strap was torn off his right foot, and his coat was even torn in many places. In extreme misery our hero went up to the table at which he had read the letter, and saw that the attendant was coming up to him with a strange and impudently peremptory expression of face. Utterly disconcerted and crestfallen, our hero began to look about the table at which he was now standing. On the table stood a dirty plate, left there from somebody's dinner, a soiled table-napkin and a knife, fork and spoon that had just been used. "Who has been having dinner?" thought our hero. "Can it have been I? Anything is possible! I must have had dinner without noticing it; what am I to do?"

Raising his eyes, Mr. Golyadkin again saw beside him the waiter who was about to address him.

"How much is my bill, my lad?" our hero inquired, in a trembling voice.

A loud laugh sounded round Mr. Golyadkin, the waiter himself grinned. Mr. Golyadkin realized that he had blundered again, and had done something dreadfully stupid. He was overcome by confusion, and to avoid standing there with nothing to do he put his hand in his pocket to get out his handkerchief; but to the indescribable amazement of himself and all surrounding him, he pulled out instead of his handkerchief the bottle of medicine which Krestyan Ivanovich had prescribed for him four days earlier. "Get the medicine at the same chemist's," floated through Mr. Golyadkin's brain. . . .

Suddenly he started and almost cried out in horror. A new light dawned. . . . The dark reddish and repulsive liquid had a sinister gleam to Mr. Golyadkin's eyes. . . . The bottle dropped from his hands and was instantly smashed. Our hero cried out and stepped back a pace to avoid the spilled medicine . . . he was trembling in every limb, and drops of sweat came out on to his brow and temples. "So my life is in danger!" Meantime there was a stir, a commotion in the room; every one surrounded Mr. Golyadkin, every one talked to Mr. Golyadkin, some even caught hold of Mr. Golyadkin. But our hero was dumb and motionless, seeing nothing, hearing nothing, feeling nothing. . . . At last, as though tearing himself from the place, he rushed out of the tavern, pushing away all and each who tried to detain him; almost unconscious, he got into the first cab that passed him and drove to his flat.

In the entry of his flat he met Mikheyev, an attendant from the office, with an official envelope in his hand.

"I know, my good man, I know all about it," our exhausted hero answered, in a weak, miserable voice; "it's official . . ."

The envelope did, in fact, contain instructions to Mr. Golyadkin, signed by Andrey Filippovich, to give up the business in his hands to Ivan Semyonovich. Taking the envelope and giving ten kopeks to the man, Mr. Golyadkin went into his flat and saw that Petrushka was collecting all his odds and ends, all his things into a heap, evidently intending to abandon Mr. Golyadkin and move to the flat of Karolina Ivanovna, who had enticed him to take the place of Yevstafy.

CHAPTER XII

Petrushka came in swaggering, with a strangely casual manner and an air of vulgar triumph on his face. It was evident that he had some idea in his head, that he felt thoroughly within his rights, and he looked like an unconcerned spectator—that is, as though he were anybody's servant rather than Mr. Golyadkin's.

"I say, you know, my good lad," our hero began breathlessly, "what time is it?"

Without speaking, Petrushka went behind his partition, then returned, and in a rather independent tone announced that it was nearly half-past seven.

"Well, that's all right, my lad, that's all right. Come, you see, my boy . . . allow me to tell you, my good lad, that everything, I fancy, is at an end between us."

Petrushka said nothing.

"Well, now as everything is over between us, tell me openly, as a friend, where you have been."

"Where I've been? To see good people, sir."

"I know, my good lad, I know. I have always been satisfied with you, and I give you a character. . . . Well, what are you doing with them now?"

"Why, sir! You know yourself. We all know a decent man won't teach you any harm."

"I know, my dear fellow, I know. Nowadays good people are rare, my lad; prize them, my friend. Well, how are they?"

"To be sure, they . . . Only I can't serve you any longer, sir; as your honour must know."

"I know, my dear fellow, I know your zeal and devotion; I have seen it all, my lad, I've noticed it. I respect you, my friend. I respect a good and honest man, even though he's a lackey."

"Why, yes, to be sure! The likes of us, of course, as you know yourself, are as good as anybody. That's so. We all know, sir, that there's no getting on without a good man."

"Very well, very well, my boy, I feel it. . . . Come, here's your money and here's your character. Now we'll kiss and say good-bye, brother. . . . Come, now, my lad, I'll ask one service of you, one last service," said Mr. Golyadkin, in a solemn voice. "You see, my dear boy, all sorts of things happen. Sorrow is concealed in gilded palaces, and there's no escaping it. You know, my boy, I've always been kind to you, my boy."

Petrushka remained mute.

"I believe I've always been kind to you, my dear fellow. . . . Come, how much linen have we now, my dear boy?"

"Well, it's all there. Linen shirts six, three pairs of socks; four shirtfronts; flannel vests; of underlinen two sets. You know all that yourself. I've got nothing of yours, sir. . . . I look after my master's belongings, sir. I am like that, sir . . . we all know . . . and I've . . . never been guilty of anything of the sort, sir, you know yourself, sir . . ."

"I trust you, my lad, I trust you. I didn't mean that, my friend, I didn't mean that, you know, my lad; I tell you what . . ."

"To be sure, sir, we know that already. Why, when I used to be in service at General Stolbnyakov's[21] . . . I lost the place through the family's going away to Saratov . . . they've an estate there . . ."

"No; I didn't mean that, my lad, I didn't mean that; don't think anything of the sort, my dear fellow . . ."

"To be sure. It's easy, as you know yourself, sir, to take away the character of folks like us. And I've always given satisfaction—ministers, generals, senators, counts—I've served them all. I've been at Prince Svinchatkin's, at Colonel Pereborkin's, at General Nedobarov's—they've gone away too, they've gone to their property. As we all know . . ."

"Yes, my lad, very good, my lad, very good. And now I'm going away, my friend. . . . A different path lies before each man, no one can tell what road he may have to take. Come, my lad, put out my clothes now, lay out my uniform too . . . and my other trousers, my sheets, quilts and pillows . . ."

"Am I to pack them all in the bag?"

"Yes, my lad, yes; the bag, please. Who knows what may happen to us. Come, my dear boy, you can go and find a carriage . . ."

"A carriage? . . ."

"Yes, my lad, a carriage; a roomy one, and take it by the hour. And don't you imagine anything . . ."

"And are you meaning to go far away, sir?"

"I don't know, my lad, I don't know that either. I think you had better pack my feather bed too. What do you think, my lad? I am relying on you, my dear fellow . . ."

"Is your honour setting off at once?"

"Yes, my friend, yes! Circumstances have turned out so . . . so it is, my dear fellow, so it is . . ."

"To be sure, sir; when we were in the regiment the same thing happened to the lieutenant; they eloped from a country gentleman's . . ."

"Eloped? . . . How! My dear fellow!"

"Yes, sir, eloped, and they were married in another house. Everything was got ready beforehand. There was a hue and cry after them; the late prince took their part, and so it was all settled . . ."

"They were married, but . . . how is it, my dear fellow. . . . How did you come to know, my boy?"

"Why, to be sure! The earth is full of rumours, sir. We know, sir, we've all . . . to be sure, there's no one without sin. Only I'll tell you now, sir, let me speak plainly and vulgarly, sir; since it has come to this, I must tell you, sir; you have an enemy—you've a rival, sir, a powerful rival, so there . . ."

"I know, my dear fellow, I know; you know yourself, my dear fellow . . . So, you see, I'm relying upon you. What are we to do now, my friend! How do you advise me?"

"Well, sir, if you are in that way now, if you've come, so to say, to such a pass, sir, you'll have to make some purchases, sir—say some sheets, pillows, another feather bed, a double one, a good quilt—here at the neighbours downstairs—she's a shopkeeper, sir—she has a good fox-fur cloak, so you might look at it and buy it, you might have a look at it at once. You'll need it now, sir; it's a good cloak, sir, satin-lined with fox . . ."

"Very good, my lad, very good, I agree; I rely upon you, I rely upon you entirely; a cloak by all means, if necessary. . . . Only make haste, make haste! For God's sake make haste! I'll buy the cloak—only please make haste! It will soon be eight o'clock. Make haste for God's sake, my dear lad! Hurry up, my lad . . ."

Petrushka ran to gather together a bundle of linen, pillows, quilt, sheets, and all sorts of odds and ends, tied them up and rushed headlong out of the room. Meanwhile, Mr. Golyadkin seized the letter once more, but he could not read it. Clutching his devoted head, he leaned against the wall in a state of stupefaction. He could not think of anything, he could do nothing either, and could not even tell what was happening to him. At last, seeing that time was passing and neither Petrushka nor the fur cloak had made their appearance, Mr. Golyadkin made up his mind to go himself. Opening the door into the entry, he heard below noise, talk, disputing, scuffling. . . . Several of the women of the neighbouring flats were shouting, talking and protesting about something—Mr. Golyadkin knew what. Petrushka's voice was heard: then there was a sound of footsteps.

"My goodness! They'll bring all the world in here," moaned Mr. Golyadkin, wringing his hands in despair and rushing back into his room. Running back into his room, he fell almost senseless on the sofa with his face in the pillow. After lying a minute in this way, he jumped up and, without waiting for Petrushka, he put on his goloshes, his hat and his greatcoat, snatched up his papers and ran headlong downstairs.

"Nothing is wanted, nothing, my dear fellow! I will manage myself—everything myself. I don't need you for the time, and meantime, things may take a better turn, perhaps," Mr. Golyadkin muttered to Petrushka, meeting him on the stairs; then he ran out into the yard, away from the house. There was a faintness at his heart, he had not yet made up his mind what was his position, what he was to do, how he was to act in the present critical position.

"Yes, how am I to act? Lord, have mercy on me! And that all this should happen!" he cried out at last in despair, tottering along the street at random; "that all this must needs happen! Why, but for this, but for just this, everything would have been put right; at one stroke, at one skilful, vigorous, firm stroke it would have been set right. I would have my finger cut off to have it set right! And I know, indeed, how it would have been settled. This is how it would have been managed: I'd have gone on the spot . . . said how it was . . . 'with your permission, sir, I'm neither here nor there in it . . . things aren't done like that,' I would say, 'my dear sir, things aren't done like that, there's no accepting an impostor in our office: an impostor . . . my dear sir, is a man . . . who is worthless and of no service to his country. Do you understand that? Do you understand that, my dear sir,' I should say! That's how it would be. . . . But no . . . after all, things are not like that . . . not a bit like that. . . . I am talking nonsense, like a fool! A suicidal fool! It's not like that at all, you suicidal fool. . . . This is how things are done, though, you profligate man! . . . Well, what am I to do with myself now? Well, what am I going to do with myself now. What am I fit for now? Come, what are you fit for now, for instance, you, Golyadkin, you, you worthless fellow! Well, what now? I must get a carriage; 'hire a carriage and bring it here,' says she, 'we shall get our feet wet without a carriage,' says she. . . . And who could ever have thought it! Fie, fie, my young lady! Fie, fie, a

young lady of virtuous behaviour! Well, well, the girl we all
thought so much of! You've distinguished yourself, madam,
there's no doubt of that! you've distinguished yourself! . . . And
it all comes from immoral education. And now that I've looked
into it and seen through it all I see that it is due to nothing else
but immorality. Instead of looking after her as a child . . . and
the rod at times . . . they stuff her with sweets and dainties, and
the old man is always doting over her: saying 'my dear, my love,
my beauty,' saying, 'we'll marry you to a count!' . . . And now
she has come forward herself and shown her cards, as though
to say that's her little game! Instead of keeping her at home as
a child, they sent her to a boarding school, to a French
madame, an émigrée, a Madame Falbalas[22] or something, and she
learned all sorts of things at that Madame Falbalas', and this is
how it always turns out. 'Come,' says she, 'and be happy! Be in
a carriage,' she says, 'at such a time, under the windows, and
sing a sentimental serenade in the Spanish style; I await you and
I know you love me, and we will fly together and live in a hut.'
But the fact is it's impossible; since it has come to that, madam,
it's impossible, it is against the law to abduct an innocent, respectable girl from her parents' roof without their sanction!
And, if you come to that, why, what for and what need is there
to do it? Come, she should marry a suitable person, the man
marked out by destiny, and that would be the end of it. But I'm
in the government service, I might lose my berth through it: I
might be arrested for it, madam! I tell you that! If you did not
know it. It's that German woman's doing. She's at the bottom of
it all, the witch; she cooked the whole kettle of fish. For they've
slandered a man, for they've invented a bit of womanish gossip
about him, a regular performance by the advice of Andrey Filippovich, that's what it came from. Otherwise how could
Petrushka be mixed up in it? What has he to do with it? What
need for that rogue to be in it? No, I cannot, madam, I cannot
possibly, not on any account. . . . No, madam, this time you
must really excuse me. It's all your doing, madam, it's not all the
German's doing, it's not the witch's doing at all, but simply
yours. For the witch is a good woman, for the witch is not to

blame in any way; it's your fault, madam; it's you who are to blame, let me tell you! I shall be charged with a crime through you, madam. . . . A man might be ruined . . . a man might lose sight of himself, and not be able to restrain himself—a wedding, indeed! And how is it all going to end? And how will it all be arranged? I would give a great deal to know all that! . . ."

So our hero reflected in his despair. Coming to himself suddenly, he observed that he was standing somewhere in Liteyny Street. The weather was awful: it was a thaw; snow and rain were falling—just as at that memorable time when at the dread hour of midnight all Mr. Golyadkin's troubles had begun. "This is a nice night for a journey!" thought Mr. Golyadkin, looking at the weather; "it's death all round. . . . Good Lord! Where am I to find a carriage, for instance? I believe there's something black there at the corner. We'll see, we'll investigate. . . . Lord, have mercy on us!" our hero went on, bending his weak and tottering steps in the direction in which he saw something that looked like a cab.

"No, I know what I'll do; I'll go straight and fall on my knees, if I can, and humbly beg, saying 'I put my fate in your hands, in the hands of my superiors'; saying, 'Your Excellency, be a protector and a benefactor'; and then I'll say this and that, and explain how it is and that it is an unlawful act; 'Do not destroy me, I look upon you as my father, do not abandon me . . . save my dignity, my honour, my name, my reputation . . . and save me from a miscreant, a vicious man. . . . He's another person, your Excellency, and I'm another person too; he's apart and I am myself by myself too; I am really myself by myself, your Excellency; really myself by myself,' that's what I shall say. 'I cannot be like him. Change him, dismiss him, give orders for him to be changed and a godless, licentious impersonation to be suppressed . . . that it may not be an example to others, your Excellency. I look upon you as a father'; those in authority over us, our benefactors and protectors, are bound, of course, to encourage such impulses. . . . There's something chivalrous about it: I shall say, 'I look upon you, my benefactor and superior, as a father, and trust my fate to you, and I will not say anything against it; I put myself in your hands, and retire from the affair myself' . . . that's what I would say."

"Well, my man, are you a cabman?"

"Yes . . ."

"I want a cab for the evening . . ."

"And does your honour want to go far?"

"For the evening, for the evening; wherever I have to go, my man, wherever I have to go."

"Does your honour want to drive out of town?"

"Yes, my friend, out of town, perhaps. I don't quite know myself yet, I can't tell you for certain, my man. Maybe you see it will all be settled for the best. We all know, my friend . . ."

"Yes, sir, of course we all know. Please God it may."

"Yes, my friend, yes; thank you, my dear fellow; come, what's your fare, my good man? . . ."

"Do you want to set off at once?"

"Yes, at once, that is, no, you must wait at a certain place. . . . A little while, not long, you'll have to wait . . ."

"Well, if you hire me for the whole time, I couldn't ask less than six rubles for weather like this . . ."

"Oh, very well, my friend; and I thank you, my dear fellow. So, come, you can take me now, my good man."

"Get in; allow me, I'll put it straight a bit—now will your honour get in. Where shall I drive?"

"To the Izmailovsky Bridge, my friend."

The driver plumped down on the box, with difficulty roused his pair of lean nags from the trough of hay, and was setting off for Izmailovsky Bridge. But suddenly Mr. Golyadkin pulled the cord, stopped the cab, and besought him in an imploring voice not to drive to Izmailovsky Bridge, but to turn back to another street. The driver turned into another street, and ten minutes later Mr. Golyadkin's newly hired equipage was standing before the house in which his Excellency had a flat. Mr. Golyadkin got out of the carriage, begged the driver to be sure to wait and with a sinking heart ran upstairs to the third storey and pulled the bell; the door was opened and our hero found himself in the entry of his Excellency's flat.

"Is his Excellency graciously pleased to be at home?" said Mr. Golyadkin, addressing the man who opened the door.

"What do you want?" asked the servant, scrutinizing Mr. Golyadkin from head to foot.

"I, my friend . . . I am Golyadkin, the titular councillor, Golyadkin. . . . To say . . . something or other . . . to explain . . ."

"You must wait; you cannot . . ."

"My friend, I cannot wait; my business is important, it's business that admits of no delay . . ."

"But from whom have you come? Have you brought papers? . . ."

"No, my friend, I am on my own account. Announce me, my friend, say something or other, explain. I'll reward you, my good man . . ."

"I cannot. His Excellency is not at home, he has visitors. Come at ten o'clock in the morning . . ."

"Take in my name, my good man, I can't wait—it is impossible. . . . You'll have to answer for it, my good man."

"Why, go and announce him! What's the matter with you; want to save your shoe leather?" said another lackey, who was lolling on the bench and had not uttered a word till then.

"Shoe leather! I was told not to show any one up, you know; their time is the morning."

"Announce him, have you lost your tongue?"

"I'll announce him all right—I've not lost my tongue. It's not my orders; I've told you, it's not my orders. Walk inside."

Mr. Golyadkin went into the outermost room; there was a clock on the table. He glanced at it: it was half-past eight. His heart ached within him. Already he wanted to turn back, but at that very moment the footman standing at the door of the next room had already boomed out Mr. Golyadkin's name.

"Oh, what lungs," thought our hero in indescribable misery. "Why, you ought to have said: 'he has come most humbly and meekly to make an explanation . . . something . . . be graciously pleased to see him.' . . . Now the whole business is ruined; all my hopes are scattered to the winds. But . . . however . . . never mind. . . ."

There was no time to think, moreover. The lackey, returning, said, "Please walk in," and led Mr. Golyadkin into the study.

When our hero went in, he felt as though he were blinded, for he could see nothing at all. . . . But three or four figures seemed flitting before his eyes: "Oh, yes, they are the visitors," flashed through Mr. Golyadkin's mind. At last our hero could distinguish clearly the star on the black coat of his Excellency, then by degrees advanced to seeing the black coat and at last gained the power of complete vision. . . .

"What is it?" said a familiar voice above Mr. Golyadkin.

"The titular councillor, Golyadkin, your Excellency."

"Well?"

"I have come to make an explanation . . ."

"How? . . . What?"

"Why, yes. This is how it is. I've come for an explanation, your Excellency . . ."

"But you . . . but who are you? . . ."

"M—m—m—mist—er Golyadkin, your Excellency, a titular councillor."

"Well, what is it you want?"

"Why, this is how it is, I look upon you as a father; I retire . . . defend me from my enemy! . . ."

"What's this? . . ."

"We all know . . ."

"What do we all know!"

Mr. Golyadkin was silent: his chin began twitching a little.

"Well?"

"I thought it was chivalrous, your Excellency. . . . 'There's something chivalrous in it,' I said, 'and I look upon my superior as a father' . . . this is what I thought; 'protect me, I tear . . . earfully . . . b . . . beg and that such imp . . . impulses ought . . . to . . . be encouraged . . ."

His Excellency turned away, our hero for some minutes could distinguish nothing. There was a weight on his chest. His breathing was laboured; he did not know where he was standing. . . . He felt ashamed and sad. God knows what followed. . . . Recovering himself, our hero noticed that his Excellency was talking with his guests, and seemed to be briskly and emphatically discussing something with them. One of the visitors Mr. Golyadkin recognized at once. This was Andrey Filippovich; he knew no one else; yet there was another person that seemed familiar—a tall, thick-set figure, middle-aged, possessed of very thick eyebrows and whiskers and a significant sharp expression. On his chest was an order and in his mouth a cigar. This gentleman was smoking and nodding significantly without taking the cigar out of his mouth, glancing from time to time at Mr. Golyadkin. Mr. Golyadkin felt awkward; he turned away his eyes and immediately saw another very strange visitor. Through a door which our hero had taken for a looking-glass, just as he had done once before—*he* made his appearance—we know who: a very intimate friend and acquaintance of Mr. Golyadkin's. Mr. Golyadkin junior had actually been till then in a little room close by, hurriedly writing something; now, apparently, he was needed—and he came in with papers under his arm, went up to his Excellency, and while waiting for exclusive attention to be paid him succeeded very adroitly in putting his spoke into the talk and consultation, taking his place a little behind Andrey Filippovich's back and partly screening him from the gentleman smoking the cigar. Apparently Mr. Golyadkin junior took an extreme interest in the conversation, to which he was listening now in a gentlemanly way, nodding his head, fidgeting with his feet, smiling, continually looking at his Excellency—as it were beseeching him with his eyes to let him put his word in.

"The scoundrel," thought Mr. Golyadkin, and involuntarily he took a step forward. At this moment his Excellency turned round, and came rather hesitatingly towards Mr. Golyadkin.

"Well, that's all right, that's all right; well, run along, now. I'll look into your case, and give orders for you to be taken . . ."

At this point his Excellency glanced at the gentleman with the thick whiskers. The latter nodded in assent.

Mr. Golyadkin felt and distinctly understood that they were

taking him for something different and not looking at him in the proper light at all.

"In one way or another I must explain myself," he thought; "I must say, 'This is how it is, your Excellency.'"

At this point in his perplexity he dropped his eyes to the floor and to his great astonishment he saw a good-sized patch of something white on his Excellency's boots.

"Can there be a hole in them?" thought Mr. Golyadkin. Mr. Golyadkin was, however, soon convinced that his Excellency's boots were not split, but were only shining brilliantly—a phenomenon fully explained by the fact that they were patent leather and highly polished.

"It is what they call blick," thought our hero; "the term is used particularly in artists' studios; in other places such a reflected light is called a rib of light."

At this point Mr. Golyadkin raised his eyes and saw that the time had come to speak, for things might easily end badly. . . .

Our hero took a step forward.

"I say this is how it is, your Excellency," he said, "and there's no accepting impostors nowadays."

His Excellency made no answer, but rang the bell violently. Our hero took another step forward.

"He is a vile, vicious man, your Excellency," said our hero, beside himself and faint with terror, though he still pointed boldly and resolutely at his unworthy twin, who was fidgeting about near his Excellency. "I say this is how it is, and I am alluding to a well-known person."

There was a general sensation at Mr. Golyadkin's words. Andrey Filippovich and the gentleman with the cigar nodded their heads; his Excellency impatiently tugged at the bell to summon the servants. At this point Mr. Golyadkin junior came forward in his turn.

"Your Excellency," he said, "I humbly beg permission to speak." There was something very resolute in Mr. Golyadkin junior's voice; everything showed that he felt himself completely in the right.

"Allow me to ask you," he began again, anticipating his Excellency's reply in his eagerness, and this time addressing Mr. Golyadkin; "allow me to ask you, in whose presence you are making this explanation? Before whom are you standing, in whose room are you? . . ."

Mr. Golyadkin junior was in a state of extraordinary excitement, flushed and glowing with wrath and indignation; there were positively tears in his eyes.

A lackey, appearing in the doorway, roared at the top of his voice the name of some new arrivals, the Bassavryukovs.

"A good aristocratic name, hailing from Little Russia," thought Mr. Golyadkin, and at that moment he felt some one lay a very friendly hand on his back, then a second hand was laid on his back. Mr. Golyadkin's infamous twin was tripping about in front leading the way; and our hero saw clearly that he was being led to the big doors of the room.

"Just as it was at Olsufy Ivanovich's," he thought, and he found himself in the hall. Looking round, he saw beside him two of his Excellency's lackeys and his twin.

"The greatcoat, the greatcoat, the greatcoat, the greatcoat, my friend! The greatcoat of my best friend!" whispered the depraved man, snatching the coat from one of the servants, and by way of a nasty and ungentlemanly joke flinging it straight at Mr. Golyadkin's head. Extricating himself from under his coat, Mr. Golyadkin distinctly heard the two lackeys snigger. But without listening to anything, or paying attention to it, he went out of the hall and found himself on the lighted stairs. Mr. Golyadkin junior following him.

"Good-bye, your Excellency!" he shouted after Mr. Golyadkin senior.

"Scoundrel!" our hero exclaimed, beside himself.

"Well, scoundrel, then . . ."

"Depraved man! . . ."

"Well, depraved man, then . . ." answered Mr. Golyadkin's unworthy enemy, and with his characteristic baseness he looked down from the top of the stairs straight into Mr. Golyadkin's face as though begging him to go on. Our hero spat with indignation and ran out of the front door; he was so shattered, so crushed, that he had no recollection of how he got into the cab or who helped him in. Coming to himself, he found that he was being driven to Fontanka. "To Izmailovsky Bridge, then," thought Mr. Golyadkin. At this point Mr. Golyadkin tried to think of something else, but could not; there was something so terrible that he could not explain it. . . . "Well, never mind," our hero concluded and he drove to Izmailovsky Bridge.

CHAPTER XIII

. . . It seemed as though the weather meant to change for the better. The snow, which had till then been coming down in regular clouds, began growing less and less and at last almost ceased. The sky became visible and here and there tiny stars sparkled in it. It was only wet, muddy, damp and stifling, especially for Mr. Golyadkin, who could hardly breathe as it was. His greatcoat, soaked and heavy with wet, sent a sort of unpleasant warm dampness all through him and weighed down his exhausted legs. A feverish shiver sent sharp, shooting pains all over him; he was in a painful cold sweat of exhaustion, so much so that Mr. Golyadkin even forgot to repeat at every suitable occasion with his characteristic firmness and resolution his favourite phrase that "it all, maybe, most likely, indeed, might turn out for the best." "But all this does not matter for the time," our hero repeated, still staunch and not downhearted, wiping from his face the cold drops that streamed in all directions from the brim of his round hat, which was so soaked that it could hold no more water. Adding that all this was nothing so far, our hero tried to sit on a rather thick clump of wood, which was lying near a heap of logs in Olsufy Ivanovich's yard. Of course, it was no good thinking of Spanish serenades or silken ladders, but it was quite necessary to think of a modest corner, snug and private, if not altogether warm. He felt greatly tempted, we may mention in passing, by that corner in the back entry of Olsufy Ivanovich's flat in which he had once, almost at the beginning of this true story, stood for two hours between a cupboard and an old screen among all sorts of domestic odds and ends and useless litter. The fact is that Mr. Golyadkin had been standing waiting for two whole hours on this occasion in Olsufy Ivanovich's yard. But in regard to that modest and snug little corner there were certain drawbacks which had not existed before. The first drawback was the fact that it was probably now a marked place and that certain precautionary measures had been taken in regard to it since the scandal at Olsufy Ivanovich's last ball. Secondly, he had to wait for a signal from Klara Olsufyevna, for there was bound to be some such signal, it was always a feature in such cases and, "it didn't begin with us and it won't end with us."

At this point Mr. Golyadkin very appropriately remembered a novel he had read long ago in which the heroine, in precisely similar circumstances, signalled to Alfred by tying a pink ribbon to her window. But now, at night, in the climate of Petersburg, famous for its dampness and unreliability, a pink ribbon was hardly appropriate and, in fact, was utterly out of the question.

"No, it's not a matter of silk ladders," thought our hero, "and I had better stay here quietly and comfortably. . . . I had better stand here."

And he selected a place in the yard exactly opposite the window, near a stack of firewood. Of course, many persons, grooms and coachmen, were continually crossing the yard, and there was, besides, the rumbling of wheels and the snorting of horses and so on; yet it was a convenient place, whether he was observed or not; but now, anyway, there was the advantage of being to some extent in shadow, and no one could see Mr. Golyadkin while he himself could see everything.

The windows were brightly lit up, there was some sort of ceremonious party at Olsufy Ivanovich's. But he could hear no music as yet.

"So it's not a ball, but a party of some other sort," thought our hero, somewhat aghast. "Is it to-day?" floated the doubt through him. "Have I made a mistake in the date? Perhaps; anything is possible. . . . Yes, to be sure, anything is possible. . . . Perhaps she wrote a letter to me yesterday, and it didn't reach me, and perhaps it did not reach me because Petrushka put his spoke in, the rascal! Or it was to-morrow in the letter, that is, that I . . . should do everything to-morrow, that is—wait with a carriage. . . ."

At this point our hero turned cold all over and felt in his pocket for the letter, to make sure. But to his surprise the letter was not in his pocket.

"How's this?" muttered Mr. Golyadkin, more dead than alive. "Where did I leave it? Then I must have lost it. That is the last straw!" he moaned at last. "Oh, if it falls into evil hands! Perhaps it has already. Good Lord! What may it not lead to! It may lead to something such that . . . Ach, my miserable fate!" At this point Mr. Golyadkin began trembling like a leaf at the thought that perhaps his vicious twin had thrown the greatcoat at him with the object of stealing the letter of which he had somehow got an inkling from Mr. Golyadkin's enemies.

"What's more, he's stealing it," thought our hero, "as evidence . . . but why evidence! . . ."

After the first shock of horror, the blood rushed to Mr. Golyadkin's head. Moaning and gnashing his teeth, he clutched his burning head, sank back on his block of wood and relapsed into brooding. . . . But he could form no coherent thoughts. Figures kept flitting through his brain, incidents came back to his memory, now vaguely, now distinctly, the tunes of some foolish songs kept ringing in his ears. . . . He was in great distress, unnatural distress!

"My God, my God!" our hero thought, recovering himself a little, and suppressing a muffled sob, "give me fortitude in the immensity of my afflictions! That I am done for, utterly destroyed—of that there can be no doubt, and that's all in the natural order of things, since it cannot be otherwise. To begin with, I've lost my berth, I've certainly lost it, I must have lost it. . . . Well, supposing things are set right somehow. Supposing I have money enough to begin with: I must have another lodging, furniture of some sort. . . . In the first place, I shan't have Petrushka. I can get on without the rascal . . . somehow, with help from the people of the house; well, that will be all right! I can go in and out when I like, and Petrushka won't grumble at my coming in late—yes, that is so; that's why it's a good thing to have the people in the house. . . . Well, supposing that's all right; but all that's nothing to do with it, all that's nothing to do with it."

At this point the thought of the real position again dawned upon Mr. Golyadkin's memory. He looked round.

"Oh, Lord, have mercy on me, have mercy on me! What am I talking about?" he thought, growing utterly desperate and clutching his burning head in his hands. . . .

"Won't you soon be going, sir?" a voice pronounced above Mr. Golyadkin. Our hero started; before him stood his cabman, who was also drenched through and shivering; growing impatient, and having nothing to do, he had thought fit to take a look at Mr. Golyadkin behind the woodstack.

"I am all right, my friend. . . . I am coming soon, soon, very soon; you wait. . . ."

The cabman walked away, grumbling to himself. "What is he grumbling about?" Mr. Golyadkin wondered through his tears. "Why, I have hired him for the evening, why, I'm . . . within my rights now . . . that's so! I've hired him for the evening, and that's the end of it. If one stands still, it's just the same. That's for me to decide. I am free to drive on or not to drive on. And my staying here by the woodstack has nothing to do with the case . . . and don't dare to say anything; think, the gentleman wants to stand behind the woodstack, and so he's standing behind it . . . and he is not disgracing any one's honour! That's the fact of the matter.

"I tell you what it is, madam, if you care to know. Nowadays, madam, nobody lives in a hut, or anything of that sort. No, indeed. And in our industrial age there's no getting on without morality, a fact of which you are a fatal example,

madam.... You say we must get a job as a collegiate registrar
and live in a hut on the sea-shore. In the first place, madam,
there are no collegiate registrars on the sea-shore, and in the
second place we can't get a job as a collegiate registrar. For
supposing, for example, I send in a petition, present myself—
saying a collegiate registrar's place or something of the sort . . .
and defend me from my enemy . . . they'll tell you, madam,
they'll say, to be sure . . . we've lots of collegiate registrars, and
here you are not at Madame Falbalas', where you learnt the
rules of good behaviour of which you are such a fatal example.
Good behaviour, madam, means staying at home, honouring
your father and not thinking about suitors prematurely. Suitors
will come in good time, madam, that's so! Of course, you are
bound to have some accomplishments, such as playing the
piano sometimes, speaking French, history, geography, scrip-
ture and arithmetic, that's the truth of it! And that's all you
need. Cooking, too, cooking certainly forms part of the education of a well-behaved girl! But as it is, in the first place, my fine
lady, they won't let you go, they'll raise a hue and cry after you,
and then they'll lock you up in a nunnery. How will it be
then, madam? What will you have me do then? Would you have
me, madam, follow the example of some stupid novels, and
melt into tears on a neighbouring hillock, gazing at the cold
walls of your prison house, and finally die, following the example of some wretched German poets and novelists. Is that it,
madam? But, to begin with, allow me to tell you, as a friend,
that things are not done like that, and in the second place I
would have given you and your parents, too, a good thrashing
for letting you read French books; for French books teach you
no good. There's a poison in them . . . a pernicious poison,
madam! Or do you imagine, allow me to ask you, or do you
imagine that we shall elope with impunity, or something of that
sort . . . that we shall have a hut on the shore of the sea and so
on; and that we shall begin billing and cooing and talking about
our feelings, and that so we shall spend our lives in happiness
and content; and then there would be little ones—so then we
shall . . . shall go to our father, the civil councillor, Olsufy

Ivanovich, and say, 'we've got a little one, and so, on this propitious occasion remove your curse, and bless the couple.' No, madam, I tell you again, that's not the way to do things, and for the first thing there'll be no billing and cooing and please don't reckon on it. Nowadays, madam, the husband is the master and a good, well-brought-up wife should try and please him in every way. And endearments, madam, are not in favour, nowadays, in our industrial age; the day of Jean Jacques Rousseau is over.[23] The husband comes home, for instance, hungry from the office, and asks, 'Isn't there something to eat, my love, a drop of vodka to drink, a bit of salt fish to eat?' So then, madam, you must have the vodka and the herring ready. Your husband will eat it with relish, and he won't so much as look at you, he'll only say 'Run into the kitchen, kitten,' he'll say, 'and look after the dinner,' and at most, once a week, he'll kiss you, even then rather indifferently. . . . That's how it will be with us, my young lady! Yes, even then indifferently. . . . That's how it will be, if one considers it, if it has come to one's looking at the thing in that way. . . . And how do I come in? Why have you mixed me up in your caprices? 'The noble man who is suffering for your sake and will be dear to your heart for ever,' and so on. But in the first place, madam, I am not suited to you, you know yourself, I'm not a great hand at compliments, I'm not fond of uttering perfumed trifles for the ladies. I'm not fond of lady-killers, and I must own I've never been a beauty to look at. You won't find any swagger or false shame in me, and I tell you so now in all sincerity. This is the fact of the matter: we can boast of nothing but a straightforward, open character and common sense; we have nothing to do with intrigues. I am not one to intrigue, I say so and I'm proud of it—that's the fact of the matter! . . . I wear no mask among straightforward people, and to tell you the whole truth . . ."

Suddenly Mr. Golyadkin started. The red and perfectly sopping beard of the cabman appeared round the woodstack again. . . .

"I am coming directly, my friend. I'm coming at once, you

know," Mr. Golyadkin responded in a trembling and failing voice.

The cabman scratched his head, then stroked his beard, and moved a step forward . . . stood still and looked suspiciously at Mr. Golyadkin.

"I am coming directly, my friend; you see, my friend . . . I . . . just a little, you see, only a second! . . . more . . . here, you see, my friend. . . ."

"Aren't you coming at all?" the cabman asked at last, definitely coming up to Mr. Golyadkin.

"No, my friend, I'm coming directly. I am waiting, you see, my friend. . . ."

"So I see. . . ."

"You see, my friend, I . . . What part of the country do you come from, my friend?"

"We are under a master . . ."

"And have you a good master? . . ."

"All right. . . ."

"Yes, my friend; you stay here, my friend, you see . . . Have you been in Petersburg long, my friend?"

"It's a year since I came. . . ."

"And are you getting on all right, my friend?"

"Middling."

"To be sure, my friend, to be sure. You must thank Providence, my friend. You must look out for straightforward people. Straightforward people are none too common nowadays, my friend; he would give you washing, food, and drink, my good fellow, a good man would. But sometimes you see tears shed for the sake of gold, my friend . . . you see a lamentable example; that's the fact of the matter, my friend. . . ."

The cabman seemed to feel sorry for Mr. Golyadkin. "Well, your honour, I'll wait. Will your honour be waiting long?"

"No, my friend, no; I . . . you know . . . I won't wait any longer, my good man. . . . What do you think, my friend? I rely upon you. I won't stay any longer."

"Aren't you going at all?"

"No, my friend, no; I'll reward you, my friend . . . that's the fact of the matter. How much ought I to give you, my dear fellow?"

"What you hired me for, please, sir. I've been waiting here a long time; don't be hard on a man, sir."

"Well, here, my good man, here."

At this point Mr. Golyadkin gave six whole rubles to the cabman, and made up his mind in earnest to waste no more time, that is, to clear off straight away, especially as the cabman was dismissed and everything was over, and so it was useless to wait longer. He rushed out of the yard, went out of the gate, turned to the left and without looking round took to his heels, breathless and rejoicing. "Perhaps it will all be for the best," he thought, "and perhaps in this way I've run away from trouble." Mr. Golyadkin suddenly became all at once light-hearted. "Oh, if only it could turn out for the best!" thought our hero, though he put little faith in his own words. "I know what I'll do . . ." he thought. "No, I know, I'd better try the other tack. . . . Or wouldn't it be better to do this? . . ." In this way, hesitating and seeking for the solution of his doubts, our hero ran to Semyonovsky Bridge; but while running to Semyonovsky Bridge he very rationally and conclusively decided to return.

"It will be better so," he thought. "I had better try the other tack, that is . . . I will just go—I'll look on simply as an outsider, and that will be the end of it; I am simply an onlooker, an outsider—and nothing more, whatever happens—it's not my fault, that's the fact of the matter! That's how it shall be now."

Deciding to return, our hero actually did return, the more readily because with this happy thought he conceived of himself now as quite an outsider.

"It's the best thing; one's not responsible for anything, and one will see all that's necessary . . . that's the fact of the matter!"

It was a safe plan and that settled it. Reassured, he crept back under the peaceful shelter of his soothing and protecting woodstack, and began gazing intently at the window. This time he was not destined to gaze and wait for long. Suddenly a strange commotion became apparent at all the windows. Figures appeared, curtains were drawn back, whole groups of people were crowding to the windows at Olsufy Ivanovich's flat. All were peeping out looking for something in the yard. From the security of his woodstack, our hero, too, began with curiosity watching the general commotion, and with interest craned forward to right and to left so far as he could within the shadow of the woodstack. Suddenly he started, held his breath and almost sat down with horror. It seemed to him—in short, he realized, that they were looking for nothing and for nobody but him, Mr. Golyadkin! Every one was looking in his direction. It was impossible to escape; they saw him. . . . In a flutter, Mr. Golyadkin huddled as closely as he could to the woodstack, and only then noticed that the treacherous shadow had betrayed him, that it did not cover him completely. Our hero would have been delighted at that moment to creep into a mouse-hole in the woodstack, and there meekly to remain, if only it had been possible. But it was absolutely impossible. In his agony he began at last staring openly and boldly at the windows, it was the best thing to do. . . . And suddenly he glowed with shame. He had been fully discovered, every one was staring at him at once, they were all waving their hands, all were nodding their heads at him, all were calling to him; then several windows creaked as they opened, several voices shouted something to him at once. . . .

"I wonder why they don't whip these naughty girls as children," our hero muttered to himself, losing his head completely. Suddenly there ran down the steps he (we know who), without his hat or greatcoat, breathless, rubbing his hands, wriggling, capering, perfidiously displaying intense joy at seeing Mr. Golyadkin.

"Yakov Petrovich," whispered this individual, so notorious for his worthlessness, "Yakov Petrovich, are you here? You'll catch cold. It's chilly here, Yakov Petrovich. Come indoors."

"Yakov Petrovich! No, I'm all right, Yakov Petrovich," our hero muttered in a submissive voice.

"No, this won't do, Yakov Petrovich, I beg you, I humbly beg you to wait with us. 'Make him welcome and bring him in,' they say, 'Yakov Petrovich.' "

"No, Yakov Petrovich, you see, I'd better. . . . I had better go home, Yakov Petrovich . . ." said our hero, burning at a slow fire and freezing at the same time with shame and terror.

"No—no—no—no!" whispered the loathsome person. "No—no—no, on no account! Come along," he said resolutely, and he dragged Mr. Golyadkin senior to the steps. Mr. Golyadkin senior did not at all want to go, but as every one was looking at them, it would have been stupid to struggle and resist; so our hero went—though, indeed, one cannot say that he went, because he did not know in the least what was being done with him. Though, after all, it made no difference!

Before our hero had time to recover himself and come to his senses, he found himself in the drawing-room. He was pale, dishevelled, harassed; with lustreless eyes he scanned the crowd—horror! The drawing-room, all the rooms—were full to overflowing. There were masses of people, a whole galaxy of ladies; and all were crowding round Mr. Golyadkin, all were pressing towards Mr. Golyadkin, all were squeezing Mr. Golyadkin and he perceived clearly that they were all forcing him in one direction.

"Not towards the door," was the thought that floated through Mr. Golyadkin's mind.

They were, in fact, forcing him not towards the door but Olsufy Ivanovich's easy chair. On one side of the armchair stood Klara Olsufyevna, pale, languid, melancholy, but gorgeously dressed. Mr. Golyadkin was particularly struck by a little white flower which rested on her superb hair. On the other side of the armchair stood Vladimir Semyonovich, clad in black, with his new order in his buttonhole. Mr. Golyadkin was led in, as we have described above, straight up to Olsufy Ivanovich—on one side of him Mr. Golyadkin junior, who had assumed an air of great decorum and propriety, to the immense relief of our hero, while on the other side was Andrey Filippovich, with a very solemn expression on his face.

"What can it mean?" Mr. Golyadkin wondered.

When he saw that he was being led to Olsufy Ivanovich, an idea struck him like a flash of lightning. The thought of the intercepted letter darted through his brain. In great agony our hero stood before Olsufy Ivanovich's chair.

"What will he say now?" he wondered to himself. "Of course, it will be all aboveboard now, that is, straightforward and, one may say, honourable; I shall say this is how it is, and so on."

But what our hero apparently feared did not happen. Olsufy Ivanovich received Mr. Golyadkin very warmly, and though he did not hold out his hand to him, yet as he gazed at our hero, he shook his grey and venerable head—shook it with an air of solemn melancholy and yet of goodwill. So, at least, it seemed to Mr. Golyadkin. He even fancied that a tear glittered in Olsufy Ivanovich's lustreless eyes; he raised his eyes and saw that there seemed to be tears, too, on the eyelashes of Klara Olsufyevna, who was standing by—that there seemed to be something of the same sort even in the eyes of Vladimir Semyonovich—that the unruffled and composed dignity of Andrey Filippovich had the same significance as the general tearful sympathy—that even the young man who was so much like a state councillor, seizing the opportunity, was sobbing bitterly. . . . Though perhaps this was only all Mr. Golyadkin's fancy, because he was so much moved himself, and distinctly felt the hot tears running down his cold cheeks. . . .

Feeling reconciled with mankind and his destiny, and filled with love at the moment, not only for Olsufy Ivanovich, not only for the whole party collected there, but even for his noxious twin (who seemed now to be by no means noxious, and not even to be his twin at all, but a person very agreeable in himself and in no way connected with him), our hero, in a voice broken with sobs, tried to express his feelings to Olsufy Ivanovich, but was too much overcome by all that he had gone through, and could not utter a word; he could only, with an expressive gesture, point meekly to his heart . . .

At last, probably to spare the feelings of the old man, Andrey

Filippovich led Mr. Golyadkin a little away, though he seemed to leave him free to do as he liked. Smiling, muttering something to himself, somewhat bewildered, yet almost completely reconciled with fate and his fellow creatures, our hero began to make his way through the crowd of guests. Every one made way for him, every one looked at him with strange curiosity and with mysterious, unaccountable sympathy. Our hero went into another room; he met with the same attention everywhere; he was vaguely conscious of the whole crowd closely following him, noting every step he took, talking in undertones among themselves of something very interesting, shaking their heads, arguing and discussing in whispers. Mr. Golyadkin wanted very much to know what they were discussing in whispers. Looking round, he saw near him Mr. Golyadkin junior. Feeling an overwhelming impulse to seize his hand and draw him aside, Mr. Golyadkin begged the other Yakov Petrovich most particularly to co-operate with him in all his future undertakings, and not to abandon him at a critical moment. Mr. Golyadkin junior nodded his head gravely and warmly pressed the hand of Mr. Golyadkin senior. Our hero's heart was quivering with the intensity of his emotion. He was gasping for breath, however; he felt so oppressed—so oppressed; he felt that all those eyes fastened upon him were oppressing and dominating him. . . . Mr. Golyadkin caught a glimpse of the councillor who wore a wig. The latter was looking at him with a stern, searching eye, not in the least softened by the general sympathy. . . .

Our hero made up his mind to go straight up to him in order to smile at him and have an immediate explanation, but this somehow did not come off. For one instant Mr. Golyadkin became almost unconscious, almost lost all memory, all feeling.

When he came to himself again he noticed that he was the centre of a large ring formed by the rest of the party round him. Suddenly Mr. Golyadkin's name was called from the other room; the shout was at once taken up by the whole crowd. All was noise and excitement, all rushed to the door of the first room, almost carrying our hero along with them. In the crush

the hard-hearted councillor in the wig was side by side with
Mr. Golyadkin, and, taking our hero by the hand, he made him
sit down beside him opposite Olsufy Ivanovich, at some distance from the latter, however. Every one in the room sat down;
the guests were arranged in rows round Mr. Golyadkin and Olsufy Ivanovich. Everything was hushed; every one preserved a
solemn silence; every one was watching Olsufy Ivanovich, evidently expecting something out of the ordinary. Mr. Golyadkin
noticed that beside Olsufy Ivanovich's chair and directly facing
the councillor sat Mr. Golyadkin junior, with Andrey Filippovich. The silence was prolonged; they were evidently expecting something.

"Just as it is in a family when some one is setting off on a
far journey. We've only to stand up and pray now," thought our
hero.

Suddenly there was a general stir which interrupted Mr.
Golyadkin's reflections. Something they had long been waiting
for happened.

"He is coming, he is coming!" passed from one to another
in the crowd.

"Who is it that is coming?" floated through Mr. Golyadkin's
mind, and he shuddered at a strange sensation. "High time
too!" said the councillor, looking intently at Andrey Filippovich.
Andrey Filippovich, for his part, glanced at Olsufy Ivanovich.
Olsufy Ivanovich gravely and solemnly nodded his head.

"Let us stand up," said the councillor, and he made Mr.
Golyadkin get up. All rose to their feet. Then the councillor
took Mr. Golyadkin senior by the hand, and Andrey Filippovich took Mr. Golyadkin junior, and in this way these two
precisely similar persons were conducted through the expec-
tant crowd surrounding them. Our hero looked about him in
perplexity; but he was at once checked and his attention was
called to Mr. Golyadkin junior, who was holding out his hand
to him.

"They want to reconcile us," thought our hero, and with
emotion he held out his hand to Mr. Golyadkin junior; and

then—then bent his head forward towards him. The other Mr. Golyadkin did the same. . . .

At this point it seemed to Mr. Golyadkin senior that his perfidious friend was smiling, that he gave a sly, hurried wink to the crowd of onlookers, and that there was something sinister in the face of the worthless Mr. Golyadkin junior, that he even made a grimace at the moment of his Judas kiss. . . .

There was a ringing in Mr. Golyadkin's ears, and a darkness before his eyes; it seemed to him that an infinite multitude, an unending series of precisely similar Golyadkins were noisily bursting in at every door of the room; but it was too late . . . the resounding, treacherous kiss was over, and . . .

Then quite an unexpected event occurred. . . . The door opened noisily, and in the doorway stood a man, the very sight of whom sent a chill to Mr. Golyadkin's heart. He stood rooted to the spot. A cry of horror died away in his choking throat. Yet Mr. Golyadkin knew it all beforehand, and had had a presentiment of something of the sort for a long time. The new arrival went up to Mr. Golyadkin gravely and solemnly. Mr. Golyadkin knew this personage very well. He had seen him before, had seen him very often, had seen him that day. . . . This personage was a tall, thick-set man in a black dress-coat with a good-sized cross on his breast, and was possessed of thick, very black whiskers; nothing was lacking but the cigar in the mouth to complete the picture. Yet this person's eyes, as we have mentioned already, sent a chill to the heart of Mr. Golyadkin. With a grave and solemn air this terrible man approached the pitiable hero of our story. . . . Our hero held out his hand to him; the stranger took his hand and drew him along with him. . . . With a crushed and desperate air our hero looked about him.

"It's . . . it's Krestyan Ivanovich Rutenspitz, doctor of medicine and surgery; your old acquaintance, Yakov Petrovich!" a detestable voice whispered in Mr. Golyadkin's ear. He looked round: it was Mr. Golyadkin's twin, so revolting in the despicable meanness of his soul. A malicious, indecent joy shone in his countenance; he was rubbing his hands with rapture, he was turning his head from side to side in ecstasy, he was fawning round every one in delight and seemed ready to dance with glee. At last he pranced forward, took a candle from one of the servants and walked in front, showing the way to Mr. Golyadkin and Krestyan Ivanovich. Mr. Golyadkin heard the whole party in the drawing-room rush out after him, crowding and squeezing one another, and all beginning to repeat after Mr. Golyadkin himself, "It is all right, don't be afraid, Yakov Petrovich; this is your old friend and acquaintance, you know, Krestyan Ivanovich Rutenspitz. . . ."

At last they came out on the brightly lighted stairs; there was a crowd of people on the stairs too. The front door was thrown open noisily, and Mr. Golyadkin found himself on the steps, together with Krestyan Ivanovich. At the entrance stood a carriage with four horses that were snorting with impatience. The malignant Mr. Golyadkin junior in three bounds flew down the stairs and opened the carriage door himself. Krestyan Ivanovich, with an impressive gesture, asked Mr. Golyadkin to get in. There was no need of the impressive gesture, however; there were plenty of people to help him in. . . . Faint with horror, Mr. Golyadkin looked back. The whole of the brightly lighted staircase was crowded with people; inquisitive eyes were looking at him from all sides; Olsufy Ivanovich himself was sitting in his easy chair on the top landing, and watching all that took place with deep interest. Every one was waiting. A murmur of impatience passed through the crowd when Mr. Golyadkin looked back.

"I hope I have done nothing . . . nothing reprehensible . . . or that can call for severity . . . and general attention in regard to my official relations," our hero brought out in desperation. A clamour of talk rose all round him, all were shaking their heads, tears started from Mr. Golyadkin's eyes.

"In that case I'm ready. . . . I have full confidence . . . and I entrust my fate to Krestyan Ivanovich. . . ."

No sooner had Mr. Golyadkin declared that he entrusted his fate to Krestyan Ivanovich than a dreadful, deafening shout of joy came from all surrounding him and was repeated in a sinister echo through the whole of the waiting crowd. Then Krestyan Ivanovich on one side and Andrey Filippovich on the other helped Mr. Golyadkin into the carriage; his double, in his usual nasty way, was helping to get him in from behind. The unhappy Mr. Golyadkin senior took his last look on all and everything, and, shivering like a kitten that has been drenched with cold water—if the comparison may be permitted—got into the carriage. Krestyan Ivanovich followed him in immediately. The carriage door slammed. There was a swish of the whip on the horses' backs . . . the horses started off. . . . The crowd dashed after Mr. Golyadkin. The shrill, furious shouts of his enemies pursued him by way of good wishes for his journey. For some time several persons were still running by the carriage that bore away Mr. Golyadkin; but by degrees they were left behind, till at last they had all disappeared. Mr. Golyadkin's unworthy twin kept up longer than any one. With his hands in the trouser pockets of his green uniform he ran on with a satisfied air, skipping first to one and then to the other side of the carriage, sometimes catching hold of the window-frame and hanging on by it, poking his head in at the window, and throwing farewell kisses to Mr. Golyadkin. But he began to get tired, he was less and less often to be seen, and at last vanished altogether. There was a dull ache in Mr. Golyadkin's heart; a hot rush of blood set Mr. Golyadkin's head throbbing; he felt stifled, he longed to unbutton himself—to bare his breast, to cover it with snow and pour cold water on it. He sank at last into forgetfulness. . . .

When he came to himself, he saw that the horses were taking him along an unfamiliar road. There were dark patches of copse on each side of it; it was desolate and deserted. Suddenly he almost swooned; two fiery eyes were staring at him in the darkness, and those two eyes were glittering with malignant, hellish glee. "That's not Krestyan Ivanovich! Who is it? Or is it he? It is. It is Krestyan Ivanovich, but not the old Krestyan Ivanovich, it's another Krestyan Ivanovich! It's a terrible Krestyan Ivanovich!" . . .

"Krestyan Ivanovich, I . . . I believe . . . I'm all right,

Krestyan Ivanovich," our hero was beginning timidly in a trembling voice, hoping by his meekness and submission to soften the terrible Krestyan Ivanovich a little.

"You get free quarters, wood, with light, and service, the which you deserve not," Krestyan Ivanovich's answer rang out, stern and terrible as a judge's sentence.

Our hero shrieked and clutched his head in his hands. Alas! For a long while he had been haunted by a presentiment of this.

WHITE NIGHTS

A SENTIMENTAL STORY
(FROM THE MEMOIRS OF A DREAMER)

FIRST NIGHT

It was a wonderful night, such a night as is only possible when we are young, dear reader. The sky was so starry, so bright that, looking at it, one could not help asking oneself whether ill-humoured and capricious people could live under such a sky. That is a youthful question too, dear reader, very youthful, but may the Lord put it more frequently into your heart! . . . Speaking of capricious and ill-humoured people, I cannot help recalling my moral condition all that day. From early morning I had been oppressed by a strange despondency. It suddenly seemed to me that I was lonely, that every one was forsaking me and going away from me. Of course, any one is entitled to ask who "every one" was. For though I had been living almost eight years in Petersburg I had hardly an acquaintance. But what did I want with acquaintances? I was acquainted with all Petersburg as it was; that was why I felt as though they were all deserting me when all Petersburg packed up and went to its summer villa. I felt afraid of being left alone, and for three whole days I wandered about the town in profound dejection, not knowing what to do with myself. Whether I walked on Nevsky Prospect, went to the Gardens or sauntered along the embankment, there was not one face of those I had been accustomed to meet at the same time and place all the year. They, of course, do not know me, but I know them. I know them intimately, I have almost made a study of their faces, and am delighted when they are gay, and downcast when they are under a cloud. I have almost struck up a friendship with one old man whom I meet every blessed day, at the same hour on the Fontanka Embankment. Such a grave, pensive countenance; he is always whispering to himself and brandishing his left arm, while in his right hand he holds a long gnarled cane with a gold knob. He even notices me and takes a warm interest in me. If I happen not to be at a certain time in the same spot on the Fontanka, I am certain he feels disappointed. That is how it is that we almost bow to each other, especially when we are both in good humour. The other day, when we had not seen each other for two days and met on the third, we were actually touching our hats, but, realizing in time, dropped our hands and passed each other with a look of interest.

I know the houses too. As I walk along they seem to run forward in the streets to look out at me from every window, and almost to say: "Good-morning! How do you do? I am quite well, thank God, and I am to have a new storey in May," or, "How are you? I am being redecorated to-morrow"; or, "I was almost burnt down and had such a fright," and so on. I have my favourites among them, some are dear friends; one of them intends to be treated by the architect this summer. I shall go every day on purpose to see that the operation is not a failure. God forbid! But I shall never forget an incident with a very pretty little house of a light pink colour. It was such a charming little brick house, it looked so hospitably at me, and so proudly at its ungainly neighbours, that my heart rejoiced whenever I happened to pass it. Suddenly last week I walked along the street, and when I looked at my friend I heard a plaintive, "They are painting me yellow!" The villains! The barbarians! They had spared nothing, neither columns, nor cornices, and my poor little friend was as yellow as a canary. It almost made me bilious. And to this day I have not had the courage to visit my poor disfigured friend, painted the colour of the Celestial Empire.*

So now you understand, reader, in what sense I am acquainted with all Petersburg.

I have mentioned already that I had felt worried for three whole days before I guessed the cause of my uneasiness. And I felt ill at ease in the street—this one had gone and that one had gone, and what had become of the other?—and at home I did not feel like myself either. For two evenings I was puzzling my brains to think what was amiss in my corner; why I felt so uncomfortable in it. And in perplexity I scanned my grimy green walls, my ceiling covered with a spider's web, the growth of

---

*Old name for China.

which Matryona has so successfully encouraged. I looked over all my furniture, examined every chair, wondering whether the trouble lay there (for if one chair is not standing in the same position as it stood the day before, I am not myself). I looked at the window, but it was all in vain . . . I was not a bit the better for it! I even bethought me to send for Matryona, and was giving her some fatherly admonitions in regard to the spider's web and sluttishness in general; but she simply stared at me in amazement and went away without saying a word, so that the spider's web is comfortably hanging in its place to this day. I only at last this morning realized what was wrong. Aie! Why, they are giving me the slip and making off to their summer villas! Forgive the triviality of the expression, but I am in no mood for fine language . . . for everything that had been in Petersburg had gone or was going away for the holidays; for every respectable gentleman of dignified appearance who took a cab was at once transformed, in my eyes, into a respectable head of a household who after his daily duties were over, was making his way to the bosom of his family, to the summer villa; for all the passers-by had now quite a peculiar air which seemed to say to every one they met: "We are only here for the moment, gentlemen, and in another two hours we shall be going off to the summer villa." If a window opened after delicate fingers, white as snow, had tapped upon the pane, and the head of a pretty girl was thrust out, calling to a street-seller with pots of flowers—at once on the spot I fancied that those flowers were being bought not simply in order to enjoy the flowers and the spring in stuffy town lodgings, but because they would all be very soon moving into the country and could take the flowers with them. What is more, I made such progress in my new peculiar sort of investigation that I could distinguish correctly from the mere air of each in what summer villa he was living. The inhabitants of Kamenny and Aptekarsky Islands or of the Peterhof Road were marked by the studied elegance of their manner, their fashionable summer suits, and the fine carriages in which they drove to town. Visitors to Pargolovo and places further away impressed one at first sight by their reasonable and dignified air; the tripper to Krestovsky Island could be recognized by his look of irrepressible gaiety.[1] If I chanced to meet a long procession of waggoners walking lazily with the reins in their hands beside waggons loaded with regular mountains of furniture, tables, chairs, ottomans and sofas and domestic utensils of all sorts, frequently with a decrepit cook sitting on the top of it all, guarding her master's property as though it were the apple of her eye; or if I saw boats heavily loaded with household goods crawling along the Neva or Fontanka to the Black River or the Islands—the waggons and the boats were multiplied tenfold, a hundredfold, in my eyes. I fancied that everything was astir and moving, everything was going in regular caravans to the summer villas. It seemed as though Petersburg threatened to become a wilderness, so that at last I felt ashamed, mortified and sad that I had nowhere to go for the holidays and no reason to go away. I was ready to go away with every waggon, to drive off with every gentleman of respectable appearance who took a cab; but no one—absolutely no one— invited me; it seemed they had forgotten me, as though really I were a stranger to them!

I took long walks, succeeding, as I usually did, in quite forgetting where I was, when I suddenly found myself at the city gates. Instantly I felt lighthearted, and I passed the barrier and walked between cultivated fields and meadows, unconscious of fatigue, and feeling only all over as though a burden were falling off my soul. All the passers-by gave me such friendly looks that they seemed almost greeting me, they all seemed so pleased at something. They were all smoking cigars, every one of them. And I felt pleased as I never had before. It was as though I had suddenly found myself in Italy—so strong was the effect of nature upon a half-sick townsman like me, almost stifling between city walls.

There is something inexpressibly touching in nature round Petersburg, when at the approach of spring she puts forth all her might, all the powers bestowed on her by Heaven, when she breaks into leaf, decks herself out and spangles herself with flowers. . . . Somehow I cannot help being reminded of a frail, consumptive girl, at whom one sometimes looks with compassion, sometimes with sympathetic love, whom sometimes one simply does not notice; though suddenly in one instant she becomes, as though by chance, inexplicably lovely and exquisite, and, impressed and intoxicated, one cannot help asking oneself what power made those sad, pensive eyes flash with such fire? What summoned the blood to those pale, wan cheeks? What bathed with passion those soft features? What set that bosom heaving? What so suddenly called strength, life and beauty into the poor girl's face, making it gleam with such a smile, kindle with such bright, sparkling laughter? You look round, you seek for some one, you conjecture. . . . But the moment passes, and next day you meet, maybe, the same pensive and preoccupied look as before, the same pale face, the same meek and timid movements, and even signs of remorse, traces of a mortal anguish and regret for the fleeting distraction. . . . And you grieve that the momentary beauty has faded so soon never to return, that it flashed upon you so treacherously, so vainly, grieve because you had not even time to love her. . . .

And yet my night was better than my day! This was how it happened.

I came back to the town very late, and it had struck ten as I was going towards my lodgings. My way lay along the canal embankment,[2] where at that hour you never meet a soul. It is true that I live in a very remote part of the town. I walked along singing, for when I am happy I am always humming to myself like every happy man who has no friend or acquaintance with whom to share his joy. Suddenly I had a most unexpected adventure.

Leaning on the canal railing stood a woman with her elbows on the rail, she was apparently looking with great attention at the muddy water of the canal. She was wearing a very charming yellow hat and a jaunty little black mantle. "She's a girl, and I am sure she is dark," I thought. She did not seem to hear my footsteps, and did not even stir when I passed by with bated breath and loudly throbbing heart.

"Strange," I thought; "she must be deeply absorbed in

something," and all at once I stopped as though petrified. I
heard a muffled sob. Yes! I was not mistaken, the girl was crying, and a minute later I heard sob after sob. Good Heavens! My
heart sank. And timid as I was with women, yet this was such a
moment! . . . I turned, took a step towards her, and should certainly have pronounced the word "Madam!" if I had not known
that that exclamation has been uttered a thousand times in
every Russian society novel. It was only that reflection stopped
me. But while I was seeking for a word, the girl came to herself, looked round, started, cast down her eyes and slipped by
me along the embankment. I at once followed her; but she, di-
vining this, left the embankment, crossed the road and walked
along the pavement. I dared not cross the street after her. My
heart was fluttering like a captured bird. All at once a chance
came to my aid.

Along the same side of the pavement there suddenly came
into sight, not far from the girl, a gentleman in evening dress,
of dignified years, though by no means of dignified carriage;
he was staggering and cautiously leaning against the wall. The
girl flew straight as an arrow, with the timid haste one sees in
all girls who do not want any one to volunteer to accompany
them home at night, and no doubt the staggering gentleman
would not have pursued her, if my good luck had not prompted
him.

Suddenly, without a word to any one, the gentleman set off
and flew full speed in pursuit of my unknown lady. She was rac-
ing like the wind, but the staggering gentleman was over-
taking—overtook her. The girl uttered a shriek, and . . . I bless
my luck for the excellent knotted stick, which happened on that
occasion to be in my right hand. In a flash I was on the other
side of the street; in a flash the obtrusive gentleman had taken
in the position, had grasped the irresistible argument, fallen
back without a word, and only when we were very far away
protested against my action in rather vigorous language. But his
words hardly reached us.

"Give me your arm," I said to the girl. "And he won't dare
to annoy us further."

She took my arm without a word, still trembling with excitement and terror. Oh, obtrusive gentleman! How I blessed you at that moment! I stole a glance at her, she was very charming and dark—I had guessed right.

On her black eyelashes there still glistened a tear—from her recent terror or her former grief—I don't know. But there was already a gleam of a smile on her lips. She too stole a glance at me, faintly blushed and looked down.

"There, you see; why did you drive me away? If I had been here, nothing would have happened . . ."

"But I did not know you; I thought that you too . . ."

"Why, do you know me now?"

"A little! Here, for instance, why are you trembling?"

"Oh, you are right at the first guess! " I answered, delighted that my girl had intelligence; that is never out of place in company with beauty. "Yes, from the first glance you have guessed the sort of man you have to do with. Precisely; I am shy with women, I am agitated, I don't deny it, as much so as you were a minute ago when that gentleman alarmed you. I am in some alarm now. It's like a dream, and I never guessed even in my sleep that I should ever talk with any woman."

"What? Really? . . ."

"Yes; if my arm trembles, it is because it has never been held by a pretty little hand like yours. I am a complete stranger to women; that is, I have never been used to them. You see, I am alone . . . I don't even know how to talk to them. Here, I don't know now whether I have not said something silly to you! Tell me frankly; I assure you beforehand that I am not quick to take offence? . . .

"No, nothing, nothing, quite the contrary. And if you insist on my speaking frankly, I will tell you that women like such timidity; and if you want to know more, I like it too, and I won't drive you away till I get home."

"You will make me," I said, breathless with delight, "lose my timidity, and then farewell to all my chances. . . ."

"Chances! What chances—of what? That's not so nice."

"I beg your pardon, I am sorry, it was a slip of the tongue;

but how can you expect one at such a moment to have no desire. . . ."

"To be liked, eh?"

"Well, yes; but do, for goodness' sake, be kind. Think what I
am! Here, I am twenty-six and I have never seen any one. How
can I speak well, tactfully, and to the point? It will seem better
to you when I have told you everything openly. . . . I don't
know how to be silent when my heart is speaking. Well, never
mind. . . . Believe me, not one woman, never, never! No acquaintance of any sort! And I do nothing but dream every day
that at last I shall meet some one. Oh, if only you knew how
often I have been in love in that way . . ."

"How? With whom? . . ."

"Why, with no one, with an ideal, with the one I dream of
in my sleep. I make up regular romances in my dreams. Ah, you
don't know me! It's true, of course, I have met two or three
women, but what sort of women were they? They were all land-
ladies, that . . . But I shall make you laugh if I tell you that I have
several times thought of speaking, just simply speaking, to
some aristocratic lady in the street, when she is alone, I need
hardly say; speaking to her, of course, timidly, respectfully, passionately; telling her that I am perishing in solitude, begging
her not to send me away; saying that I have no chance of making the acquaintance of any woman; impressing upon her that
it is a positive duty for a woman not to repulse so timid a prayer
from such a luckless man as me. That, in fact, all I ask is, that
she should say two or three sisterly words with sympathy,
should not repulse me at first sight; should take me on trust and
listen to what I say; should laugh at me if she likes, encourage
me, say two words to me, only two words, even though we
never meet again afterwards! . . . But you are laughing; however, that is why I am telling you. . . ."

"Don't be vexed; I am only laughing at your being your own
enemy, and if you had tried you would have succeeded, perhaps, even though it had been in the street; the simpler the better. . . . No kind-hearted woman, unless she were stupid or, still
more, vexed about something at the moment, could bring her-

self to send you away without those two words which you ask for so timidly. . . . But what am I saying? Of course she would take you for a madman. I was judging by myself; I know a good deal about other people's lives."

"Oh, thank you," I cried; "you don't know what you have done for me now!"

"I am glad! I am glad! But tell me how did you find out that I was the sort of woman with whom . . . well, whom you think worthy . . . of attention and friendship . . . in fact, not a land-lady as you say? What made you decide to come up to me?"

"What made me? . . . But you were alone; that gentleman was too insolent; it's night. You must admit that it was a duty. . . ."

"No, no; I mean before, on the other side—you know you meant to come up to me."

"On the other side? Really I don't know how to answer; I am afraid to. . . . Do you know I have been happy to-day? I walked along singing; I went out into the country; I have never had such happy moments. You . . . perhaps it was my fancy. . . . For-give me for referring to it; I fancied you were crying, and I . . . could not bear to hear it . . . it made my heart ache. . . . Oh, my goodness! Surely I might be troubled about you? Surely there was no harm in feeling brotherly compassion for you. . . . I beg your pardon, I said compassion. . . . Well, in short, surely you would not be offended at my involuntary impulse to go up to you? . . ."

"Stop, that's enough, don't talk of it," said the girl, looking down, and pressing my hand. "It's my fault for having spoken of it; but I am glad I was not mistaken in you. . . . But here I am home; I must go down this turning, it's two steps from here. . . . Good-bye, thank you! . . ."

"Surely . . . surely you don't mean . . . that we shall never see each other again? . . . Surely this is not to be the end?"

"You see," said the girl, laughing, "at first you only wanted two words, and now . . . However, I won't say anything . . . perhaps we shall meet. . . ."

"I shall come here to-morrow," I said. "Oh, forgive me, I am already making demands. . . ."

"Yes, you are not very patient . . . you are almost insisting."

"Listen, listen!" I interrupted her. "Forgive me if I tell you something else. . . . I tell you what, I can't help coming here to-morrow, I am a dreamer; I have so little real life that I look upon such moments as this now, as so rare, that I cannot help going over such moments again in my dreams. I shall be dreaming of you all night, a whole week, a whole year. I shall certainly come here to-morrow, just here to this place, just at the same hour, and I shall be happy remembering to-day. This place is dear to me already. I have already two or three such places in Petersburg. I once shed tears over memories . . . like you. . . . Who knows, perhaps you were weeping ten minutes ago over some memory. . . . But, forgive me, I have forgotten myself again; perhaps you have once been particularly happy here. . . ."

"Very good," said the girl, "perhaps I will come here to-morrow, too, at ten o'clock. I see that I can't forbid you. . . . The fact is, I have to be here; don't imagine that I am making an appointment with you; I tell you beforehand that I have to be here on my own account. But . . . well, I tell you straight out, I don't mind if you do come. To begin with, something unpleasant might happen as it did to-day, but never mind that. . . . In short, I should simply like to see you . . . to say two words to you. Only, mind, you must not think the worse of me now! Don't think I make appointments so lightly. . . . I shouldn't make it except that . . . But let that be my secret! Only a compact beforehand . . ."

"A compact! Speak, tell me, tell me all beforehand; I agree to anything, I am ready for anything," I cried delighted. "I answer for myself, I will be obedient, respectful . . . you know me. . . ."

"It's just because I do know you that I ask you to come to-morrow," said the girl, laughing. "I know you perfectly. But mind you will come on the condition, in the first place (only be good, do what I ask—you see, I speak frankly), you won't fall in love with me. . . . That's impossible, I assure you. I am ready for friendship; here's my hand. . . . But you mustn't fall in love with me, I beg you!"

"I swear," I cried, gripping her hand. . . .

"Hush, don't swear, I know you are ready to flare up like gunpowder. Don't think ill of me for saying so. If only you knew. . . . I, too, have no one to whom I can say a word, whose advice I can ask. Of course, one does not look for an adviser in the street; but you are an exception. I know you as though we had been friends for twenty years. . . . You won't deceive me, will you? . . ."

"You will see . . . the only thing is, I don't know how I am going to survive the next twenty-four hours."

"Sleep soundly. Good-night, and remember that I have trusted you already. But you exclaimed so nicely just now, 'Surely one can't be held responsible for every feeling, even for brotherly sympathy!' Do you know, that was so nicely said, that the idea struck me at once, that I might confide in you?"

"For God's sake do; but about what? What is it?"

"Wait till to-morrow. Meanwhile, let that be a secret. So much the better for you; it will give it a faint flavour of romance. Perhaps I will tell you to-morrow, and perhaps not. . . . I will talk to you a little more beforehand; we will get to know each other better. . . ."

"Oh yes, I will tell you all about myself to-morrow! But what has happened? It is as though a miracle had befallen me. . . . My God, where am I? Come, tell me aren't you glad that you were not angry and did not drive me away at the first moment, as any other woman would have done? In two minutes you have made me happy for ever. Yes, happy; who knows, perhaps, you have reconciled me with myself, solved my doubts! . . . Perhaps such moments come upon me. . . . But there I will tell you all about it to-morrow, you shall know everything, everything. . . ."

"Very well, I consent; you shall begin . . ."

"Agreed."

"Good-bye till to-morrow!"

"Till to-morrow!"

And we parted. I walked about all night; I could not make up my mind to go home. I was so happy. . . . To-morrow!

SECOND NIGHT

"Well, so you have survived!" she said, pressing both my hands.

"I've been here for the last two hours; you don't know what a state I have been in all day."

"I know, I know. But to business. Do you know why I have come? Not to talk nonsense, as I did yesterday. I tell you what, we must behave more sensibly in future. I thought a great deal about it last night."

"In what way—in what must we be more sensible? I am ready for my part; but, really, nothing more sensible has happened to me in my life than this, now."

"Really? In the first place, I beg you not to squeeze my hands so; secondly, I must tell you that I spent a long time thinking about you and feeling doubtful to-day."

"And how did it end?"

"How did it end? The upshot of it is that we must begin all over again, because the conclusion I reached to-day was that I don't know you at all; that I behaved like a baby last night, like a little girl; and, of course, the fact of it is, that it's my soft heart that is to blame—that is, I sang my own praises, as one always does in the end when one analyses one's conduct. And therefore to correct my mistake, I've made up my mind to find out all about you minutely. But as I have no one from whom I can find out anything, you must tell me everything fully yourself. Well, what sort of man are you? Come, make haste—begin—tell me your whole history."

"My history!" I cried in alarm. "My history! But who has told you I have a history? I have no history. . . ."

"Then how have you lived, if you have no history?" she interrupted, laughing.

"Absolutely without any history! I have lived, as they say, keeping myself to myself, that is, utterly alone—alone, entirely alone. Do you know what it means to be alone?"

"But how alone? Do you mean you never saw any one?"

"Oh no, I see people, of course; but still I am alone."

"Why, do you never talk to any one?"

"Strictly speaking, with no one."

"Who are you then? Explain yourself! Stay, I guess: most likely, like me you have a grandmother. She is blind and will never let me go anywhere, so that I have almost forgotten how to talk; and when I played some pranks two years ago, and she saw there was no holding me in, she called me up and pinned my dress to hers, and ever since we sit like that for days together; she knits a stocking, though she's blind, and I sit beside her, sew or read aloud to her—it's such a queer habit, here for two years I've been pinned to her. . . ."

"Good Heavens! what misery! But no, I haven't a grandmother like that."

"Well, if you haven't why do you sit at home? . . ."

"Listen, do you want to know the sort of man I am?"

"Yes, yes!"

"In the strict sense of the word?"

"In the very strictest sense of the word."

"Very well, I am a type!"

"Type, type! What sort of type?" cried the girl, laughing, as though she had not had a chance of laughing for a whole year. "Yes, it's very amusing talking to you. Look, here's a seat, let us sit down. No one is passing here, no one will hear us, and—begin your history. For it's no good your telling me, I know you have a history; only you are concealing it. To begin with, what is a type?"

"A type? A type is an original, it's a ridiculous man!" I said, infected by her childish laughter. "It's a character. Listen; do you know what is meant by a dreamer?"

"A dreamer! Indeed I should think I do know. I am a

dreamer myself. Sometimes, as I sit by grandmother, all sorts of
things come into my head. Why, when one begins dreaming
one lets one's fancy run away with one—why, I marry a Chinese Prince! . . . Though sometimes it is a good thing to dream!
But, goodness knows! Especially when one has something to
think of apart from dreams," added the girl, this time rather seriously.

"Excellent! If you have been married to a Chinese Emperor,
you will quite understand me. Come, listen. . . . But one
minute, I don't know your name yet."

"At last! You have been in no hurry to think of it!"

"Oh, my goodness! It never entered my head, I felt quite
happy as it was. . . ."

"My name is Nastenka."

"Nastenka! And nothing else?"

"Nothing else! Why, is not that enough for you, you insa-
tiable person?"

"Not enough? On the contrary, it's a great deal, a very great
deal, Nastenka; you kind girl, if you are Nastenka for me from
the first."

"Quite so! Well?"

"Well, listen, Nastenka, now for this ridiculous history."

I sat down beside her, assumed a pedantically serious attitude, and began as though reading from a manuscript:—

"There are, Nastenka, though you may not know it, strange
nooks in Petersburg. It seems as though the same sun as shines
for all Petersburg people does not peep into those spots, but
some other different new one, bespoken expressly for those
nooks, and it throws a different light on everything. In these
corners, dear Nastenka, quite a different life is lived, quite unlike the life that is surging round us, but such as perhaps exists
in some unknown realm, not among us in our serious, over-
serious time. Well, that life is a mixture of something purely
fantastic, fervently ideal, with something (alas! Nastenka)
dingily prosaic and ordinary, not to say incredibly vulgar."

"Foo! Good Heavens! What a preface! What do I hear?"

"Listen, Nastenka. (It seems to me I shall never be tired of calling you Nastenka.) Let me tell you that in these corners live strange people—dreamers. The dreamer—if you want an exact definition—is not a human being, but a creature of an intermediate sort. For the most part he settles in some inaccessible corner, as though hiding from the light of day; once he slips into his corner, he grows to it like a snail, or, anyway, he is in that respect very much like that remarkable creature, which is an animal and a house both at once, and is called a tortoise. Why do you suppose he is so fond of his four walls, which are invariably painted green, grimy, dismal and reeking unpardonably of tobacco smoke? Why is it that when this ridiculous gentleman is visited by one of his few acquaintances (and he ends by getting rid of all his friends), why does this ridiculous person meet him with such embarrassment, changing countenance and overcome with confusion, as though he had only just committed some crime within his four walls; as though he had been forging counterfeit notes, or as though he were writing verses to be sent to a journal with an anonymous letter, in which he states that the real poet is dead, and that his friend thinks it his sacred duty to publish his things? Why, tell me, Nastenka, why is it conversation is not easy between the two friends? Why is there no laughter? Why does no lively word fly from the tongue of the perplexed newcomer, who at other times may be very fond of laughter, lively words, conversation about the fair sex, and other cheerful subjects? And why does this friend, probably a new friend and on his first visit—for there will hardly be a second, and the friend will never come again—why is the friend himself so confused, so tongue-tied, in spite of his wit (if he has any), as he looks at the downcast face of his host, who in his turn becomes utterly helpless and at his wits' end after gigantic but fruitless efforts to smooth things over and enliven the conversation, to show his knowledge of polite society, to talk, too, of the fair sex, and by such humble endeavour, to please the poor man, who like a fish out of water has mistakenly come to visit him? Why does the gentleman, all at once remembering some very necessary business which never existed, suddenly seize his hat and hurriedly make off, snatching away his hand from the warm grip of his host, who was trying his utmost to show his regret and retrieve the lost position? Why does the friend chuckle as he goes out of the door, and swear never to come and see this queer fellow again, though the queer fellow is really a very good fellow, and at the same time he cannot refuse his imagination the little diversion of comparing the queer fellow's countenance during their conversation with the expression of an unhappy kitten treacherously captured, roughly handled, frightened and subjected to all sorts of indignities by children, till, utterly crestfallen, it hides away from them under a chair in the dark, and there must needs at its leisure bristle up, spit, and wash its insulted face with both paws, and long afterwards look angrily at life and nature, and even at the bits saved from the master's dinner for it by the sympathetic housekeeper?"

"Listen," interrupted Nastenka, who had listened to me all the time in amazement, opening her eyes and her little mouth. "Listen; I don't know in the least why it happened and why you ask me such absurd questions; all I know is, that this adventure must have happened word for word to you."

"Doubtless," I answered, with the gravest face.

"Well, since there is no doubt about it, go on," said Nastenka, "because I want very much to know how it will end."

"You want to know, Nastenka, what our hero, that is I—for the hero of the whole business was my humble self—did in his corner? You want to know why I lost my head and was upset for the whole day by the unexpected visit of a friend? You want to know why I was so startled, why I blushed when the door of my room was opened, why I was not able to entertain my visitor, and why I was crushed under the weight of my own hospitality?"

"Why, yes, yes," answered Nastenka, "that's the point. Listen. You describe it all splendidly, but couldn't you perhaps describe it a little less splendidly? You talk as though you were reading it out of a book."

"Nastenka," I answered in a stern and dignified voice, hardly able to keep from laughing, "dear Nastenka, I know I describe splendidly, but, excuse me, I don't know how else to do it. At this moment, dear Nastenka, at this moment I am like the djinn of King Solomon when, after lying a thousand years under seven seals in his urn, those seven seals were at last taken off.[3] At this moment, Nastenka, when we have met at last after such a long separation—for I have known you for ages, Nastenka, because I have been looking for some one for ages, and that is a sign that it was you I was looking for, and it was ordained that we should meet now—at this moment a thousand valves have opened in my head, and I must let myself flow in a river of words, or I shall choke. And so I beg you not to interrupt me, Nastenka, but listen humbly and obediently, or I will be silent."

"No, no, no! Not at all. Go on! I won't say a word!"

"I will continue. There is, my friend Nastenka, one hour in my day which I like extremely. That is the hour when almost all business, work and duties are over, and every one is hurrying home to dinner, to lie down, to rest, and on the way all are cogitating on other more cheerful subjects relating to their evenings, their nights, and all the rest of their free time. At that hour our hero—for allow me, Nastenka, to tell my story in the third person, for one feels awfully ashamed to tell it in the first person—and so at that hour our hero, who had his work too, was pacing along after the others. But a strange feeling of pleasure set his pale, rather crumpled-looking face working. He looked not with indifference on the evening glow which was slowly fading on the cold Petersburg sky. When I say he looked, I am lying: he did not look at it, but saw it as it were without realizing, as though tired or preoccupied with some other more interesting subject, so that he could scarcely spare a glance for anything about him. He was pleased because till next day he was released from business irksome to him, and happy as a schoolboy let out from the class-room to his games and mischief. Take a look at him, Nastenka; you will see at once that joyful emotion has already had an effect on his weak nerves and morbidly excited fancy. You see he is thinking of something. . . . Of dinner, do you imagine? Of the evening? What is he looking at like that? Is it at that gentleman of dignified appearance who is bowing so picturesquely to the lady who rolls by in a carriage drawn by prancing horses? No, Nastenka; what are all those trivialities to him now! He is rich now with his *own individual* life; he has suddenly become rich, and it is not for nothing that the fading sunset sheds its farewell gleams so gaily before him, and calls forth a swarm of impressions from his warmed heart. Now he hardly notices the road, on which the tiniest details at other times would strike him. Now 'the Goddess of Fancy' (if you have read Zhukovsky,[4] dear Nastenka) has already with fantastic hand spun her golden warp and begun weaving upon it patterns of marvellous magic life—and who knows, maybe, her fantastic hand has borne him to the seventh crystal heaven far from the excellent granite pavement on which he was walking his way? Try stopping him now, ask him suddenly where he is standing now, through what streets he is going—he will, probably remember nothing, neither where he is going nor where he is standing now, and flushing with vexation he will certainly tell some lie to save appearances. That is why he starts, almost cries out, and looks round with horror when a respectable old lady stops him politely in the middle of the pavement and asks her way. Frowning with vexation he strides on, scarcely noticing that more than one passer-by smiles and turns round to look after him, and that a little girl, moving out of his way in alarm, laughs aloud, gazing open-eyed at his broad meditative smile and gesticulations. But fancy catches up in its playful flight the old woman, the curious passers-by, and the laughing child, and the peasants spending their nights in their barges on the Fontanka River (our hero, let us suppose, is walking along the canal-side at that moment), and capriciously weaves every one and everything into the canvas like a fly in a spider's web. And it is only after the queer fellow has returned to his comfortable den with fresh stores for his mind to work on, has sat down and finished his dinner, that he comes to himself, when Matryona who waits upon him—always thoughtful and depressed—clears the table and gives him his pipe; he comes to himself then and recalls with surprise that he has dined, though he has absolutely no notion how it has happened. It has grown dark in the room; his soul is sad and empty; the whole kingdom of fancies drops to pieces about him, drops to pieces without a trace, without a sound, floats away like a dream, and he cannot himself remember what he was dreaming. But a vague sensation faintly stirs his heart and sets it aching, some new desire temptingly tickles and excites his fancy, and imperceptibly evokes a swarm of fresh phantoms. Stillness reigns in the little room; imagination is fostered by solitude and idleness; it is faintly smouldering, faintly simmering, like the water with which old Matryona is making her coffee as she moves quietly about in the kitchen close by. Now it breaks out spasmodically; and the book, picked up aimlessly and at random, drops from my dreamer's hand before he has reached the third page. His imagination is again stirred and at work, and again a new world, a new fascinating life opens vistas before him. A fresh dream—fresh happiness! A fresh rush of delicate, voluptuous poison! What is real life to him! To his corrupted eyes we live, you and I, Nastenka, so torpidly, slowly, insipidly; in his eyes we are all so dissatisfied with our fate, so exhausted by our life! And, truly, see how at first sight everything is cold, morose, as though ill-humoured among us. . . . Poor things! thinks our dreamer. And it is no wonder that he thinks it! Look at these magic phantasms, which so enchantingly, so whimsically, so carelessly and freely group before him in such a magic, animated picture, in which the most prominent figure in the foreground is of course himself, our dreamer, in his precious person. See what varied adventures, what an endless swarm of ecstatic dreams. You ask, perhaps, what he is dreaming of.[5] Why ask that?—why, of everything . . . of the lot of the poet, first unrecognized, then crowned with laurels; of friendship with Hoffmann, St. Bartholomew's Night, of Diana Vernon, of playing the hero at the taking of Kazan by Ivan Vassilyevich, of Clara Mowbray, of Effie Deans, of the council of the prelates and Hus before them, of the rising of the dead in 'Robert the Devil' (do you remember the music, it smells of the church-yard!), of Minna and Brenda, of the battle of Berezina, of the reading of a poem at Countess V. D.'s, of Danton, of Cleopatra *ei suoi amanti*, of a little house in Kolomna, of a little home of one's own and beside one a dear creature who listens to one on a winter's evening, opening her little mouth and eyes as you are listening to me now, my angel. . . . No, Nastenka, what is there, what is there for him, voluptuous sluggard, in this life, for which you and I have such a longing? He thinks that this is a poor pitiful life, not foreseeing that for him too, maybe, sometime the mournful hour may strike, when for one day of that pitiful life he would give all his years of fantasy, and would give them not only for joy and for happiness, but without caring to make distinctions in that hour of sadness, remorse and unchecked grief. But so far that threatening time has not arrived—he desires nothing, because he is superior to all desire, because he has everything, because he is satiated, because he is the artist of his own life, and creates it for himself every hour to suit his latest whim. And you know this fantastic world of fairyland is so easily, so naturally created! As though it were not a delusion! Indeed, he is ready to believe at some moments that all this life is not suggested by feeling, is not mirage, not a delusion of the imagination, but that it is concrete, real, substantial! Why is it, Nastenka, why is it at such moments one holds one's breath? Why, by what sorcery, through what incomprehensible caprice, is the pulse quickened, does a tear start from the dreamer's eye, while his pale moist cheeks glow, while his whole being is suffused with an inexpressible sense of consolation? Why is it that whole sleepless nights pass like a flash in inexhaustible gladness and happiness, and when the dawn gleams rosy at the window and daybreak floods the gloomy room with uncertain, fantastic light, as in Petersburg, our dreamer, worn out and exhausted, flings himself on his bed and drops asleep with thrills of delight in his morbidly overwrought spirit, and with a weary sweet ache in his heart? Yes, Nastenka, one deceives oneself and unconsciously believes that real true passion is stirring one's soul; one unconsciously believes that there is something living, tangible in one's immaterial dreams! And is it delusion? Here love, for instance, is bound up with all its fathomless joy, all its torturing agonies in his bosom. . . . Only look at him, and you will be convinced! Would you believe, looking at him, dear Nastenka, that he has never known her whom he loves in his ecstatic dreams? Can it be that he has only seen her in seductive visions, and that this passion has been nothing but a dream? Surely they must have spent years hand in hand together—alone the two of them, casting off all the world and each uniting his or her life with the other's? Surely when the hour of parting came she must have lain sobbing and grieving on his bosom, heedless of the tempest raging under the sullen sky, heedless of the wind which snatches and bears away the tears from her black eyelashes? Can all of that have been a dream—and that garden, dejected, forsaken, run wild, with its little moss-grown paths, solitary, gloomy, where they used to walk so happily together, where they hoped, grieved, loved, loved each other so long, 'so long and so fondly?'[6] And that strange ancestral house where she spent so many years lonely and sad with her morose old husband, always silent and splenetic, who frightened them, while timid as children they hid their love from each other? What torments they suffered, what agonies of terror, how innocent, how pure was their love, and how (I need hardly say Nastenka) malicious people were! And, good Heavens! surely he met her afterwards, far from their native shores, under alien skies, in the hot south in the divinely eternal city, in the dazzling splendour of the ball to the crash of music, in a *palazzo* (it must be in a *palazzo*), drowned in a sea of lights, on the balcony wreathed in myrtle and roses, where, recognizing him, she hurriedly removes her mask and whispering, 'I am free,' flings herself trembling into his arms, and with a cry of rapture, clinging to one another, in one instant they forget their sorrow and their parting and all their agonies, and the gloomy house and the old man and the dismal garden in that distant land, and the seat on which with a last passionate kiss she tore herself away from his arms numb with anguish and despair. . . . Oh, Nastenka, you must admit that one would start, betray confusion, and blush like a schoolboy who has just stuffed in his pocket an apple stolen from a neighbour's garden, when your uninvited visitor, some stalwart, lanky fellow, a festive soul fond of a joke, opens your door and shouts out as though nothing were happening; 'My dear boy, I have this minute come from Pavlovsk.' My goodness! the old count is dead, unutterable happiness is close at hand—and people arrive from Pavlovsk!"

Finishing my pathetic appeal, I paused pathetically. I remembered that I had an intense desire to force myself to laugh, for I was already feeling that a malignant demon was stirring within me, that there was a lump in my throat, that my chin was beginning to twitch, and that my eyes were growing more and more moist.

I expected Nastenka, who listened to me opening her clever eyes, would break into her childish, irrepressible laugh; and I was already regretting that I had gone so far, that I had unnecessarily described what had long been simmering in my heart, about which I could speak as though from a written account of it, because I had long ago passed judgment on myself and now could not resist reading it, making my confession, without expecting to be understood; but to my surprise she was silent, waiting a little, then she faintly pressed my hand and with timid sympathy asked—

"Surely you haven't lived like that all your life?"

"All my life, Nastenka," I answered; "all my life, and, it seems to me I shall go on so to the end."

"No, that won't do," she said uneasily, "that must not be; and so, maybe, I shall spend all my life beside grandmother. Do you know, it is not at all good to live like that?"

"I know, Nastenka, I know!" I cried, unable to restrain my feelings longer. "And I realize now, more than ever, that I have lost all my best years! And now I know it and feel it more painfully from recognizing that God has sent me you, my good angel, to tell me that and show it. Now that I sit beside you and talk to you it is strange for me to think of the future, for in the future—there is loneliness again, again this musty, useless life; and what shall I have to dream of when I have been so happy in reality beside you! Oh, may you be blessed, dear girl, for not having repulsed me at first, for enabling me to say that for two evenings, at least, I have lived."

"Oh, no, no!" cried Nastenka and tears glistened in her eyes. "No, it mustn't be so any more; we must not part like that! what are two evenings?"

"Oh, Nastenka, Nastenka! Do you know how far you have reconciled me to myself? Do you know now that I shall not think so ill of myself, as I have at some moments? Do you know that, maybe, I shall leave off grieving over the crime and sin of my life? for such a life is a crime and a sin. And do not imagine that I have been exaggerating anything—for goodness' sake don't think that, Nastenka: for at times such misery comes over me, such misery. . . . Because it begins to seem to me at such times that I am incapable of beginning a life in real life, because it has seemed to me that I have lost all touch, all instinct for the actual, the real; because at last I have cursed myself; because after my fantastic nights I have moments of returning sobriety, which are awful! Meanwhile, you hear the whirl and roar of the crowd in the vortex of life around you; you hear, you see, men living in reality; you see that life for them is not forbidden, that their life does not float away like a dream, like a vision; that their life is being eternally renewed, eternally youthful, and not one hour of it is the same as another; while fancy is so spiritless, monotonous to vulgarity and easily scared, the slave of shadows, of the idea, the slave of the first cloud that shrouds the sun, and overcasts with depression the true Petersburg heart so devoted to the sun—and what is fancy in depression! One feels that this inexhaustible fancy is weary at last and worn out with continual exercise, because one is growing into manhood, outgrowing one's old ideals: they are being shattered into fragments, into dust; if there is no other life one must build one up from the fragments. And meanwhile the soul longs and craves for something else! And in vain the dreamer rakes over his old dreams, as though seeking a spark among the embers, to fan them into flame, to warm his chilled heart by the rekindled fire, and to rouse up in it again all that was so sweet, that touched his heart, that set his blood boiling, drew tears from his eyes, and so luxuriously deceived him! Do you know, Nastenka, the point I have reached? Do you know that I am forced now to cel-

ebrate the anniversary of my own sensations, the anniversary of
that which was once so sweet, which never existed in reality—
for this anniversary is kept in memory of those same foolish,
shadowy dreams—and to do this because those foolish dreams
are no more, because I have nothing to earn them with; you
know even dreams do not come for nothing! Do you know that
I love now to recall and visit at certain dates the places where I
was once happy in my own way? I love to build up my present
in harmony with the irrevocable past, and I often wander like a
shadow, aimless, sad and dejected, about the streets and
crooked lanes of Petersburg. What memories they are! To remember, for instance, that here just a year ago, just at this time,
at this hour, on this pavement, I wandered just as lonely, just as
dejected as to-day. And one remembers that then one's dreams
were sad, and though the past was no better one feels as though
it had somehow been better, and that life was more peaceful,
that one was free from the black thoughts that haunt one now;
that one was free from the gnawing of conscience—the
gloomy, sullen gnawing which now gives me no rest by day or
by night. And one asks oneself where are one's dreams. And one
shakes one's head and says how rapidly the years fly by! And
again one asks oneself what has one done with one's years.
Where have you buried your best days? Have you lived or not?
Look, one says to oneself, look how cold the world is growing.
Some more years will pass, and after them will come gloomy
solitude; then will come old age trembling on its crutch, and
after it misery and desolation. Your fantastic world will grow
pale, your dreams will fade and die and will fall like the yellow
leaves from the trees. . . . Oh, Nastenka! you know it will be sad
to be left alone, utterly alone, and to have not even anything to
regret—nothing, absolutely nothing . . . for all that you have
lost, all that, all was nothing, stupid, simple nullity, there has
been nothing but dreams!"

   "Come, don't work on my feelings any more," said Nastenka, wiping away a tear which was trickling down her cheek.
"Now it's over! Now we shall be two together. Now, whatever
happens to me, we will never part. Listen; I am a simple girl, I

have not had much education, though grandmother did get a teacher for me, but truly I understand you, for all that you have described I have been through myself, when grandmother pinned me to her dress. Of course, I should not have described it so well as you have; I am not educated," she added timidly, for she was still feeling a sort of respect for my pathetic eloquence and lofty style; "but I am very glad that you have been quite open with me. Now I know you thoroughly, all of you. And do you know what? I want to tell you my history too, all without concealment, and after that you must give me advice. You are a very clever man; will you promise to give me advice?"

"Ah, Nastenka," I cried, "though I have never given advice, still less sensible advice, yet I see now that if we always go on like this that it will be very sensible, and that each of us will give the other a great deal of sensible advice! Well, my pretty Nastenka, what sort of advice do you want? Tell me frankly; at this moment I am so gay and happy, so bold and sensible, that it won't be difficult for me to find words."

"No, no!" Nastenka interrupted, laughing. "I don't only want sensible advice, I want warm brotherly advice, as though you had been fond of me all your life!"

"Agreed, Nastenka, agreed!" I cried delighted; "and if I had been fond of you for twenty years, I couldn't have been fonder of you than I am now."

"Your hand," said Nastenka.

"Here it is," said I, giving her my hand.

"And so let us begin my history!"

Nastenka's History

"Half my story you know already—that is, you know that I have an old grandmother. . . ."

"If the other half is as brief as that . . ." I interrupted, laughing.

"Be quiet and listen. First of all you must agree not to interrupt me, or else, perhaps I shall get in a muddle! Come, listen quietly.

"I have an old grandmother. I came into her hands when I was quite a little girl, for my father and mother are dead. It must be supposed that grandmother was once richer, for now she recalls better days. She taught me French, and then got a teacher for me. When I was fifteen (and now I am seventeen) we gave up having lessons. It was at that time that I got into mischief; what I did I won't tell you; it's enough to say that it wasn't very important. But grandmother called me to her one morning and said that as she was blind she could not look after me; she took a pin and pinned my dress to hers, and said that we should sit like that for the rest of our lives if, of course, I did not become a better girl. In fact, at first it was impossible to get away from her: I had to work, to read and to study all beside grandmother. I tried to deceive her once, and persuaded Fyokla to sit in my place. Fyokla is our charwoman, she is deaf. Fyokla sat there instead of me; grandmother was asleep in her arm-chair at the time, and I went off to see a friend close by. Well, it ended in trouble. Grandmother woke up while I was out, and asked some questions; she thought I was still sitting quietly in my place. Fyokla saw that grandmother was asking her some-thing, but could not tell what it was; she wondered what to do, undid the pin and ran away. . . ."

At this point Nastenka stopped and began laughing. I laughed with her. She left off at once.

"I tell you what, don't you laugh at grandmother. I laugh be-cause it's funny. . . . What can I do, since grandmother is like that; but yet I am fond of her in a way. Oh, well, I did catch it that time. I had to sit down in my place at once, and after that I was not allowed to stir.

"Oh, I forgot to tell you that our house belongs to us, that is to grandmother; it is a little wooden house with three win-dows as old as grandmother herself, with a little upper storey; well, there moved into our upper storey a new lodger."

"Then you had an old lodger," I observed casually.

"Yes, of course," answered Nastenka, "and one who knew how to hold his tongue better than you do. In fact, he hardly ever used his tongue at all. He was a dumb, blind, lame, dried-up little old man, so that at last he could not go on living, he died; so then we had to find a new lodger, for we could not live without a lodger—the rent, together with grandmother's pension, is almost all we have. But the new lodger, as luck would have it, was a young man, a stranger not of these parts. As he did not haggle over the rent, grandmother accepted him, and only afterwards she asked me: 'Tell me, Nastenka, what is our lodger like—is he young or old?' I did not want to lie, so I told grandmother that he wasn't exactly young and that he wasn't old.

" 'And is he pleasant looking?' asked grandmother.

"Again I did not want to tell a lie: 'Yes, he is pleasant looking, grandmother,' I said. And grandmother said: 'Oh, what a nuisance, what a nuisance! I tell you this, grandchild, that you may not be looking after him. What times these are! Why a paltry lodger like this, and he must be pleasant looking too; it was very different in the old days!'

"Grandmother was always regretting the old days—she was younger in old days, and the sun was warmer in old days, and cream did not turn so sour in old days—it was always the old days! I would sit still and hold my tongue and think to myself: why did grandmother suggest it to me? Why did she ask whether the lodger was young and good-looking? But that was all, I just thought it, began counting my stitches again, went on knitting my stocking, and forgot all about it.

"Well one morning the lodger came in to see us; he asked about a promise to paper his rooms. One thing led to another. Grandmother was talkative, and she said: 'Go, Nastenka, into my bedroom and bring me my abacus.' I jumped up at once; I blushed all over, I don't know why, and forgot I was sitting pinned to grandmother; instead of quietly undoing the pin, so that the lodger should not see—I jumped so that grandmother's chair moved. When I saw that the lodger knew all about me now, I blushed, stood still as though I had been shot, and suddenly began to cry—I felt so ashamed and miserable at that minute, that I didn't know where to look! Grandmother called out, 'What are you waiting for?' and I went on worse than ever.

When the lodger saw, saw that I was ashamed on his account, he bowed and went away at once!

"After that I felt ready to die at the least sound in the passage. 'It's the lodger,' I kept thinking; I stealthily undid the pin in case. But it always turned out not to be, he never came. A fortnight passed; the lodger sent word through Fyokla that he had a great number of French books, and that they were all good books that I might read, so would not grandmother like me to read them that I might not be dull? Grandmother agreed with gratitude, but kept asking if they were moral books, for if the books were immoral it would be out of the question, one would learn evil from them.

"'And what should I learn, grandmother? What is there written in them?'

"'Ah,' she said, 'what's described in them, is how young men seduce virtuous girls; how, on the excuse that they want to marry them, they carry them off from their parents' houses; how afterwards they leave these unhappy girls to their fate, and they perish in the most pitiful way. I read a great many books,' said grandmother, 'and it is all so well described that one sits up all night and reads them on the sly. So mind you don't read them, Nastenka,' said she. 'What books has he sent?'

"'They are all Walter Scott's novels, grandmother.'

"'Walter Scott's novels! But stay, isn't there some trick about it? Look, hasn't he stuck a love-letter among them?'

"'No, grandmother,' I said, 'there isn't a love-letter.'

"'But look under the binding; they sometimes stuff it under the bindings, the rascals!'

"'No, grandmother, there is nothing under the binding.'

"'Well, that's all right.'

"So we began reading Walter Scott, and in a month or so we had read almost half. Then he sent us more and more. He sent us Pushkin, too; so that at last I could not get on without a book, and left off dreaming of how fine it would be to marry a Chinese Prince.

"That's how things were when I chanced one day to meet our lodger on the stairs. Grandmother had sent me to fetch something. He stopped, I blushed and he blushed; he laughed, though, said good-morning to me, asked after grandmother, and said, 'Well, have you read the books?' I answered that I had. 'Which did you like best?' he asked. I said, 'Ivanhoe, and Pushkin best of all,' and so our talk ended for that time.

"A week later I met him again on the stairs. That time grandmother had not sent me, I wanted to get something for myself. It was past two, and the lodger used to come home at that time. 'Good-afternoon,' said he. I said good-afternoon, too.

" 'Aren't you dull,' he said, 'sitting all day with your grandmother?'

"When he asked that, I blushed, I don't know why; I felt ashamed, and again I felt offended—I suppose because other people had begun to ask me about that. I wanted to go away without answering, but I hadn't the strength.

" 'Listen,' he said, 'you are a good girl. Excuse my speaking to you like that, but I assure you that I wish for your welfare quite as much as your grandmother. Have you no friends that you could go and visit?'

"I told him I hadn't any, that I had had no friend but Mashenka, and she had gone away to Pskov.

" 'Listen,' he said, 'would you like to go to the theatre with me?'

" 'To the theatre. What about grandmother?'

" 'But you must go without your grandmother's knowing it,' he said.

" 'No,' I said, 'I don't want to deceive grandmother. Good-bye.'

" 'Well, good-bye,' he answered, and said nothing more.

"Only after dinner he came to see us; sat a long time talking to grandmother; asked her whether she ever went out anywhere, whether she had acquaintances, and suddenly said: 'I have taken a box at the opera for this evening; they are putting on *The Barber of Seville*.[7] My friends meant to go, but afterwards refused, so the ticket is left on my hands.' '*The Barber of Seville*,' cried grandmother; 'why, the same they used to act in old days?'

" 'Yes, it's the same barber,' he said, and glanced at me. I saw what it meant and turned crimson, and my heart began throbbing with suspense.

" 'To be sure, I know it,' said grandmother; 'why, I took the part of Rosina myself in old days, at a private performance!'

" 'So wouldn't you like to go to-day?' said the lodger. 'Or my ticket will be wasted.'

" 'By all means let us go,' said grandmother; why shouldn't we? And my Nastenka here has never been to the theatre.'

"My goodness, what joy! We got ready at once, put on our best clothes, and set off. Though grandmother was blind, still she wanted to hear the music; besides, she is a kind old soul, what she cared most for was to amuse me, we should never have gone of ourselves.

"What my impressions of *The Barber of Seville* were I won't tell you; but all that evening our lodger looked at me so nicely, talked so nicely, that I saw at once that he had meant to test me in the morning when he proposed that I should go with him alone. Well, it was joy! I went to bed so proud, so gay, my heart beat so that I was a little feverish, and all night I was raving about *The Barber of Seville*.

"I expected that he would come and see us more and more often after that, but it wasn't so at all. He almost entirely gave up coming. He would just come in about once a month, and then only to invite us to the theatre. We went twice again. Only I wasn't at all pleased with that; I saw that he was simply sorry for me because I was so hardly treated by grandmother, and that was all. As time went on, I grew more and more restless, I couldn't sit still, I couldn't read, I couldn't work; sometimes I laughed and did something to annoy grandmother, at another time I would cry. At last I grew thin and was very nearly ill. The opera season was over, and our lodger had quite given up coming to see us; whenever we met—always on the same staircase, of course—he would bow so silently, so gravely, as though he did not want to speak, and go down to the front door, while I went on standing in the middle of the stairs, as red as a cherry, for all the blood rushed to my head at the sight of him.

"Now the end is near. Just a year ago, in May, the lodger

came to us and said to grandmother that he had finished his business here, and that he must go back to Moscow for a year. When I heard that, I sank into a chair half dead; grandmother did not notice anything; and having informed us that he should be leaving us, he bowed and went away.

"What was I to do? I thought and thought and fretted and fretted, and at last I made up my mind. Next day he was to go away, and I made up my mind to end it all that evening when grandmother went to bed. And so it happened. I made up all my clothes in a parcel—all the linen I needed—and with the parcel in my hand, more dead than alive, went upstairs to our lodger. I believe I must have stayed an hour on the staircase. When I opened his door he cried out as he looked at me. He thought I was a ghost, and rushed to give me some water, for I could hardly stand up. My heart beat so violently that my head ached, and I did not know what I was doing. When I recovered I began by laying my parcel on his bed, sat down beside it, hid my face in my hands and went into floods of tears. I think he understood it all at once, and looked at me so sadly that my heart was torn.

" 'Listen,' he began, 'listen, Nastenka, I can't do anything; I am a poor man, for I have nothing, not even a decent berth. How could we live, if I were to marry you?'

"We talked a long time; but at last I got quite frantic, I said I could not go on living with grandmother, that I should run away from her, that I did not want to be pinned to her, and that I would go to Moscow if he liked, because I could not live without him. Shame and pride and love were all clamouring in me at once, and I fell on the bed almost in convulsions, I was so afraid of a refusal.

"He sat for some minutes in silence, then got up, came up to me and took me by the hand.

" 'Listen, my dear good Nastenka, listen; I swear to you that if I am ever in a position to marry, you shall make my happiness. I assure you that now you are the only one who could make me happy. Listen, I am going to Moscow and shall be there just a year; I hope to establish my position. When I come

back, if you still love me, I swear that we will be happy. Now it
is impossible, I am not able, I have not the right to promise anything. Well, I repeat, if it is not within a year it will certainly be
some time; that is, of course, if you do not prefer any one else,
for I cannot and dare not bind you by any sort of promise.'

"That was what he said to me, and next day he went away.
We agreed together not to say a word to grandmother: that was
his wish. Well, my history is nearly finished now. Just a year
has past. He has arrived; he has been here three days, and—
and—"

"And what?" I cried, impatient to hear the end.

"And up to now has not shown himself!" answered Nastenka, as though screwing up all her courage. "There's no sign
or sound of him."

Here she stopped, paused for a minute, bent her head, and
covering her face with her hands broke into such sobs that it
sent a pang to my heart to hear them. I had not in the least expected such a dénouement.

"Nastenka," I began timidly in an ingratiating voice, "Nastenka! For goodness' sake don't cry! How do you know? Perhaps he is not here yet. . . ."

"He is, he is," Nastenka repeated. "He is here, and I know it.
We made an agreement at the time, that evening, before he went
away: when we said all that I have told you, and had come to
an understanding, then we came out here for a walk on this
embankment. It was ten o'clock; we sat on this seat. I was not
crying then; it was sweet to me to hear what he said. . . . And
he said that he would come to us directly he arrived, and if I
did not refuse him, then we would tell grandmother about it
all. Now he is here, I know it, and yet he does not come!"

And again she burst into tears.

"Good God, can I do nothing to help you in your sorrow?"
I cried, jumping up from the seat in utter despair. "Tell me, Nastenka, wouldn't it be possible for me to go to him?"

"Would that be possible?" she asked suddenly, raising her
head.

"No, of course not," I said pulling myself up; "but I tell you what, write a letter."

"No, that's impossible, I can't do that," she answered with decision, bending her head and not looking at me.

"How impossible—why is it impossible?" I went on, clinging to my idea. "But, Nastenka, it depends what sort of letter; there are letters and letters and. . . . Ah, Nastenka, I am right; trust to me, trust to me, I will not give you bad advice. It can all be arranged! You took the first step—why not now?"

"I can't. I can't! It would seem as though I were forcing myself on him. . . ."

"Ah, my good little Nastenka," I said, hardly able to conceal a smile; "no, no, you have a right to, in fact, because he made you a promise. Besides, I can see from everything that he is a man of delicate feeling; that he behaved very well," I went on, more and more carried away by the logic of my own arguments and convictions. "How did he behave? He bound himself by a promise: he said that if he married at all he would marry no one but you; he gave you full liberty to refuse him at once. . . . Under such circumstances you may take the first step; you have the right; you are in the privileged position—if, for instance, you wanted to free him from his promise. . . ."

"Listen; how would you write?"

"Write what?"

"This letter."

"I tell you how I would write: 'Dear Sir' . . ."

"Must I really begin like that, 'Dear Sir'?"

"You certainly must! Though, after all, I don't know, I imagine. . . ."

"Well, well, what next?"

" 'Dear Sir,—I must apologize for——' But, no, there's no need to apologize; the fact itself justifies everything. Write simply:—

" 'I am writing to you. Forgive me my impatience; but I have been happy for a whole year in hope; am I to blame for being unable to endure a day of doubt now? Now that you have come, perhaps you have changed your mind. If so, this letter is to tell

you that I do not repine, nor blame you. I do not blame you because I have no power over your heart, such is my fate!

" 'You are an honourable man. You will not smile or be
vexed at these impatient lines. Remember they are written by a
poor girl; that she is alone; that she has no one to direct her, no
one to advise her, and that she herself could never control her
heart. But forgive me that a doubt has stolen—if only for one
instant—into my heart. You are not capable of insulting, even in
thought, her who so loved and so loves you.' "

"Yes, yes; that's exactly what I was thinking!" cried Nastenka, and her eyes beamed with delight. "Oh, you have solved
my difficulties: God has sent you to me! Thank you, thank you!"

"What for? What for? For God's sending me?" I answered
looking delighted at her joyful little face.

"Why, yes; for that too."

"Ah, Nastenka! Why, one thanks some people for being alive
at the same time with one; I thank you for having met me for
my being able to remember you all my life!"

"Well, enough, enough! But now I tell you what, listen: we
made an agreement then that as soon as he arrived he would let
me know, by leaving a letter with some good simple people of
my acquaintance who know nothing about it; or, if it were impossible to write a letter to me, for a letter does not always tell
everything, he would be here at ten o'clock on the day he arrived, where we had arranged to meet. I know he has arrived
already; but now it's the third day, and there's no sign of him
and no letter. It's impossible for me to get away from grandmother in the morning. Give my letter to-morrow to those kind
people I spoke to you about: they will send it on to him, and if
there is an answer you bring it to-morrow at ten o'clock."

"But the letter, the letter! You see, you must write the letter
first! So perhaps it must all be the day after to-morrow."

"The letter . . ." said Nastenka, a little confused, "the letter . . . but . . ."

But she did not finish. At first she turned her little face away
from me, flushed like a rose, and suddenly I felt in my hand a

letter which had evidently been written long before, all ready and sealed up. A familiar sweet and charming reminiscence floated through my mind.

"R, o—Ro; s, i—si; n, a—na,"[8] I began.

"Rosina!" we both hummed together; I almost embracing her with delight, while she blushed as only she could blush, and laughed through the tears which gleamed like pearls on her black eyelashes.

"Come, enough, enough! Good-bye now," she said, speaking rapidly. "Here is the letter, here is the address to which you are to take it. Good-bye, till we meet again! Till to-morrow!"

She pressed both my hands warmly, nodded her head, and flew like an arrow down her side street. I stood still for a long time following her with my eyes.

"Till to-morrow! till to-morrow!" was ringing in my ears as she vanished from my sight.

THIRD NIGHT

To-day was a gloomy, rainy day without a glimmer of sunlight, like the old age before me. I am oppressed by such strange thoughts, such gloomy sensations; questions still so obscure to me are crowding into my brain—and I seem to have neither power nor will to settle them. It's not for me to settle all this!

To-day we shall not meet. Yesterday, when we said good-bye, the clouds began gathering over the sky and a mist rose. I said that to-morrow it would be a bad day; she made no answer, she did not want to speak against her wishes; for her that day was bright and clear, not one cloud should obscure her happiness.

"If it rains we shall not see each other," she said, "I shall not come."

I thought that she would not notice to-day's rain, and yet she has not come.

Yesterday was our third interview, our third white night. . . .

But how fine joy and happiness makes any one! How brimming over with love the heart is! One seems longing to pour out one's whole heart; one wants everything to be gay, everything to be laughing. And how infectious that joy is! There was such a softness in her words, such a kindly feeling in her heart towards me yesterday. . . . How solicitous and friendly she was; how tenderly she tried to give me courage! Oh, the coquetry of happiness! While I . . . I took it all for the genuine thing, I thought that she. . . .

But, my God, how could I have thought it? How could I have been so blind, when everything had been taken by another already, when nothing was mine; when, in fact, her very tenderness to me, her anxiety, her love . . . yes, love for me, was nothing else but joy at the thought of seeing another man so soon, desire to include me, too, in her happiness? . . . When he did not come, when we waited in vain, she frowned, she grew timid and discouraged. Her movements, her words, were no longer so light, so playful, so gay; and, strange to say, she redoubled her attentiveness to me, as though instinctively desiring to lavish on me what she desired for herself so anxiously, if her wishes were not accomplished. My Nastenka was so downcast, so dismayed, that I think she realized at last that I loved her, and was sorry for my poor love. So when we are unhappy we feel the unhappiness of others more; feeling is not destroyed but concentrated. . . .

I went to meet her with a full heart, and was all impatience. I had no presentiment that I should feel as I do now, that it would not all end happily. She was beaming with pleasure; she was expecting an answer. The answer was himself. He was to come, to run at her call. She arrived a whole hour before I did. At first she giggled at everything, laughed at every word I said. I began talking, but relapsed into silence.

"Do you know why I am so glad," she said, "so glad to look at you?—why I like you so much to-day?"

"Well?" I asked, and my heart began throbbing.

"I like you because you have not fallen in love with me. You know that some men in your place would have been pestering and worrying me, would have been sighing and miserable, while you are so nice!"

Then she wrung my hand so hard that I almost cried out. She laughed.

"Goodness, what a friend you are!" she began gravely a minute later. "God sent you to me. What would have happened to me if you had not been with me now? How disinterested you are! How truly you care for me! When I am married we will be great friends, more than brother and sister. I shall care almost as I do for him. . . ."

I felt horribly sad at that moment, yet something like laughter was stirring in my soul.

"You are very much upset," I said; "you are frightened, you think he won't come."

"Oh dear!" she answered; "if I were less happy, I believe I should cry at your lack of faith, at your reproaches. However, you have made me think and have given me a lot to think about, but I shall think later, and now I will own that you are right. Yes, I am somehow not myself; I am all suspense, and feel everything as it were too lightly. But hush! that's enough about feelings. . . ."

At that moment we heard footsteps, and in the darkness we saw a figure coming towards us. We both started; she almost cried out; I dropped her hand and made a movement as though to walk away. But we were mistaken, it was not he.

"What are you afraid of? Why did you let go of my hand?" she said, giving it to me again. "Come, what is it? We will meet him together; I want him to see how fond we are of each other."

"How fond we are of each other!" I cried. ("Oh, Nastenka, Nastenka," I thought, "how much you have told me in that saying! Such fondness at *certain* moments makes the heart cold and the soul heavy. Your hand is cold, mine burns like fire. How blind you are, Nastenka! . . . Oh, how unbearable a happy person is sometimes! But I could not be angry with you!")

At last my heart was too full.

"Listen, Nastenka!" I cried. "Do you know how it has been with me all day?"

"Why, how, how? Tell me quickly! Why have you said nothing all this time?"

"To begin with, Nastenka, when I had carried out all your commissions, given the letter, gone to see your good friends, then . . . then I went home and went to bed."

"Is that all?" she interrupted, laughing.

"Yes, almost all," I answered restraining myself, for foolish tears were already starting into my eyes. "I woke an hour before our appointment, and yet, as it were, I had not been asleep. I don't know what happened to me. I came to tell you all about it, feeling as though time were standing still, feeling as though one sensation, one feeling must remain with me from that time for ever; feeling as though one minute must go on for all eternity, and as though all life had come to a standstill for me. . . . When I woke up it seemed as though some musical motive long familiar, heard somewhere in the past, forgotten and voluptuously sweet, had come back to me now. It seemed to me that it had been clamouring at my heart all my life, and only now. . . ."

"Oh my goodness, my goodness," Nastenka interrupted, "what does all that mean? I don't understand a word."

"Ah, Nastenka, I wanted somehow to convey to you that strange impression. . . ." I began in a plaintive voice, in which there still lay hid a hope, though a very faint one.

"Leave off. Hush!" she said, and in one instant the sly puss had guessed.

Suddenly she became extraordinarily talkative, gay, mischievous; she took my arm, laughed, wanted me to laugh too, and every confused word I uttered evoked from her prolonged ringing laughter. . . . I began to feel angry, she had suddenly begun flirting.

"Do you know," she began, "I feel a little vexed that you are not in love with me? There's no understanding human nature! But all the same, Mr. Unapproachable, you cannot blame me for being so simple; I tell you everything, everything, whatever foolish thought comes into my head."

"Listen! That's eleven, I believe," I said as the slow chime of a bell rang out from a distant tower. She suddenly stopped, left off laughing and began to count.

"Yes, it's eleven," she said at last in a timid, uncertain voice.

I regretted at once that I had frightened her, making her count the strokes, and I cursed myself for my spiteful impulse. I felt sorry for her, and did not know how to atone for what I had done.

I began comforting her, seeking for reasons for his not coming, advancing various arguments, proofs. No one could have been easier to deceive than she was at that moment; and, indeed, anyone at such a moment listens gladly to any consolation, whatever it may be, and is overjoyed if a shadow of excuse can be found.

"And indeed it's an absurd thing," I began, warming to my task and admiring the extraordinary clearness of my argument, "why, he could not have come; you have muddled and confused me, Nastenka, so that I too, have lost count of the time. . . . Only think: he can scarcely have received the letter; suppose he is not able to come, suppose he is going to answer the letter, could not come before to-morrow. I will go for it as soon as it's light to-morrow and let you know at once. Consider, there are thousands of possibilities; perhaps he was not at home when the letter came, and may not have read it even now! Anything may happen, you know."

"Yes, yes!" said Nastenka. "I did not think of that. Of course anything may happen?" she went on in a tone that offered no opposition, though some other far-away thought could be heard like a vexatious discord in it. "I tell you what you must do," she said, "you go as early as possible to-morrow morning, and if you get anything let me know at once. You know where I live, don't you?"

And she began repeating her address to me.

Then she suddenly became so tender, so solicitous with me. She seemed to listen attentively to what I told her; but when I asked her some question she was silent, was confused, and turned her head away. I looked into her eyes—yes, she was crying.

"How can you? How can you? Oh, what a baby you are! what childishness! . . . Come, come!"

She tried to smile, to calm herself, but her chin was quivering and her bosom was still heaving.

"I was thinking about you," she said after a minute's silence. "You are so kind that I should be a stone if I did not feel it. Do you know what has occurred to me now? I was comparing you two. Why isn't he you? Why isn't he like you? He is not as good as you, though I love him more than you."

I made no answer. She seemed to expect me to say something.

"Of course, it may be that I don't understand him fully yet. You know I was always as it were afraid of him; he was always so grave, as it were so proud. Of course I know it's only that he seems like that, I know there is more tenderness in his heart than in mine . . . I remember how he looked at me when I went in to him—do you remember?—with my bundle; but yet I respect him too much, and doesn't that show that we are not equals?"

"No, Nastenka, no," I answered, "it shows that you love him more than anything in the world, and far more than yourself."

"Yes, supposing that is so," answered Nastentka naïvely. "But do you know what strikes me now? Only I am not talking about him now, but speaking generally; all this came into my mind some time ago. Tell me, how is it that we can't all be like brothers together? Why is it that even the best of men always seem to hide something from other people and to keep something back? Why not say straight out what is in one's heart, when one knows that one is not speaking idly? As it is every one seems harsher than he really is, as though all were afraid of doing injustice to their feelings, by being too quick to express them."

"Oh, Nastenka, what you say is true; but there are many reasons for that," I broke in suppressing my own feelings at that moment more than ever.

"No, no!" she answered with deep feeling. "Here you, for instance, are not like other people! I really don't know how to tell you what I feel; but it seems to me that you, for instance . . . at the present moment . . . it seems to me that you are sacrificing something for me," she added timidly, with a fleeting glance at me. "Forgive me for saying so, I am a simple girl you know. I have seen very little of life, and I really sometimes don't know how to say things," she added in a voice that quivered with some hidden feeling, while she tried to smile; "but I only wanted to tell you that I am grateful, that I feel it all too . . . Oh, may God give you happiness for it! What you told me about your dreamer is quite untrue now—that is, I mean, it's not true of you. You are recovering, you are quite a different man from what you described. If you ever fall in love with some one, God give you happiness with her! I won't wish anything for her, for she will be happy with you. I know, I am a woman myself, so you must believe me when I tell you so."

She ceased speaking, and pressed my hand warmly. I too could not speak without emotion. Some minutes passed.

"Yes, it's clear he won't come to-night," she said at last raising her head. "It's late."

"He will come to-morrow," I said in the most firm and convincing tone.

"Yes," she added with no sign of her former depression. "I see for myself now that he could not come till to-morrow. Well, good-bye, till to-morrow. If it rains perhaps I shall not come. But the day after to-morrow, I shall come. I shall come for certain, whatever happens; be sure to be here, I want to see you, I will tell you everything."

And then when we parted she gave me her hand and said, looking at me candidly: "We shall always be together, shan't we?"

Oh, Nastenka, Nastenka! If only you knew how lonely I am now!

As soon as it struck nine o'clock I could not stay indoors,

but put on my things, and went out in spite of the weather. I was there, sitting on our seat. I went to her street, but I felt ashamed, and turned back without looking at their windows, when I was two steps from her door. I went home more depressed than I had ever been before. What a damp, dreary day! If it had been fine I should have walked about all night. . . .

But to-morrow, to-morrow! To-morrow she will tell me everything. The letter has not come to-day, however. But that was to be expected. They are together by now. . . .

FOURTH NIGHT

My God, how it has all ended! What it has all ended in! I arrived at nine o'clock. She was already there. I noticed her a good way off; she was standing as she had been that first time, with her elbows on the railing, and she did not hear me coming up to her.

"Nastenka!" I called to her, suppressing my agitation with an effort.

She turned to me quickly.

"Well?" she said. "Well? Make haste!"

I looked at her in perplexity.

"Well, where is the letter? Have you brought the letter?" she repeated clutching at the railing.

"No, there is no letter," I said at last. "Hasn't he been to you yet?" She turned fearfully pale and looked at me for a long time without moving. I had shattered her last hope.

"Well, God be with him," she said at last in a breaking voice; "God be with him if he leaves me like that."

She dropped her eyes, then tried to look at me and could not. For several minutes she was struggling with her emotion. All at once she turned away, leaning her elbows against the railing and burst into tears.

"Oh don't, don't!" I began; but looking at her I had not the heart to go on, and what was I to say to her?

"Don't try and comfort me," she said; "don't talk about him; don't tell me that he will come, that he has not cast me off so cruelly and so inhumanly as he has. What for—what for? Can there have been something in my letter, that unlucky letter?"

At that point sobs stifled her voice; my heart was torn as I looked at her.

"Oh, how inhumanly cruel it is!" she began again. "And not a line, not a line! He might at least have written that he does not want me, that he rejects me—but not a line for three days! How easy it is for him to wound, to insult a poor, defenceless girl, whose only fault is that she loves him! Oh, what I've suffered during these three days! Oh, dear! When I think that I was the first to go to him, that I humbled myself before him, cried, that I begged of him a little love! . . . and after that, Listen," she said, turning to me, and her black eyes flashed, "it isn't so! It can't be so; it isn't natural. Either you are mistaken or I; perhaps he has not received the letter? Perhaps he still knows nothing about it? How could any one—judge for yourself, tell me, for goodness' sake explain it to me, I can't understand it—how could any one behave with such barbarous coarseness as he has behaved to me? Not one word! Why, the lowest creature on earth is treated more compassionately. Perhaps he has heard something, perhaps some one has told him something about me," she cried, turning to me inquiringly: "What do you think?"

"Listen, Nastenka, I shall go to him to-morrow in your name."

"Yes?"

"I will question him about everything; I will tell him everything."

"Yes, yes?"

"You write a letter. Don't say no, Nastenka, don't say no! I will make him respect your action, he shall hear all about it, and if——"

"No, my friend, no," she interrupted. "Enough! Not another

word, not another line from me—enough! I don't know him; I
don't love him any more. I will . . . forget him."

She could not go on.

"Calm yourself, calm yourself! Sit here, Nastenka," I said,
making her sit down on the seat.

"I am calm. Don't trouble. It's nothing! It's only tears, they
will soon dry. Why, do you imagine I shall do away with myself,
that I shall throw myself into the river?"

My heart was full: I tried to speak, but I could not.

"Listen," she said taking my hand. "Tell me: you wouldn't
have behaved like this, would you? You would not have abandoned a girl who had come to you of herself, you would not
have thrown into her face a shameless taunt at her weak foolish
heart? You would have taken care of her? You would have realized that she was alone, that she did not know how to look after
herself, that she could not guard herself from loving you, that
it was not her fault, not her fault—that she had done nothing. . . . Oh dear, oh dear!"

"Nastenka!" I cried at last, unable to control my emotion.
"Nastenka, you torture me! You wound my heart, you are
killing me, Nastenka! I cannot be silent! I must speak at last,
give utterance to what is surging in my heart!"

As I said this I got up from the seat. She took my hand and
looked at me in surprise.

"What is the matter with you?" she said at last.

"Listen," I said resolutely. "Listen to me, Nastenka! What I
am going to say to you now is all nonsense, all impossible, all
stupid! I know that this can never be, but I cannot be silent. For
the sake of what you are suffering now, I beg you beforehand
to forgive me!"

"What is it? What is it?" she said, drying her tears and looking at me intently, while a strange curiosity gleamed in her astonished eyes. "What is the matter?"

"It's impossible, but I love you, Nastenka! There it is! Now
everything is told," I said with a wave of my hand. "Now you
will see whether you can go on talking to me as you did just

now, whether you can listen to what I am going to say to you." . . .

"Well, what then?" Nastenka interrupted me. "What of it? I knew you loved me long ago, only I always thought that you simply liked me very much. . . . Oh dear, oh dear!"

"At first it was simply liking, Nastenka, but now, now! I am just in the same position as you were when you went to him with your bundle. In a worse position than you, Nastenka, because he cared for no one else as you do."

"What are you saying to me! I don't understand you in the least. But tell me, what's this for; I don't mean what for, but why are you . . . so suddenly. . . . Oh dear, I am talking nonsense! But you . . ."

And Nastenka broke off in confusion. Her cheeks flamed; she dropped her eyes.

"What's to be done, Nastenka, what am I to do? I am to blame. I have abused your . . . But no, no, I am not to blame, Nastenka; I feel that, I know that, because my heart tells me I am right, for I cannot hurt you in any way, I cannot wound you! I was your friend, but I am still your friend, I have betrayed no trust. Here my tears are falling, Nastenka. Let them flow, let them flow—they don't hurt anybody. They will dry, Nastenka."

"Sit down, sit down," she said, making me sit down on the seat. "Oh, my God!"

"No, Nastenka, I won't sit down; I cannot stay here any longer, you cannot see me again; I will tell you everything and go away. I only want to say that you would never have found out that I loved you. I should have kept my secret. I would not have worried you at such a moment with my egoism. No! But I could not resist it now; you spoke of it yourself, it is your fault, your fault and not mine. You cannot drive me away from you. . . ."

"No, no, I don't drive you away, no!" said Nastenka, concealing her confusion as best she could, poor child.

"You don't drive me away? No! But I meant to run from you myself. I will go away, but first I will tell you all, for when you were crying here I could not sit unmoved, when you wept, when you were in torture at being—at being—I will speak of it, Nastenka—at being forsaken, at your love being repulsed, I felt that in my heart there was so much love for you, Nastenka, so much love! And it seemed so bitter that I could not help you with my love, that my heart was breaking and I . . . I could not be silent, I had to speak, Nastenka, I had to speak!"

"Yes, yes! tell me, talk to me," said Nastenka with an indescribable gesture. "Perhaps you think it strange that I talk to you like this, but . . . speak! I will tell you afterwards! I will tell you everything."

"You are sorry for me, Nastenka, you are simply sorry for me, my dear little friend! What's done can't be mended. What is said cannot be taken back. Isn't that so? Well, now you know. That's the starting-point. Very well. Now it's all right, only listen. When you were sitting crying I thought to myself (oh, let me tell you what I was thinking!), I thought, that (of course it cannot be, Nastenka), I thought that you . . . I thought that you somehow . . . quite apart from me, had ceased to love him. Then—I thought that yesterday and the day before yesterday, Nastenka—then I would—I certainly would—have succeeded in making you love me; you know, you said yourself, Nastenka, that you almost loved me. Well, what next? Well, that's nearly all I wanted to tell you; all that is left to say is how it would be if you loved me, only that, nothing more! Listen, my friend—for any way you are my friend—I am, of course, a poor, humble man, of no great consequence; but that's not the point (I don't seem to be able to say what I mean, Nastenka, I am so confused), only I would love you, I would love you so, that even if you still loved him, even if you went on loving the man I don't know, you would never feel that my love was a burden to you. You would only feel every minute that at your side was beating a grateful, grateful heart, a warm heart ready for your sake. . . . Oh Nastenka, Nastenka! What have you done to me?"

"Don't cry; I don't want you to cry," said Nastenka, getting up quickly from the seat. "Come along, get up, come with me, don't cry, don't cry," she said, drying her tears with her handkerchief; "let us go now; maybe I will tell you something. . . .

If he has forsaken me now, if he has forgotten me, though I still love him (I do not want to deceive you) . . . but listen, answer me. If I were to love you, for instance, that is, if I only. . . . Oh my friend, my friend! To think, to think how I wounded you, when I laughed at your love, when I praised you for not falling in love with me. Oh dear! How was it I did not foresee this, how was it I did not foresee this, how could I have been so stupid? But . . . Well, I have made up my mind, I will tell you."

"Look here, Nastenka, do you know what? I'll go away, that's what I'll do. I am simply tormenting you. Here you are remorseful for having laughed at me, and I won't have you . . . in addition to your sorrow. . . . Of course it is my fault, Nastenka, but good-bye!"

"Stay, listen to me: can you wait?"

"What for? How?"

"I love him; but I shall get over it, I must get over it, I cannot fail to get over it; I am getting over it, I feel that. . . . Who knows? Perhaps it will all end to-day, for I hate him, for he has been laughing at me, while you have been weeping here with me, for you have not repulsed me as he has, for you love me while he has never loved me, for in fact, I love you myself. . . . Yes, I love you! I love you as you love me; I have told you so before, you heard it yourself—I love you because you are better than he is, because you are nobler than he is, because, because he——"

The poor girl's emotion was so violent that she could not say more; she laid her head upon my shoulder, then upon my bosom, and wept bitterly. I comforted her, I persuaded her, but she could not stop crying; she kept pressing my hand, and saying between her sobs: "Wait, wait, it will be over in a minute! I want to tell you . . . you mustn't think that these tears—it's nothing, it's weakness, wait till it's over." . . . At last she left off crying, dried her eyes and we walked on again. I wanted to speak, but she still begged me to wait. We were silent. . . . At last she plucked up courage and began to speak.

"It's like this," she began in a weak and quivering voice, in which, however, there was a note that pierced my heart with a

sweet pang; "don't think that I am so light and inconstant, don't
think that I can forget and change so quickly. I have loved him
for a whole year, and I swear by God that I have never, never,
even in thought, been unfaithful to him. . . . He has despised
me, he has been laughing at me—God forgive him! But he has
insulted me and wounded my heart. I . . . I do not love him, for
I can only love what is magnanimous, what understands me,
what is generous; for I am like that myself and he is not worthy of me—well, that's enough of him. He has done better than
if he had deceived my expectations later, and shown me later
what he was. . . . Well, it's over! But who knows, my dear
friend," she went on pressing my hand, "who knows, perhaps
my whole love was a mistaken feeling, a delusion—perhaps it
began in mischief, in nonsense, because I was kept so strictly by
grandmother? Perhaps I ought to love another man, not him, a
different man, who would have pity on me and . . . and . . . But
don't let us say any more about that," Nastenka broke off,
breathless with emotion, "I only wanted to tell you . . . I
wanted to tell you that if, although I love him (no, did love
him), if, in spite of this you still say. . . . If you feel that your
love is so great that it may at last drive from my heart my old
feeling—if you will have pity on me—if you do not want to
leave me alone to my fate, without hope, without consolation—
if you are ready to love me always as you do now—I swear to
you that gratitude . . . that my love will be at last worthy of
your love. . . . Will you take my hand?"

"Nastenka!" I cried breathless with sobs. "Nastenka, oh,
Nastenka!"

"Enough, enough! Well, now it's quite enough," she said,
hardly able to control herself. "Well, now all has been said,
hasn't it? Hasn't it? You are happy—I am happy too. Not another
word about it, wait; spare me. . . . talk of something else, for
God's sake."

"Yes, Nastenka, yes! Enough about that, now I am happy.
I—— Yes, Nastenka, yes, let us talk of other things, let us make
haste and talk. Yes! I am ready."

And we did not know what to say: we laughed, we wept, we

said thousands of things meaningless and incoherent; at one moment we walked along the pavement, then suddenly turned back and crossed the road; then we stopped and went back again to the embankment; we were like children.

"I am living alone now, Nastenka," I began, "but to-morrow! Of course you know, Nastenka, I am poor, I have only got twelve hundred rubles, but that doesn't matter."

"Of course not, and granny has her pension, so she will be no burden. We must take granny."

"Of course we must take granny. But there's Matryona."

"Yes and we've got Fyokla too!"

"Matryona is a good woman, but she has one fault: she has no imagination, Nastenka, absolutely none; but that doesn't matter."

"That's all right—they can live together; only you must move to us to-morrow."

"To you? How so? All right, I am ready."

"Yes, hire a room from us. We have a top floor, it's empty. We had an old lady lodging there, but she has gone away; and I know granny would like to have a young man. I said to her, 'Why a young man?' And she said, 'Oh, because I am old; only don't you fancy, Nastenka, that I want him as a husband for you.' So I guessed it was with that idea."

"Oh, Nastenka!"

And we both laughed.

"Come, that's enough, that's enough. But where do you live? I've forgotten."

"Over that way, near X bridge, Barannikov's Buildings."

"It's that big house?"

"Yes, that big house."

"Oh, I know, a nice house; only you know you had better give it up and come to us as soon as possible."

"To-morrow, Nastenka, to-morrow; I owe a little for my rent there, but that doesn't matter. I shall soon get my salary."

"And do you know I will perhaps give lessons; I will learn something myself and then give lessons."

"Capital! And I shall soon get a bonus."

"So by to-morrow you will be my lodger."

"And we will go to *The Barber of Seville*, for they are soon going to put it on again."

"Yes, we'll go," said Nastenka "but better see something else and not *The Barber of Seville*."

"Very well, something else. Of course that will be better, I did not think——"

As we talked like this we walked along in a sort of delirium, a sort of intoxication, as though we did not know what was happening to us. At one moment we stopped and talked for a long time at the same place; then we went on again, and goodness knows where we went; and again tears and again laughter. All of a sudden Nastenka would want to go home, and I would not dare to detain her but would want to see her to the house; we set off, and in a quarter of an hour found ourselves at the embankment by our seat. Then she would sigh, and tears would come into her eyes again; I would turn chill with dismay. . . . But she would press my hand and force me to walk, to talk, to chatter as before.

"It's time I was home at last; I think it must be very late," Nastenka said at last. "We must give over being childish."

"Yes, Nastenka, only I shan't sleep to-night; I am not going home."

"I don't think I shall sleep either; only see me home."

"I should think so!"

"Only this time we really must get to the house."

"We must, we must."

"Honour bright? For you know one must go home some time!"

"Honour bright," I answered laughing.

"Well, come along!"

"Come along! Look at the sky, Nastenka. Look! To-morrow it will be a lovely day; what a blue sky, what a moon! Look; that yellow cloud is covering it now, look, look! No, it has passed by. Look, look!"

But Nastenka did not look at the cloud; she stood mute as though turned to stone; a minute later she huddled timidly close up to me. Her hand trembled in my hand; I looked at her. She pressed still more closely to me.

At that moment a young man passed by us. He suddenly stopped, looked at us intently, and then again took a few steps on. My heart began throbbing.

"Who is it, Nastenka?" I said in an undertone.

"It's he," she answered in a whisper, huddling up to me, still more closely, still more tremulously. . . . I could hardly stand on my feet.

"Nastenka, Nastenka! It's you!" I heard a voice behind us and at the same moment the young man took several steps towards us.

My God, how she cried out! How she started! How she tore herself out of my arms and rushed to meet him! I stood and looked at them, utterly crushed. But she had hardly given him her hand, had hardly flung herself into his arms, when she turned to me again, was beside me again in a flash, and before I knew where I was she threw both arms round my neck and gave me a warm, tender kiss. Then, without saying a word to me, she rushed back to him again, took his hand, and drew him after her.

I stood a long time looking after them. At last the two vanished from my sight.

MORNING

My night ended with the morning. It was a wet day. The rain was falling and beating disconsolately upon my window pane; it was dark in the room and grey outside. My head ached and I was giddy; fever was stealing over my limbs.

"There's a letter for you, sir; the postman brought it," Matryona said stooping over me.

"A letter? From whom?" I cried, jumping up from my chair.

"I don't know, sir, better look—maybe it is written there whom it is from."

I broke the seal. It was from her!

"Oh, forgive me, forgive me! I beg you on my knees to forgive me! I deceived you and myself. It was a dream, a mirage. . . . My heart aches for you to-day; forgive me, forgive me!

"Don't blame me, for I have not changed to you in the least. I told you that I would love you, I love you now, I more than love you. Oh, my God! If only I could love you both at once! Oh, if only you were he!"

["Oh, if only he were you," echoed in my mind. I remembered your words, Nastenka!]

"God knows what I would do for you now! I know that you are sad and dreary. I have wounded you, but you know when one loves a wrong is soon forgotten. And you love me.

"Thank you, yes, thank you for that love! For it will live in my memory like a sweet dream which lingers long after awakening; for I shall remember for ever that instant when you opened your heart to me like a brother and so generously accepted the gift of my shattered heart to care for it, nurse it, and heal it . . . If you forgive me, the memory of you will be exalted by a feeling of everlasting gratitude which will never be effaced from my soul. . . . I will treasure that memory: I will be true to it, I will not betray it, I will not betray my heart: it is too constant. It returned so quickly yesterday to him to whom it has always belonged.

"We shall meet, you will come to us, you will not leave us, you will be for ever a friend, a brother to me. And when you see me you will give me your hand. . . . yes? You will give it to me, you have forgiven me, haven't you? You love me *as before?*

"Oh, love me, do not forsake me, because I love you so at this moment, because I am worthy of your love, because I will deserve it . . . my dear! Next week I am to be married to him. He has come back in love, he has never forgotten me. You will

not be angry at my writing about him. But I want to come and
see you with him; you will like him, won't you?

"Forgive me, remember and love your
"NASTENKA."

I read that letter over and over again for a long time; tears
gushed to my eyes. At last it fell from my hands and I hid my
face.

"Dearie! I say, dearie——" Matryona began.

"What is it, Matryona?"

"I have taken all the cobwebs off the ceiling; you can have a
wedding or give a party."

I looked at Matryona. She was still a hearty, youngish old
woman, but I don't know why all at once I suddenly pictured
her with lustreless eyes, a wrinkled face, bent, decrepit. . . . I
don't know why I suddenly pictured my room grown old like
Matryona. The walls and the floors looked discoloured, everything seemed dingy; the spiders' webs were thicker than ever. I
don't know why, but when I looked out of the window it
seemed to me that the house opposite had grown old and dingy
too, that the stucco on the columns was peeling off and crum-
bling, that the cornices were cracked and blackened, and that
the walls, of a vivid deep yellow, were patchy.

Either the sunbeams suddenly peeping out from the clouds
for a moment were hidden again behind a veil of rain, and
everything had grown dingy again before my eyes; or perhaps
the whole vista of my future flashed before me so sad and for-
bidding, and I saw myself just as I was now, fifteen years hence,
older, in the same room, just as solitary, with the same Matryona grown no cleverer for those fifteen years.

But to imagine that I should bear you a grudge, Nastenka!
That I should cast a dark cloud over your serene, untroubled
happiness; that by my bitter reproaches I should cause distress
to your heart, should poison it with secret remorse and should
force it to throb with anguish at the moment of bliss; that I
should crush a single one of those tender blossoms which you
have twined in your dark tresses when you go with him to the

altar . . . Oh never, never! May your sky be clear, may your sweet smile be bright and untroubled, and may you be blessed for that moment of blissful happiness which you gave to another, lonely and grateful heart!

My God, a whole moment of happiness! Is that too little for the whole of a man's life?

NOTES FROM UNDERGROUND[*]

A NOVEL

---

[*]The author of the diary and the diary itself are, of course, imaginary. Nevertheless it is clear that such persons as the writer of these notes not only may, but positively must, exist in our society, when we consider the circumstances in the midst of which our society is formed. I have tried to expose to the view of the public more distinctly than is commonly done, one of the characters of the recent past. He is one of the representatives of a generation still living. In this fragment, entitled "Underground," this person introduces himself and his views, and, as it were, tries to explain the causes owing to which he has made his appearance and was bound to make his appearance in our midst. In the second fragment there are added the actual notes of this person concerning certain events in his life.—AUTHOR'S NOTE.

PART I

UNDERGROUND

I

I am a sick man . . . I am a spiteful man. I am an unattractive man. I believe my liver is diseased. However I know nothing at all about my disease, and do not know for certain what ails me. I don't consult a doctor for it and never have, though I have a respect for medicine and doctors. Besides, I am extremely superstitious, sufficiently so to respect medicine, anyway (I am well-educated enough not to be superstitious, but I am superstitious). No, I refuse to consult a doctor from spite. That you probably will not understand. Well, I understand it, though. Of course I can't explain who it is precisely that I am mortifying in this case by my spite: I am perfectly well aware that I cannot "pay out" the doctors by not consulting them; I know better than any one that by all this I am only injuring myself and no one else. But still, if I don't consult a doctor it is from spite. My liver is bad, well—let it get worse!

I have been going on like that for a long time—twenty years. Now I am forty. I used to be in the government service, but am no longer. I was a spiteful official. I was rude and took pleasure in being so. I did not take bribes, you see, so I was bound to find a recompense in that, at least. (A poor jest, but I will not scratch it out. I wrote it thinking it would sound very witty; but now that I have seen myself that I only wanted to show off in a despicable way, I will not scratch it out on purpose!)

When petitioners used to come for information to the table at which I sat, I used to grind my teeth at them, and felt intense enjoyment when I succeeded in making anybody unhappy. I almost always did succeed. For the most part they were all timid people—of course, they were petitioners. But of the uppish ones there was one officer in particular I could not endure. He simply would not be humble, and clanked his sword in a disgusting way. I carried on a feud with him for eighteen months over that sword. At last I got the better of him. He left off clanking it. That happened in my youth, though.

But do you know, gentlemen, what was the chief point

about my spite? Why, the whole point, the real sting of it lay in
the fact that continually, even in the moment of the acutest
spleen, I was inwardly conscious with shame that I was not
only not a spiteful but not even an embittered man, that I was
simply scaring sparrows at random and amusing myself by it. I
might foam at the mouth, but bring me a doll to play with, give
me a cup of tea with sugar in it, and maybe I should be appeased. I might even be genuinely touched, though probably I
should grind my teeth at myself afterwards and lie awake at
night with shame for months after. That was my way.

I was lying when I said just now that I was a spiteful official.
I was lying from spite. I was simply amusing myself with the petitioners and with the officer, and in reality I never could become
spiteful. I was conscious every moment in myself of many, very
many elements absolutely opposite to that. I felt them positively
swarming in me, these opposite elements. I knew that they had
been swarming in me all my life and craving some outlet from
me, but I would not let them, would not let them, purposely
would not let them come out. They tormented me till I was
ashamed: they drove me to convulsions and—sickened me, at
last, how they sickened me! Now, are not you fancying, gentlemen, that I am expressing remorse for something now, that I am
asking your forgiveness for something? I am sure you are fancying that . . . However, I assure you I do not care if you are. . . .

It was not only that I could not become spiteful, I did not
know how to become anything: neither spiteful nor kind, neither
a rascal nor an honest man, neither a hero nor an insect. Now, I
am living out my life in my corner, taunting myself with the
spiteful and useless consolation that an intelligent man cannot
become anything seriously, and it is only the fool who becomes
anything. Yes, a man in the nineteenth century must and morally
ought to be pre-eminently a characterless creature; a man of
character, an active man is pre-eminently a limited creature. That
is my conviction of forty years. I am forty years old now, and you
know forty years is a whole life-time; you know it is extreme old
age. To live longer than forty years is bad manners, is vulgar, immoral. Who does live beyond forty? Answer that, sincerely and

honestly. I will tell you who do: fools and worthless fellows. I tell
all old men that to their face, all these venerable old men, all these
silver-haired and reverend seniors! I tell the whole world that to
its face! I have a right to say so, for I shall go on living to sixty
myself. To seventy! To eighty! . . . Stay, let me take breath. . . .

You imagine no doubt, gentlemen, that I want to amuse you.
You are mistaken in that, too. I am by no means such a mirthful
person as you imagine, or as you may imagine; however, irritated
by all this babble (and I feel that you are irritated) you think fit
to ask me who am I—then my answer is, I am a collegiate assessor.[1] I was in the service that I might have something to eat (and
solely for that reason), and when last year a distant relation left
me six thousand rubles in his will I immediately retired from the
service and settled down in my corner. I used to live in this corner before, but now I have settled down in it. My room is a
wretched, horrid one in the outskirts of the town. My servant is
an old country-woman, ill-natured from stupidity, and, moreover, there is always a nasty smell about her. I am told that the Petersburg climate is bad for me, and that with my small means it
is very expensive to live in Petersburg. I know all that better than
all these sage and experienced counsellors and monitors. . . . But
I am remaining in Petersburg; I am not going away from Petersburg! I am not going away because . . . ech! Why, it is absolutely
no matter whether I am going away or not going away.

But what can a decent man speak of with most pleasure?

Answer: Of himself.

Well, so I will talk about myself.

II

I want now to tell you, gentlemen, whether you care to hear
it or not, why I could not even become an insect. I tell you
solemnly, that I have many times tried to become an insect.

But I was not equal even to that. I swear, gentlemen, that to be too conscious is an illness—a real thorough-going illness. For man's everyday needs, it would have been quite enough to have the ordinary human consciousness, that is, half or a quarter of the amount which falls to the lot of a cultivated man of our unhappy nineteenth century, especially one who has the fatal ill-luck to inhabit Petersburg, the most abstract and premeditated city on the whole earth. (There are premeditated and unpremeditated cities.) It would have been quite enough, for instance, to have the consciousness by which all so-called direct persons and men of action live. I bet you think I am writing all this from affectation, to be witty at the expense of men of action; and what is more, that from ill-bred affectation, I am clanking a sword like my officer. But, gentlemen, whoever can pride himself on his diseases and even swagger over them?

Though, after all, every one does do that; people do pride themselves on their diseases, and I do, may be, more than any one. We will not dispute it; my contention was absurd. But yet I am firmly persuaded that a great deal of consciousness, every sort of consciousness, in fact, is a disease. I stick to that. Let us leave that, too, for a minute. Tell me this: why does it happen that at the very, yes, at the very moments when I am most capable of feeling every refinement of all that is "good and beautiful," as they used to say at one time, it would, as though of design, happen to me not only to feel but to do such ugly things, such that . . . Well, in short, actions that all, perhaps, commit; but which, as though purposely, occurred to me at the very time when I was most conscious that they ought not to be committed. The more conscious I was of goodness and of all that was "beautiful and sublime,"[2] the more deeply I sank into my mire and the more ready I was to sink in it altogether. But the chief point was that all this was, as it were, not accidental in me, but as though it were bound to be so. It was as though it were my most normal condition, and not in the least disease or depravity, so that at last all desire in me to struggle against this depravity passed. It ended by my almost believing (perhaps actually believing) that this was perhaps my normal condition. But at first, in the beginning, what agonies I endured in that struggle! I did not believe it was the same with other people, and all my life I hid this fact about myself as a secret. I was ashamed (even now, perhaps, I am ashamed): I got to the point of feeling a sort of secret abnormal, despicable enjoyment in returning home to my corner on some disgusting Petersburg night, acutely conscious that that day I had committed a loathsome action again, that what was done could never be undone, and secretly, inwardly gnawing, gnawing at myself for it, tearing and consuming myself till at last the bitterness turned into a sort of shameful accursed sweetness, and at last—into positive real enjoyment! Yes, into enjoyment, into enjoyment! I insist upon that. I have spoken of this because I keep wanting to know for a fact whether other people feel such enjoyment? I will explain; the enjoyment was just from the too intense consciousness of one's own degradation; it was from feeling oneself that one had reached the last barrier, that it was horrible, but that it could not be otherwise; that there was no escape for you; that you never could become a different man; that even if time and faith were still left you to change into something different you would most likely not wish to change; or if you did wish to, even then you would do nothing; because perhaps in reality there was nothing for you to change into.

And the worst of it was, and the root of it all, that it was all in accord with the normal fundamental laws of over-acute consciousness, and with the inertia that was the direct result of those laws, and that consequently one was not only unable to change but could do absolutely nothing. Thus it would follow, as the result of acute consciousness, that one is not to blame in being a scoundrel; as though that were any consolation to the scoundrel once he has come to realize that he actually is a scoundrel. But enough. . . . Ech, I have talked a lot of nonsense, but what have I explained? How is enjoyment in this to be explained? But I will explain it. I will get to the bottom of it! That is why I have taken up my pen. . . .

I, for instance, have a great deal of *amour propre*.* I am as suspicious and prone to take offence as a humpback or a dwarf. But upon my word I sometimes have had moments when if I had happened to be slapped in the face I should, perhaps, have been positively glad of it. I say, in earnest, that I should probably have been able to discover even in that a peculiar sort of enjoyment—the enjoyment, of course, of despair; but in despair there are the most intense enjoyments, especially when one is very acutely conscious of the hopelessness of one's position. And when one is slapped in the face—why then the consciousness of being rubbed into a pulp would positively overwhelm one. The worst of it is, look at it which way one will, it still turns out that I was always the most to blame in everything. And what is most humiliating of all, to blame for no fault of my own but, so to say, through the laws of nature. In the first place, to blame because I am cleverer than any of the people surrounding me. (I have always considered myself cleverer than any of the people surrounding me, and sometimes, would you believe it, have been positively ashamed of it. At any rate, I have all my life, as it were, turned my eyes away and never could look people straight in the face.) To blame, finally, because even if I had had magnanimity, I should only have had more suffering from the sense of its uselessness. I should certainly have never been able to do anything from being magnanimous—neither to forgive, for my assailant would perhaps have slapped me from the laws of nature, and one cannot forgive the laws of nature; nor to forget, for even if it were owing to the laws of nature, it is insulting all the same. Finally, even if I had wanted to be anything but magnanimous, had desired on the contrary to revenge myself on my assailant, I could not have revenged myself on any one for anything because I should certainly never have made up my mind to do anything, even if I had been able to. Why should I not have

---

*Pride, self-respect (French).

made up my mind? About that in particular I want to say a few words.

III

With people who know how to revenge themselves and to stand up for themselves in general, how is it done? Why, when they are possessed, let us suppose, by the feeling of revenge, then for the time there is nothing else but that feeling left in their whole being. Such a gentleman simply dashes straight for his object like an infuriated bull with its horns down, and nothing but a wall will stop him. (By the way: facing the wall, such gentlemen—that is, the "direct" persons and men of action—are genuinely nonplussed. For them a wall is not an evasion, as for us people who think and consequently do nothing; it is not an excuse for turning aside, an excuse for which we are always very glad, though we scarcely believe in it ourselves, as a rule. No, they are nonplussed in all sincerity. The wall has for them something tranquillizing, morally soothing, final—maybe even something mysterious . . . but of the wall later.)

Well, such a direct person I regard as the real normal man, as his tender mother nature wished to see him when she graciously brought him into being on the earth. I envy such a man till I am green in the face. He is stupid. I am not disputing that, but perhaps the normal man should be stupid, how do you know? Perhaps it is very beautiful, in fact. And I am the more persuaded of that suspicion, if one can call it so, by the fact that if you take, for instance, the antithesis of the normal man, that is, the man of acute consciousness, who has come, of course, not out of the lap of nature but out of a retort (this is almost mysticism, gentlemen, but I suspect this, too), this retort-made man is sometimes so nonplussed in the presence

of his antithesis that with all his exaggerated consciousness he
genuinely thinks of himself as a mouse and not a man. It may
be an acutely conscious mouse, yet it is a mouse, while the
other is a man, and therefore, et cætera, et cætera. And the
worst of it is, he himself, his very own self, looks on himself
as a mouse; no one asks him to do so; and that is an important point. Now let us look at this mouse in action. Let us suppose, for instance, that it feels insulted, too (and it almost
always does feel insulted), and wants to revenge itself, too.
There may even be a greater accumulation of spite in it than
in l'homme de la nature et de la vérité.[3] The base and nasty desire to
vent that spite on its assailant rankles perhaps even more nas-
tily in it than in l'homme de la nature et de la vérité. For through his
innate stupidity the latter looks upon his revenge as justice
pure and simple; while in consequence of his acute consciousness the mouse does not believe in the justice of it. To
come at last to the deed itself, to the very act of revenge. Apart
from the one fundamental nastiness the luckless mouse suc-
ceeds in creating around it so many other nastinesses in the
form of doubts and questions, adds to the one question so
many unsettled questions that there inevitably works up
around it a sort of fatal brew, a stinking mess, made up of its
doubts, emotions, and of the contempt spat upon it by the direct men of action who stand solemnly about it as judges and
arbitrators, laughing at it till their healthy sides ache. Of
course the only thing left for it is to dismiss all that with a
wave of its paw, and, with a smile of assumed contempt in
which it does not even itself believe, creep ignominiously into
its mouse-hole. There in its nasty, stinking, underground
home our insulted, crushed and ridiculed mouse promptly
becomes absorbed in cold, malignant and, above all, everlasting spite. For forty years together it will remember its injury
down to the smallest, most ignominious details, and every
time will add, of itself, details still more ignominious, spite-
fully teasing and tormenting itself with its own imagination.
It will itself be ashamed of its imaginings, but yet it will recall it all, it will go over and over every detail, it will invent

unheard of things against itself, pretending that those things might happen, and will forgive nothing. Maybe it will begin to revenge itself, too, but, as it were, piecemeal, in trivial ways, from behind the stove, incognito, without believing either in its own right to vengeance, or in the success of its revenge, knowing that from all its efforts at revenge it will suffer a hundred times more than he on whom it revenges itself, while he, I daresay, will not even scratch himself. On its deathbed it will recall it all over again, with interest accumulated over all the years and. . . .

But it is just in that cold, abominable half despair, half belief, in that conscious burying oneself alive for grief in the underworld for forty years, in that acutely recognized and yet partly doubtful hopelessness of one's position, in that hell of unsatisfied desires turned inward, in that fever of oscillations, of resolution determined for ever and repented of again a minute later—that the savour of that strange enjoyment of which I have spoken lies. It is so subtle, so difficult of analysis, that persons who are a little limited, or even simply persons of strong nerves, will not understand a single atom of it. "Possibly," you will add on your own account with a grin, "people will not understand it either who have never received a slap in the face," and in that way you will politely hint to me that I, too, perhaps, have had the experience of a slap in the face in my life, and so I speak as one who knows. I bet that you are thinking that. But set your minds at rest, gentlemen, I have not received a slap in the face, though it is absolutely a matter of indifference to me what you may think about it. Possibly, I even regret myself, that I have given so few slaps in the face during my life. But enough . . . not another word on that subject of such extreme interest to you.

I will continue calmly concerning persons with strong nerves who do not understand a certain refinement of enjoyment. Though in certain circumstances these gentlemen bellow their loudest like bulls, though this, let us suppose, does them the greatest credit, yet, as I have said already, confronted with the impossible they subside at once. The impossible means the stone wall! What stone wall? Why, of course, the laws of nature, the deductions of natural science, mathematics. As soon as they prove to you, for instance, that you are descended from a monkey,[4] then it is no use scowling, accept it for a fact. When they prove to you that in reality one drop of your own fat must be dearer to you than a hundred thousand of your fellow-creatures, and that this conclusion is the final solution of all so-called virtues and duties and all such prejudices and fancies, then you have just to accept it, there is no help for it for twice two is a law of mathematics. Just try refuting it.

"Upon my word, they will shout at you, it is no use protesting: it is a case of twice two makes four! Nature does not ask your permission, she has nothing to do with your wishes, and whether you like her laws or dislike them, you are bound to accept her as she is, and consequently all her conclusions. A wall, you see, is a wall . . . and so on, and so on."

Merciful Heavens! but what do I care for the laws of nature and arithmetic, when, for some reason I dislike those laws and the fact that twice two makes four? Of course I cannot break through the wall by battering my head against it if I really have not the strength to knock it down, but I am not going to be reconciled to it simply because it is a stone wall and I have not the strength.

As though such a stone wall really were a consolation, and really did contain some word of conciliation, simply because it is as true as twice two makes four. Oh, absurdity of absurdities! How much better it is to understand it all, to recognize it all, all the impossibilities and the stone wall; not to be reconciled to one of those impossibilities and stone walls if it disgusts you to be reconciled to it; by the way of the most inevitable, logical combinations to reach the most revolting conclusions on the everlasting theme, that even for the stone wall you are yourself somehow to blame, though again it is as clear as day you are not to blame in the least, and therefore grinding your teeth in silent impotence to sink into luxurious inertia, brooding on the fact that there is no one even for you to feel vindictive against, that you have not, and perhaps never will have, an object for your spite, that it is a sleight of hand, a bit of juggling, a card-sharper's trick, that it is simply a mess, no knowing what and no knowing who, but in spite of all these uncertainties and jugglings, still there is an ache in you, and the more you do not know, the worse the ache.

IV

"Ha, ha, ha! You will be finding enjoyment in toothache next," you cry, with a laugh.

"Well? Even in toothache there is enjoyment," I answer. I had toothache for a whole month and I know there is. In that case, of course, people are not spiteful in silence, but moan; but they are not candid moans, they are malignant moans, and the malignancy is the whole point. The enjoyment of the sufferer finds expression in those moans; if he did not feel enjoyment in them he would not moan. It is a good example, gentlemen, and I will develop it. Those moans express in the first place all the aimlessness of your pain, which is so humiliating to your consciousness; the whole legal system of nature on which you spit disdainfully, of course, but from which you suffer at the same while she does not. They express the consciousness that you have no enemy to punish, but that you have pain; the consciousness that in spite of all possible Vagenheims[5] you are in complete slavery to your teeth; that if some one wishes it, your teeth will leave off aching, and if he does not, they will go on aching another three months; and that finally if you are still contumacious and still protest, all that is left you for your own gratification is to thrash yourself or beat your wall with your fist as hard as you can, and absolutely nothing more. Well these mortal insults, these jeers on the part of some one unknown end at last in an enjoyment which sometimes reaches the highest degree of voluptuousness. I ask you, gentlemen, listen some-times to the moans of an educated man of the nineteenth century suffering from toothache, on the second or third day of the attack, when he is beginning to moan, not as he moaned on the first day, that is, not simply because he has toothache, not just as any coarse peasant, but as a man af-fected by progress and European civilization, a man who is "divorced from the soil and one's national origins,"[6] as they express it now-a-days. His moans become nasty, disgustingly malignant, and go on for whole days and nights. And of course he knows himself that he is doing himself no sort of good with his moans; he knows better than any one that he is only lacerating and harassing himself and others for noth-ing; he knows that even the audience before whom he is making his efforts, and his whole family, listen to him with loathing, do not put a ha'porth of faith in him, and inwardly understand that he might moan differently, more simply, without trills and flourishes, and that he is only amusing himself like that from ill-humour, from malignancy. Well, in all these recognitions and disgraces it is that there lies a voluptuous pleasure. As though he would say: "I am worry-ing you, I am lacerating your hearts, I am keeping every one in the house awake. Well, stay awake then, you, too, feel every minute that I have toothache. I am not a hero to you now, as I tried to seem before, but simply a nasty person, an impos-tor. Well, so be it, then! I am very glad that you see through me. It is nasty for you to hear my despicable moans: well, let it be nasty; here I will let you have a nastier flourish in a minute. . . ." You do not understand even now, gentlemen? No, it seems our development and our consciousness must go further to understand all the intricacies of this pleasure. You laugh? Delighted. My jests, gentlemen, are of course in bad taste, jerky, involved, lacking self-confidence. But of course that is because I do not respect myself. Can a man of perception respect himself at all?

V

Come, can a man who attempts to find enjoyment in the very feeling of his own degradation possibly have a spark of respect for himself? I am not saying this now from any mawkish kind of remorse. And, indeed, I could never endure saying, "Forgive me, Papa, I won't do it again," not because I am incapable of saying that—on the contrary, perhaps just because I have been too capable of it, and in what a way, too! As though of design I used to get into trouble in cases when I was not to blame in any way. That was the nastiest part of it. At the same time I was genuinely touched and penitent, I used to shed tears and, of course, deceived myself, though I was not acting in the least and there was a sick feeling in my heart at the time. . . . For that one could not blame even the laws of nature, though the laws of nature have continually all my life offended me more than anything. It is loathsome to remember it all, but it was loathsome even then. Of course, a minute or so later I would realize wrathfully that it was all a lie, a revolting lie, an affected lie, that is, all this penitence, this emotion, these vows of reform. You will ask why did I worry myself with such antics: answer, because it was very dull to sit with one's hands folded, and so one began cutting capers. That is really it. Observe yourselves more carefully, gentlemen, then you will understand that it is so. I invented adventures for myself and made up a life, so as at least to live in some way. How many times it has happened to me—well, for instance, to take offence simply on purpose, for nothing; and one knows oneself, of course, that one is offended at nothing, that one is putting it on, but yet one brings oneself, at last to the point of being really offended. All my life I have had an impulse to play such pranks, so that in the end I could not control it in myself. Another time, twice, in fact, I tried hard to be in love. I suffered, too, gentlemen, I assure you. In the depth of my heart there was no faith in my suffering, only a faint stir of mockery, but yet I did suffer, and in the real, orthodox way; I was jealous, beside myself . . . and it was all from boredom, gentlemen, all from boredom; inertia overcame me. You know the direct, legitimate fruit of consciousness is inertia, that is, conscious sitting-with-the-hands-folded. I have referred to this already. I repeat, I repeat with emphasis: all "direct" persons and men of action are active just because they are stupid and limited. How explain that? I will tell you: in consequence of their limitation they take immediate and secondary causes for primary ones, and in that way persuade themselves more quickly and easily than other people do that they have found an infallible foundation for their activity, and their minds are at ease and you know that is the chief thing. To begin to act, you know, you must first have your mind completely at ease and no trace of doubt left in it. Why, how am I, for example to set my mind at rest? Where are the primary causes on which I am to build? Where are my foundations? Where am I to get them from? I exercise myself in reflection, and consequently with me every primary cause at once draws after itself another still more primary, and so on to infinity. That is just the essence of every sort of consciousness and reflection. It must be a case of the laws of nature again. What is the result of it in the end? Why, just the same. Remember I spoke just now of vengeance. (I am sure you did not take it in.) I said that a man revenges himself because he sees justice in it. Therefore he has found a primary cause, that is, justice. And so he is at rest on all sides, and consequently he carries out his revenge calmly and successfully, being persuaded that he is doing a just and honest thing. But I see no justice in it, I find no sort of virtue in it either, and consequently if I attempt to revenge myself, it is only out of spite. Spite, of course, might overcome everything, all my doubts, and so might serve quite successfully in place of a primary cause, precisely because it is not a cause. But what is to be done[7] if I have not even spite (I began with that just now, you know). In consequence again of those accursed laws of consciousness, anger in me is subject to chemical disintegration. You look into it, the object flies off into air, your reasons evaporate, the criminal is not to be found, the wrong becomes not a wrong but a phantom, something like the toothache, for which no one is to blame, and consequently there is only the same outlet left again—that is, to beat the wall as hard as you can. So you give it up with a wave of the hand because you have not found a fundamental cause. And try letting yourself be carried away by your feelings, blindly, without reflection, without a primary cause, repelling consciousness at least for a time; hate or love, if only not to sit with your hands folded. The day after to-morrow, at the latest, you will begin despising yourself for having knowingly deceived yourself. Result: a soap-bubble and inertia. Oh, gentlemen, do you know, perhaps I consider myself an intelligent man, only because all my life I have been able neither to begin nor to finish anything. Granted I am a babbler, a harmless vexatious babbler, like all of us. But what is to be done if the direct and sole vocation of every intelligent man is babble, that is, the intentional pouring of water through a sieve?

VI

Oh, if I had done nothing simply from laziness! Heavens, how I should have respected myself, then. I should have respected myself because I should at least have been capable of being lazy; there would at least have been one quality, as it were, positive in me, in which I could have believed myself. Question: What is he? Answer: A sluggard; how very pleasant it would have been to hear that of oneself! It would mean that I was positively defined, it would mean that there was something to say about me. "Sluggard"—why, it is a calling and vocation, it is a career. Do not jest, it is so. I should then be a member of the best club by right, and should find my occupation in continually respecting myself. I knew a gentleman who prided himself all his life on being a connoisseur of Lafitte.* He considered this as his positive virtue, and never doubted himself. He died, not simply with a tranquil, but with a triumphant, conscience, and he was quite right, too. Then I should have chosen a career for myself, I should have been a sluggard and a glutton, not a simple one, but, for instance, one with sympathies for everything good and beautiful. How do you like that? I have long had visions of it. That "good and beautiful" weighs heavily on my mind at forty. But that is at forty; then—oh, then it would have been different! I should have found for myself a form of activity in keeping with it, to be precise, drinking to the health of everything "good and beautiful." I should have snatched at every opportunity to drop a tear into my glass and then to drain it to all that is "good and beautiful." I should then have turned everything into the good and the beautiful; in the nastiest, unquestionable trash, I should have sought out the good and the beautiful. I should have exuded tears like a wet sponge. An artist, for instance, paints a picture worthy of Ge.[8] At once I drink to the health of the artist who painted the picture worthy of Ge, because I love all that is "beautiful and sublime." An author has written *As you will*:[9] at once I drink to the health of "any one you will" because I love all that is "beautiful and sublime."

I should claim respect for doing so. I should persecute any one who would not show me respect. I should live at ease, I should die with dignity, why, it is charming, perfectly charming! And what a good round belly I should have grown, what a treble chin I should have established, what a ruby nose I should have coloured for myself, so that every one would have said, looking at me: "Here is an asset! Here is something real and

---

*A French red wine.

solid!" And, say what you like, it is very agreeable to hear such remarks about oneself in this negative age.

VII

But these are all golden dreams. Oh, tell me, who was it first announced, who was it first proclaimed, that man only does nasty things because he does not know his own interests; and that if he were enlightened, if his eyes were opened to his real normal interests, man would at once cease to do nasty things, would at once become good and noble because, being enlightened and understanding his real advantage, he would see his own advantage in the good and nothing else, and we all know that not one man can, consciously, act against his own interests, consequently, so to say, through necessity, he would begin doing good? Oh, the babe! Oh, the pure, innocent child! Why, in the first place, when in all these thousands of years has there been a time when man has acted only from his own interest? What is to be done with the millions of facts that bear witness that men, *consciously*, that is fully understanding their real interests, have left them in the background and have rushed headlong on another path, to meet peril and danger, compelled to this course by nobody and by nothing, but, as it were, simply disliking the beaten track, and have obstinately, wilfully, struck out another difficult, absurd way, seeking it almost in the darkness. So, I suppose, this obstinacy and perversity were pleasanter to them than any advantage. . . . Advantage! What is advantage? And will you take it upon yourself to define with perfect accuracy in what the advantage of man consists? And what if it so happens that a man's advantage, *sometimes*, not only may, but even must, consist in his desiring in certain cases what is harmful to himself and not advantageous. And if so, if there can be such a case, the whole principle falls into dust.

What do you think—are there such cases? You laugh; laugh
away, gentlemen, but only answer me: have man's advantages
been reckoned up with perfect certainty? Are there not some
which not only have not been included but cannot possibly be
included under any classification? You see, you gentlemen have,
to the best of my knowledge, taken your whole register of
human advantages from the averages of statistical figures and
politico-economical formulas. Your advantages are prosperity,
wealth, freedom, peace—and so on, and so on. So that the man
who should, for instance, go openly and knowingly in opposition to all that list would, to your thinking, and indeed mine,
too, of course, be an obscurantist or an absolute madman:
would not he? But, you know, this is what is surprising: why
does it so happen that all these statisticians, sages and lovers of
humanity, when they reckon up human advantages invariably
leave out one? They don't even take it into their reckoning in the
form in which it should be taken, and the whole reckoning depends upon that. It would be no great matter, they would simply have to take it, this advantage, and add it to the list. But the
trouble is, that this strange advantage does not fall under any
classification and is not in place in any list. I have a friend for
instance . . . Ech! gentlemen, but of course he is your friend,
too; and indeed there is no one, no one, to whom he is not a
friend! When he prepares for any undertaking this gentleman
immediately explains to you, elegantly and clearly, exactly how
he must act in accordance with the laws of reason and truth.
What is more, he will talk to you with excitement and passion
of the true normal interests of man; with irony he will upbraid
the shortsighted fools who do not understand their own interests nor the true significance of virtue; and, within a quarter of
an hour, without any sudden outside provocation, but simply
through something inside him which is stronger than all his interests—he will go off on quite a different tack—that is, act in
dire opposition to what he has just been saying about himself
in opposition to the laws of reason, in opposition to his own
advantage, in fact in opposition to everything . . . I warn you
that my friend is a compound personality, and therefore it is

difficult to blame him as an individual. The fact is, gentlemen, it seems there must really exist something that is dear to almost every man than his greatest advantages, or (not to be illogical) there is a most advantageous advantage (the very one omitted of which we spoke just now) which is more important and more advantageous than all other advantages, for the sake of which a man if necessary is ready to act in opposition to all laws; that is, in opposition to reason, honour, peace, prosperity—in fact, in opposition to all those excellent and useful things if only he can attain that fundamental, most advantageous advantage which is dearer to him than all. "Yes, but it is advantage all the same," you will retort. But excuse me, I'll make the point clear, and it is not a case of playing upon words. What matters is, that this advantage is remarkable from the very fact that it breaks down all our classifications, and continually shatters every system constructed by lovers of mankind for their benefit of mankind. In fact, it upsets everything. But before I mention this advantage to you, I want to compromise myself personally, and therefore I boldly declare that all these fine systems, all these theories for explaining to mankind their real normal interests, in order that inevitably striving to pursue these interests they may at once become good and noble—are in my opinion, so far, mere logical exercises! Yes, logical exercises. Why, to maintain this theory of the regeneration of mankind by means of the pursuit of his own advantage is to my mind almost the same thing as . . . as to affirm, for instance, following Buckle, that through civilization mankind becomes softer, and consequently less bloodthirsty and less fitted for warfare.[10] Logically it does not seem to follow from his arguments. But man has such a predilection for systems and abstract deductions that he is ready to distort the truth intentionally, he is ready to deny the evidence of his senses only to justify his logic. I take this example because it is the most glaring instance of it. Only look about you: blood is being spilt in streams, and in the merriest way, as though it were champagne. Take the whole of the nineteenth century in which Buckle lived. Take Napoleon—the Great and also the present one. Take North America—the eter-

nal union. Take the farce of Schleswig-Holstein[11]. . . . And what
is it that civilization softens in us? The only gain of civilization
for mankind is the greater capacity for variety of sensations—
and absolutely nothing more. And through the development of
this many-sidedness man may come to finding enjoyment in
bloodshed. In fact, this has already happened to him. Have you
noticed that it is the most civilized gentlemen who have been
the subtlest slaughterers, to whom the Attilas and Stenka Razins
could not hold a candle,[12] and if they are not so conspicuous as
the Attilas and Stenka Razins it is simply because they are so
often met with, are so ordinary and have become so familiar to
us. In any case civilization has made mankind if not more
bloodthirsty, at least more vilely, more loathsomely bloodthirsty.
In old days he saw justice in bloodshed and with his conscience
at peace exterminated those he thought proper. Now we do
think bloodshed abominable and yet we engage in this abomi-
nation, and with more energy than ever. Which is worse? Decide that for yourselves. They say that Cleopatra (excuse an
instance from Roman history) was fond of sticking gold pins
into her slave-girls' breasts and derived gratification from their
screams and writhings.[13] You will say that that was in the comparatively barbarous times; that these are barbarous times too,
because also, comparatively speaking, pins are stuck in even
now; that though man has now learned to see more clearly than
in barbarous ages, he is still far from having learnt to act as reason and science would dictate. But yet you are fully convinced
that he will be sure to learn when he gets rid of certain old bad
habits, and when common sense and science have completely
re-educated human nature and turned it in a normal direction.
You are confident that then man will cease from intentional error
and will, some say, be compelled not to want to set his will
against his normal interests. That is not all; then, you say, science
itself will teach man (though to my mind it's a superfluous luxury) that he never has really had any caprice or will of his own,
and that he himself is something of the nature of a piano-key
or the stop of an organ[14] and that there are, besides, things
called the laws of nature so that everything he does is not done

by his willing it, but done of itself, by the laws of nature. Consequently we have only to discover these laws of nature, and man will no longer have to answer for his actions and life will become exceedingly easy for him. All human actions will then, of course, be tabulated according to these laws, mathematically, like tables of logarithms up to 108,000, and entered in an index; or, better still, there would be published certain edifying works of the nature of encyclopedic lexicons, in which everything will be so clearly calculated and explained that there will be no more incidents or adventures in the world.

Then—this is all what you say—new economic relations will be established, all ready-made and worked out with mathematical exactitude, so that every possible question will vanish in the twinkling of an eye, simply because every possible answer then will be provided. Then a cystal palace[15] will be built Then. . . . In fact, those will be halcyon days. Of course there is no guaranteeing (this is my comment) that it will not be, for instance, frightfully dull then (for what will one have to do when everything will be calculated and tabulated), but on the other hand everything will be extraordinary rational. Of course, boredom may lead you to anything. It is boredom sets our sticking golden pins into people, but all that would not matter. What is bad (this is my comment again) is that I dare say people will be thankful for the gold pins then. Man is stupid, you know, phenomenally stupid; or rather he is not at all stupid but he is so ungrateful that you could not find another like him in all creation. I, for instance, would not be in the least surprised if all of a sudden, à propos of nothing, in the midst of general prosperity a gentleman with an ignoble, or rather with a reactionary and ironical, countenance were to arise and putting his arms akimbo, say to us all: "I say, gentlemen, hadn't we better kick over the whole show and scatter rationalism to the winds, simply to send these logarithms to the devil, and to enable us to live once more at our own sweet foolish will!" That again would not matter; but what is annoying is that he would be sure to find followers—such is the nature of man. And all that for the most foolish reason, which, one would think, was hardly worth

mentioning: that is, that man everywhere and at all times, whoever he may be, has preferred to act as he chose and not in the
least as his reason and advantage dictated. And one may choose
what is contrary to one's own interests, and sometimes one positively ought (that is my idea). One's own free unfettered choice,
one's own caprice, however wild it may be, one's own fancy
worked up at times to frenzy—is that very "most advantageous
advantage" which we have overlooked, which comes under no
classification and against which all systems and theories are
continually being shattered to atoms. And how do these
wiseacres know that man wants a normal, a virtuous choice?
What has made them conceive that man must want a rationally
advantageous choice? What man wants is simply independent
choice, whatever that independence may cost and wherever it
may lead. And choice, of course, the devil only knows what
choice.

VIII

"Ha! ha! ha! But you know there is no such thing as
choice in reality, say what you like," you will inter-
pose with a chuckle. "Science has succeeded in so far
analysing man that we know already that choice and what is
called freedom of will is nothing else than——"

Stay, gentlemen, I meant to begin with that myself. I confess,
I was rather frightened. I was just going to say that the devil
only knows what choice depends on, and that perhaps that was
a very good thing, but I remembered the teaching of science . . . and pulled myself up. And here you have begun upon
it. Indeed, if there really is some day discovered a formula for
all our desires and caprices—that is, an explanation of what
they depend upon, by what laws they arise, how they develop,
what they are aiming at in one case and in another and so on,

that is a real mathematical formula—then, most likely man will at once cease to feel desire, indeed, he will be certain to. For who would want to choose by rule? Besides, he will at once be transformed from a human being into an organ-stop or something of the sort; for what is a man without desires, without free will and without choice, if not a stop in an organ? What do you think? Let us reckon the chances—can such a thing happen or not?

"H'm!" you decide. "Our choice is usually mistaken from a false view of our advantage. We sometimes choose absolute nonsense because in our foolishness we see in that nonsense the easiest means for attaining a supposed advantage. But when all that is explained and worked out on paper (which is perfectly possible, for it is contemptible and senseless to suppose that some laws of nature man will never understand), then certainly so-called desires will no longer exist. For if a desire should come into conflict with reason we shall then reason and not desire because it will be impossible retaining our reason to be *senseless* in our desires, and in that way knowingly act against reason and desire to injure ourselves. And as all choice and reasoning can be really calculated—because there will some day be discovered the laws of our so-called free will—so, joking apart there may one day be something like a table constructed of them, so that we really shall choose in accordance with it. If for instance, some day they calculate and prove to me that I have made a fig at some one[16] because I could not help making it and that I had to do it in that particular way, what remains *free* in me, especially if I am a learned man and have taken my degree somewhere? Then I should be able to calculate my whole life for thirty years beforehand. In short, if this could be arranged there would be nothing left for us to do anyway, we should have to understand that. And, in fact, we ought unwearyingly to repeat to ourselves that at such and such time and in such and such circumstances nature does not ask our leave; that we have got to take her as she is and not fashion her to suit our fancy, and if we really aspire to formulas and tables of rules, and well, even . . . to the chemical retort, there's no help for it, we must accept the retort too, or else we will be accepted without our consent. . . ."

Yes, but here I come to a stop! Gentlemen, you must excuse me for being over-philosophical: it's the result of forty years underground! Allow me to indulge my fancy. You see, gentlemen, reason is an excellent thing, there's no disputing that, but reason is nothing but reason and satisfies only the rational side of man's nature, while will is a manifestation of the whole life, that is, of the whole human life including reason and all the impulses. And although our life, in this manifestation of it, is often worthless, yet it is life and not simply extracting square roots. Here I, for instance, quite naturally want to live, in order to satisfy all my capacities for life, and not simply my capacity for reasoning, that is, not simply one twentieth of my capacity for life. What does reason know? Reason only knows what it has succeeded in learning (some things, perhaps, it will never learn; this is a poor comfort, but why not say so frankly?) and human nature acts as a whole, with everything that is in it, consciously or unconsciously, and, even if it goes wrong, it lives. I suspect, gentlemen, that you are looking at me with compassion; you tell me again that an enlightened and developed man, such, in short, as the future man will be, cannot consciously desire anything disadvantageous to himself, that that can be proved mathematically. I thoroughly agree, it can—by mathematics. But I repeat for the hundredth time, there is one case, one only, when man may consciously, purposely, desire what is injurious to himself, what is stupid, very stupid—simply in order to have the right to desire for himself even what is very stupid and not to be bound by an obligation to desire only what is sensible. Of course, this very stupid thing, this caprice of ours, may be in reality, gentlemen, more advantageous for us than anything else on earth, especially in certain cases. And in particular it may be more advantageous than any advantage even when it does us obvious harm, and contradicts the soundest conclusions of our reason concerning our advantage—for in any circumstances it preserves for us what is most precious and most important—that is, our personality, our individuality.

Some, you see, maintain that this really is the most precious thing for mankind; choice can, of course, if it chooses, be in agreement with reason; and especially if this be not abused but kept within bounds. It is profitable and sometimes even praiseworthy. But very often, and even most often, choice is utterly and stubbornly opposed to reason . . . and . . . and . . . do you know that that, too, is profitable, sometimes even praiseworthy? Gentlemen, let us suppose that man is not stupid. (Indeed one cannot refuse to suppose that, if only from the one consideration, that, if man is stupid, then who is wise?) But if he is not stupid, he is monstrously ungrateful! Phenomenally ungrateful. In fact, I believe that the best definition of man is the ungrateful biped. But that is not all, that is not his worst defect; his worst defect is his perpetual moral obliquity, perpetual—from the days of the Flood to the Schleswig-Holstein period. Moral obliquity and consequently lack of good sense for it has long been accepted that lack of good sense is due to no other cause than moral obliquity. Put it to the test and cast your eyes upon the history of mankind. What will you see? Is it a grand spectacle? Grand, if you like. Take the Colossus of Rhodes, for instance, that's worth something. With good reason Mr. Anaevsky[17] testifies of it that some say that it is the work of man's hands, while others maintain that it has been created by nature herself. Is it many-coloured? May be it is many-coloured, too: if one takes the dress uniforms, military and civilian, of all peoples in all ages—that alone is worth something, and if you take the undress uniforms you will never get to the end of it; no historian would be equal to the job. Is it monotonous? May be it's monotonous too: it's fighting and fighting; they are fighting now, they fought first and they fought last—you will admit, that it is almost too monotonous. In short, one may say anything about the history of the world—anything that might enter the most disordered imagination. The only thing one can't say is that it's rational. The very word sticks in one's throat. And, indeed, this is the odd thing that is continually happening: there are continually turning up in life moral and rational persons, sages and lovers of humanity who make it their object to live all their lives as morally and rationally as possible, to be, so to speak, a light to their neighbours simply in order to show them that it is possible to live morally and rationally in this world. And yet we all know that those very people sooner or later have been false to themselves, playing some queer trick, often a most unseemly one. Now I ask you: what can be expected of man since he is a being endowed with such strange qualities? Shower upon him every earthly blessing, drown him in a sea of happiness, so that nothing but bubbles of bliss can be seen on the surface; give him economic prosperity, such that he should have nothing else to do but sleep, eat cakes and busy himself with the continuation of his species, and even then out of sheer ingratitude, sheer spite, man would play you some nasty trick. He would even risk his cakes and would deliberately desire the most fatal rubbish, the most uneconomical absurdity, simply to introduce into all this positive good sense his fatal fantastic element. It is just his fantastic dreams, his vulgar folly that he will desire to retain, simply in order to prove to himself—as though that were so necessary—that men still are men and not the keys of a piano, which the laws of nature threaten to control so completely that soon one will be able to desire nothing but by the calendar. And that is not all: even if man really were nothing but a piano-key, even if this were proved to him by natural science and mathematics, even then he would not become reasonable, but would purposely do something perverse out of simple ingratitude, simply to gain his point. And if he does not find means he will contrive destruction and chaos, will contrive sufferings of all sorts, only to gain his point! He will launch a curse upon the world, and as only man can curse (it is his privilege, the primary distinction between him and other animals), may be by his curse alone he will attain his object—that is, convince himself that he is a man and not a piano-key! If you say that all this, too, can be calculated and tabulated—chaos and darkness and curses, so that the mere possibility of calculating it all beforehand would stop it all, and reason would reassert itself, then man would purposely go mad in order to be rid of reason and gain his point! I believe in it, I answer for it, for the whole work of man really seems to consist in nothing but proving to himself every minute that he is a man and not a piano-key! It may be at the cost of his skin, it may be by cannibalism! And this being so, can one help being tempted to rejoice that it has not yet come off, and that desire still depends on something we don't know?

You will scream at me (that is, if you condescend to do so) that no one is touching my free will, that all they are concerned with is that my will should of itself, of its own free will, coincide with my own normal interests, with the laws of nature and arithmetic.

Good Heavens, gentlemen, what sort of free will is left when we come to tabulation and arithmetic, when it will all be a case of twice two make four? Twice two makes four without my will. As if free will meant that!

IX

Gentlemen, I am joking, and I know myself that my jokes are not brilliant, but you know one can't take everything as a joke. I am, perhaps, jesting against the grain. Gentlemen, I am tormented by questions; answer them for me. You, for instance, want to cure men of their old habits and reform their will in accordance with science and good sense. But how do you know, not only that it is possible, but also that it is *desirable* to reform man in that way? And what leads you to the conclusion that man's inclinations *need* reforming? In short, how do you know that such a reformation will be a benefit to man? And to go to the root of the matter, why are you so positively convinced that not to act against his real normal interests guaranteed by the conclusions of reason and arithmetic is certainly always advantageous for man and must always be a law for mankind? So far, you know, this is only your supposition. It may be the law of logic, but not the law of humanity. You think, gentlemen, perhaps that I am mad. Allow me to defend myself. I agree that man is pre-eminently a creative animal, predestined to strive consciously for an object and to engage in engineering—that is, incessantly and eternally to make new roads, *wherever they may lead*. But the reason why he wants sometimes to go off at a tangent may just be that he is *predestined* to make the road, and perhaps, too, that however stupid the "direct" practical man may be, the thought sometimes will occur to him that the road almost always does lead *somewhere*, and that the destination it leads to is less important than the process of making it, and that the chief thing is to save the well-conducted child from despising engineering, and so giving way to the fatal idleness, which, as we all know, is the mother of all the vices. Man likes to make roads and to create, that is a fact beyond dispute. But why has he such a passionate love for destruction and chaos also? Tell me that! But on that point I want to say a couple of words myself. May it not be that he loves chaos and destruction (there can be no disputing that he does sometimes love it) because he is instinctively afraid of attaining his object and completing the edifice he is constructing? Who knows, perhaps he only loves that edifice from a distance, and is by no means in love with it at close quarters; perhaps he only loves building it and does not want to live in it, but will leave it, when completed, for the use of *les animaux domestiques** such as the ants, the sheep, and so on. Now the ants have quite a different taste. They have a marvellous edifice of that pattern which endures for ever—the ant-hill.

With the ant-hill the respectable race of ants began and with the ant-hill they will probably end, which does the greatest credit to their perseverance and good sense. But man is a frivolous and incongruous creature, and perhaps, like a chess player, loves the process of the game, not the end of it. And who knows (there is no saying with certainty), perhaps the only goal on

---

*The domestic animals (French).

earth to which mankind is striving lies in this incessant process of attaining, in other words, in life itself, and not in the thing to be attained, which must always be expressed as a formula, as positive as twice two makes four, and such positiveness is not life, gentlemen, but is the beginning of death. Anyway, man has always been afraid of this mathematical certainty, and I am afraid of it now. Granted that man does nothing but seek that mathematical certainty, he traverses oceans, sacrifices his life in the quest, but to succeed, really to find it, he dreads, I assure you. He feels that when he has found it there will be nothing for him to look for. When workmen have finished their work they do at least receive their pay, they go to the tavern, then they are taken to the police-station—and there is occupation for a week. But where can man go? Anyway, one can observe a certain awkwardness about him when he has attained such objects. He loves the process of attaining, but does not quite like to have attained, and that, of course, is very absurd. In fact, man is a comical creature; there seems to be a kind of jest in it all. But yet mathematical certainty is, after all, something insufferable. Twice two makes four seems to me simply a piece of insolence. Twice two makes four is a pert coxcomb who stands with arms akimbo barring your path and spitting. I admit that twice two makes four is an excellent thing, but if we are to give everything its due, twice two makes five is sometimes a very charming thing too.

And why are you so firmly, so triumphantly, convinced that only the normal and the positive—in other words, only what is conducive to welfare—is for the advantage of man? Is not reason in error as regards advantage? Does not man, perhaps, love something besides well-being? Perhaps he is just as fond of suffering? Perhaps suffering is just as great a benefit to him as well-being? Man is sometimes extraordinarily, passionately, in love with suffering, and that is a fact. There is no need to appeal to universal history to prove that; only ask yourself, if you are a man and have lived at all. As far as my personal opinion is concerned, to care only for well-being seems to me positively ill-bred. Whether it's good or bad, it is sometimes very pleasant, too, to smash things. I hold no brief for suffering nor for well-being either. I am standing for . . . my caprice, and for its being guaranteed to me when necessary. Suffering would be out of place in vaudevilles, for instance; I know that. In a crystal palace it is unthinkable; suffering means doubt, negation, and what would be the good of a crystal palace if there could be any doubt about it? And yet I think man will never renounce real suffering, that is, destruction and chaos. Why, suffering is the sole origin of consciousness. Though I did lay it down at the beginning that consciousness is the greatest misfortune for man, yet I know man prizes it and would not give it up for any satisfaction. Consciousness, for instance, is infinitely superior to twice two makes four. Once you have mathematical certainty there is nothing left to do or to understand. There will be nothing left but to bottle up your five senses and plunge into contemplation. While if you stick to consciousness, even though the same result is attained, you can at least flog yourself at times, and that will, at any rate, liven you up. Reactionary as it is, corporal punishment is better than nothing.

X

You believe in a crystal palace that can never be destroyed—a palace at which one will not be able to put out one's tongue on the sly or make a fig in one's pocket. And perhaps that is just why I am afraid of this edifice, that it is of crystal and can never be destroyed and that one cannot put one's tongue out at it even on the sly.

You see, if it were not a palace, but a hen-house, I might creep into it to avoid getting wet, and yet I would not call the hen-house a palace out of gratitude to it for keeping me dry. You laugh and say that in such circumstances a hen-house is as good as a mansion. Yes, I answer, if one had to live simply to keep out of the rain.

But what is to be done if I have taken it into my head that that is not the only object in life, and that if one must live one had better live in a mansion. That is my choice, my desire. You will only eradicate it when you have changed my preference. Well, do change it, allure me with something else, give me another ideal. But meanwhile I will not take a hen-house for a mansion. The crystal palace may be an idle dream, it may be that it is inconsistent with the laws of nature and that I have invented it only through my own stupidity, through the old-fashioned irrational habits of my generation. But what does it matter to me that it is inconsistent? That makes no difference since it exists in my desires, or rather exists as long as my desires exist. Perhaps you are laughing again? Laugh away; I will put up with any mockery rather than pretend that I am satisfied when I am hungry. I know, anyway, that I will not be put off with a compromise, with a recurring zero, simply because it is consistent with the laws of nature and actually exists. I will not accept as the crown of my desires a block of buildings with tenements for the poor on a lease of a thousand years, and perhaps with a sign-board of a dentist hanging out. Destroy my desires, eradicate my ideals, show me something better, and I will follow you. You will say, perhaps, that it is not worth your trouble; but in that case I can give you the same answer. We are discussing things seriously; but if you won't deign to give me your attention, I will drop your acquaintance. I can retreat into my underground hole.

But while I am alive and have desires I would rather my hand were withered off than bring one brick to such a building! Don't remind me that I have just rejected the crystal palace for the sole reason that one cannot put out one's tongue at it. I did not say because I am so fond of putting my tongue out. Perhaps the thing I resented was, that of all your edifices there has not been one at which one could not put out one's tongue. On the contrary, I would let my tongue be cut off out of gratitude if things could be so arranged that I should lose all desire to put it out. It is not my fault that things cannot be so arranged, and that one must be satisfied with model flats. Then why am I made with such desires? Can I have been constructed simply in order to come to the conclusion that all my construction is a cheat? Can this be my whole purpose? I do not believe it.

But do you know what: I am convinced that we underground folk ought to be kept on a curb. Though we may sit forty years underground without speaking, when we do come out into the light of day and break out we talk and talk and talk. . . .

XI

The long and the short of it is, gentlemen, that it is better to do nothing! Better conscious inertia! And so hurrah for underground! Though I have said that I envy the normal man to the last drop of my bile, yet I should not care to be in his place such as he is now (though I shall not cease envying him). No, no; anyway the underground life is more advantageous. There, at any rate, one can. . . . Oh, but even now I am lying. I am lying because I know myself just like two times two that the underground is not better, something different is, something quite different, which I thirst for, but which I cannot find at all! To the devil with the underground!

I will tell you another thing that would be better, and that is, if I myself believed in anything of what I have just written. I swear to you, gentlemen, there is not one thing, not one word of what I have written that I really believe. That is, I believe it, perhaps, but at the same time I feel and suspect that I am lying like a cobbler.

"Then why have you written all this?" you will say to me. "I ought to put you underground for forty years without anything to do and then come to you in your cellar, to find out what stage you have reached! How can a man be left alone with nothing to do for forty years?"

"Isn't that shameful, isn't that humiliating?" you will say, perhaps, wagging your heads contemptuously. "You thirst for life and try to settle the problems of life by a logical tangle. And how persistent, how insolent are your sallies, and at the same time what a scare you are in! You talk nonsense and are pleased with it; you say impudent things and are in continual alarm and apologizing for them. You declare that you are afraid of nothing and at the same time try to ingratiate yourself in our good opinion. You declare that you are gnashing your teeth and at the same time you try to be witty so as to amuse us. You know that your witticisms are not witty, but you are evidently well satisfied with their literary value. You may, perhaps, have really suffered, but you have no respect for your own suffering. You may have sincerity, but you have no modesty; out of the pettiest vanity you expose your sincerity to publicity and ignominy. You doubtlessly mean to say something, but hide your last word through fear, because you have not the resolution to utter it, and only have a cowardly impudence. You boast of consciousness, but you are not sure of your ground, for though your mind works, yet your heart is darkened and corrupt, and you cannot have a full, genuine consciousness without a pure heart. And how intrusive you are, how you insist and grimace! Lies, lies, lies!"

Of course I have myself made up all the things you say. That, too, is from underground. I have been for forty years listening to you through a crack under the floor. I have invented them myself, there was nothing else I could invent. It is no wonder that I have learned it by heart and it has taken a literary form . . .

But can you really be so credulous as to think that I will print all this and give it to you to read too? And another problem: why do I call you "gentlemen," why do I address you as though you really were my readers? Such confessions as I intend to make are never printed nor given to other people to read. Anyway, I am not strong-minded enough for that, and I don't see why I should be. But you see a fancy has occurred to me and I want to realize it at all costs. Let me explain.

Every man has memories which he would not tell to everyone, but only to his friends. He has other matters in his mind which he would not reveal even to his friends, but only to himself, and that in secret. But there are other things which a man is afraid to tell even to himself, and every decent man has a number of such things stored away in his mind. The more decent he is, the greater the number of such things in his mind. Anyway, I have only lately determined to remember some of my early adventures. Till now I have always avoided them, even with a certain uneasiness. Now, when I am not only recalling them, but have actually decided to write an account of them, I want to try the experiment whether one can, even with oneself, be perfectly open and not take fright at the whole truth. I will observe, in parenthesis, that Heine says that a true autobiography is almost an impossibility, and that man is bound to lie about himself. He considers that Rousseau certainly told lies about himself in his confessions, and even intentionally lied, out of vanity.[18] I am convinced that Heine is right; I quite understand how sometimes one may, out of sheer vanity, attribute regular crimes to oneself, and indeed I can very well conceive that kind of vanity. But Heine judged of people who made their confessions to the public. I write only for myself, and I wish to declare once and for all that if I write as though I were addressing readers, that is simply because it is easier for me to write in that form. It is a form, an empty form—I shall never have readers. I have made this plain already . . .

I don't wish to be hampered by any restrictions in the compilation of my notes. I shall not attempt any system or method. I will jot things down as I remember them.

But here, perhaps, some one will catch at the word and ask me: if you really don't reckon on readers, why do you make such compacts with yourself—and on paper too—that is, that you won't attempt any system or method, that you jot things down as you remember them, and so on, and so on? Why are you explaining? Why do you apologize?

Well, there it is, I answer.

There is a whole psychology in all this, though. Perhaps it is simply that I am a coward. And perhaps that I purposely imagine an audience before me in order that I may be more dignified while I write. There are perhaps thousands of reasons. Again, what is my object precisely in writing? If it is not for the benefit of the public why should I not simply recall these incidents in my own mind without putting them on paper?

Quite so; but yet it is more imposing on paper. There is something more impressive in it; I shall be better able to criticize and improve my style. Besides, I shall perhaps obtain actual relief from writing. To-day, for instance, I am particularly oppressed by one memory of a distant past. It came back vividly to my mind a few days ago, and has remained haunting me like an annoying tune that one cannot get rid of. And yet I must get rid of it somehow. I have hundreds of such reminiscences; but at times some one stands out from the hundred and oppresses me. For some reason I believe that if I write it down I should get rid of it. Why not try?

Besides, I am bored, and I never have anything to do. Writing will be a sort of work. They say work makes man kind-hearted and honest. Well, here is a chance for me, anyway.

Snow is falling to-day, yellow and dingy. It fell yesterday, too, and a few days ago. I fancy it is the wet snow that has reminded me of that incident which I cannot shake off now. And so let it be a story *à propos* of the falling snow.

PART II

À PROPOS OF THE WET SNOW[19]

When from dark error's subjugation
My words of passionate exhortation
    Had wrenched thy fainting spirit free;
And writhing prone in thine affliction
Thou didst recall with malediction
    The vice that had encompassed thee:
And when thy slumbering conscience, fretting
    By recollection's torturing flame,
Thou didst reveal the hideous setting
    Of thy life's current ere I came:
When suddenly I saw thee sicken,
    And weeping, hide thine anguished face,
Revolted, maddened, horror-stricken,
    At memories of foul disgrace.[20]

            NEKRASOV (translated by Juliet Soskice).

I

At that time I was only twenty-four. My life was even then gloomy, ill-regulated, and as solitary as that of a savage. I made friends with no one and positively avoided talking, and buried myself more and more in my hole. At work in the office I never looked at any one, and I was perfectly well aware that my companions looked upon me, not only as a queer fellow, but even looked upon me—I always fancied this—with a sort of loathing. I sometimes wondered why it was that nobody except me fancied that he was looked upon with aversion? One of the clerks had a most repulsive, pock-marked face, which looked positively villainous. I believe I should not have dared to look at any one with such an unsightly face. Another had such a very dirty old uniform that there was an unpleasant odour in his proximity. Yet not one of these gentlemen showed the slightest self-consciousness—either about their clothes or their face or their character in any way. Neither of them ever imagined that they were looked at with repulsion; if they had imagined it they would not have minded—so long as their superiors did not look at them in that way. It is clear to me now that, owing to my unbounded vanity and to the high standard I set for myself, I often looked at myself with furious discontent, which verged on loathing, and so I inwardly attributed the same feeling to every one. I hated my face, for instance: I thought it disgusting, and even suspected that there was something base in my expression, and so every day when I turned up at the office I tried to behave as independently as possible, and to assume a lofty expression, so that I might not be suspected of being abject. "My face may be ugly," I thought, "but let it be lofty, expressive, and, above all, *extremely* intelligent." But I was positively and painfully certain that it was impossible for my face ever to express those qualities. And what was worst of all, I thought it actually stupid looking, and I would have been quite satisfied if I could have looked intelligent. In fact, I would even have put up with looking base if, at the same time, my face could have been thought strikingly intelligent.

Of course, I hated my fellow clerks one and all, and I despised them all, yet at the same time I was, as it were, afraid of them. In fact, it happened at times that I thought more highly of them than of myself. It somehow happened quite suddenly that I alternated between despising them and thinking them superior to myself. A cultivated and decent man cannot be vain without setting a fearfully high standard for himself, and without despising and almost hating himself at certain moments. But whether I despised them or thought them superior I dropped my eyes almost every time I met any one. I even made experiments whether I could face so and so's looking at me, and I was always the first to drop my eyes. This worried me to distraction. I had a sickly dread, too, of being ridiculous, and so had a slavish passion for the conventional in everything external. I loved to fall into the common rut, and had a wholehearted terror of any kind of eccentricity in myself. But how could I live up to it? I was morbidly sensitive, as a man of our age should be. They were all stupid, and as like one another as so many sheep. Perhaps I was the only one in the office who fancied that I was a coward and a slave, and I fancied it just because I was more highly developed. But it was not only that I fancied it, it really was so. I was a coward and a slave. I say this without the slightest embarrassment. Every decent man of our age must be a coward and a slave. That is his normal condition. Of that I am firmly persuaded. He is made and constructed to that very end. And not only at the present time owing to some casual circumstances, but always, at all times, a decent man is bound to be a coward and a slave. It is the law of nature for all decent people all over the earth. If any one of them happens to be valiant about something, he need not be comforted nor carried away by that; he would show the white feather just the same before something else. That is how it invariably and inevitably ends. Only donkeys and mules are valiant, and they only till they are pushed up to the wall. It is not worth while to pay attention to them for they really are of no consequence.

Another circumstance, too, worried me in those days: that there was no one like me and I was unlike any one else. "I am alone and they are *every one*," I thought—and pondered.

From that it is evident that I was still a youngster.

The very opposite sometimes happened. It was loathsome sometimes to go to the office; things reached such a point that I often came home ill. But all at once, *à propos* of nothing, there would come a phase of scepticism and indifference (everything happened in phases to me), and I would laugh myself at my intolerance and fastidiousness, I would reproach myself with being *romantic*. At one time I was unwilling to speak to any one, while at other times I would not only talk, but go to the length of contemplating making friends with them. All my fastidiousness would suddenly, for no rhyme or reason, vanish. Who knows, perhaps I never had really had it, and it had simply been affected, and got out of books. I have not decided that question even now. Once I quite made friends with them, visited their homes, played preference,* drank vodka, talked of promotions. . . . But here let me make a digression.

We Russians, speaking generally, have never had those foolish transcendental "romantics"—German, and still more French—on whom nothing produces any effect; if there were an earthquake, if all France perished at the barricades, they would still be the same, they would not even have the decency to affect a change, but would still go on singing their transcendental songs to the hour of their death, because they are fools. We, in Russia, have no fools; that is well known. That is what distinguishes us from foreign lands. Consequently these transcendental natures are not found amongst us in their pure form. The idea that they are is due to our "realistic" journalists and critics of that day, always on the look out for Kostanzhoglos and Uncle Pyotr Ivanichs[21] and foolishly accepting them as our ideal; they have slandered our romantics, taking them for the same transcendental sort as in Germany or France. On the

---

*A card game.

contrary, the characteristics of our "romantics" are absolutely and directly opposed to the transcendental European type, and no European standard can be applied to them. (Allow me to make use of this word "romantic"—an old-fashioned and much respected word which has done good service and is familiar to all). The characteristics of our romantic are to understand everything, *to see everything and to see it often incomparably more clearly than our most realistic minds see* it; to refuse to accept anyone or anything, but at the same time not to despise anything; to give way, to yield, from policy; never to lose sight of a useful practical object (such as rent-free quarters at the government expense, pensions, decorations), to keep their eye on that object through all the enthusiasms and volumes of lyrical poems, and at the same time to preserve "the good and the beautiful" inviolate within them to the hour of their death, and to preserve themselves also, incidentally, like some precious jewel wrapped in cotton wool if only for the benefit of "the good and the beautiful." Our "romantic" is a man of great breadth and the greatest rogue of all our rogues, I assure you. . . . I can assure you from experience, indeed. Of course, that is, if he is intelligent. But what am I saying! The romantic is always intelligent, and I only meant to observe that although we have had foolish romantics they don't count, and they were only so because in the flower of their youth they degenerated into Germans, and to preserve their precious jewel more comfortably, settled somewhere out there—by preference in Weimar or the Black Forest.[22]

I, for instance, genuinely despised my official work and did not openly abuse it simply because I was in it myself and got a salary for it. Anyway, take note, I did not openly abuse it. Our romantic would rather go out of his mind—a thing, however, which very rarely happens—than take to open abuse, unless he had some other career in view; and he is never kicked out. At most, they would take him to the lunatic asylum as "the King of Spain"[23] if he should go very mad. But it is only the thin, fair people who go out of their minds in Russia. Innumerable "romantics" attain later in life to considerable rank in the service.

Their many-sidedness is remarkable! And what a faculty they have for the most contradictory sensations! I was comforted by this thought even in those days, and I am of the same opinion now. That is why there are so many "broad natures" among us who never lose their ideal even in the depths of degradation; and though they never stir a finger for their ideal, though they are arrant thieves and knaves, yet they tearfully cherish their first ideal and are extraordinarily honest at heart. Yes, it is only among us that the most incorrigible rogue can be absolutely and loftily honest at heart without in the least ceasing to be a rogue. I repeat, our romantics, frequently, become such accomplished rascals (I use the term "rascals" affectionately), suddenly display such a sense of reality and practical knowledge that their bewildered superiors and the public can only stand in amazement and cluck their tongues.

Their many-sidedness is really amazing, and goodness knows what it may develop into later on, and what the future has in store for us. It is not a poor material! I do not say this from any foolish or boastful patriotism. But I feel sure that you are again imagining that I am joking. Or perhaps it's just the contrary and you are convinced that I really think so. Anyway, gentlemen, I shall welcome both views as an honor and a special favour. And do forgive my digression.

I did not, of course, maintain friendly relations with my comrades and soon was at loggerheads with them, and in my youth and inexperience I even gave up bowing to them, as though I had cut off all relations. That, however, only happened to me once. As a rule, I was always alone.

In the first place I spent most of my time at home, reading. I tried to stifle all that was continually seething within me by means of external impressions. And the only external means I had was reading. Reading, of course, was a great help—exciting me, giving me pleasure and pain. But at times it bored me fearfully. One longed for movement in spite of everything and I plunged all at once into dark, underground, loathsome vice of the pettiest kind. My wretched passions were acute, smarting, from my continual, sickly irritability. I had hysterical impulses, with tears and convulsions. I had no resource except reading, that is, there was nothing in my surroundings which I could respect and which attracted me. I was overwhelmed with depression, too; I had an hysterical craving for incongruity and for contrast, and so I took to vice. I have not said all this to justify myself. . . . But, no! I am lying. I did want to justify myself. I make that little observation for my own benefit gentlemen. I don't want to lie. I vowed to myself I would not.

And so, furtively, timidly, in solitude, at night, I indulged a filthy vice, with a feeling of shame which never deserted me even at the most loathsome moments, and which at such moments nearly made me curse. Already even then I had my underground world in my soul. I was fearfully afraid of being seen, of being met, of being recognized. I visited various obscure haunts.

One night as I was passing a tavern I saw through a lighted window some gentlemen fighting with billiard cues, and saw one of them thrown out of window. At other times I should have felt very much disgusted, but I was in such a mood at the time that I actually envied the gentleman thrown out of window—and I envied him so much that I even went into the tavern and into the billiard-room. "Perhaps," I thought, "I'll have a fight, too, and they'll throw me out of window."

I was not drunk—but what is one to do—depression will drive a man to such a pitch of hysteria? But nothing happened. It seemed that I was not even equal to being thrown out of window and I went away without having my fight.

An officer put me in my place from the first moment.

I was standing by the billiard-table and in my ignorance blocking up the way, and he wanted to pass; he took me by the shoulders and without a word—without a warning or explanation—moved me from where I was standing to another spot and passed by as though he had not noticed me. I could have forgiven blows, but I could not forgive his having moved me without noticing me.

Devil knows what I would have given for a real regular quarrel—a more decent, a more literary one, so to speak. I had been treated like a fly. This officer was over six foot, while I was a spindly little fellow. But the quarrel was in my hands. I had only to protest and I certainly would have been thrown out of the window. But I changed my mind and preferred to beat a resentful retreat.

I went out of the tavern straight home, confused and troubled, and the next night I went out again with the same lewd intentions, still more furtively, abjectly and miserably than before, as it were, with tears in my eyes—but still I did go out again. Don't imagine, though, it was cowardice made me slink away from the officer: I never have been a coward at heart, though I have always been a coward in action. Don't be in a hurry to laugh—I assure you I can explain it all.

Oh, if only that officer had been one of the sort who would consent to fight a duel! But no, he was one of those gentlemen (alas, long extinct!) who preferred fighting with cues or, like Gogol's Lieutenant Pirogov,[24] appealing to the police. They did not fight duels and would have thought a duel with a civilian like me an utterly unseemly procedure in any case—and they looked upon the duel altogether as something impossible, something free-thinking and French. But they were quite ready to bully, especially when they were over six foot.

I did not slink away through cowardice, but through an unbounded vanity. I was afraid not of his six foot, not of getting a sound thrashing and being thrown out of the window; I should have had physical courage enough, I assure you; but I had not the moral courage. What I was afraid of was that every one present, from the insolent marker down to the lowest little stinking, pimply clerk in a greasy collar, would jeer at me and fail to understand when I began to protest and to address them in literary language. For of the point of honour—not of honour, but of the point of honour (*point d'honneur*)[25]—one cannot speak among us except in literary language. You can't allude to the "point of honour" in ordinary language. I was fully convinced (the sense of reality, in spite of all my romanticism!) that they would all simply split their sides with laughter, and that the of-

ficer would not simply beat me, that is, without insulting me,
but would certainly prod me in the back with his knee, kick me
round the billiard-table, and only then perhaps have pity and
drop me out of the window.

Of course, this trivial incident could not with me end in
that. I often met that officer afterwards in the street and noticed him very carefully. I am not quite sure whether he recognized me, I imagine not; I judge from certain signs. But
I—I stared at him with spite and hatred and so it went on . . .
for several years! My resentment grew even deeper with
years. At first I began making stealthy inquiries about this officer. It was difficult for me to do so, for I knew no one. But
one day I heard some one shout his surname in the street as
I was following him at a distance, as though I were tied to
him—and so I learnt his surname. Another time I followed
him to his flat, and for ten kopeks learned from the porter
where he lived, on which storey, whether he lived alone or
with others, and so on—in fact, everything one could learn
from a porter. One morning, though I had never tried my
hand with the pen, it suddenly occurred to me to describe
this officer in an exposé, as a caricature, in the form of a
story. I wrote the story with pleasure. I exposed, even slandered him; at first I so altered his surname that it could easily be recognized, but on second thoughts I changed it, and
sent the story to *Fatherland Notes*.[26] But at that time such attacks
were not the fashion and my story was not printed. That was
a great vexation to me.

Sometimes I was positively choked with resentment. At
last I determined to challenge my enemy to a duel. I composed a splendid, charming letter to him, imploring him to
apologize to me, and hinting rather plainly at a duel in case
of refusal. The letter was so composed that if the officer had
had the least understanding of the good and the beautiful he
would certainly have flung himself on my neck and have offered me his friendship. And how fine that would have been!
How we should have got on together! "He could have
shielded me with his higher rank, while I could have im-

proved his mind with my culture, and, well . . . my ideas, and all sorts of things might have happened." Only fancy, this was two years after his insult to me, and my challenge would have been a ridiculous anachronism, in spite of all the ingenuity of my letter in disguising and explaining away the anachronism. But, thank God (to this day I thank the Almighty with tears in my eyes) I did not send the letter to him. Cold shivers run down my back when I think of what might have happened if I had sent it.

And all at once I revenged myself in the simplest way, by a stroke of genius! A brilliant thought suddenly dawned upon me. Sometimes on holidays I used to stroll along the sunny side of Nevsky Prospect about four o'clock in the afternoon. Though it was hardly a stroll so much as a series of innumerable miseries, humiliations and resentments; but no doubt that was just what I wanted. I used to wriggle along in a most unseemly fashion, like an eel, continually moving aside to make way for generals, for officers of the guards and the hussars, or for ladies. At such minutes there used to be a convulsive twinge at my heart, and I used to feel hot all down my back at the mere thought of the wretchedness of my attire, of the wretchedness and abjectness of my little scurrying figure. This was a regular martyrdom, a continual, intolerable humiliation at the thought, which passed into an incessant and direct sensation, that I was a mere fly in the eyes of all this world, a nasty, disgusting fly—more intelligent, more highly developed, more refined in feeling than any of them, of course—but a fly that was continually making way for every one, insulted and injured by every one. Why I inflicted this torture upon myself, why I went to Nevsky Prospect, I don't know. I felt simply drawn there at every possible opportunity.

Already then I began to experience a rush of the enjoyment of which I spoke in the first chapter. After my affair with the officer I felt even more drawn there than before: it was on Nevsky that I met him most frequently, there I could admire him. He, too, went there chiefly on holidays. He, too, turned out of his path for generals and persons of high rank, and he, too, wriggled between them like an eel; but people, like me, or even better dressed like me, he simply walked over; he made straight for them as though there was nothing but empty space before him, and never, under any circumstances, turned aside. I gloated over my resentment watching him and . . . always resentfully made way for him. It exasperated me that even in the street I could not be on an even footing with him.

"Why must you invariably be the first to move aside?" I kept asking myself in hysterical rage, waking up sometimes at three o'clock in the morning. "Why is it you and not he? There's no regulation about it; there's no written law. Let the making way be equal as it usually is when refined people meet: he moves half-way and you move half-way; you pass with mutual respect."

But that never happened, and I always moved aside, while he did not even notice my making way for him. And lo and behold a bright idea dawned upon me! "What," I thought, "if I meet him and don't move to one side? What if I don't move aside on purpose, even if I knock up against him? How would that be?" This audacious idea took such a hold on me that it gave me no peace. I was dreaming of it continually, horribly, and I purposely went more frequently to Nevsky in order to picture more vividly how I should do it when I did do it. I was delighted. This intention seemed to me more and more practical and possible.

"Of course I shall not really push him," I thought, already more good-natured in my joy. "I will simply not turn aside, will run up against him, not very violently, but just shouldering each other—just as much as decency permits. I will push against him just as much as he pushes against me." At last I made up my mind completely. But my preparations took a great deal of time. To begin with, when I carried out my plan I should need to be looking rather more decent, and so I had to think of my get-up. "In case of emergency, if, for instance, there were any sort of public scandal (and the public there is of the most *recherche:** the Countess walks there; Prince D. walks there; all the

---

*Sought after, in demand (French).

literary world is there), I must be well dressed; that inspires respect and of itself puts us on an equal footing in the eyes of society."

With this object I asked for some of my salary in advance,
and bought at Churkin's a pair of black gloves and a decent
hat. Black gloves seemed to me both more dignified and *bon
ton** than the lemon-coloured ones which I had contemplated
at first. "The colour is too gaudy, it looks as though one were
trying to be conspicuous," and I did not take the lemon-
coloured ones. I had got ready long beforehand a good shirt,
with white bone studs; my overcoat was the only thing that
held me back. The coat in itself was a very good one, it kept
me warm; but it was wadded and it had a raccoon collar
which was the height of vulgarity. I had to change the collar
at any sacrifice, and to have a beaver one like an officer's. For
this purpose I began visiting the Gostiny Dvor and after several attempts I pitched upon a piece of cheap German beaver.
Though these German beavers soon grow shabby and look
wretched, yet at first they look exceedingly well, and I only
needed it for one occasion. I asked the price; even so, it was
too expensive. After thinking it over thoroughly I decided to
sell my raccoon collar. The rest of the money—a considerable
sum for me, I decided to borrow from Anton Antonich
Syetochkin, my immediate superior, an unassuming person,
though grave and judicious. He never lent money to any one,
but I had, on entering the service, been specially recom-
mended to him by an important personage who had got me
my berth. I was horribly worried. To borrow from Anton Antonich seemed to me monstrous and shameful. I did not sleep
for two or three nights. Indeed, I did not sleep well at that
time, I was in a fever; I had a vague sinking at my heart or else
a sudden throbbing, throbbing, throbbing! Anton Antonich
was surprised at first, then he frowned, then he reflected, and
did after all lend me the money, receiving from me a written

---

*In good taste (French).

authorization to take from my salary a fortnight later the sum that he had lent me.

In this way everything was at last ready. The handsome beaver replaced the mean-looking raccoon, and I began by degrees to get to work. It would never have done to act off-hand, at random; the plan had to be carried out skilfully, by degrees. But I must confess that after many efforts I began to despair: we simply could not run into each other. I made every preparation, I was quite determined—it seemed as though we should run into one another directly—and before I knew what I was doing I had stepped aside for him again and he had passed without noticing me. I even prayed as I approached him that God would grant me determination. One time I had made up my mind thoroughly, but it ended in my stumbling and falling at his feet because at the very last instant when I was six inches from him my courage failed me. He very calmly stepped over me, while I flew on one side like a ball. That night I was ill again, feverish and delirious.

And suddenly it ended most happily. The night before I had made up my mind not to carry out my fatal plan and to abandon it all, and with that object I went to Nevsky for the last time, just to see how I would abandon it all. Suddenly, three paces from my enemy, I unexpectedly made up my mind—I closed my eyes, and we ran full tilt, shoulder to shoulder, against one another! I did not budge an inch and passed him on a perfectly equal footing! He did not even look round and pretended not to notice it; but he was only pretending, I am convinced of that. I am convinced of that to this day! Of course, I got the worst of it—he was stronger, but that was not the point. The point was that I had attained my object, I had kept up my dignity, I had not yielded a step, and had put myself publicly on an equal social footing with him. I returned home feeling that I was fully avenged for everything. I was delighted. I was triumphant and sang Italian arias. Of course, I will not describe to you what happened to me three days later; if you have read my first chapter you can guess that for yourself. The officer was afterwards transferred; I have not seen him now for fourteen years. What is the dear fellow doing now? Whom is he walking over?

II

But the period of my dissipation would end and I always felt very sick afterwards. It was followed by remorse—I tried to drive it away: I felt too sick. By degrees, however, I grew used to that too. I grew used to everything, or rather I voluntarily resigned myself to enduring it. But I had a means of escape that reconciled everything—that was to find refuge in "the good and the beautiful," in dreams, of course. I was a terrible dreamer, I would dream for three months on end, tucked away in my corner, and you may believe me that at those moments I had no resemblance to the gentleman who, in the perturbation of his chicken heart, put a collar of German beaver on his great coat. I suddenly became a hero. I would not have admitted my six-foot lieutenant even if he had called on me. I could not even picture him before me then. What were my dreams and how I could satisfy myself with them—it is hard to say now, but at the time I was satisfied with them. Though, indeed, even now, I am to some extent satisfied with them. Dreams were particularly sweet and vivid after a spell of dissipation; they came with remorse and with tears, with curses and transports. There were moments of such positive intoxication, of such happiness, that there was not the faintest trace of irony within me, on my honour. I had faith, hope, love. I believed blindly at such times that by some miracle, by some external circumstance, all this would suddenly open out, expand; that suddenly a vista of suitable activity—beneficent, good, and, above all, *ready made* (what sort of activity I had no idea, but the great thing was that it should be all ready for me)—would rise up before me—and I should come out into the light of day, almost riding a white horse and crowned with laurel. Anything but the foremost place I could not conceive for myself, and for that very reason I quite contentedly occupied the lowest in reality. Either to be a hero or to grovel in the mud—there was nothing between. That was my ruin, for when I was in the mud I comforted myself with the thought that at other times I was a hero, and the hero was a cloak for the mud: for an ordinary man it was shameful to defile himself, but a hero was too lofty to be utterly defiled, and so he might defile himself. It is worth noting that these attacks of the "good and the beautiful" visited me even during the period of dissipation and just at the times when I was touching the bottom. They came in separate spurts, as though reminding me of themselves, but did not banish the dissipation by their appearance. On the contrary, they seemed to add a zest to it by contrast, and were only sufficiently present to serve as an appetizing sauce. That sauce was made up of contradictions and sufferings, of agonizing inward analysis, and all these pangs and pin-pricks gave a certain piquancy, even a significance to my dissipation—in fact, completely answered the purpose of an appetizing sauce. There was a certain depth of meaning in it. And I could hardly have resigned myself to the simple, vulgar, direct debauchery of a clerk and have endured all the filthiness of it. What could have allured me about it then and have drawn me at night into the street? No, I had a lofty way of getting out of it all.

And what loving-kindness, oh Lord, what loving-kindness I felt at times in those dreams of mine! in those "flights into the good and the beautiful:" though it was fantastic love, though it was never applied to anything human in reality, yet there was so much of this love that one did not feel afterwards even the impulse to apply it in reality; that would have been superfluous. Everything, however, passed satisfactorily by a lazy and fascinating transition into the sphere of art, that is, into the beautiful forms of life, lying ready, largely stolen from the poets and novelists and adapted to all sorts of needs and uses. I, for instance, was triumphant over every one; every one, of course, was in dust and ashes, and was forced spontaneously to recog-

nize my superiority, and I forgave them all. I was a poet and a
grand gentleman, I fell in love; I came in for countless millions
and immediately devoted them to humanity, and at the same
time I confessed before all the people my shameful deeds,
which, of course, were not merely shameful, but had in them
much that was "good and beautiful," something in the Manfred
style.[27] Every one would kiss me and weep (what idiots they
would be if they did not), while I should go barefoot and hungry preaching new ideas and fighting a victorious Austerlitz
against the obscurantists. Then the band would play a march, an
amnesty would be declared, the Pope would agree to retire
from Rome to Brazil; then there would be a ball for the whole
of Italy at the Villa Borghese on the shores of the Lake of Como,
the Lake of Como being for that purpose transferred to the
neighbourhood of Rome;[28] then would come a scene in the
bushes, and so on, and so on—as though you did not know all
about it? You will say that it is vulgar and contemptible to drag
all this into public after all the tears and transports which I have
myself confessed. But why is it contemptible? Can you imagine
that I am ashamed of it all, and that it was stupider than anything in your life, gentlemen? And I can assure you that some
of these fancies were by no means badly composed. . . . It did
not all happen on the shores of Lake Como. And yet you are
right—it really is vulgar and contemptible. And most contemptible of all it is that now I am attempting to justify myself
to you. And even more contemptible than that is my making
this remark now. But that's enough, or there will be no end to
it: each step will be more contemptible than the last. . . .

I could never stand more than three months of dreaming at
a time without feeling an irresistible desire to plunge into society. To plunge into society meant to visit my superior at the
office, Anton Antonich Syetochkin. He was the only permanent
acquaintance I have had in my life, and wonder at the fact myself now. But I only went to see him when that phase came over
me, and when my dreams had reached such a point of bliss that
it became essential at once to embrace my fellows and all
mankind; and for that purpose I needed, at least, one human

being, actually existing. I had to call on Anton Antonich, however, on Tuesday—his at-home day; so I had always to time my
passionate desire to embrace humanity so that it might fall on
a Tuesday.

This Anton Antonich lived on the fourth storey in a house
in Five Corners, in four low-pitched rooms, one smaller than
the other, of a particularly frugal and sallow appearance. He
had two daughters and their aunt, who used to pour out the
tea. Of the daughters one was thirteen and another fourteen,
they both had snub noses, and I was awfully shy of them because they were always whispering and giggling together. The
master of the house usually sat in his study on a leather couch
in front of the table with some grey-headed gentleman, usually a colleague from our office or some other department. I
never saw more than two or three visitors there, always the
same. They talked about the excise duty; about business in the
senate, about salaries, about promotions, about His Excellency, and the best means of pleasing him, and so on. I had the
patience to sit like a fool beside these people for four hours at
a stretch, listening to them without knowing what to say to
them or venturing to say a word. I became stupified, several
times I felt myself perspiring, I was overcome by a sort of
paralysis; but this was pleasant and good for me. On returning home I deferred for a time my desire to embrace all
mankind.

I had however one other acquaintance of a sort, Simonov,
who was an old schoolfellow. I had a number of schoolfellows, indeed, in Petersburg, but I did not associate with them
and had even given up nodding to them in the street. I believe I had transferred into the department I was in simply to
avoid their company and to cut off all connection with my
hateful childhood. Curses on that school and all those terrible years of penal servitude! In short, I parted from my
schoolfellows as soon as I got out into the world. There were
two or three left to whom I nodded in the street. One of
them was Simonov who had been in no way distinguished at
school, was of a quiet and equable disposition; but I discov-

ered in him a certain independence of character and even honesty. I don't even suppose that he was particularly stupid. I had at one time spent some rather soulful moments with him, but these had not lasted long and had somehow been suddenly clouded over. He was evidently uncomfortable at these reminiscences, and was, I fancy, always afraid that I might take up the same tone again. I suspected that he had an aversion for me, but still I went on going to see him, not being quite certain of it.

And so on one occasion, unable to endure my solitude and knowing that as it was Thursday Anton Antonich's door would be closed, I thought of Simonov. Climbing up to his fourth storey I was thinking that the man disliked me and that it was a mistake to go and see him. But as it always happened that such reflections impelled me, as though purposely, to put myself into a false position, I went in. It was almost a year since I had last seen Simonov.

III

I found two of my old schoolfellows with him. They seemed to be discussing an important matter. All of them took scarcely any notice of my entrance, which was strange, for I had not met them for years. Evidently they looked upon me as something on the level of a common fly. I had not been treated like that even at school, though they all hated me. I knew, of course, that they must despise me now for my lack of success in the service, and for my having let myself sink so low, going about badly dressed and so on—which seemed to them a sign of my incapacity and insignificance. But I had not expected such contempt. Simonov was positively surprised at my turning up. Even in old days he had always seemed surprised at my coming. All this disconcerted me: I sat down, feeling rather miserable, and began listening to what they were saying.

They were engaged in warm and earnest conversation about a farewell dinner which they wanted to arrange for the next day to a comrade of theirs called Zverkov, an officer in the army, who was going away to a distant province. This Zverkov had been all the time at school with me too. I had begun to hate him particularly in the upper forms. In the lower forms he had simply been a pretty, playful boy whom everybody liked. I had hated him, however, even in the lower forms, just because he was a pretty and playful boy. He was always bad at his lessons and got worse and worse as he went on; however, he left with a good certificate, as he had powerful interest. During his last year at school he came in for an estate of two hundred serfs, and as almost all of us were poor he took up a swaggering tone among us. He was vulgar in the extreme, but at the same time he was a good-natured fellow, even in his swaggering. In spite of superficial, fantastic and sham notions of honour and dignity, all but very few of us positively grovelled before Zverkov, and the more so the more he swaggered. And it was not from any interested motive that they grovelled, but simply because he had been favoured by the gifts of nature. Moreover, it was, as it were, an accepted idea among us that Zverkov was a specialist in regard to tact and the social graces. This last fact particularly infuriated me. I hated the abrupt self-confident tone of his voice, his admiration of his own witticisms, which were often frightfully stupid, though he was bold in his language; I hated his handsome, but stupid face (for which I would, however, have gladly exchanged my intelligent one), and the free-and-easy military manners in fashion in the " 'forties." I hated the way in which he used to talk of his future conquests of women (he did not venture to begin his attack upon women until he had the epaulettes of an officer, and was looking forward to them with impatience), and boasted of the duels he would constantly be fighting. I remember how I, invariably so taciturn, suddenly fastened upon Zverkov, when one day talking at a leisure moment with his schoolfellows of his future relations with the fair sex, and growing as sportive as a puppy in the sun, he all at once declared that he would not leave a single village girl on his estate unnoticed, that that was his *droit de seigneur*,* and that if the peasants dared to protest he would have them all flogged and double the tax on them, the bearded rascals. Our servile rabble applauded, but I attacked him, not from compassion for the girls and their fathers, but simply because they were applauding such an insect. I got the better of him on that occasion, but though Zverkov was stupid he was lively and impudent, and so laughed it off, and in such a way that my victory was not really complete: the laugh was on his side. He got the better of me on several occasions afterwards, but without malice, jestingly, casually. I remained angrily and contemptuously silent and would not answer him. When we left school he made advances to me; I did not rebuff them, for I was flattered, but we soon parted and quite naturally. Afterwards I heard of his barrack-room success as a lieutenant, and of his carousing. Then there came other rumours—of his successes in the service. By then he had taken to cutting me in the street, and I suspected that he was afraid of compromising himself by greeting a personage as insignificant as me. I saw him once in the theatre, in the third tier of boxes. By then he was wearing aglets. He was twisting and twirling about, ingratiating himself with the daughters of an ancient General. In three years he had gone off considerably, though he was still rather handsome and adroit. One could see that by the time he was thirty he would be corpulent. So it was to this Zverkov that my schoolfellows were going to give a dinner on his departure. They had kept up with him for those three years, though privately they did not consider themselves on an equal footing with him, I am convinced of that.

---

*Master's right (French); that is, it is his right to deflower his servants' brides.

Of Simonov's two visitors, one was Ferfichkin, a Russian-ized German—a little fellow with the face of a monkey, a blockhead who was always deriding every one, a very bitter enemy of mine from our days in the lower forms—a vulgar, impudent, swaggering fellow, who affected a most sensitive feeling of personal honour, though, of course, he was a wretched little coward at heart. He was one of those worship-pers of Zverkov who made up to the latter from interested mo-tives, and often borrowed money from him. Simonov's other visitor, Trudolyubov, was a person in no way remarkable—a tall young fellow, in the army, with a cold face, fairly honest, though he worshipped success of every sort, and was only ca-pable of thinking of promotion. He was some sort of distant relation of Zverkov's, and this, foolish as it seems, gave him a certain importance among us. He always thought me of no consequence whatever; his behaviour to me, though not quite courteous, was tolerable.

"Well, with seven rubles each," said Trudolyubov, "twenty-one rubles between the three of us, we ought to be able to get a good dinner. Zverkov, of course, won't pay."

"Of course not, since we are inviting him," Simonov de-cided.

"Can you imagine," Ferfichkin interrupted hotly and con-ceitedly, like some insolent flunkey boasting of his master the General's decorations, "can you imagine that Zverkov will let us pay alone? He will accept from delicacy, but he will order half a dozen bottles of champagne."

"Do we want half a dozen for the four of us?" observed Tru-dolyubov, taking notice only of the half dozen.

"So the three of us, with Zverkov for the fourth, twenty-one rubles, at the Hôtel de Paris at five o'clock to-morrow," Si-monov, who had been asked to make the arrangements, con-cluded finally.

"How twenty-one rubles?" I asked in some agitation, with a show of being offended; "if you count me it will not be twenty-one, but twenty-eight rubles."

It seemed to me that to invite myself so suddenly and unexpectedly would be positively graceful, and that they would all be conquered at once and would look at me with respect.

"Do you want to join, too?" Simonov observed, with no appearance of pleasure, seeming to avoid looking at me. He knew me through and through.

It infuriated me that he knew me so thoroughly.

"Why not? I am an old schoolfellow of his, too, I believe, and I must own I feel hurt that you have left me out," I said, boiling over again.

"And where were we to find you?" Ferfichkin put in roughly.

"You never were on good terms with Zverkov," Trudolyubov added, frowning.

But I had already clutched at the idea and would not give it up.

"It seems to me that no one has a right to form an opinion upon that," I retorted in a shaking voice, as though something tremendous had happened. "Perhaps that is just my reason for wishing it now, that I have not always been on good terms with him."

"Oh, there's no making you out . . . with these refinements," Trudolyubov jeered.

"We'll put your name down," Simonov decided, addressing me. "To-morrow at five o'clock at the Hôtel de Paris."

"What about the money?" Ferfichkin began in an undertone, indicating me to Simonov, but he broke off, for even Simonov was embarrassed.

"That will do," said Trudolyubov, getting up. "If he wants to come so much, let him."

"But it's a private thing, between us friends," Ferfichkin said crossly, as he, too, picked up his hat. "It's not an official gathering."

"We do not want at all, perhaps . . ."

They went away. Ferfichkin did not greet me in any way as he went out, Trudolyubov barely nodded. Simonov, with whom I was left tête-à-tête, was in a state of vexation and perplexity, and

looked at me queerly. He did not sit down and did not ask
me to.

"H'm . . . yes . . . to-morrow, then. Will you pay your
money now? I just ask so as to know," he muttered in embarrassment.

I flushed crimson, and as I did so I remembered that I had
owed Simonov fifteen rubles for ages—which I had, indeed,
never forgotten, though I had not paid it.

"You will understand, Simonov, that I could have no idea
when I came here. . . . I am very much vexed that I have forgotten. . . ."

"All right, all right, that doesn't matter. You can pay to-
morrow after the dinner. I simply wanted to know. . . . Please
don't . . ."

He broke off and began pacing the room still more vexed.
As he walked he began to stamp with his heels.

"Am I keeping you?" I asked, after two minutes of silence.

"Oh!" he said, starting, "that is—to be truthful—yes. I have
to go and see some one . . . not far from here," he added in an
apologetic voice, somewhat abashed.

"My goodness, why didn't you say so?" I cried, seizing my
cap, with an astonishingly free-and-easy air, which was the last
thing I should have expected of myself.

"It's close by . . . not two paces away," Simonov repeated, accompanying me to the front door with a fussy air which did
not suit him at all. "So five o'clock, punctually, to-morrow," he
called down the stairs after me. He was very glad to get rid of
me. I was in a fury.

"What possessed me, what possessed me to force myself
upon them?" I wondered, grinding my teeth as I strode along
the street, "for a scoundrel, a pig like that Zverkov! Of course, I
had better not go; of course, I must just snap my fingers at
them. I am not bound in any way. I'll send Simonov a note by
to-morrow's post. . . ."

But what made me furious was that I knew for certain that
I should go, that I should make a point of going; and the more

tactless, the more unseemly my going would be, the more certainly I would go.

And there was a positive obstacle to my going: I had no money. All I had was nine rubles, I had to give seven of that to my servant, Apollon, for his monthly wages. That was all I paid him—he had to keep himself.

Not to pay him was impossible, considering his character. But I will talk about that fellow, about that plague of mine, another time.

However, I knew I should go and should not pay him his wages.

That night I had the most hideous dreams. No wonder; all evening I had been oppressed by memories of my miserable days at school, and I could not shake them off. I was sent to the school by distant relations, upon whom I was dependent and of whom I have heard nothing since—they sent me there a forlorn, silent boy, already crushed by their reproaches, already troubled by doubt, and looking with savage distrust at every one. My schoolfellows met me with spiteful and merciless jibes because I was not like any of them. But I could not endure their taunts; I could not give in to them with the ignoble readiness with which they gave in to one another. I hated them from the first, and shut myself away from every one in timid, wounded and disproportionate pride. Their coarseness revolted me. They laughed cynically at my face, at my clumsy figure; and yet what stupid faces they had themselves. In our school the boys' faces seemed in a special way to degenerate and grow stupider. How many fine-looking boys came to us! In a few years they became repulsive. Even at sixteen I wondered at them morosely; even then I was struck by the pettiness of their thoughts, the stupidity of their pursuits, their games, their conversations. They had no understanding of essential things, they took no interest in striking, impressive subjects, that I could not help considering them inferior to myself. It was not wounded vanity that drove me to it, and for God's sake do not thrust upon me your hackneyed remarks, repeated to nausea, that "I was only a dreamer," while they even then had an understanding of life. They understood nothing, they had no idea of real life, and I swear that that was what made me most indignant with them. On the contrary, the most obvious, striking reality they accepted with fantastic stupidity and even at that time were accustomed to respect success. Everything that was just, but oppressed and looked down upon, they laughed at heartlessly and shamefully. They took rank for intelligence; even at sixteen they were already talking about a snug berth. Of course, a great deal of it was due to their stupidity, to the bad examples with which they had always been surrounded in their childhood and boyhood. They were monstrously depraved. Of course a great deal of that, too, was superficial and an assumption of cynicism; of course there were glimpses of youth and freshness even in their depravity; but even that freshness was not attractive, and showed itself in a certain rakishness. I hated them horribly, though perhaps I was worse than any of them. They repaid me in the same way, and did not conceal their aversion for me. But by then I did not desire their affection: on the contrary I continually longed for their humiliation. To escape from their derision I purposely began to make all the progress I could with my studies and forced my way to the very top. This impressed them. Moreover, they all began by degrees to grasp that I had already read books none of them could read, and understood things (not forming part of our school curriculum) of which they had not even heard. They took a savage and sarcastic view of it, but were morally impressed, especially as the teachers began to notice me on those grounds. The mockery ceased, but the hostility remained, and cold and strained relations became permanent between us. In the end I could not put up with it: with years a craving for society, for friends, developed in me. I attempted to get on friendly terms with some of my schoolfellows; but somehow or other my intimacy with them was always strained and soon ended of itself. Once, indeed, I did have a friend. But I was already a tyrant at heart; I wanted to exercise unbounded sway over him; I tried to instil into him a contempt for his surroundings; I required of him a disdainful and complete break with those surroundings. I frightened him with my passionate affection; I reduced him to tears, to hysterics. He was a simple and devoted soul; but when he devoted himself to me entirely I began to hate him immediately and repulsed him— as though all I needed him for was to win a victory over him, to subjugate him and nothing else. But I could not subjugate all of them; my friend was not at all like them either, he was, in fact, a rare exception. The first thing I did on leaving school was to give up the special job for which I had been destined so as to break all ties, to curse my past and shake the dust from off my feet. . . . And goodness knows why, after all that, I should go trudging off to Simonov's!

Early next morning I roused myself and jumped out of bed with excitement, as though it were all about to happen at once. But I believed that some radical change in my life was coming, and would inevitably come that day. Owing to its rarity, perhaps, any external event, however trivial, always made me feel as though some radical change in my life were at hand. I went to the office, however, as usual, but sneaked away home two hours earlier to get ready. The great thing, I thought, is not to be the first to arrive, or they will think I am overjoyed at coming. But there were thousands of such great points to consider, and they all agitated and overwhelmed me. I polished my boots a second time with my own hands; nothing in the world would have induced Apollon to clean them twice a day, as he considered that it was more than his duties required of him. I stole the brushes to clean them from the passage, being careful he should not detect it, for fear of his contempt. Then I minutely examined my clothes and thought that everything looked old, worn and threadbare. I had let myself get too slovenly. My uniform, perhaps, was tidy, but I could not go out to dinner in my uniform. The worst of it was that on the knee of my trousers was a big yellow stain. I had a foreboding that that stain would deprive me of nine-tenths of my personal dignity. I knew, too, that it was very poor to think so. "But this is no time for

thinking: now I am in for the real thing," I thought, and my
heart sank. I knew, too, perfectly well even then, that I was
monstrously exaggerating the facts. But how could I help it?
I could not control myself and was already shaking with
fever. With despair I pictured to myself how coldly and disdainfully that "scoundrel" Zverkov would meet me; with
what dull-witted, invincible contempt the blockhead Trudolyubov would look at me; with what impudent rudeness
the insect Ferfichkin would snigger at me in order to curry
favour with Zverkov; how completely Simonov would take it
all in, and how he would despise me for the abjectness of my
vanity and lack of spirit—and, worst of all, how paltry, unlit-
erary, commonplace it would all be. Of course, the best thing
would be not to go at all. But that was most impossible of all:
if I feel impelled to do anything, I seem to be pitchforked
into it. I should have jeered at myself ever afterwards: "So you
turned coward, faced with reality you turned coward, turned
coward!" On the contrary, I passionately longed to show all
that "rabble" that I was by no means such a coward as I
seemed to myself. What is more, even in the acutest paroxysm
of this cowardly fever, I dreamed of getting the upper hand,
of dominating them, carrying them away, making them like
me—if only for my "elevation of thought and unmistakable
wit." They would abandon Zverkov, he would sit on one side,
silent and ashamed, while I should crush him. Then, perhaps,
we would be reconciled and drink to our everlasting friendship; but what was most bitter and most humiliating for me
was that I knew even then, knew fully and for certain, that I
needed nothing of all this really, that I did not really want to
crush, to subdue, to attract them, and that I did not care a
straw really for the result, even if I did achieve it. Oh, how I
prayed for the day to pass quickly! In unutterable anguish I
went to the window, opened the movable pane and looked
out into the troubled darkness of the thickly falling wet snow.
At last my wretched little clock hissed out five. I seized my
hat and trying not to look at Apollon, who had been all day
expecting his month's wages, but in his foolishness was un-

willing to be the first to speak about it, I slipt between him and the door and jumping into a high-class sledge, on which I spent my last half ruble, I drove up in grand style to the Hôtel de Paris.

IV

I had been certain the day before that I should be the first to arrive. But it was not a question of being the first to arrive. Not only were they not there, but I had difficulty in finding our room. The table was not laid even. What did it mean? After a good many questions I elicited from the waiters that the dinner had been ordered not for five, but for six o'clock. This was confirmed at the buffet too. I felt really ashamed to go on questioning them. It was only twenty-five minutes past five. If they changed the dinner hour they ought at least to have let me know—that is what the post is for, and not to have put me in an absurd position in my own eyes and . . . and even before the waiters. I sat down; the servant began laying the table; I felt even more humiliated when he was present. Towards six o'clock they brought in candles, though there were lamps burning in the room. It had not occurred to the waiter, however, to bring them in at once when I arrived. In the next room two gloomy, angry-looking persons were eating their dinners in silence at two different tables. There was a great deal of noise, even shouting, in a room further away; one could hear the laughter of a crowd of people, and nasty little shrieks in French: there were ladies at the dinner. It was sickening, in fact. I rarely passed more unpleasant moments, so much so that when they did arrive all together punctually at six I was overjoyed to see them, as though they were my deliverers, and even forgot that it was incumbent upon me to show resentment.

Zverkov walked in at the head of them; evidently he was the

leading spirit. He and all of them were laughing; but, seeing
me, Zverkov drew himself up a little, walked up to me deliberately with a slight, rather jaunty bend from the waist. He shook
hands with me in a friendly, but not over-friendly, fashion, with
a sort of circumspect courtesy like that of a General, as though
in giving me his hand he were warding off something. I had
imagined, on the contrary, that on coming in he would at once
break into his habitual thin, shrill laugh and fall to making his
insipid jokes and witticisms. I had been preparing for them ever
since the previous day, but I had not expected such condescen-
sion, such high-official courtesy. So, then, he felt himself inef-
fably superior to me in every respect! If he only meant to insult
me by that high-official tone, it would not matter, I thought—
I could pay him back for it one way or another. But what if, in
reality, without the least desire to be offensive, that sheepshead
had a notion in earnest that he was superior to me and could
only look at me in a patronizing way? The very supposition
made me gasp.

"I was surprised to hear of your desire to join us," he began,
lisping and drawling, which was something new. "You and I
seem to have seen nothing of one another. You fight shy of us.
You shouldn't. We are not such terrible people as you think.
Well, anyway, I am glad to renew our acquaintance."

And he turned carelessly to put down his hat on the window.

"Have you been waiting long?" Trudolyubov inquired.

"I arrived at five o'clock as you told me yesterday," I answered aloud, with an irritability that threatened an explosion.

"Didn't you let him know that we had changed the hour?"
said Trudolyubov to Simonov.

"No, I didn't. I forgot," the latter replied, with no sign of regret, and without even apologizing to me he went off to order
the hors d'œuvres.

"So you've been here a whole hour? Oh, poor fellow!"
Zverkov cried ironically, for to his notions this was bound to be
extremely funny. That rascal Ferfichkin followed with his nasty

little snigger like a puppy yapping. My position struck him, too, as ridiculous and embarrassing.

"It isn't funny at all!" I cried to Ferfichkin, more and more irritated. "It wasn't my fault, but other people's. They neglected to let me know. It was . . . it was . . . it was simply absurd."

"It's not only absurd, but something else as well," muttered Trudolyubov, naïvely taking my part. "You are not hard enough upon it. It was simply rudeness—unintentional, of course. And how could Simonov . . . h'm!"

"If a trick like that had been played on me," observed Ferfichkin, "I should . . ."

"But you should have ordered something for yourself," Zverkov interrupted, "or simply asked for dinner without waiting for us."

"You will allow that I might have done that without your permission," I rapped out. "If I waited, it was . . ."

"Let us sit down, gentlemen," cried Simonov, coming in. "Everything is ready; I can answer for the champagne; it is capitally chilled. . . . You see, I did not know your address, where was I to look for you?" he suddenly turned to me, but again he seemed to avoid looking at me. Evidently he had something against me. It must have been what happened yesterday.

All sat down; I did the same. It was a round table. Trudolyubov was on my left, Simonov on my right. Zverkov was sitting opposite, Ferfichkin next to him, between him and Trudolyubov.

"Tell me, are you . . . in a government office?" Zverkov went on attending to me. Seeing that I was embarrassed he seriously thought that he ought to be friendly to me, and, so to speak, cheer me up.

"Does he want me to throw a bottle at his head?" I thought, in a fury. In my novel surroundings I was unnaturally ready to be irritated.

"In the N—— office," I answered jerkily, with my eyes on my plate.

"And ha-ave you a go-od berth? I say, what ma-a-de you leave your original job?"

"What ma-a-de me was that I wanted to leave my original job," I drawled more than he, hardly able to control myself. Ferfichkin went off into a guffaw. Simonov looked at me ironically. Trudolyubov left off eating and began looking at me with curiosity.

Zverkov winced, but he tried not to notice it.

"And the remuneration?"

"What remuneration?"

"I mean, your sa-a-lary?"

"Why are you cross-examining me?" However, I told him at once what my salary was. I turned horribly red.

"It is not very handsome," Zverkov observed majestically.

"Yes, you can't afford to dine at cafés on that," Ferfichkin added insolently.

"To my thinking it's very poor," Trudolyubov observed gravely.

"And how thin you have grown! How you have changed!" added Zverkov, with a shade of venom in his voice, scanning me and my attire with a sort of insolent compassion.

"Oh, spare his blushes," cried Ferfichkin, sniggering.

"My dear sir, allow me to tell you I am not blushing," I broke out at last; "do you hear? I am dining here, at this café, at my own expense, not at other people's—note that, Mr. Ferfichkin."

"Wha-at? Isn't every one here dining at his own expense? You would seem to be . . ." Ferfichkin flew out at me, turning as red as a lobster, and looking me in the face with fury.

"Tha-at," I answered, feeling I had gone too far, "and I imagine it would be better to talk of something more intelligent."

"You intend to show off your intelligence, I suppose?"

"Don't disturb yourself, that would be quite out of place here."

"Why are you clacking away like that, my good sir, eh? Have you gone out of your wits in your office?"

"Enough, gentlemen, enough!" Zverkov cried, authoritatively.

"How stupid it is!" muttered Simonov.

"It really is stupid. We have met here, a company of friends, for a farewell dinner to a comrade and you carry on an altercation," said Trudolyubov, rudely addressing himself to me alone. "You invited yourself to join us, so don't disturb the general harmony."

"Enough, enough!" cried Zverkov. "Give over, gentlemen, it's out of place. Better let me tell you how I nearly got married the day before yesterday. . . ."

And then followed a burlesque narrative of how this gentleman had almost been married two days before. There was not a word about the marriage, however, but the story was adorned with generals, colonels and court attendants, while Zverkov almost took the lead among them. It was greeted with approving laughter; Ferfichkin positively squealed.

No one paid any attention to me, and I sat crushed and humiliated.

"Good Heavens, these are not the people for me!" I thought. "And what a fool I have made of myself before them! I let Ferfichkin go too far, though. The brutes imagine they are doing me an honour in letting me sit down with them. They don't understand that it's an honour to them and not to me! I've grown thinner! My clothes! Oh, damn my trousers! Zverkov noticed the yellow stain on the knee as soon as he came in. . . . But what's the use! I must get up at once, this very minute, take my hat and simply go without a word . . . with contempt! And tomorrow I can send a challenge. The scoundrels! As though I cared about the seven rubles. They may think. . . . Damn it! I don't care about the seven rubles. I'll go this minute!"

Of course I remained. I drank sherry and Lafitte by the glassful in my discomfiture. Being unaccustomed to it, I was quickly affected. My annoyance increased as the wine went to my head. I longed all at once to insult them all in a most flagrant manner and then go away. To seize the moment and show what I could do, so that they would say, "He's clever, though he is ridiculous," and . . . and . . . in fact, damn them all!

I scanned them all insolently with my drowsy eyes. But they seemed to have forgotten me altogether. They were noisy, vociferous, cheerful. Zverkov was talking all the time. I began listening. Zverkov was talking of some exuberant lady whom he had at last led on to declaring her love (of course, he was lying like a horse), and how he had been helped in this affair by an intimate friend of his, a Prince Kolya, an officer in the hussars, who had three thousand serfs.

"And yet this Kolya, who has three thousand serfs, has not put in an appearance here to-night to see you off," I cut in suddenly.

For a minute every one was silent. "You are drunk already." Trudolyubov deigned to notice me at last, glancing contemptuously in my direction. Zverkov, without a word, examined me as though I were an insect. I dropped my eyes. Simonov made haste to fill up the glasses with champagne.

Trudolyubov raised his glass, as did every one else but me.

"Your health and good luck on the journey!" he cried to Zverkov. "To old times, to our future, hurrah!"

They all tossed off their glasses, and crowded round Zverkov to kiss him. I did not move; my full glass stood untouched before me.

"Why, aren't you going to drink it?" roared Trudolyubov losing patience and turning menacingly to me.

"I want to make a speech separately, on my own account . . . and then I'll drink it, Mr. Trudolyubov."

"Spiteful brute!" muttered Simonov. I drew myself up in my chair and feverishly seized my glass, prepared for something extraordinary, though I did not know myself precisely what I was going to say.

"*Silence!*" cried Ferfichkin. "Now for a display of wit!"

Zverkov waited very gravely, knowing what was coming.

"Mr. Lieutenant Zverkov," I began, "let me tell you that I hate phrases, phrasemongers and men in corsets . . . that's the first point, and there is a second one to follow it."

There was a general stir.

"The second point is: I hate ribaldry and ribald talkers. Especially ribald talkers! The third point: I love justice, truth and honesty." I went on almost mechanically, for I was beginning to shiver with horror myself and had no idea how I came to be talking like this. "I love thought, Monsieur Zverkov; I love true comradeship, on an equal footing and not ... H'm ... I love. ... But, however, why not? I will drink your health, too, Mr. Zverkov. Seduce the Circassian girls, shoot the enemies of the fatherland and ... and ... to your health, Monsieur Zverkov!"

Zverkov got up from his seat, bowed to me and said:

"I am very much obliged to you." He was frightfully offended and turned pale.

"Damn the fellow!" roared Trudolyubov, bringing his fist down on the table.

"Well, he wants a punch in the face for that," squealed Ferfichkin.

"We ought to turn him out," muttered Simonov.

"Not a word, gentlemen, not a movement!" cried Zverkov solemnly, checking the general indignation. "I thank you all, but I can show him for myself how much value I attach to his words."

"Mr. Ferfichkin, you will give me satisfaction to-morrow for your words just now!" I said aloud, turning with dignity to Ferfichkin.

"A duel, you mean? Certainly," he answered. But probably I was so ridiculous as I challenged him and it was so out of keeping with my appearance that everyone, including Ferfichkin, was prostrate with laughter.

"Yes, let him alone, of course! He is quite drunk," Trudolyubov said with disgust.

"I shall never forgive myself for letting him join us," Simonov muttered again.

"Now is the time to throw a bottle at their heads," I thought to myself. I picked up the bottle ... and filled my glass. ... "No, I'd better sit on to the end," I went on thinking; "you would be pleased, my friends, if I went away. Nothing will induce me to go. I'll go on sitting here and drinking to the end, on purpose, as a sign that I don't think you of the slightest consequence. I will go on sitting and drinking, because this is a

public-house and I paid my entrance money. I'll sit here and
drink, for I look upon you as so many pawns, as inanimate
pawns. I'll sit here and drink . . . and sing if I want to, yes, sing,
for I have the right to . . . to sing . . . H'm!"

But I did not sing. I simply tried not to look at any of them.
I assumed most unconcerned attitudes and waited with impatience for them to speak first. But alas, they did not address me!
And oh, how I wished, how I wished at that moment to be reconciled to them! It struck eight, at last nine. They moved from
the table to the sofa. Zverkov stretched himself on a lounge and
put one foot on a round table. Wine was brought there. He did,
as a fact, order three bottles on his own account. I, of course,
was not invited to join them. They all sat round him on the sofa.
They listened to him, almost with reverence. It was evident that
they were fond of him. "What for? What for?" I wondered.
From time to time they were moved to drunken enthusiasm
and kissed each other. They talked of the Caucasus, of the nature
of true passion, of snug berths in the service, of the income of
an hussar called Podkharzhevsky, whom none of them knew
personally, and rejoiced in the largeness of it, of the extraordinary grace and beauty of a Princess D., whom none of them had
ever seen; then it came to Shakespeare's being immortal.

I smiled contemptuously and walked up and down the other
side of the room, opposite the sofa, from the table to the stove
and back again. I tried my very utmost to show them that I
could do without them, and yet I purposely made a noise with
my boots, thumping with my heels. But it was all in vain. They
paid no attention. I had the patience to walk up and down in
front of them from eight o'clock till eleven, in the same place,
from the table to the stove and back again. "I walk up and down
to please myself and no one can prevent me." The waiter who
came into the room stopped, from time to time, to look at me.
I was somewhat giddy from turning round so often; at moments it seemed to me that I was in delirium. During those
three hours I was three times soaked with sweat and dry again.
At times, with an intense, acute pang I was stabbed to the heart
by the thought that ten years, twenty years, forty years would

pass, and that even in forty years I would remember with loathing and humiliation those filthiest, most ridiculous, and most awful moments of my life. No one could have gone out of his way to degrade himself more shamelessly, and I fully realized it, fully, and yet I went on pacing up and down from the table to the stove. "Oh, if you only knew what thoughts and feelings I am capable of, how cultured I am!" I thought at moments, mentally addressing the sofa on which my enemies were sitting. But my enemies behaved as though I were not in the room. Once—only once—they turned towards me, just when Zverkov was talking about Shakespeare, and I suddenly gave a contemptuous laugh. I laughed in such an affected and disgusting way that they all at once broke off their conversation, and silently and gravely for two minutes watched me walking up and down from the table to the stove, *taking no notice of them*. But nothing came of it: they said nothing, and two minutes later they ceased to notice me again. It struck eleven.

"Friends," cried Zverkov getting up from the sofa, "let us all be off now, *there!*"

"Of course, of course," the others assented. I turned sharply to Zverkov. I was so harassed, so exhausted, that I would have cut my throat to put an end to it. I was in a fever; my hair, soaked with perspiration, stuck to my forehead and temples.

"Zverkov, I beg your pardon," I said abruptly and resolutely. "Ferfichkin, yours too, and every one's, every one's: I have insulted you all!"

"Aha! A duel is not in your line, old man," Ferfichkin hissed venomously.

It sent a sharp pang to my heart.

"No, it's not the duel I am afraid of, Ferfichkin! I am ready to fight you to-morrow, after we are reconciled. I insist upon it, in fact, and you cannot refuse. I want to show you that I am not afraid of a duel. You shall fire first and I shall fire into the air."

"He is comforting himself," said Simonov.

"He's simply raving," said Trudolyubov.

"But let us pass. Why are you barring our way? What do you want?" Zverkov answered disdainfully.

They were all flushed; their eyes were bright: they had been drinking heavily.

"I ask for your friendship, Zverkov; I insulted you, but . . ."

"Insulted? *You* insulted *me*? Understand, sir, that you never, under any circumstances, could possibly insult *me*."

"And that's enough for you. Out of the way!" concluded Trudolyubov.

"Olympia is mine, friends, that's agreed!" cried Zverkov.

"We won't dispute your right, we won't dispute your right," the others answered, laughing.

I stood as though spat upon. The party went noisily out of the room. Trudolyubov struck up some stupid song. Simonov remained behind for a moment to tip the waiters. I suddenly went up to him.

"Simonov! give me six rubles!" I said, with desperate resolution.

He looked at me in extreme amazement, with vacant eyes. He, too, was drunk.

"You don't mean you are coming with us?"

"Yes."

"I've no money," he snapped out, and with a scornful laugh he went out of the room.

I clutched at his overcoat. It was a nightmare.

"Simonov, I saw you had money. Why do you refuse me? Am I a scoundrel? Beware of refusing me: if you knew, if you knew why I am asking! My whole future, my whole plans depend upon it!"

Simonov pulled out the money and almost flung it at me.

"Take it, if you have no sense of shame!" he pronounced pitilessly, and ran to overtake them.

I was left for a moment alone. Disorder, the remains of dinner, a broken wine-glass on the floor, spilt wine, cigarette ends, fumes of drink and delirium in my brain, an agonizing misery in my heart and finally the waiter, who had seen and heard all and was looking inquisitively into my face.

"I am going there!" I cried. "Either they shall all go down

on their knees to beg for my friendship, or I will give Zverkov
a slap in the face!"

V

"So this is it, this is it at last—contact with real life," I muttered as I ran headlong downstairs. "This is very different from the Pope's leaving Rome and going to Brazil,
very different from the ball on Lake Como!"

"You are a scoundrel," a thought flashed through my mind,
"if you laugh at this now."

"No matter!" I cried, answering myself. "Now everything is
lost!"

There was no trace to be seen of them, but that made no difference—I knew where they had gone.

At the steps was standing a solitary night sledge-driver in a
rough peasant coat, powdered over with the still falling, wet,
and as it were warm, snow. It was hot and steamy. The little
shaggy piebald horse was also covered with snow and cough-
ing, I remember that very well. I made a rush for the roughly
made sledge; but as soon as I raised my foot to get into it, the
recollection of how Simonov had just given me six rubles
seemed to double me up and I tumbled into the sledge like a
sack.

"No, I must do a great deal to make up for all that," I cried.
"But I will make up for it or perish on the spot this very night.
Start!"

We set off. There was a perfect whirl in my head.

"They won't go down on their knees to beg for my friendship. That is a mirage, cheap mirage, revolting, romantic and
fantastical—that's another ball on Lake Como. And so I am
bound to slap Zverkov's face! It is my duty to. And so it is settled; I am flying to give him a slap in the face. Hurry up!"

The driver tugged at the reins.

"As soon as I go in I'll give it him. Ought I before giving him the slap to say a few words by way of preface? No. I'll simply go in and give it him. They will all be sitting in the drawing-room, and he with Olympia on the sofa. That damned Olympia! She laughed at my looks on one occasion and refused me. I'll pull Olympia's hair, pull Zverkov's ears! No, better one ear, and pull him by it round the room. Maybe they will all begin beating me and will kick me out. That's most likely, indeed. No matter! Anyway, I shall first slap him; the initiative will be mine; and by the laws of honour that is everything: he will be branded and cannot wipe off the slap by any blows, by nothing but a duel. He will be forced to fight. And let them beat me now. Let them, the ungrateful wretches! Trudolyubov will beat me hardest, he is so strong; Ferfichkin will be sure to catch hold sideways and tug at my hair. But no matter, no matter! That's what I am going for. The blockheads will be forced at last to see the tragedy of it all! When they drag me to the door I shall call out to them that in reality they are not worth my little finger. Get on, driver, get on!" I cried to the driver. He started and flicked his whip, I shouted so savagely.

"We shall fight at daybreak, that's a settled thing. I've done with the office. Ferfichkin made a joke about it just now. But where can I get pistols? Nonsense! I'll get my salary in advance and buy them. And powder, and bullets? That's the second's business. And how can it all be done by daybreak? And where am I to get a second? I have no friends. Nonsense!" I cried, lashing myself up more and more. "It's of no consequence! the first person I meet in the street is bound to be my second, just as he would be bound to pull a drowning man out of water. The most eccentric things must be allowed. Even if I were to ask the director himself to be my second tomorrow, he would be bound to consent, if only from a feeling of chivalry, and to keep the secret! Anton Antonich. . . ."

The fact is, that at that very minute the disgusting absurdity of my plan and the other side of the question was clearer and more vivid to my imagination than it could be to any one on earth. But. . . .

"Get on, driver, get on, you rascal, get on!"

"Ugh, sir!" said the son of toil.

Cold shivers suddenly ran down me. Wouldn't it be better . . . to go straight home? My God, my God! Why did I invite myself to this dinner yesterday? But no, it's impossible. And my walking up and down for three hours from the table to the stove? No, they, they and no one else must pay for my walking up and down! They must wipe out this dishonour! Drive on!

And what if they give me into custody? They won't dare! They'll be afraid of the scandal. And what if Zverkov is so contemptuous that he refuses to fight a duel? He is sure to; but in that case I'll show them . . . I will turn up at the posting station when he is setting off to-morrow, I'll catch him by the leg, I'll pull off his coat when he gets into the carriage. I'll get my teeth into his hand, I'll bite him. "See what lengths you can drive a desperate man to!" He may hit me on the head and they may belabour me from behind. I will shout to the assembled multitude: "Look at this young puppy who is driving off to captivate the Circassian girls after letting me spit in his face!"

Of course, after that everything will be over! The office will have vanished off the face of the earth. I shall be arrested, I shall be tried, I shall be dismissed from the service, thrown in prison, sent to Siberia. Never mind! In fifteen years when they let me out of prison I will trudge off to him, a beggar, in rags. I shall find him in some provincial town. He will be married and happy. He will have a grown-up daughter. . . . I shall say to him: "Look, monster, at my hollow cheeks and my rags! I've lost everything—my career, my happiness, art, science, *the woman I loved*, and all through you. Here are pistols. I have come to discharge my pistol and . . . and I . . . forgive you. Then I shall fire into the air and he will hear nothing more of me. . . ."

I was actually on the point of tears, though I knew perfectly well at that moment that all this was out of Pushkin's *Silvio* and Lermontov's *Masquerade*.[29] And all at once I felt horribly ashamed, so ashamed that I stopped the horse, got out of the sledge, and stood still in the snow in the middle of the street. The driver gazed at me, sighing and astonished.

What was I to do? I could not go on there—it was evidently stupid, and I could not leave things as they were, because that would seem as though . . . Heavens, how could I leave things! And after such insults! "No!" I cried, throwing myself into the sledge again. "It is ordained! It is fate! Drive on, drive on!"

And in my impatience I punched the sledge-driver on the back of the neck.

"What are you up to? What are you hitting me for?" the peasant shouted, but he whipped up his nag so that it began kicking.

The wet snow was falling in big flakes; I unbuttoned myself, regardless of it. I forgot everything else, for I had finally decided on the slap, and felt with horror that it was going to happen *now, at once*, and that *no force could stop* it. The deserted street lamps gleamed sullenly in the snowy darkness like torches at a funeral. The snow drifted under my great-coat, under my coat, under my cravat, and melted there. I did not wrap myself up— all was lost, anyway.

At last we arrived. I jumped out, almost unconscious, ran up the steps and began knocking and kicking at the door. I felt fearfully weak, particularly in my legs and my knees. The door was opened quickly as though they knew I was coming. In fact, Simonov had warned them that perhaps another gentleman would arrive, and this was a place in which one had to give notice and to observe certain precautions. It was one of those "millinery establishments" which were abolished by the police a good time ago. By day it really was a shop; but at night, if one had an introduction, one might visit it for other purposes.

I walked rapidly through the dark shop into the familiar drawing-room, where there was only one candle burning, and stood still in amazement: there was no one there. "Where are they?" I asked somebody. But by now, of course, they had separated. Before me was standing a person with a stupid smile, the "madam" herself, who had seen me before. A minute later a door opened and another person came in.

Taking no notice of anything I strode about the room, and, I believe, I talked to myself. I felt as though I had been saved from death and was conscious of this, joyfully, all over: I should have given that slap, I should certainly, certainly have given it! But now they were not here and . . . everything had vanished and changed! I looked round. I could not grasp it yet. I looked mechanically at the girl who had come in: and had a glimpse of a fresh, young, rather pale face, with straight, dark eyebrows, and with grave, as it were wondering, eyes that attracted me at once; I should have hated her if she had been smiling. I began looking at her more intently and, as it were, with effort. I had not fully collected my thoughts. There was something simple and good-natured in her face, but something strangely grave. I am sure that this stood in her way here, and no one of those fools had noticed her. She could not, however, have been called a beauty, though she was tall, strong-looking, and well built. She was very simply dressed. Something loathsome stirred within me. I went straight up to her.

I chanced to look into the glass. My harassed face struck me as revolting in the extreme, pale, angry, abject, with dishevelled hair. "No matter, I am glad of it," I thought; "I am glad that I shall seem repulsive to her; I like that."

VI

. . . Somewhere behind a screen a clock began wheezing, as though oppressed by something, as though some one were strangling it. After an unnaturally prolonged wheezing there followed a shrill, nasty, and as it were unexpectedly rapid, chime—as though some one were suddenly jumping forward. It struck two. I woke up, though I had indeed not been asleep but lying half conscious.

It was almost completely dark in the narrow, cramped, low-pitched room, cumbered up with an enormous wardrobe and piles of cardboard boxes and all sorts of frippery and litter. The candle end that had been burning on the table was going out and gave a faint flicker from time to time. In a few minutes there would be complete darkness.

I was not long in coming to myself; everything came back to my mind at once, without an effort, as though it had been in ambush to pounce upon me again. And, indeed, even while I was unconscious a point seemed continually to remain in my memory unforgotten, and round it my dreams moved drearily. But strange to say, everything that had happened to me in that day seemed to me now, on waking, to be in the far, far away past, as though I had long, long ago lived all that down.

My head was full of fumes. Something seemed to be hovering over me, rousing me, exciting me, and making me restless. Misery and spite seemed surging up in me again and seeking an outlet. Suddenly I saw beside me two wide open eyes scrutinizing me curiously and persistently. The look in those eyes was coldly detached, sullen, as it were utterly remote; it weighed upon me.

A grim idea came into my brain and passed all over my body, as a horrible sensation, such as one feels when one goes into a damp and mouldy cellar. There was something unnatural in those two eyes, beginning to look at me only now. I recalled, too, that during those two hours I had not said a single word to this creature, and had, in fact, considered it utterly superfluous; in fact, the silence had for some reason gratified me. Now I suddenly realized vividly the hideous idea—revolting as a spider—of vice, which, without love, grossly and shamelessly begins with that in which true love finds its consummation. For a long time we gazed at each other like that, but she did not drop her eyes before mine and her expression did not change, so that at last I felt uncomfortable.

"What is your name?" I asked abruptly, to put an end to it.

"Liza," she answered almost in a whisper, but somehow far from graciously, and she turned her eyes away.

I was silent.

"What weather! The snow . . . it's disgusting!" I said, almost to myself, putting my arm under my head despondently, and gazing at the ceiling.

She made no answer. This was horrible.

"Have you always lived in Petersburg?" I asked a minute later, almost angrily, turning my head slightly towards her.

"No."

"Where do you come from?"

"From Riga," she answered reluctantly.

"Are you a German?"

"No, Russian."

"Have you been here long?"

"Where?"

"In this house?"

"A fortnight."

She spoke more and more jerkily. The candle went out; I could no longer distinguish her face.

"Have you a father and mother?"

"Yes . . . no . . . I have."

"Where are they?"

"There . . . in Riga."

"What are they?"

"Oh, nothing."

"Nothing? Why, what class are they?"

"Tradespeople."

"Have you always lived with them?"

"Yes."

"How old are you?"

"Twenty."

"Why did you leave them?"

"Oh, for no reason."

That answer meant "Let me alone; I feel sick, sad."

We were silent.

God knows why I did not go away. I felt myself more and more sick and dreary. The images of the previous day began of themselves, apart from my will, flitting through my memory in confusion. I suddenly recalled something I had seen that morning when, full of anxious thoughts, I was hurrying to the office.

"I saw them carrying a coffin out yesterday and they nearly dropped it," I suddenly said aloud, not that I desired to open the conversation, but as it were by accident.

"A coffin?"

"Yes, in the Haymarket;[30] they were bringing it up out of a cellar."

"From a cellar?"

"Not from a cellar, but from a basement. Oh, you know . . . down below . . . from a house of ill-fame. It was filthy all round . . . Egg-shells, litter . . . a stench. It was loathsome."

Silence.

"A nasty day to be buried," I began, simply to avoid being silent.

"Nasty, in what way?"

"The snow, the wet." (I yawned.)

"It makes no difference," she said suddenly, after a brief silence.

"No, it's horrid." (I yawned again.) "The gravediggers must have sworn at getting drenched by the snow. And there must have been water in the grave."

"Why water in the grave?" she asked, with a sort of curiosity, but speaking even more harshly and abruptly than before.

I suddenly began to feel provoked.

"Why, there must have been water at the bottom a foot deep. You can't dig a dry grave in Volkovo Cemetery."

"Why?"

"Why? Why, the place is waterlogged. It's a regular marsh. So they bury them in water. I've seen it myself . . . many times."

(I had never seen it once, indeed I had never been in Volkovo, and had only heard stories of it.)

"Do you mean to say, you don't mind how you die?"

"But why should I die?" she answered, as though defending herself.

"Why, some day you will die, and you will die just the same

as that dead woman. She was . . . a girl like you. She died of consumption."

"A wench would have died in hospital . . ." (She knows all about it already: she said "wench," not "girl.")

"She was in debt to her madam," I retorted, more and more provoked by the discussion; "and went on earning money for her up to the end, though she was in consumption. Some sledge-drivers standing by were talking about her to some soldiers and telling them so. No doubt they knew her. They were laughing. They were going to meet in a pot-house to drink to her memory."

A great deal of this was my invention. Silence followed, profound silence. She did not stir.

"And is it better to die in a hospital?"

"Isn't it just the same? Besides, why should I die?" she added irritably.

"If not now, a little later."

"Why a little later?"

"Why, indeed? Now you are young, pretty, fresh, you fetch a high price. But after another year of this life you will be very different—you will go off."

"In a year?"

"Anyway, in a year you will be worth less," I continued malignantly. "You will go from here to something lower, another house; a year later—to a third, lower and lower, and in seven years you will come to a basement in the Haymarket. That will be if you were lucky. But it would be much worse if you got some disease, consumption, say . . . and caught a chill, or something or other. It's not easy to get over an illness in your way of life. If you catch anything you may not get rid of it. And so you would die."

"Oh, well, then I shall die," she answered, quite vindictively, and she made a quick movement.

"But one is sorry."

"Sorry for whom?"

"Sorry for life."

Silence.

"Have you been engaged to be married? Eh?"

"What's that to you?"

"Oh, I am not cross-examining you. It's nothing to me. Why are you so cross? Of course you may have had your own troubles. What is it to me? It's simply that I felt sorry."

"Sorry for whom?"

"Sorry for you."

"No need," she whispered hardly audibly, and again made a faint movement.

That incensed me at once. What! I was so gentle with her, and she. . . .

"Why, do you think that you are on the right path?"

"I don't think anything."

"That's what's wrong, that you don't think. Realize it while there is still time. There still is time. You are still young, good-looking; you might love, be married, be happy. . . ."

"Not all married women are happy," she snapped out in the rude abrupt tone she had used at first.

"Not all, of course, but anyway it is much better than the life here. Infinitely better. Besides, with love one can live even without happiness. Even in sorrow life is sweet; life is sweet, however one lives. But here what is there but . . . foulness? Phew!"

I turned away with disgust; I was no longer reasoning coldly. I began to feel myself what I was saying and warmed to the subject. I was already longing to expound the cherished ideas I had brooded over in my corner. Something suddenly flared up in me. An object had appeared before me.

"Never mind my being here, I am not an example for you. I am, perhaps, worse than you are. I was drunk when I came here, though," I hastened, however, to say in self-defence. "Besides, a man is no example for a woman. It's a different thing. I may degrade and defile myself, but I am not any one's slave. I come and go, and that's an end of it. I shake it off, and I am a different man. But you are a slave from the start. Yes, a slave! You give up everything, your whole freedom. If you want to break your chains afterwards, you won't be able to: you will be more and more fast in the snares. It is an accursed bondage. I know it. I won't speak of anything else, maybe you won't understand, but tell me: no doubt you are in debt to your madam? There, you see," I added, though she made no answer, but only listened in silence, entirely absorbed, "that's a bondage for you! You will never buy your freedom. They will see to that. It's like selling your soul to the devil. . . . And besides . . . perhaps I, too, am just as unlucky—how do you know—and wallow in the mud on purpose, out of misery? You know, men take to drink from grief; well, maybe I am here from grief. Come, tell me, what is there good here? Here you and I . . . came together . . . just now and did not say one word to one another all the time, and it was only afterwards you began staring at me like a wild creature, and I at you. Is that loving? Is that how one human being should meet another? It's hideous, that's what it is!"

"Yes!" she assented sharply and hurriedly.

I was positively astounded by the promptitude of this "Yes." So the same thought may have been straying through her mind when she was staring at me just before. So she, too, was capable of certain thoughts? "Damn it all, this was interesting, this was a point of likeness!" I thought, almost rubbing my hands. And indeed it's easy to turn a young soul like that!

It was the exercise of my power that attracted me most.

She turned her head nearer to me, and it seemed to me in the darkness that she propped herself on her arm. Perhaps she was scrutinizing me. How I regretted that I could not see her eyes. I heard her deep breathing.

"Why have you come here?" I asked her, with a note of authority already in my voice.

"Oh, I don't know."

"But how nice it would be to be living in your father's house! It's warm and free; you have a home of your own."

"But what if it's worse than this?"

"I must take the right tone," flashed through my mind. "I may not get far with sentimentality." But it was only a momentary thought. I swear she really did interest me. Besides, I was exhausted and moody. And cunning so easily goes hand-in-hand with feeling.

"Who denies it!" I hastened to answer. "Anything may happen. I am convinced that some one has wronged you, and that you are more sinned against than sinning. Of course, I know nothing of your story, but it's not likely a girl like you has come here of her own inclination. . . ."

"A girl like me?" she whispered, hardly audibly; but I heard it.

Damn it all, I was flattering her. That was horrid. But perhaps it was a good thing. . . . She was silent.

"See, Liza, I will tell you about myself. If I had had a home from childhood, I shouldn't be what I am now. I often think that. However bad it may be at home, anyway they are your father and mother, and not enemies, strangers. Once a year at least, they'll show their love of you. Anyway, you know you are at home. I grew up without a home; and perhaps that's why I've turned so . . . unfeeling."

I waited again. "Perhaps she doesn't understand," I thought, "and, indeed, it is absurd—it's moralizing."

"If I were a father and had a daughter, I believe I should love my daughter more than my sons, really," I began indirectly, as though talking of something else, to distract her attention. I must confess I blushed.

"Why so?" she asked.

Ah! so she was listening!

"I don't know, Liza. I knew a father who was a stern, austere man, but used to go down on his knees to his daughter, used to kiss her hands, her feet, he couldn't make enough of her, really. When she danced at parties he used to stand for five hours at a stretch, gazing at her. He was mad over her: I understand that! She would fall asleep tired at night, and he would wake to kiss her in her sleep and make the sign of the cross over her. He would go about in a dirty old coat, he was stingy to every one else, but would spend his last penny for her, giving her expensive presents, and it was his greatest delight when she was pleased with what he gave her. Fathers always love their daughters more than the mothers do. Some girls live happily at home! And I believe I should never let my daughters marry."

"What next?" she said, with a faint smile.

"I should be jealous, I really should. To think that she should kiss any one else! That she should love a stranger more than her father! It's painful to imagine it. Of course, that's all nonsense, of course every father would be reasonable at last. But I believe before I should let her marry, I should worry myself to death; I should find fault with all her suitors. But I should end by letting her marry whom she herself loved. The one whom the daughter loves always seems the worst to the father, you know. That is always so. So many family troubles come from that."

"Some are glad to sell their daughters, rather than marrying them honourably."

Ah, so that was it!

"Such a thing, Liza, happens in those accursed families in which there is neither love nor God," I retorted warmly, "and where there is no love, there is no sense either. There are such families, it's true, but I am not speaking of them. You must have seen wickedness in your own family, if you talk like that. Truly, you must have been unlucky. H'm! . . . that sort of thing mostly comes about through poverty."

"And is it any better with the gentry? Even among the poor, honest people live happily."

"H'm . . . yes. Perhaps. Another thing, Liza, man is fond of reckoning up his troubles, but does not count his joys. If he counted them up as he ought, he would see that every lot has enough happiness provided for it. And what if all goes well with the family, if the blessing of God is upon it, if the husband is a good one, loves you, cherishes you, never leaves you! There is happiness in such a family! Even sometimes there is happiness in the midst of sorrow; and indeed sorrow is everywhere. If you marry you will find out for yourself. But think of the first years of married life with one you love: what happiness, what happiness there sometimes is in it! And indeed it's the ordinary thing. In those early days even quarrels with one's husband end happily. Some women get up quarrels with their husbands just because they love them. Indeed, I knew a woman like that: she seemed to say that because she loved him, she would torment

him and make him feel it. You know that you may torment a
man on purpose through love. Women are particularly given to
that, thinking to themselves 'I will love him so, I will make so
much of him afterwards, that it's no sin to torment him a little
now.' And all in the house rejoice in the sight of you, and you
are happy and gay and peaceful and honourable. . . . Then there
are some women who are jealous. If he went off anywhere—I
knew one such woman, she couldn't restrain herself, but would
jump up at night and run off on the sly to find out where he
was, whether he was with some other woman. That's a pity. And
the woman knows herself it's wrong, and her heart fails her and
she suffers, but she loves—it's all through love. And how sweet
it is to make it up after quarrels, to own herself in the wrong
or to forgive him! And they are both so happy all at once—as
though they had met anew, been married over again; as though
their love had begun afresh. And no one, no one should know
what passes between husband and wife if they love one another.
And whatever quarrels there may be between them they ought
not to call in their own mother to judge between them and tell
tales of one another. They are their own judges. Love is a holy
mystery and ought to be hidden from all other eyes, whatever
happens. That makes it holier and better. They respect one another more, and much is built on respect. And if once there has
been love, if they have been married for love, why should love
pass away? Surely one can keep it! It is rare that one cannot keep
it. And if the husband is kind and straightforward, why should
not love last? The first phase of married love will pass, it is true,
but then there will come a love that is better still. Then there
will be the union of souls, they will have everything in common, there will be no secrets between them. And once they
have children, the most difficult times will seem to them happy,
so long as there is love and courage. Even toil will be a joy, you
may deny yourself bread for your children and even that will be
a joy. They will love you for it afterwards; so you are laying by
for your future. As the children grow up you feel that you are
an example, a support for them; that even after you die your
children will always keep your thoughts and feelings, because

they have received them from you, they will take on your semblance and likeness. So you see this is a great duty. How can it
fail to draw the father and mother nearer? People say it's a trial
to have children. Who says that? It is heavenly happiness! Are
you fond of little children, Liza? I am awfully fond of them. You
know—a little rosy baby boy at your bosom, and what husband's heart is not touched, seeing his wife nursing his child!
A plump little rosy baby, sprawling and snuggling, chubby little hands and feet, clean tiny little nails, so tiny that it makes one
laugh to look at them; eyes that look as if they understand
everything. And while it sucks it clutches at your bosom with
its little hand, plays. When its father comes up, the child tears
itself away from the bosom, flings itself back, looks at its father,
laughs, as though it were fearfully funny and falls to sucking
again. Or it will bite its mother's breast when its little teeth are
coming, while it looks sideways at her with its little eyes as
though to say, 'Look, I am biting!' Is not all that happiness when
they are the three together, husband, wife and child? One can
forgive a great deal for the sake of such moments. Yes, Liza, one
must first learn to live oneself before one blames others!"

"It's by pictures, pictures like that one must get at you," I
thought to myself, though I did speak with real feeling, and all
at once I flushed crimson. "What if she were suddenly to burst
out laughing, what should I do then?" That idea drove me to
fury. Towards the end of my speech I really was excited, and
now my vanity was somehow wounded. The silence continued.
I almost nudged her.

"Why are you——" she began and stopped. But I understood: there was a quiver of something different in her voice,
not abrupt, harsh and unyielding as before, but something soft
and shamefaced, so shamefaced that I suddenly felt ashamed
and guilty.

"What?" I asked, with tender curiosity.

"Why, you . . ."

"What?"

"Why, you . . . speak somehow like a book," she said, and
again there was a note of irony in her voice.

That remark sent a pang to my heart. It was not what I was expecting.

I did not understand that she was hiding her feelings under irony, that this is usually the last refuge of modest and chaste-souled people when the privacy of their soul is coarsely and intrusively invaded, and that their pride makes them refuse to surrender till the last moment and shrink from giving expression to their feelings before you. I ought to have guessed the truth from the timidity with which she had repeatedly approached her sarcasm, only bringing herself to utter it at last with an effort. But I did not guess, and an evil feeling took possession of me.

"Wait a bit!" I thought.

VII

"Oh, hush, Liza! How can you talk about being like a book, when it makes even me, an outsider, feel sick? Though I don't look at it as an outsider, for, indeed, it touches me to the heart. . . . Is it possible, is it possible that you do not feel sick at being here yourself? Evidently habit does wonders! God knows what habit can do with any one. Can you seriously think that you will never grow old, that you will always be good-looking, and that they will keep you here for ever and ever? I say nothing of the loathsomeness of the life here. . . . Though let me tell you this about it—about your present life, I mean; here though you are young now, attractive, nice, with soul and feeling, yet you know as soon as I came to myself just now I felt at once sick at being here with you! One can only come here when one is drunk. But if you were anywhere else, living as good people live, I should perhaps be more than attracted by you, should fall in love with you, should be glad of a look from you, let alone a word; I should hang about your door, should go down on my knees to you, should look upon you as my betrothed and think it an honour to be allowed to. I should not dare to have an impure thought about you. But here, you see, I know that I have only to whistle and you have to come with me whether you like it or not. I don't consult your wishes, but you mine. The lowest labourer hires himself as a workman, but he doesn't make a slave of himself altogether; besides, he knows that he will be free again presently. But when are you free? Only think what you are giving up here? What is it you are making a slave of? It is your soul, together with your body; you are selling your soul which you have no right to dispose of! You give your love to be outraged by every drunkard! Love! But that's everything, you know, it's a priceless diamond, it's a maiden's treasure, love—why, a man would be ready to give his soul, to face death to gain that love. But how much is your love worth now? You are sold, all of you, body and soul, and there is no need to strive for love when you can have everything without love. And you know there is no greater insult to a girl than that, do you understand? To be sure, I have heard that they comfort you, poor fools, they let you have lovers of your own here. But you know that's simply a farce, that's simply a sham, it's just laughing at you, and you are taken in by it! Why, do you suppose he really loves you, that lover of yours? I don't believe it. How can he love you when he knows you may be called away from him any minute? He would be a low fellow if he did! Will he have a grain of respect for you? What have you in common with him? He laughs at you and robs you—that is all his love amounts to! You are lucky if he does not beat you. Very likely he does beat you, too. Ask him, if you have got one, whether he will marry you. He will laugh in your face, if he doesn't spit in it or give you a blow—though maybe he is not worth a bad halfpenny himself. And for what have you ruined your life, if you come to think of it? For the coffee they give you to drink and the plentiful meals? But with what object are they feeding you up? An honest girl couldn't swallow the food, for she would know what she was being fed for. You are in debt here, and, of course, you will always be in debt, and you will go on in debt to the end, till the visitors here begin to scorn you. And that will soon happen, don't rely upon your youth—all that flies by express train here, you know. You will be kicked out. And not simply kicked out; long before that she'll begin nagging at you, scolding you, abusing you, as though you had not sacrificed your health for her, had not thrown away your youth and your soul for her benefit, but as though you had ruined her, beggared her, robbed her. And don't expect any one to take your part: the others, your companions, will attack you, too, to win her favour, for all are in slavery here, and have lost all conscience and pity here long ago. They have become utterly vile, and nothing on earth is viler, more loathsome, and more insulting than their abuse. And you are laying down everything here, unconditionally, youth and health and beauty and hope, and at twenty-two you will look like a woman of five-and-thirty, and you will be lucky if you are not diseased, pray to God for that! No doubt you are thinking now that you have a gay time and no work to do! Yet there is no work harder or more dreadful in the world or ever has been. One would think that the heart alone would be worn out with tears. And you won't dare to say a word, not half a word when they drive you away from here; you will go away as though you were to blame. You will change to another house, then to a third, then somewhere else, till you come down at last to the Haymarket. There you will be beaten at every turn; that is good manners there, the visitors don't know how to be friendly without beating you. You don't believe that it is so hateful there? Go and look for yourself some time, you can see with your own eyes. Once, one New Year's Day, I saw a woman at a door. They had turned her out as a joke, to give her a taste of the frost because she had been crying so much, and they shut the door behind her. At nine o'clock in the morning she was already quite drunk, dishevelled, half-naked, covered with bruises, her face was powdered, but she had a black eye, blood was trickling from her nose and her teeth; some cabman had just given her a drubbing. She was sitting on the stone steps, a salt fish of some sort was in her hand; she was crying, wailing something about her luck and beating with the fish on the steps, and cabmen and drunken soldiers were crowding in the doorway taunting her. You don't believe that you will ever be like that? I should be sorry to believe it, too, but how do you know; maybe ten years, eight years ago that very woman with the salt fish came here fresh as a cherub, innocent, pure, knowing no evil, blushing at every word. Perhaps she was like you, proud, ready to take offence, not like the others; perhaps she looked like a queen, and knew what happiness was in store for the man who should love her and whom she should love. Do you see how it ended? And what if at that very minute when she was beating on the filthy steps with that fish, drunken and dishevelled—what if at that very minute she recalled the pure early days in her father's house, when she used to go to school and the neighbour's son watched for her on the way, declaring that he would love her as long as he lived, that he would devote his life to her, and when they vowed to love one another for ever and be married as soon as they were grown up! No, Liza, it would be happy for you if you were to die soon of consumption in some corner, in some cellar like that woman just now. In the hospital, do you say? You will be lucky if they take you, but what if you are still of use to the madam here? Consumption is a queer disease, it is not like fever. The patient goes on hoping till the last minute and says he is all right. He deludes himself. And that just suits your madam. Don't doubt it, that's how it is; you have sold your soul, and what is more you owe money, so you daren't say a word. But when you are dying, all will abandon you, all will turn away from you, for then there will be nothing to get from you. What's more, they will reproach you for cumbering the place, for being so long over dying. However you beg you won't get a drink of water without abuse: 'Whenever are you going off, you nasty hussy, you won't let us sleep with your moaning, you make the gentlemen sick.' That's true, I have heard such things said myself. They will thrust you dying into the filthiest corner in the cellar—in the damp and darkness; what will your thoughts be, lying there alone? When you die, strange hands will lay you out, with grumbling and impatience; no one will bless you, no one will sigh for you, they only want to get rid of you as soon as may be; they will buy a coffin, take you to the grave as they did that poor woman to-day, and celebrate your memory at the tavern. In the grave, sleet, filth, wet snow—no need to put themselves out for you—'Let her down, Vanukha; it's just like her luck—even here, she is head-foremost, the hussy. Shorten the cord, you rascal.' 'It's all right as it is.' 'All right, is it? Why, she's on her side! She was a fellow creature, after all! But, never mind, throw the earth on her.' And they won't care to waste much time quarrelling over you. They will scatter the wet blue clay as quick as they can and go off to the tavern . . . and there your memory on earth will end; other women have children to go to their graves, fathers, husbands. While for you neither tear, nor sigh, nor remembrance; no one in the whole world will ever come to you, your name will vanish from the face of the earth—as though you had never existed, never been born at all! Nothing but filth and mud, however you knock at your coffin lid at night, when the dead arise, however you cry: 'Let me out, kind people, to live in the light of day! My life was no life at all; my life has been thrown away like a dishclout; it was drunk away in the tavern at the Haymarket; let me out, kind people, to live in the world again.'"

And I worked myself up to such a pitch that I began to have a lump in my throat myself, and . . . and all at once I stopped, sat up in dismay, and bending over apprehensively, began to listen with a beating heart. I had reason to be troubled.

I had felt for some time that I was turning her soul upside down and rending her heart, and—and the more I was convinced of it, the more eagerly I desired to gain my object as quickly and as effectually as possible. It was the exercise of my skill that carried me away; yet it was not merely sport. . . .

I knew I was speaking stiffly, artificially, even bookishly, in fact, I could not speak except "like a book." But that did not trouble me: I knew, I felt that I should be understood and that this very bookishness might be an assistance. But now, having attained my effect, I was suddenly panic-stricken. Never before had I witnessed such despair! She was lying on her face, thrusting her face into the pillow and clutching it in both hands. Her heart was being torn. Her youthful body was shuddering all over as though in convulsions. Suppressed sobs rent her bosom and suddenly burst out in weeping and wailing, then she pressed closer into the pillow: she did not want any one here, not a living soul, to know of her anguish and her tears. She bit the pillow, bit her hand till it bled (I saw that afterwards), or, thrusting her fingers into her dishevelled hair seemed rigid with the effort of restraint, holding her breath and clenching her teeth. I began saying something, begging her to calm herself, but felt that I did not dare; and all at once, in a sort of cold shiver, almost in terror, began fumbling in the dark, trying hurriedly to get dressed to go. It was dark: though I tried my best I could not finish dressing quickly. Suddenly I felt a box of matches and a candlestick with a whole candle in it. As soon as the room was lighted up, Liza sprang up, sat up in bed, and with a contorted face, with a half insane smile, looked at me almost senselessly. I sat down beside her and took her hands; she came to herself, made an impulsive movement towards me, would have caught hold of me, but did not dare, and slowly bowed her head before me.

"Liza, my dear, I was wrong . . . forgive me, my dear," I began, but she squeezed my hand in her fingers so tightly that I felt I was saying the wrong thing and stopped.

"This is my address, Liza, come to me."

"I will come," she answered resolutely, her head still bowed.

"But now I am going, good-bye . . . till we meet again."

I got up; she, too, stood up and suddenly flushed all over, gave a shudder, snatched up a shawl that was lying on a chair and muffled herself in it to her chin. As she did this she gave another sickly smile, blushed and looked at me strangely. I felt wretched; I was in haste to get away—to disappear.

"Wait a minute," she said suddenly, in the passage just at the doorway, stopping me with her hand on my overcoat. She put down the candle in hot haste and ran off; evidently she had thought of something or wanted to show me something. As she ran away she flushed, her eyes shone, and there was a smile on her lips—what was the meaning of it? Against my will I waited: she came back a minute later with an expression that seemed to ask forgiveness for something. In fact, it was not the same face, not the same look as the evening before: sullen, mistrustful and obstinate. Her eyes now were imploring, soft, and at the same time trustful, caressing, timid. The expression with which children look at people they are very fond of, of whom they are asking a favour. Her eyes were a light hazel, they were lovely eyes, full of life, and capable of expressing love as well as sullen hatred.

Making no explanation, as though I, as a sort of higher being, must understand everything without explanations, she held out a piece of paper to me. Her whole face was positively beaming at that instant with naïve, almost childish, triumph. I unfolded it. It was a letter to her from a medical student or some one of that sort—a very high-flown and flowery, but extremely respectful, love-letter. I don't recall the words now, but I remember well that through the high-flown phrases there was apparent a genuine feeling, which cannot be feigned. When I had finished reading it I met her glowing, questioning, and childishly impatient eyes fixed upon me. She fastened her eyes upon my face and waited impatiently for what I should say. In a few words, hurriedly, but with a sort of joy and pride, she explained to me that she bad been to a dance somewhere in a private house, a family of "very nice people, who knew nothing, absolutely nothing, for she had only come here so lately and it had all happened . . . and she hadn't made up her mind to stay and was certainly going away as soon as she had paid her debt . . ." and at that party there had been the student who had danced with her all the evening. He had talked to her, and it turned out that he had known her in old days at Riga when he was a child, they had played together, but a very long time ago—and he knew her parents, but about this he knew nothing, nothing whatever, and had no suspicion! And the day after the dance (three days ago) he had sent her that letter through the friend with whom she had gone to the party . . . and . . . well, that was all."

She dropped her shining eyes with a sort of bashfulness as she finished.

The poor girl was keeping that student's letter as a precious treasure, and had run to fetch it, her only treasure, because she did not want me to go away without knowing that she, too, was honestly and genuinely loved; that she, too, was addressed respectfully. No doubt that letter was destined to lie in her box and lead to nothing. But none the less, I am certain that she would keep it all her life as a precious treasure, as her pride and justification, and now at such a minute she had thought of that letter and brought it with naïve pride to raise herself in my eyes that I might see, that I, too, might think well of her. I said nothing, pressed her hand and went out. I so longed to get away. . . . I walked all the way home, in spite of the fact that the melting snow was still falling in heavy flakes. I was exhausted, shattered, in bewilderment. But behind the bewilderment the truth was already gleaming. The loathsome truth.

VIII

It was some time, however, before I consented to recognize that truth. Waking up in the morning after some hours of heavy, leaden sleep, and immediately realizing all that had happened on the previous day, I was positively amazed at my last night's *sentimentality* with Liza, at all those "outcries of horror and pity." "To think of having such an attack of womanish hysteria, pah!" I concluded. And what did I thrust my address upon her for? What if she comes? Let her come, though; it doesn't matter. . . . But *obviously*, that was not now the chief and the most important matter: I had to make haste and at all costs save my reputation in the eyes of Zverkov and Simonov as quickly as possible; that was the chief business. And I was so taken up that morning that I actually forgot all about Liza.

First of all I had at once to repay what I had borrowed the day before from Simonov. I resolved on a desperate measure: to borrow fifteen rubles straight off from Anton Antonich. As luck would have it he was in the best of humours that morning, and gave it to me at once, on the first asking. I was so delighted at this that, as I signed the I O U with a swaggering air, I told him casually that the night before "I had been keeping it up with some friends at the Hôtel de Paris; we were giving a farewell party to a comrade, in fact, I might say a friend of my child-hood, and you know—a desperate rake, fearfully spoilt—of course, he belongs to a good family, and has considerable means, a brilliant career; he is witty, charming, a regular Lovelace,[31] you understand; we drank an extra 'half-dozen' and . . ."

And it went off all right; all this was uttered very easily, un-constrainedly and complacently.

On reaching home I promptly wrote to Simonov.

To this hour I am lost in admiration when I recall the truly gentlemanly, good-humoured, candid tone of my letter. With tact and good-breeding, and, above all, entirely without super-fluous words, I blamed myself for all that had happened. I de-fended myself, "if I really may be allowed to defend myself," by alleging that being utterly unaccustomed to wine, I had been intoxicated with the first glass, which I said, I had drunk before they arrived, while I was waiting for them at the Hôtel de Paris between five and six o'clock. I begged Simonov's pardon espe-cially; I asked him to convey my explanations to all the others, especially to Zverkov, whom "I seemed to remember as though in a dream" I had insulted. I added that I would have called upon all of them myself, but my head ached, and besides I had not the face to. I was particularly pleased with a certain light-ness, almost carelessness (strictly within the bounds of polite-ness, however), which was apparent in my style, and better than any possible arguments, gave them at once to understand that I took rather an independent view of "all that unpleasantness last night;" that I was by no means so utterly crushed as you, my friends, probably imagine; but on the contrary, looked upon it as a gentleman serenely respecting himself should look upon it. "On a young hero's past no censure is cast!"

"There is actually an aristocratic playfulness about it!" I thought admiringly, as I read over the letter. And it's all because I am an intellectual and cultivated man! Another man in my place would not have known how to extricate himself, but here I have got out of it and am as jolly as ever again, and all because I am "a cultivated and educated man of our day." And, indeed, perhaps, everything was due to the wine yesterday. H'm! . . . no, it was not the wine. I did not drink anything at all between five and six when I was waiting for them. I had lied to Simonov; I had lied shamelessly; and indeed I wasn't ashamed now. . . . Hang it all though, the great thing was that I was rid of it.

I put six rubles in the letter, sealed it up, and asked Apollon to take it to Simonov. When he learned that there was money in the letter, Apollon became more respectful and agreed to take it. Towards evening I went out for a walk. My head was still aching and giddy after yesterday. But as evening came on and the twilight grew denser, my impressions and, following them, my thoughts, grew more and more different and confused. Something was not dead within me, in the depths of my heart and conscience it would not die, and it showed itself in acute depression. For the most part I jostled my way through the most crowded business streets, along Myeshchansky Street, along Sadovy Street and in Yusupov Garden. I always liked particularly sauntering along these streets in the dusk, just when there were crowds of working people of all sorts going home from their daily work, with faces looking cross with anxiety. What I liked was just that cheap bustle, that bare prose. On this occasion the jostling of the streets irritated me more than ever. I could not make out what was wrong with me, I could not find the clue, something seemed rising up continually in my soul, painfully, and refusing to be appeased. I returned home completely upset, it was just as though some crime were lying on my conscience.

The thought that Liza was coming worried me continually. It seemed queer to me that of all my recollections of yesterday this tormented me, as it were, especially, as it were, quite separately. Everything else I had quite succeeded in forgetting by the evening; I dismissed it all and was still perfectly satisfied with my letter to Simonov. But on this point I was not satisfied at all. It was as though I were worried only by Liza. "What if she comes," I thought incessantly, "well, it doesn't matter, let her come! H'm! it's horrid that she should see, for instance, how I live. Yesterday I seemed such a hero to her, while now, h'm! It's horrid, though, that I have let myself go so, the room looks like a beggar's. And I brought myself to go out to dinner in such a suit! And my Turkish divan with the stuffing sticking out. And my dressing-gown, which will not cover me, such tatters, and she will see all this and she will see Apollon. That beast is certain to insult her. He will fasten upon her in order to be rude to me. And I, of course, shall be panic-stricken as usual, I shall begin bowing and scraping before her and pulling my dressing-gown round me, I shall begin smiling, telling lies. Oh, the beastliness! And it isn't the beastliness of it that matters most! There is something more important, more loathsome, viler! Yes, viler! And to put on that dishonest lying mask again!" . . .

When I reached that thought I fired up all at once.

"Why dishonest? How dishonest? I was speaking sincerely last night. I remember there was real feeling in me, too. What I wanted was to excite an honourable feeling in her. . . . Her crying was a good thing, it will have a good effect."

Yet I could not feel at ease. All that evening, even when I had come back home, even after nine o'clock, when I calculated that Liza could not possibly come, she still haunted me, and what was worse, she came back to my mind always in the same position. One moment out of all that had happened last night stood vividly before my imagination; the moment when I struck a match and saw her pale, distorted face, with its look of torture. And what a pitiful, what an unnatural, what a distorted smile she had at that moment! But I did not know then, that fifteen years later I should still in my imagination see Liza, always with the pitiful, distorted, inappropriate smile which was on her face at that minute.

Next day I was ready again to look upon it all as nonsense, due to over-excited nerves, and, above all, as *exaggerated*. I was always conscious of that weak point of mine, and sometimes very much afraid of it. "I exaggerate everything, that is where I go wrong," I repeated to myself every hour. But, however, "Liza will very likely come all the same," was the refrain with which all my reflections ended. I was so uneasy that I sometimes flew into a fury: "She'll come, she is certain to come!" I cried, running about the room, "if not to-day, she will come to-morrow; she'll find me out! The damnable romanticism of these pure hearts! Oh, the vileness—oh, the silliness—oh, the stupidity of these 'wretched sentimental souls!' Why, how fail to understand? How could one fail to understand? . . ."

But at this point I stopped short, and in great confusion, indeed.

And how few, how few words, I thought, in passing, were needed; how little of the idyllic (and affectedly, bookishly, artificially idyllic too) had sufficed to turn a whole human life at once according to my will. That's virginity, to be sure! Freshness of soil!

At times a thought occurred to me, to go to her, "to tell her all," and beg her not to come to me. But this thought stirred such wrath in me that I believed I should have crushed that "damned" Liza if she had chanced to be near me at the time. I should have insulted her, have spat at her, have turned her out, have struck her!

One day passed, however, another and another; she did not come and I began to grow calmer. I felt particularly bold and cheerful after nine o'clock, I even sometimes began dreaming, and rather sweetly: I, for instance, became the salvation of Liza, simply through her coming to me and my talking to her. . . . I develop her, educate her. Finally, I notice that she loves me, loves me passionately. I pretend not to understand (I don't know, however, why I pretend, just for effect, perhaps). At last all confusion, transfigured, trembling and sobbing, she flings herself at my feet and says that I am her saviour, and that she loves me better than anything in the world. I am amazed, but. . . . "Liza," I say, "can you imagine that I have not noticed your love, I saw it all, I divined it, but I did not dare to approach you first, because I had an influence over you and was afraid that you would force yourself, from gratitude, to respond to my love, would try to rouse in your heart a feeling which was perhaps absent, and I did not wish that . . . because it would be tyranny . . . it would be indelicate (in short, I launch off at that point into European, inexplicably lofty subtleties à la George Sand),[32] but now, now you are mine, you are my creation, you are pure, you are good, you are my noble wife.

> 'Into my house come bold and free,
> Its rightful mistress there to be.' "[33]

Then we begin living together, go abroad and so on, and so on. In fact, in the end it seemed vulgar to me myself, and I began putting out my tongue at myself.

Besides, they won't let her out, "the hussy!" I thought. They don't let them go out very readily, especially in the evening (for some reason I fancied she would come in the evening, and at seven o'clock precisely). Though she did say she was not altogether a slave there yet, and had certain rights; so, h'm! Damn it all, she will come, she is sure to come!

It was a good thing, in fact, that Apollon distracted my attention at that time by his rudeness. He drove me beyond all patience! He was the bane of my life, the curse laid upon me by Providence. We had been squabbling continually for years, and I hated him. My God, how I hated him! I believe I had never hated any one in my life as I hated him, especially at some moments. He was an elderly, dignified man, who worked part of his time as a tailor. But for some unknown reason he despised me beyond all measure, and looked down upon me insufferably. Though, indeed, he looked down upon every one. Simply to glance at that flaxen, smoothly brushed head, at the tuft of hair he combed up on his forehead and oiled with sunflower oil, at that dignified mouth, compressed into the shape of the letter V, made one feel one was confronting a man who never doubted of himself. He was a pedant, to the most extreme point, the greatest pedant I had met on earth, and with that had a vanity only befitting Alexander of Macedon.* He was in love with every button on his coat, every nail on his fingers—absolutely in love with them, and he looked it! In his behaviour to me he was a perfect tyrant, he spoke very little to me, and if he chanced to glance at me he gave me a firm, majestically self-confident and invariably ironical look that drove me sometimes to fury. He did his work with the air of doing me the greatest favour. Though he did scarcely anything for me, and did not, indeed, consider himself bound to do anything. There could be no doubt that he looked upon me as the greatest fool on earth, and that "he did not get rid of me" was simply that he could get wages from me every month. He consented to do nothing for me for seven rubles a month. Many sins should be forgiven me for what I suffered from him. My hatred reached such a point that sometimes his very step almost threw me into convulsions. What I loathed particularly was his lisp. His tongue must have been a little too long or something of that sort, for he continually lisped, and seemed to be very proud of it, imagining that it greatly added to his dignity. He spoke in a slow, measured tone, with his hands behind his back and his eyes fixed on the ground. He maddened me particularly when he read aloud the psalms to himself behind his partition. Many a battle I waged over that reading! But he was awfully fond of reading aloud in the evenings, in a slow, even, sing-song voice, as though over the dead. It is interesting that that is how he has ended: he hires himself out to read the psalms over the dead, and at the same time he kills rats and makes blacking. But at that time I could not get rid of him, it was as though he were chemically combined with my existence. Besides, nothing would

---

*King of Macedonia (356–323 B.C.); better known as Alexander the Great.

have induced him to consent to leave me. I could not live in furnished lodgings: my lodging was my private solitude, my shell, my cave, in which I concealed myself from all mankind, and Apollon seemed to me, for some reason, an integral part of that flat, and for seven years I could not turn him away.

To be two or three days behind with his wages, for instance, was impossible. He would have made such a fuss, I should not have known where to hide my head. But I was so exasperated with every one during those days, that I made up my mind for some reason and with some object to punish Apollon and not to pay him for a fortnight the wages that were owing him. I had for a long time—for the last two years—been intending to do this, simply in order to teach him not to give himself airs with me, and to show him that if I liked I could withhold his wages. I purposed to say nothing to him about it, and was purposely silent indeed, in order to score off his pride and force him to be the first to speak of his wages. Then I would take the seven rubles out of a drawer, show him I have the money put aside on purpose, but that I won't, I won't, I simply won't pay him his wages, I won't just because that is "what I wish," because "I am master, and it is for me to decide," because he has been disrespectful, because he has been rude; but if he were to ask respectfully I might be softened and give it to him, otherwise he might wait another fortnight, another three weeks, a whole month. . . .

But angry as I was, yet he got the better of me. I could not hold out for four days. He began as he always did begin in such cases, for there had been such cases already, there had been attempts (and it may be observed I knew all this beforehand, I knew his nasty tactics by heart). He would begin by fixing upon me an exceedingly severe stare, keeping it up for several minutes at a time, particularly on meeting me or seeing me out of the house. If I held out and pretended not to notice these stares, he would, still in silence, proceed to further tortures. All at once, *à propos* of nothing, he would walk softly and smoothly into my room, when I was pacing up and down or reading, stand at the door, one hand behind his back and one foot behind the other, and fix upon me a stare more than severe, utterly contemptuous. If I suddenly asked him what he wanted, he would make me no answer, but continue staring at me persistently for some seconds, then, with a peculiar compression of his lips and a most significant air, deliberately turn round and deliberately go back to his room. Two hours later he would come out again and again present himself before me in the same way. It had happened that in my fury I did not even ask him what he wanted, but simply raised my head sharply and imperiously and began staring back at him. So we stared at one another for two minutes; at last he turned with deliberation and dignity and went back again for two hours.

If I were still not brought to reason by all this, but persisted in my revolt, he would suddenly begin sighing while he looked at me, long, deep sighs as though measuring by them the depths of my moral degradation, and, of course, it ended at last by his triumphing completely: I raged and shouted, but still was forced to do what he wanted.

This time the usual staring manœuvres had scarcely begun when I lost my temper and flew at him in a fury. I was irritated beyond endurance apart from him.

"Stay," I cried, in a frenzy, as he was slowly and silently turning, with one hand behind his back, to go to his room, "stay! Come back, come back, I tell you!" and I must have bawled so unnaturally, that he turned round and even looked at me with some wonder. However, he persisted in saying nothing, and that infuriated me.

"How dare you come and look at me like that without being sent for? Answer!"

After looking at me calmly for half a minute, he began turning round again.

"Stay!" I roared, running up to him, "don't stir! There. Answer, now: what did you come in to look at?"

"If you have any order to give me it's my duty to carry it out," he answered, after another silent pause, with a slow, measured lisp, raising his eyebrows and calmly twisting his head from one side to another, all this with exasperating composure.

"That's not what I am asking you about, you torturer!" I shouted, turning crimson with anger. "I'll tell you why you came here myself: you see, I don't give you your wages, you are so proud you don't want to bow down and ask for it, and so you come to punish me with your stupid stares, to worry me and you have no sus . . . pic . . . ion how stupid it is—stupid, stupid, stupid, stupid!" . . .

He would have turned round again without a word, but I seized him.

"Listen," I shouted to him. "Here's the money, do you see, here it is" (I took it out of the table drawer); "here's the seven rubles complete, but you are not going to have it, you . . . are . . . not . . . going . . . to . . . have it until you come respectfully with bowed head to beg my pardon. Do you hear?"

"That cannot be," he answered, with the most unnatural self-confidence.

"It shall be so," I said, "I give you my word of honour, it shall be!"

"And there's nothing for me to beg your pardon for," he went on, as though he had not noticed my exclamations at all. "Why, besides, you called me a 'torturer,' for which I can summon you at the police-station at any time for insulting behaviour."

"Go, summon me," I roared, "go at once, this very minute, this very second! You are a torturer all the same! a torturer!"

But he merely looked at me, then turned, and regardless of my loud calls to him, he walked to his room with an even step and without looking round.

"If it had not been for Liza nothing of this would have happened," I decided inwardly. Then, after waiting a minute, I went myself behind his screen with a dignified and solemn air, though my heart was beating slowly and violently.

"Apollon," I said quietly and emphatically, though I was breathless, "go at once without a minute's delay and fetch the police-officer."

He had meanwhile settled himself at his table, put on his

spectacles and taken up some sewing. But, hearing my order, he burst into a guffaw.

"At once, go this minute! Go on, or else you can't imagine what will happen."

"You are certainly out of your mind," he observed, without even raising his head, lisping as deliberately as ever and threading his needle. "Whoever heard of a man sending for the police against himself? And as for being frightened—you are upsetting yourself about nothing, for nothing will come of it."

"Go!" I shrieked, clutching him by the shoulder. I felt I should strike him in a minute.

But I did not notice the door from the passage softly and slowly open at that instant and a figure come in, stop short, and begin staring at us in perplexity. I glanced, nearly swooned with shame, and rushed back to my room. There, clutching at my hair with both hands, I leaned my head against the wall and stood motionless in that position.

Two minutes later I heard Apollon's deliberate footsteps. "There is some woman asking for you," he said, looking at me with peculiar severity. Then he stood aside and let in Liza. He would not go away, but stared at us sarcastically.

"Go away, go away," I commanded in desperation. At that moment my clock began whirring and wheezing and struck seven.

IX

"Into my house come bold and free,
  Its rightful mistress there to be."

I stood before her crushed, crestfallen, revoltingly confused, and I believe I smiled as I did my utmost to wrap myself in the skirts of my ragged wadded dressing-gown—exactly as I

had imagined the scene not long before in a fit of depression.
After standing over us for a couple of minutes Apollon went away,
but that did not make me more at ease. What made it worse was
that she, too, was overwhelmed with confusion, more so, in fact,
than I should have expected. At the sight of me, of course.

"Sit down," I said mechanically, moving a chair up to the
table, and I sat down on the sofa. She obediently sat down at
once and gazed at me open-eyed, evidently expecting something from me at once. This naïveté of expectation drove me to
fury, but I restrained myself.

She ought to have tried not to notice, as though everything
had been as usual, while instead of that, she . . . and I dimly felt
that I should make her pay dearly for all this.

"You have found me in a strange position, Liza," I began,
stammering and knowing that this was the wrong way to
begin. "No, no, don't imagine anything," I cried, seeing that she
had suddenly flushed. "I am not ashamed of my poverty. On the
contrary I look with pride on my poverty. I am poor but honourable. . . . One can be poor and honourable," I muttered.
"However . . . would you like tea?" . . .

"No," she was beginning.

"Wait a minute."

I leapt up and ran to Apollon. I had to get out of the room
somehow.

"Apollon," I whispered in feverish haste, flinging down before him the seven rubles which had remained all the time in
my clenched fist, "here are your wages, you see I give them to
you; but for that you must come to my rescue: bring me tea and
a dozen rusks from the restaurant. If you won't go, you'll make
me a miserable man! You don't know what this woman is. . . .
This is—everything! You may be imagining something. . . . But
you don't know what that woman is!" . . .

Apollon, who had already sat down to his work and put on
his spectacles again, at first glanced askance at the money without speaking or putting down his needle; then, without paying
the slightest attention to me or making any answer he went on
busying himself with his needle, which he had not yet

threaded. I waited before him for three minutes with my arms crossed à la Napoléon. My temples were moist with sweat. I was pale, I felt it. But, thank God, he must have been moved to pity, looking at me. Having threaded his needle he deliberately got up from his seat, deliberately moved back his chair, deliberately took off his spectacles, deliberately counted the money, and finally asking me over his shoulder: "Shall I get a whole portion?" deliberately walked out of the room. As I was going back to Liza, the thought occurred to me on the way: shouldn't I run away just as I was in my dressing-gown, no matter where, and then let happen what would?

I sat down again. She looked at me uneasily. For some minutes we were silent.

"I will kill him," I shouted suddenly, striking the table with my fist so that the ink spurted out of the inkstand.

"What are you saying!" she cried, starting.

"I will kill him! kill him!" I shrieked, suddenly striking the table in absolute frenzy, and at the same time fully understanding how stupid it was to be in such a frenzy. "You don't know, Liza, what that torturer is to me. He is my torturer . . . He has gone now to fetch some rusks; he . . ."

And suddenly I burst into tears. It was an hysterical attack. How ashamed I felt in the midst of my sobs; but still I could not restrain them.

She was frightened.

"What is the matter? What is wrong?" she cried, fussing about me.

"Water, give me water, over there!" I muttered in a faint voice, though I was inwardly conscious that I could have got on very well without water and without muttering in a faint voice. But I was, what is called, putting it on, to save appearances, though the attack was a genuine one.

She gave me water, looking at me in bewilderment. At that moment Apollon brought in the tea. It suddenly seemed to me that this commonplace, prosaic tea was horribly undignified and paltry after all that had happened, and I blushed crimson.

Liza looked at Apollon with positive alarm. He went out without a glance at either of us.

"Liza, do you despise me?" I asked, looking at her fixedly, trembling with impatience to know what she was thinking.

She was confused, and did not know what to answer.

"Drink your tea," I said to her angrily. I was angry with myself, but, of course, it was she who would have to pay for it. A horrible spite against her suddenly surged up in my heart; I believe I could have killed her. To revenge myself on her I swore inwardly not to say a word to her all the time. "She is the cause of it all," I thought.

Our silence lasted for five minutes. The tea stood on the table; we did not touch it. I had got to the point of purposely refraining from beginning in order to embarrass her further; it was awkward for her to begin alone. Several times she glanced at me with mournful perplexity. I was obstinately silent. I was, of course, myself the chief sufferer, because I was fully conscious of the disgusting meanness of my spiteful stupidity, and yet at the same time I could not restrain myself.

"I want to . . . get away . . . from there altogether," she began, to break the silence in some way, but, poor girl, that was just what she ought not to have spoken about at such a stupid moment to a man so stupid as I was. My heart positively ached with pity for her tactless and unnecessary straightforwardness. But something hideous at once stifled all compassion in me; it even provoked me to greater venom. I did not care what happened. Another five minutes passed.

"Perhaps I am in your way," she began timidly, hardly audibly, and was getting up.

But as soon as I saw this first impulse of wounded dignity I positively trembled with spite, and at once burst out.

"Why have you come to me, tell me that, please?" I began, gasping for breath and regardless of logical connection in my words. I longed to have it all out at once, at one burst; I did not even trouble how to begin. "Why have you come? Answer, answer," I cried, hardly knowing what I was doing. "I'll tell you, my good girl, why you have come. You've come because I talked sentimental stuff to you then. So now you are soft as butter and longing for fine sentiments again. So you may as well know that I was laughing at you then. And I am laughing at you now. Why are you shuddering? Yes, I was laughing at you! I had been insulted just before, at dinner, by the fellows who came that evening before me. I came to you, meaning to thrash one of them, an officer; but I didn't succeed, I didn't find him; I had to avenge the insult on some one to get back my own again; you turned up, I vented my spleen on you and laughed at you. I had been humiliated, so I wanted to humiliate; I had been treated like a rag, so I wanted to show my power. . . . That's what it was, and you imagined I had come there on purpose to save you. Yes? You imagined that? You imagined that?"

I knew that she would perhaps be muddled and not take it all in exactly, but I knew, too, that she would grasp the gist of it, very well indeed. And so, indeed, she did. She turned white as a handkerchief, tried to say something, and her lips worked painfully; but she sank on a chair as though she had been felled by an axe. And all the time afterwards she listened to me with her lips parted and her eyes wide open, shuddering with awful terror. The cynicism, the cynicism of my words overwhelmed her. . . .

"Save you!" I went on, jumping up from my chair and running up and down the room before her. "Save you from what? But perhaps I am worse than you myself. Why didn't you throw it in my teeth when I was giving you that sermon: 'But what did you come here yourself for? was it to read us a sermon?' Power, power was what I wanted then, sport was what I wanted, I wanted to wring out your tears, your humiliation, your hysteria—that was what I wanted then! Of course, I couldn't keep it up then, because I am a wretched creature, I was frightened, and, the devil knows why, gave you my address in my folly. Afterwards, before I got home, I was cursing and swearing at you because of that address, I hated you already because of the lies I had told you. Because I only like playing with words, only dreaming, but, do you know, what I really want is that you should all go to hell. That is what I want. I want peace; yes, I'd sell the whole world for a farthing, straight off, so long as I was left in peace. Is the world to go to pot, or am I to go without my tea? I say that the world may go to pot for me so long as I always get my tea. Did you know that, or not? Well, anyway, I know that I am a blackguard, a scoundrel, an egoist, a sluggard. Here I have been shuddering for the last three days at the thought of your coming. And do you know what has worried me particularly for these three days? That I posed as such a hero to you, and now you would see me in a wretched torn dressing-gown, beggarly, loathsome. I told you just now that I was not ashamed of my poverty; so you may as well know that I am ashamed of it; I am more ashamed of it than of anything, more afraid of it than of being found out if I were a thief, because I am as vain as though I had been skinned and the very air blowing on me hurt. Surely by now you must realize that I shall never forgive you for having found me in this wretched dressing-gown, just as I was flying at Apollon like a spiteful cur. The saviour, the former hero, was flying like a mangy, unkempt sheep-dog at his lackey, and the lackey was jeering at him! And I shall never forgive you for the tears I could not help shedding before you just now, like some silly woman put to shame! And for what I am confessing to you now, I shall never forgive you either! Yes—you must answer for it all because you turned up like this, because I am a blackguard, because I am the nastiest, stupidest, absurdest and most envious of all the worms on earth, who are not a bit better than I am, but, the devil knows why, are never put to confusion; while I shall always be insulted by every louse, that is my doom! And what is it to me that you don't understand a word of this! And what do I care, what do I care about you, and whether you go to ruin there or not? Do you understand? How I shall hate you now after saying this, for having been here and listening. Why, it's not once in a lifetime a man speaks out like this, and then it is in hysterics! . . . What more do you want? Why do you still stand confronting me, after all this? Why are you worrying me? Why don't you go?"

But at this point a strange thing happened. I was so accustomed to think and imagine everything from books, and to picture everything in the world to myself just as I had made it up in my dreams beforehand, that I could not all at once take in this strange circumstance. What happened was this: Liza, insulted and crushed by me, understood a great deal more than I imagined. She understood from all this what a woman understands first of all, if she feels genuine love, that is, that I was myself unhappy.

The frightened and wounded expression on her face was followed first by a look of sorrowful perplexity. When I began calling myself a scoundrel and a blackguard and my tears flowed (the tirade was accompanied throughout by tears) her whole face worked convulsively. She was on the point of getting up and stopping me; when I finished she took no notice of my shouting: "Why are you here, why don't you go away?" but realized only that it must have been very bitter to me to say all this. Besides, she was so crushed, poor girl; she considered herself infinitely beneath me; how could she feel anger or resentment? She suddenly leapt up from her chair with an irresistible impulse and held out her hands, yearning towards me, though still timid and not daring to stir. . . . At this point there was a revulsion in my heart, too. Then she suddenly rushed to me, threw her arms round me and burst into tears. I, too, could not restrain myself, and sobbed as I never had before.

"They won't let me . . . I can't be good!" I managed to articulate; then I went to the sofa, fell on it face downwards, and sobbed on it for a quarter of an hour in genuine hysterics. She came close to me, put her arms round me and stayed motionless in that position. But the trouble was that the hysterics could not go on for ever, and (I am writing the loathsome truth) lying face downwards on the sofa with my face thrust into my nasty leather pillow, I began by degrees to be aware of a far-away, involuntary but irresistible feeling that it would be awkward now for me to raise my head and look Liza straight in the face. Why was I ashamed? I don't know, but I was ashamed. The thought, too, came into my overwrought brain that our parts now were completely changed, that she was now the heroine, while I was just such a crushed and humiliated creature as she had been be-

fore me that night—four days before. . . . And all this came into
my mind during the minutes I was lying on my face on the
sofa.

My God! surely I was not envious of her then.

I don't know, to this day I cannot decide, and at the time, of
course, I was still less able to understand what I was feeling than
now. I cannot get on without domineering and tyrannizing
over some one, but . . . there is no explaining anything by reasoning and so it is useless to reason.

I conquered myself, however, and raised my head; I had to
do so sooner or later . . . and I am convinced to this day that it
was just because I was ashamed to look at her that another feeling was suddenly kindled and flamed up in my heart . . . a feeling of mastery and possession. My eyes gleamed with passion,
and I gripped her hands tightly. How I hated her and how I was
drawn to her at that minute! The one feeling intensified the
other. It was almost like an act of vengeance. At first there was
a look of amazement, even of terror on her face, but only for
one instant. She warmly and rapturously embraced me.

X

A quarter of an hour later I was rushing up and down the
room in frenzied impatience, from minute to minute I
went up to the screen and peeped through the crack at
Liza. She was sitting on the ground with her head leaning
against the bed, and must have been crying. But she did not go
away, and that irritated me. This time she understood it all. I had
insulted her finally, but . . . there's no need to describe it. She
realized that my outburst of passion had been simply revenge,
a fresh humiliation, and that to my earlier, almost causeless hatred was added now a *personal hatred*, born of envy. . . . Though I
do not maintain positively that she understood all this dis-

tinctly; but she certainly did fully understand that I was a despicable man, and what was worse, incapable of loving her.

I know I shall be told that this is incredible—but it is incredible to be as spiteful and stupid as I was; it may be added that it was strange I should not love her, or at any rate, appreciate her love. Why is it strange? In the first place, by then I was incapable of love, for I repeat, with me loving meant tyrannizing and showing my moral superiority. I have never in my life been able to imagine any other sort of love, and have nowadays come to the point of sometimes thinking that love really consists in the right—freely given by the beloved object—to tyrannize over her.

Even in my underground dreams I did not imagine love except as a struggle. I began it always with hatred and ended it with moral subjugation, and afterwards I never knew what to do with the subjugated object. And what is there to wonder at in that, since I had succeeded in so corrupting myself, since I was so out of touch with "real life," as to have actually thought of reproaching her, and putting her to shame for having come to me to hear "fine sentiments"; and did not even guess that she had come not to hear fine sentiments, but to love me, because to a woman all reformation, all salvation from any sort of ruin, and all moral renewal is included in love and can only show itself in that form.

I did not hate her so much, however, when I was running about the room and peeping through the crack in the screen. I was only insufferably oppressed by her being here. I wanted her to disappear. I wanted "peace," to be left alone in my underground world. Real life oppressed me with its novelty so much that I could hardly breathe.

But several minutes passed and she still remained, without stirring, as though she were unconscious. I had the shamelessness to tap softly at the screen as though to remind her. . . . She started, sprang up, and flew to seek her kerchief, her hat, her coat, as though making her escape from me. . . . Two minutes later she came from behind the screen and looked with heavy eyes at me. I gave a spiteful grin, which was forced, however, to keep up appearances, and I turned away from her eyes.

"Good-bye," she said, going towards the door.

I ran up to her, seized her hand, opened it, thrust something in it and closed it again. Then I turned at once and dashed away in haste to the other corner of the room to avoid seeing, anyway. . . .

I did mean a moment since to tell a lie—to write that I did this accidentally, not knowing what I was doing through foolishness, through losing my head. But I don't want to lie, and so I will say straight out that I opened her hand and put the money in it . . . from spite. It came into my head to do this while I was running up and down the room and she was sitting behind the screen. But this I can say for certain: though I did that cruel thing purposely, it was not an impulse from the heart, but came from my evil brain. This cruelty was so affected, so purposely made up, so completely a product of the brain, of books, that I could not even keep it up a minute—first I dashed away to avoid seeing her, and then in shame and despair rushed after Liza. I opened the door in the passage and began listening.

"Liza! Liza!" I cried on the stairs, but in a low voice, not boldly.

There was no answer, but I fancied I heard her footsteps, lower down on the stairs.

"Liza!" I cried, more loudly.

No answer. But at that minute I heard the stiff outer glass door open heavily with a creak and slam violently, the sound echoed up the stairs.

She had gone. I went back to my room in hesitation. I felt horribly oppressed.

I stood still at the table, beside the chair on which she had sat and looked aimlessly before me. A minute passed, suddenly I started; straight before me on the table I saw. . . . In short, I saw a crumpled blue five-ruble note, the one I had thrust into her hand a minute before. It was the same note; it could be no other, there was no other in the flat. So she had managed to fling it from her hand on the table at the moment when I had dashed into the further corner.

Well! I might have expected that she would do that. Might I have expected it? No, I was such an egoist, I was so lacking in respect for my fellow-creatures that I could not even imagine she would do so. I could not endure it. A minute later I flew like a madman to dress, flinging on what I could at random and ran headlong after her. She could not have got two hundred paces away when I ran out into the street.

It was a still night and the snow was coming down in masses and falling almost perpendicularly, covering the pavement and the empty street as though with a pillow. There was no one in the street, no sound was to be heard. The street lamps gave a disconsolate and useless glimmer. I ran two hundred paces to the cross-roads and stopped short.

Where had she gone? And why was I running after her?

Why? To fall down before her, to sob with remorse, to kiss her feet, to entreat her forgiveness! I longed for that, my whole breast was being rent to pieces, and never, never shall I recall that minute with indifference. But—what for? I thought. Should I not begin to hate her, perhaps, even to-morrow, just because I had kissed her feet to-day? Should I give her happiness? Had I not recognized that day, for the hundredth time, what I was worth? Should I not torture her?

I stood in the snow, gazing into the troubled darkness and pondered this.

"And will it not be better?" I mused fantastically, afterwards at home, stifling the living pang of my heart with fantastic dreams. "Will it not be better that she should keep the resentment of the insult for ever? Resentment—why, it is purification; it is a most stinging and painful consciousness! To-morrow I should have defiled her soul and have exhausted her heart, while now the feeling of insult will never die in her heart, and however loathsome the filth awaiting her—the feeling of insult will elevate and purify her . . . by hatred . . . h'm! . . . perhaps, too, by forgiveness. . . . Will all that make things easier for her though? . . ."

And, indeed, I will ask on my own account here, an idle question: which is better—cheap happiness or exalted sufferings? Well, which is better?

So I dreamed as I sat at home that evening, almost dead with the pain in my soul. Never had I endured such suffering and remorse, yet could there have been the faintest doubt when I ran out from my lodging that I should turn back half-way? I never met Liza again and I have heard nothing of her. I will add, too, that I remained for a long time afterwards pleased with the phrase about the benefit from resentment and hatred in spite of the fact that I almost fell ill from misery.

Even now, so many years later, all this is somehow a very evil memory. I have many evil memories now, but . . . hadn't I better end my "Notes" here? I believe I made a mistake in beginning to write them, anyway I have felt ashamed all the time I've been writing this story; so it's hardly literature so much as a corrective punishment. Why, to tell long stories, showing how I have spoiled my life through morally rotting in my corner, through lack of fitting environment, through divorce from real life, and rankling spite in my underground world, would certainly not be interesting; a novel needs a hero, and all the traits for an anti-hero are *expressly* gathered together here, and what matters most, it all produces an unpleasant impression, for we are all divorced from life, we are all cripples, every one of us, more or less. We are so divorced from it that we feel at once a sort of loathing for real life, and so cannot bear to be reminded of it. Why, we have come almost to looking upon real life as an effort, almost as hard work, and we are all privately agreed that it is better in books. And why do we fuss and fume sometimes? Why are we perverse and ask for something else? We don't know what ourselves. It would be the worse for us if our petulant prayers were answered. Come, try, give any one of us, for instance, a little more independence, untie our hands, widen the spheres of our activity, relax the control and we . . . yes, I assure you . . . we should be begging to be under control again at once. I know that you will very likely be angry with me for that, and will begin shouting and stamping. Speak for yourself, you will say, and for your miseries in your underground holes, and don't dare to say all of us—excuse me, gentlemen, I am not justifying myself with that "all of us." As for what concerns me in particular I have only in my life carried to an extreme what you have not dared to carry halfway, and what's more, you have taken your cowardice for good sense, and have found comfort in deceiving yourselves. So that perhaps, after all, there is more life in me than in you. Look into it more carefully! Why, we don't even know what living means now, what it is, and what it is called? Leave us alone without books and we shall be lost and in confusion at once. We shall not know what to join on to, what to cling to, what to love and what to hate, what to respect and what to despise. We are oppressed at being humans, humans with our own real bodies and blood; we are ashamed of it, we think it a disgrace, and we keep trying to be some sort of fairy-tale universal beings. We are stillborn, and for generations past have been begotten, not by living fathers, and that suits us better and better. We are developing a taste for it. Soon we shall contrive to be born somehow from an idea. But enough; I don't want to write more from "Underground."

[The notes of this paradoxalist do not end here, however. He could not refrain from going on with them, but it seems to us that we may stop here.]

THE MEEK ONE

A FANTASTIC STORY

FROM THE AUTHOR

I beg my readers' forgiveness that instead of the *Diary* in its usual form I am only providing a tale. But I was truly occupied with this tale for the greater part of the month. In any case, I beg readers' indulgence.

Now about the story itself. I have titled it "fantastic," even though I consider it realistic to the highest degree. But the fantastic is really there, in the story's very form, something I find it necessary to clarify in advance.

In fact, it is neither a story nor notes. Imagine to yourself a husband, whose wife, a suicide, is lying on a table, having thrown herself out a window several hours earlier. He is agitated and has not yet collected his thoughts. He is walking about his room and trying to make sense of what happened, "to collect his thoughts together." Moreover, he is an inveterate hypochondriac, one of those who talk to themselves. So here he is talking to himself, narrating the case, *explaining* it to himself. Despite the seeming coherence of his speech, he contradicts himself several times, both in logic and in feelings. He justifies himself, and he blames her, and proposes extraneous interpretations: Here is coarseness of thought and of heart, here is deep feeling. Little by little, he really *explains* the case to himself and collects "his thoughts together." The series of memories he summons irresistibly leads him at last to *the truth*; the truth irresistibly elevates his mind and heart. Toward the story's end, the tone changes compared with its disordered beginning. The truth is revealed sufficiently clearly and definitively to the unfortunate, at least for himself.

That is the subject. Of course, the story's legal trial continues for several hours, with fits and starts, with gaps, and in contradictory form: Sometimes he speaks to himself, sometimes he turns as though to an invisible reader, to some kind of judge. It is always thus in reality. If a stenographer had been able to overhear him and record it all, then it would have come out a bit more rough, a bit less polished than I have represented it, but insofar as it seems to me, the psychological order, perhaps, would remain the same. This presupposition about a stenographer recording it all (after which I would polish the transcription) is what I call the fantastic in the story. Yet something partly similar has already more than once been allowed in art heretofore: Victor Hugo, for instance, in his masterpiece *The Last Day of a Man Condemned to Death*, used almost the same technique, and though he did not introduce a stenographer, he did allow an even greater inverisimilitude, proposing that a condemned man might (and had time) to carry on his notes not only to his final day, but even to his final hour, and literally to his final minute. But without allowing that fantasy, the story would not exist—the most real and most truthful work of all he wrote.

PART I

CHAPTER I

Who I Was and Who She Was

. . . Oh, while she is still here, it is still all right; I go up and look at her every minute; but to-morrow they will take her away— and how shall I be left alone? Now she is on the table in the drawing-room, they put two card tables together, the coffin will be here to-morrow—white, pure white "gros de Naples"—but that's not it . . . I keep walking and walking, trying to explain it to myself. For the last six hours, I have been trying to explain, but I still can't collect my thoughts. The fact is, I walk, and walk, and walk. This is how it was. I will simply tell it in order. (Order!) Gentlemen, I am far from being a literary man and you will see that; but no matter, I'll tell it as I understand it myself. The horror of it for me is that I understand it all!

It was, if you care to know, that is to take it from the begin- ning, that she used to come to me simply to pawn things, to pay for advertising in the *Voice*[1] to the effect that a governess was quite willing to travel, to give lessons at home, and so on, and so on. That was at the very beginning, and I, of course, made no difference between her and the others: "She comes," I thought, "like any one else," and so on. But afterwards I began to see a difference. She was such a slender, fair little thing, rather tall, al- ways a little awkward with me, as though embarrassed (I fancy she was the same with all strangers, and in her eyes, of course, I was exactly like anybody else—that is, not as a pawnbroker but as a man). As soon as she received the money she would turn round at once and go away. And always in silence. Other women argue so, entreat, haggle for me to give them more; this one did not ask for more. . . . I believe I am muddling it up . . . Yes; I was struck first of all by the things she brought: poor lit- tle silver gilt earrings, a trashy little locket, things not worth sixpence. She knew herself that they were worth next to noth- ing, but I could see from her face that they were treasures to

her, and I found out afterwards as a fact that they were all that
was left her belonging to her father and mother. Only once I allowed myself to scoff at her things. You see I never allow myself
to behave like that. I keep up a gentlemanly tone with my
clients: few words, politeness and sternness. "Sternness, sternness, and sternness!"[2] But she suddenly ventured to bring her
last rag, that is, literally the remains of an old hareskin jacket, and
I could not resist saying something by way of a joke. My goodness! how she flared up! Her eyes were large, blue and dreamy
but—how they blazed. But she did not drop one word; picking
up her "rags" she walked out. It was then for the first time I noticed her particularly, and thought something of the kind about
her—that is, something of a particular kind. Yes, I remember another impression—that is, if you will have it, perhaps the chief
impression, that summed up everything. It was that she was terribly young, so young that she looked just fourteen. And yet she was
within three months of sixteen. I didn't mean that, though, that
wasn't what summed it all up. Next day she came again. I found
out later that she had been to Dobronravov's and to Mozer's with
that jacket, but they take nothing but gold and would have nothing to say to it. I once took some stones from her (rubbishy little
ones) and, thinking it over afterwards, I wondered: I, too, only
lend on gold and silver, yet from her I accepted stones. That was
my second thought about her then; that I remember.

That time, that is when she came from Mozer's, she brought
an amber cigar-holder. It was a connoisseur's article, not bad,
but, again, of no value to us, because we only deal in gold. As
it was the day after her rebellion, I received her sternly. Sternness
with me takes the form of dryness. As I gave her two rubles,
however, I could not resist saying, with a certain irritation, "I
only do it for you, of course; Mozer wouldn't take such a thing."
The words "for you" I emphasized particularly, and with a certain
implication. I was spiteful. She flared up again when she heard
that "for you," but she did not say a word, she did not throw
down the money, she took it—that is poverty! But how she
flared up! I saw I had stung her. And when she had gone out, I
suddenly asked myself whether my triumph over her was worth

two rubles. He-he-he! I remember I put that question to myself twice over, "Was it worth it? was it worth it?" And, laughing, I inwardly answered it in the affirmative. And I felt very much elated. But that was not an evil feeling; I said it with design, with a motive; I wanted to test her, because certain ideas with regard to her had suddenly come into my mind. That was the third thing I thought particularly about her.

. . . Well, it was from that time it all began. Of course, I tried at once to find out all her circumstances indirectly, and awaited her coming with a special impatience. I had a presentiment that she would come soon. When she came, I entered into affable conversation with her, speaking with unusual politeness. I have not been badly brought up and have manners. H'm. It was then I guessed that she was kind and meek.[3] The kind and meek do not resist long, and though they are by no means very ready to reveal themselves, they do not know how to escape from a conversation; they are niggardly in their answers, but they do answer, and the more readily the longer you go on. Only, on your side you must not flag, if you want them to talk. I need hardly say that she did not explain anything to me then. About the *Voice* and all that I found out afterwards. She was at that time spending her last farthing on advertising, haughtily at first, of course. "A governess prepared to travel and will send terms on application," but, later on: "willing to do anything, to teach, to be a companion, to be a housekeeper, to wait on an invalid, plain sewing, and so on, and so on," the usual thing! Of course, all this was added to the advertisement a bit at a time, and finally, when she was reduced to despair, it came to: "without salary in return for board." No, she could not find a situation. I made up my mind then to test her for the last time. I suddenly took up the *Voice* of the day and showed her an advertisement. "A young person, without friends and relations, seeks a situation as a governess to young children, preferably in the family of middle-aged widower. Might be a comfort in the home."

"Look here how this lady has advertised this morning, and by the evening she will certainly have found a situation. That's the way to advertise." Again she flared up and her eyes blazed, she turned

round and went straight out. I was very much pleased, though by
that time I felt sure of everything and had no apprehensions; nobody will take her cigar-holders, I thought. Besides, she has got rid
of them all. And so it was, two days later, she came in again, such
a pale little creature, all agitation—I saw that something had happened to her at home, and something really had. I will explain directly what had happened, but now I only want to recall how I did
something chic, and rose in her opinion. I suddenly decided to do
it. The fact is she was pawning the ikon (she had brought herself
to pawn it!) . . . Ah, listen! listen! This is the beginning now, I've
been in a muddle. You see I want to recall all this, every detail,
every little point. I still want to collect my thoughts together and—
I cannot, instead there are these little things, little things. . . .

It was an ikon of the Madonna. A Madonna with the Babe,
an old-fashioned, homely one, and the setting was silver gilt,
worth—well, six rubles, perhaps. I could see the ikon was precious to her; she was pawning it whole, not taking it out of the
setting. I said to her—

"You had better take it out of the setting, and take the ikon
home; for it's not the thing to pawn."

"Why, are you forbidden to take them?"

"No, it's not that we are forbidden, but you might, perhaps,
yourself . . ."

"Well, take it out."

"I tell you what. I will not take it out, but I'll set it here in
the shrine with the other ikons," I said, on reflection. "Under
the little lamp" (I always had the lamp burning as soon as the
shop was opened), "and you simply take ten rubles."

"Don't give me ten rubles. I only want five; I shall certainly
redeem it."

"You don't want ten? The ikon's worth it," I added, noticing
that her eyes flashed again.

She was silent. I brought out five rubles.

"Don't despise any one; I've been in such straits myself; and
worse too, and that you see me here in this business . . . is
owing to what I've been through in the past. . . ."

"You're revenging yourself on society? Yes?" she interrupted suddenly with rather sarcastic mockery, which, however, was to a great extent innocent (that is, it was general, because certainly at that time she did not distinguish me from others, so that she said it almost without malice).

"Aha," thought I; "so that's what you're like. You've got character; you belong to the new movement."

"You see!" I remarked at once, half-jestingly, half-mysteriously, "I am part of that part of the Whole that seeks to do ill, but does good.…"

Quickly and with great curiosity, in which, however, there was something very childlike, she looked at me.

"Stay … what's that idea? Where does it come from? I've heard it somewhere …"

"Don't rack your brains. In those words Mephistopheles introduces himself to Faust. Have you read *Faust*?"[4]

"Not … not attentively."

"That is, you have not read it at all. You must read it. But I see an ironical look in your face again. Please don't imagine that I've so little taste as to try to use Mephistopheles to commend myself to you and grace the role of pawnbroker. A pawnbroker will still be a pawnbroker. We know."

"You're so strange … I didn't mean to say anything of that sort."

She meant to say: "I didn't expect to find you were an educated man"; but she didn't say it; I knew, though, that she thought that. I had pleased her very much.

"You see," I observed, "one may do good in any calling— I'm not speaking of myself, of course. Let us grant that I'm doing nothing but harm, yet.…"

"Of course, one can do good in every position," she said, glancing at me with a rapid, profound look. "Yes, in any position," she added suddenly.

Oh, I remember, I remember all those moments! And I want to add, too, that when such young creatures, such sweet young creatures want to say something so clever and profound, they show at once so truthfully and naïvely in their faces, "Here I am saying something clever and profound now"—and that is not from vanity, as it is with any one like me, but one sees that she appreciates it awfully herself, and believes in it, and thinks a lot of it, and imagines that you think a lot of all that, just as she does. Oh, sincerity! it's by that they conquer us. How exquisite it was in her!

I remember it, I have forgotten nothing! As soon as she had gone, I made up my mind. That same day I made my last investigations and found out every detail of her position at the moment; every detail of her past I had learned already from Lukerya, at that time a servant in the family, whom I had bribed a few days before. This position was so awful that I can't understand how she could laugh as she had done that day and feel interest in the words of Mephistopheles, when she was in such horrible straits. But—that's youth! That is just what I thought about her at the time with pride and joy; for, you know, there's a greatness of soul in it—to be able to say, "Though I am on the edge of the abyss, yet Goethe's grand words are radiant with light." Youth always has some greatness of soul, if it's only a spark and that distorted. Though it's of her I am speaking, of her alone. And, above all, I looked upon her then as mine and did not doubt of my power. You know that's a voluptuous idea when you feel no doubt of it.

But what is the matter with me? If I go on like this, when shall I put it all together and look at it as a whole. I must make haste, make haste—that is not what matters, oh, my God!

CHAPTER II

The Offer of Marriage

The "details" I learned about her I will tell in one word: her father and mother were dead, they had died three years before, and she had been left with two disorderly aunts:

though it is saying too little to call them disorderly. One aunt was a widow with a large family (six children, one smaller than another), the other a horrid old maid. Both were horrid. Her father was in the service, but only as a copying clerk, and was only a gentleman by courtesy; in fact, everything was in my favour. I came as though from a higher world; I was anyway a retired lieutenant of a brilliant regiment, a gentleman by birth, independent and all the rest of it, and as for my pawnbroker's shop, her aunts could only have looked on that with respect. She had been living in slavery at her aunts' for those three years: yet she had managed to pass an examination somewhere—she managed to pass it, she wrung the time for it, weighed down as she was by the pitiless burden of daily drudgery, and that proved something in the way of striving for what was higher and better on her part! Why, what made me want to marry her? Never mind me, though; of that later on . . . As though that mattered!—She taught her aunt's children; she made their clothes; and towards the end not only washed the clothes, but with her weak chest even scrubbed the floors. To put it plainly, they used to beat her, and taunt her with eating their bread. It ended by their scheming to sell her. Tfoo! I omit the filthy details. She told me all about it afterwards. All this had been watched for a whole year by a neighbour, a fat shopkeeper, and not a humble one but the owner of two grocer's shops. He had ill-treated two wives and now he was looking for a third, and so he cast his eye on her. "She's a quiet one," he thought; "she's grown up in poverty, and I am marrying for the sake of my motherless children." He really had children. He began trying to make the match and negotiating with the aunts. He was fifty years old, besides. She was aghast with horror. It was then she began coming so often to me to advertise in the *Voice*. At last she began begging the aunts to give her just a little time to think it over. They granted her that little time, but would not let her have more; they were always at her: "We don't know where to turn to find food for ourselves, without an extra mouth to feed." I had found all this out already, and the same day, after what had happened in the morning, I made up my mind. That evening the shopkeeper came, bringing with him a pound of sweets from the shop; she was sitting with him, and I called Lukerya out of the kitchen and told her to go and whisper to her that I was at the gate and wanted to say something to her without delay. I felt pleased with myself. And altogether I felt awfully pleased all that day.

On the spot, at the gate, in the presence of Lukerya, before she had recovered from her amazement at my sending for her, I informed her that I should look upon it as an honour and happiness . . . telling her, in the next place, not to be surprised at the manner of my declaration and at my speaking at the gate, saying that I was a straightforward man and had learned the position of affairs. And I was not lying when I said I was straightforward. Well, hang it all. I did not only speak with propriety—that is, showing I was a man of decent breeding, but I spoke with originality and that was the chief thing. After all, is there any harm in admitting it? I want to judge myself and am judging myself. I must speak pro and contra, and I do. I remembered afterwards with enjoyment, though it was stupid, that I frankly declared, without the least embarrassment, that, in the first place, I was not particularly talented, not particularly intelligent, perhaps not particularly good-natured, rather a cheap egoist (I remember that expression, I thought of it on the way and was pleased with it) and that very probably there was a great deal that was disagreeable in me in other respects. All this was said with a special sort of pride—we all know how that sort of thing is said. Of course, I had good taste enough not to proceed to enlarge on my virtues after honourably enumerating my defects, not to say "to make up for that I have this and that and the other." I saw that she was still horribly frightened, but I softened nothing; on the contrary, seeing she was frightened I purposely exaggerated. I told her straight out that she would have enough to eat, but that fine clothes, theatres, balls—she would have none of, at any rate not till later on, when I had attained my object. This severe tone was a positive delight to me. I added as cursorily as possible, that in adopting such a calling—that is, in keeping a pawnbroker's shop, I had only one object, hinting there was a special circumstance . . . But I really had a right to say so: I really had such an aim and there really was such a circumstance. Wait a minute, gentlemen; I have always been the first to hate this pawnbroking business, but in reality, though it is absurd to talk about oneself in such mysterious phrases, yet, you know, I was "revenging myself on society," I really was, I was, I was! So that her gibe that morning at the idea of my revenging myself was unjust. That is, do you see, if I had said to her straight out in words: "Yes, I am revenging myself on society," she would have laughed as she did that morning, and it would, in fact, have been absurd. But by indirect hints, by dropping mysterious phrases, it appeared that it was possible to work upon her imagination. Besides, I had no fears then: I knew that the fat shopkeeper was anyway more repulsive to her than I was, and that I, standing at the gate, had appeared as a deliverer. I understood that, of course. Oh, what is base a man understands particularly well! But was it base? How can a man judge? Didn't I love her even then?

Wait a bit: of course, I didn't breathe a word to her of doing her a benefit; the opposite, oh, quite the opposite; I made out that it was I that would be under an obligation to her, not she to me. Indeed, I said as much—I couldn't resist saying it—and it sounded stupid, perhaps, for I noticed a shade flit across her face. But altogether I won the day completely. Wait a bit, if I am to recall all that vileness, then I will tell of that worst beastliness. As I stood there what was stirring in my mind was, "You are tall, a good figure, educated and—speaking without conceit—good-looking." That is what was at work in my mind. I need hardly say that, on the spot, out there at the gate she said "*yes*." But . . . but I ought to add: that out there by the gate she thought a long time before she said "*yes*." She pondered for so long that I said to her, "Well?"—and could not even refrain from asking it with a certain swagger.

"Wait a little. I'm thinking."

And her little face was so serious, so serious that even then I might have read it! And I was mortified: "Can she be choosing between me and the grocer!" I thought. Oh, I did not understand then! I did not understand anything, anything, then! I did not understand till to-day! I remember Lukerya ran after me as I was going away, stopped me on the road and said, breathlessly: "God will reward you, sir, for taking our dear young lady; only don't speak of that to her—she's proud."

Proud, is she! "I like proud people," I thought. Proud people are particularly nice when . . . well, when one has no doubt of one's power over them, eh? Oh, base, tactless man! Oh, how pleased I was! You know, when she was standing there at the gate, hesitating whether to say "yes" to me, and I was wondering at it, you know, she may have had some such thought as this: "If it is to be misery either way, isn't it best to choose the very worst"— that is, let the fat grocer beat her to death when he was drunk! Eh! what do you think, could there have been a thought like that?

And, indeed, I don't understand it now, I don't understand it at all, even now. I have only just said that she may have had that thought: of two evils choose the worst—that is, the grocer. But which was the worst for her then—the grocer or I? The grocer or the pawnbroker who quoted Goethe? That's another question! What a question! And even that you don't understand: the answer is lying on the table and you call it a question! Never mind me, though. It's not a question of me at all . . . and, by the way, what is there left for me now—whether it's a question of me or whether it is not? That's what I am utterly unable to answer. I had better go to bed. My head aches. . . .

CHAPTER III

The Noblest of Men,
Though I Don't Believe It Myself

I could not sleep. And how should I? There is a pulse throbbing in my head. One longs to master it all, all that degradation. Oh, the degradation! Oh, what degradation I dragged her out of then! Of course, she must have realized that, she must have appreciated my action! I was pleased, too, by various thoughts—for instance, the reflection that I was forty-one and she was only sixteen. That fascinated me, that feeling of inequality was very sweet, was very sweet.

I wanted, for instance, to have a wedding *à l'anglaise*,* that is only the two of us, with just the two necessary witnesses, one of them Lukerya, and from the wedding straight to the train to Moscow (I happened to have business there, by the way), and then a fortnight at the hotel. She opposed it, she would not have it, and I had to visit her aunts and treat them with respect as though they were relations from whom I was taking her. I gave way, and all befitting respect was paid the aunts. I even made the creatures a present of a hundred rubles each and promised them more—not telling her anything about it, of course, that I might not make her feel humiliated by the lowness of her surroundings. The aunts were as soft as silk at once. There was a wrangle about the trousseau too; she had nothing, almost literally, but she did not want to have anything. I succeeded in proving to her, though, that she must have something, and I made up the trousseau, for who would have given her anything? But there, enough of me. I did, however, succeed in communicating some of my ideas to her then, so that she knew them anyway. I was in too great a hurry, perhaps. The best of it was that, from the very beginning, she rushed to meet me with love, greeted me with rapture, when I went to see her in the evening, told me in her chatter (the enchanting chatter of innocence) all about her childhood and girlhood, her old home, her father and mother. But I poured cold water upon all that at once. That was my idea. I met her enthusiasm with silence, friendly silence, of course . . . but, all the same, she could quickly see that we were different and that I was—an enigma. And being an enigma was what I made a point of most of all! Why, it was just for the sake of being an enigma, perhaps—that I have been

---

*English-style (French).

guilty of all this stupidity. The first thing was sternness—it was with an air of sternness that I took her into my house. In fact, as I went about then feeling satisfied, I framed a complete system. Oh, it came of itself without any effort. And it could not have been otherwise. I was bound to create that system owing to one inevitable fact—why should I libel myself, indeed! The system was a genuine one. Yes, listen; if you must judge a man, better judge him knowing all about it . . . listen.

How am I to begin this, for it is very difficult. When you begin to justify yourself—then it is difficult. You see, for instance, young people despise money—I made money of importance at once; I laid special stress on money. And laid such stress on it that she became more and more silent. She opened her eyes wide, listened, gazed and said nothing. You see, the young are heroic, that is the good among them are heroic and impulsive, but they have little tolerance; if the least thing is not quite right they are full of contempt. And I wanted breadth, I wanted to instil breadth into her very heart, to make it part of her inmost feeling, did I not? I'll take a trivial example: how should I explain my pawnbroker's shop to a character like that? Of course, I did not speak of it directly, or it would have appeared that I was apologizing, and I, so to speak, worked it through pride, I almost spoke without words, and I am masterly at speaking without words. All my life I have spoken without words, and I have passed through whole tragedies on my own account without words. Why, I, too, have been unhappy! I was abandoned by every one, abandoned and forgotten, and no one, no one knew it! And all at once this sixteen-year-old girl picked up details about me from vulgar people and thought she knew all about me, and, meanwhile, what was precious remained hidden in this heart! I went on being silent, with her especially I was silent, with her especially, right up to yesterday—why was I silent? Because I was proud. I wanted her to find out for herself, without my help, and not from the tales of low people; I wanted her to *divine of herself* what manner of man I was and to understand me! Taking her into my house I wanted all her respect, I wanted her to be standing before me in homage for the sake of my sufferings—and I deserved it. Oh, I have always been proud, I always wanted all or nothing! You see it was just because I am not one who will accept half a happiness, but always wanted all, that I was forced to act like that then: it was as much as to say, "See into me for yourself and appreciate me!" For you must see that if I had begun explaining myself to her and prompting her, ingratiating myself and asking for her respect—it would have been as good as asking for charity . . . But . . . but why am I talking of that!

Stupid, stupid, stupid, stupid! I explained to her then, in two words, directly, ruthlessly (and I emphasize the fact that it was ruthlessly) that the heroism of youth was charming, but—not worth a farthing. Why not? Because it costs them so little, because it is not gained through life; it is, so to say, merely "first impressions of existence,"[5] but just let us see you at work! Cheap heroism is always easy, and even to sacrifice life is easy too; because it is only a case of hot blood and an overflow of energy, and there is such a longing for what is beautiful! No, take the deed of heroism that is laborious, obscure, without noise or flourish, slandered, in which there is a great deal of sacrifice and not one grain of glory—in which you, a splendid man, are made to look like a scoundrel before every one, though you might be the most honest man in the world—you try that sort of heroism and you'll soon give it up! While I—have been bearing the burden of that all my life. At first she argued—ough, how she argued—but afterwards she began to be silent, completely silent, in fact, only opened her eyes wide as she listened, such big, big eyes, so attentive. And . . . and what is more, I suddenly saw a smile, mistrustful, silent, an evil smile. Well, it was with that smile on her face I brought her into my house. It is true that she had nowhere else to go. . . .

CHAPTER IV

Plans and Plans

Which of us began it first?

Neither. It began of itself from the very first. I have said that with sternness I brought her into the house. From the first step, however, I softened it. Before she was married it was explained to her that she would have to take pledges and pay out money, and she said nothing at the time (note that). What is more, she set to work with positive zeal. Well, of course, my lodging, my furniture all remained as before. My lodging consisted of two rooms, a large room from which the shop was partitioned off, and a second one, also large, our living room and bedroom. My furniture is scanty: even her aunts had better things. My shrine of ikons with the lamp was in the outer room where the shop is; in the inner room my bookcase with a few books in and a trunk of which I keep the key; of course, there is a bed, tables and chairs. Before she was married I told her that one ruble a day and not more, was to be spent on our board—that is, on food for me, her and Lukerya whom I had enticed to come to us. "I must have thirty thousand in three years," said I, "and we can't save the money if we spend more." She fell in with this, but I raised the sum by thirty kopeks a day. It was the same with the theatre. I told her before marriage that she would not go to the theatre, and yet I decided once a month to go to the theatre, and in a decent way, to the stalls. We went together. We went three times and saw *The Hunt after Happiness*, and *Singing Birds*,[6] I believe. (Oh, what does it matter!) We went in silence and in silence we returned. Why, why, from the very beginning, did we take to being silent? From the very first, you know, we had no quarrels, but always the same silence. She was always, I remember, watching me stealthily in those days; as soon as I noticed it I became more silent than before. It is true that it was I insisted on the silence, not she. On her part there were one or two outbursts, she rushed to embrace me; but as these outbursts were hysterical, painful, and I wanted secure happiness, with respect from her, I received them coldly. And indeed, I was right; each time the outburst was followed next day by a quarrel.

Though, again, there were no quarrels, but there was silence and—and on her side a more and more defiant air. "Rebellion and independence," that's what it was, only she didn't know how to show it. Yes, that meek face was becoming more and more defiant. Would you believe it, I was becoming revolting to her? I learned that. And there could be no doubt that she was moved to frenzy at times. Think, for instance, of her beginning to sniff at our poverty, after her coming from such sordidness and destitution—from scrubbing the floors! You see, there was no poverty; there was frugality, but there was abundance of what was necessary, of linen, for instance, and the greatest cleanliness. I always used to dream that cleanliness in a husband attracts a wife. It was not our poverty she was scornful of, but my supposed miserliness in the housekeeping: "He has his objects," she seemed to say, "he is showing his strength of will." She suddenly refused to go to the theatre. And more and more often an ironical look. . . . And I was more silent, more and more silent.

I could not begin justifying myself, could I? What was at the bottom of all this was the pawnbroking business. Allow me, I knew that a woman, above all at sixteen, must be in complete subordination to a man. Women have no originality. That—that is an axiom; even now, even now, for me it is an axiom! What does it prove that she is lying there in the outer room? Truth is truth, and even Mill is no use against it![7] And a woman who loves, oh, a woman who loves idealizes even the vices, even the villanies of the man she loves. He would not himself even succeed in finding such justification for his villanies as she will find for him. That is generous but not original. It is the lack of originality alone that has been the ruin of women. And, I repeat, what is the use of your pointing to that table? Why, what is there original in her being on that table? O—O—Oh!

Listen. I was convinced of her love at that time. Why, she

used to throw herself on my neck in those days. She loved me; that is, more accurately, she wanted to love. Yes, that's just what it was, she wanted to love; she was trying to love. And the point was that in this case there were no villanies for which she had to find justification. You will say, I'm a pawnbroker; and every one says the same. But what if I am a pawnbroker? It follows that there must be reasons since the most generous of men had become a pawnbroker. You see, gentlemen, there are ideas . . . that is, if one expresses some ideas, utters them in words, the effect is very stupid. The effect is to make one ashamed. For what reason? For no reason. Because we are all wretched creatures and cannot hear the truth, or I do not know why. I said just now, "the most generous of men"—that is absurd, and yet that is how it was. It's the truth, that is, the absolute, absolute truth! Yes, I *had the right* to want to make myself secure and open that pawnbroker's shop: "You have rejected me, you—people, I mean—you have cast me out with contemptuous silence. My passionate yearning towards you you have met with insult all my life. Now I have the right to put up a wall against you, to save up that thirty thousand rubles and end my life somewhere in the Crimea, on the south coast, among the mountains and vineyards, on my own estate bought with that thirty thousand, and above everything, far away from you all, living without malice against you, with an ideal in my soul, with a beloved woman at my heart, and a family, if God sends one, and—helping the inhabitants all around." Of course, it is quite right that I say this to myself now, but what could have been more stupid than describing all that aloud to her? That was the cause of my proud silence, that's why we sat in silence. For what could she have understood? Sixteen years old, the earliest youth—yes, what could she have understood of my justification, of my sufferings? Undeviating straightness, ignorance of life, the cheap convictions of youth, the hen-like blindness of those "noble hearts," and what stood for most was—the pawnbroker's shop and—enough! (And was I a villain in the pawnbroker's shop? Did not she see how I acted? Did I extort too much?) Oh, how awful is truth on earth! That exquisite creature, that meek one, that heaven—she was a tyrant, she was the insufferable tyrant and torture of my soul! I should be unfair to myself if I didn't say so! You imagine I didn't love her? Who can say that I did not love her! Do you see, it was a case of irony, the malignant irony of fate and nature! We were under a curse, the life of men in general is under a curse! (mine in particular). Of course, I understand now that I made some mistake! Something went wrong. Everything was clear, my plan was clear as daylight: "Austere and proud, asking for no moral comfort, but suffering in silence." And that was how it was. I was not lying, I was not lying! "She will see for herself, later on, that it was heroic, only that she had not known how to see it, and when, some day, she divines it she will prize me ten times more and will abase herself in the dust and fold her hands in homage"—that was my plan. But I forgot something or lost sight of it. There was something I failed to manage. But, enough, enough! And whose forgiveness am I to ask now? What is done is done. Be bolder, man, and have some pride! It is not your fault! . . .

Well, I will tell the truth, I am not afraid to face the truth; it was *her fault, her fault!* . . .

V

The Meek One Rebels

Quarrels began from her suddenly beginning to pay out loans on her own account, to price things above their worth, and even, on two occasions, she deigned to enter into a dispute about it with me. I did not agree. But then the captain's widow turned up.

This old widow brought a medallion—a present from her

dead husband, a souvenir, of course. I lent her thirty rubles on it. She fell to complaining, begged me to keep the thing for her—of course, we do keep things. Well, in short, she came again to exchange it for a bracelet that was not worth eight rubles; I, of course, refused. She must have guessed something from my wife's eyes, anyway she came again when I was not there and my wife changed it for the medallion.

Discovering it the same day, I spoke mildly but firmly and reasonably. She was sitting on the bed, looking at the ground and tapping with her right foot on the carpet (her characteristic movement); there was an ugly smile on her lips. Then, without raising my voice in the least, I explained calmly that the money was mine, that I had a right to look at life with my own eyes and—and that when I had offered to take her into my house, I had hidden nothing from her.

She suddenly leapt up, suddenly began shaking all over and—what do you think—she suddenly stamped her foot at me; it was a wild animal, it was a frenzy, it was the frenzy of a wild animal. I was petrified with astonishment; I had never expected such an outburst. But I did not lose my head. I made no movement even, and again, in the same calm voice, I announced plainly that from that time forth I should deprive her of the part she took in my work. She laughed in my face, and walked out of the house.

The fact is, she had not the right to walk out of the house. Nowhere without me, such was the agreement before she was married. In the evening she returned; I did not utter a word.

The next day, too, she went out in the morning, and the day after again. I shut the shop and went off to her aunts. I had cut off all relations with them from the time of the wedding—I would not have them to see me, and I would not go to see them. But it turned out that she had not been with them. They listened to me with curiosity and laughed in my face: "It serves you right," they said. But I expected their laughter. At that point, then, I bought over the younger aunt, the unmarried one, for a hundred rubles, giving her twenty-five in advance. Two days later she came to me: "There's an officer called Efimovich mixed up in this," she said; "a lieutenant who was a comrade of yours in the regiment." I was greatly amazed. That Efimovich had done me more harm than any one in the regiment, and about a month ago, being a shameless fellow, he once or twice came into the shop with a pretence of pawning something, and, I remember, began laughing with my wife. I went up at the time and told him not to dare to come to me, recalling our relations; but there was no thought of anything in my head, I simply thought that he was insolent. Now the aunt suddenly informed me that she had already appointed to see him and that the whole business had been arranged by a former friend of the aunt's, the widow of a colonel, called Yulia Samsonovna. "It's to her," she said, "your wife goes now."

I will cut the story short. The business cost me three hundred rubles, but in a couple of days it had been arranged that I should stand in an adjoining room, behind closed doors, and listen to the first *rendezvous* between my wife and Efimovich, tête-à-tête. Meanwhile, the evening before, a scene, brief but very memorable for me, took place between us.

She returned towards evening, sat down on the bed, looked at me sarcastically, and tapped on the carpet with her foot. Looking at her, the idea suddenly came into my mind that for the whole of the last month, or rather, the last fortnight, her character had not been her own; one might even say that it had been the opposite of her own; she had suddenly shown herself a mutinous, aggressive creature; I cannot say shameless, but regardless of decorum and eager for trouble. She went out of her way to stir up trouble. Her meekness hindered her, though. When a girl like that rebels, however outrageously she may behave, one can always see that she is forcing herself to do it, that she is driving herself to do it, and that it is impossible for her to master and overcome her own modesty and shamefacedness. That is why such people go such lengths at times, so that one can hardly believe one's eyes. One who is accustomed to depravity, on the contrary, always softens things, acts more disgustingly, but with a show of decorum and seemliness by which she claims to be superior to you.

"Is it true that you were turned out of the regiment because you were afraid to fight a duel?" she asked suddenly, apropos of nothing—and her eyes flashed.

"It is true that by the sentence of the officers I was asked to give up my commission, though, as a fact, I had sent in my papers before that."

"You were turned out as a coward?"

"Yes, they sentenced me as a coward. But I refused to fight a duel, not from cowardice, but because I would not submit to their tyrannical decision and send a challenge when I did not consider myself insulted. You know," I could not refrain from adding, "that to resist such tyranny and to accept the consequences meant showing far more manliness than fighting any kind of duel."

I could not resist it. I dropped this phrase, as it were, in self-defence, and that was all she wanted, this fresh humiliation for me.

She laughed maliciously.

"And is it true that for three years afterwards you wandered about the streets of Petersburg like a tramp, begging for coppers and spending your nights in billiard-rooms?"

"I even spent the night in Vyazemsky's House[8] in the Haymarket. Yes, it is true; there was much disgrace and degradation in my life after I left the regiment, but not moral degradation, because even at the time I hated what I did more than any one. It was only the degradation of my will and my mind, and it was only caused by the desperateness of my position. But that is over. . . ."

"Oh, now you are a personage—a financier!"

A hint at the pawnbroker's shop. But by then I had succeeded in recovering my mastery of myself. I saw that she was thirsting for explanations that would be humiliating to me and—I did not give them. A customer rang the bell very opportunely, and I went out into the shop. An hour later, when she was dressed to go out, she stood still, facing me, and said—

"You didn't tell me anything about that, though, before our marriage?"

I made no answer and she went away.

And so next day I was standing in that room, the other side of the door, listening to hear how my fate was being decided, and in my pocket I had a revolver. She was dressed better than usual and sitting at the table, and Efimovich was showing off before her. And, after all, it turned out exactly (I say it to my credit) as I had foreseen and had assumed it would, though I was not conscious of having foreseen and assumed it. I do not know whether I express myself intelligibly.

This is what happened. I listened for a whole hour. For a whole hour I was present at a duel between a noble, lofty woman and a worldly, corrupt, dense man with a crawling soul. And how, I wondered in amazement, how could that naïve, meek, silent girl have come to know all that? The wittiest author of a society comedy could not have created such a scene of mockery, of naïve laughter, and of the holy contempt of virtue for vice. And how brilliant her sayings, her little phrases were: what wit there was in her rapid answers, what truths in her condemnation. And, at the same time, what almost girlish simplicity. She laughed in his face at his declarations of love, at his gestures, at his proposals. Coming coarsely to the point at once, and not expecting to meet with opposition, he was utterly nonplussed. At first I might have imagined that it was simply coquetry on her part—"the coquetry of a witty, though depraved creature to enhance her own value." But no, the truth shone out like the sun, and to doubt was impossible. It was only an exaggerated and impulsive hatred for me that had led her, in her inexperience, to arrange this interview, but, when it came off—her eyes were opened at once. She was simply in desperate haste to mortify me, come what might, but though she had brought herself to do something so low she could not endure unseemliness. And could she, so pure and sinless, with an ideal in her heart, have been seduced by Efimovich or any worthless snob? On the contrary, she was only moved to laughter by him. All her goodness rose up from her soul and her indignation

roused her to sarcasm. I repeat, the buffoon was completely
nonplussed at last and sat frowning, scarcely answering, so
much so that I began to be afraid that he might dare to insult
her, from a mean desire for revenge. And I repeat again: to my
credit, I listened to that scene almost without surprise. I met, as
it were, nothing but what I knew well. I had gone, as it were,
on purpose to meet it, believing not a word of it, not a word
said against her, though I did take the revolver in my pocket—
that is the truth. And could I have imagined her different? For
what did I love her, for what did I prize her, for what had I married her? Oh, of course, I was quite convinced of her hate for
me, but at the same time I was quite convinced of her sinless-
ness. I suddenly cut short the scene by opening the door. Efimovich leapt up. I took her by the hand and suggested she
should go home with me. Efimovich recovered himself and
suddenly burst into loud peals of laughter.

"Oh, to sacred conjugal rights I offer no opposition; take her
away, take her away! And you know," he shouted after me,
"though no decent man could fight you, yet from respect to
your lady I am at your service . . . If you are ready to risk yourself."

"Do you hear?" I said, stopping her for a second in the
doorway.

After which not a word was said all the way home. I led her
by the arm and she did not resist. On the contrary, she was
greatly impressed, and this lasted after she got home. On reaching home she sat down in a chair and fixed her eyes upon me.
She was extremely pale; though her lips were compressed ironically yet she looked at me with solemn and austere defiance
and seemed convinced in earnest, for the first minute, that I
should kill her with the revolver. But I took the revolver from
my pocket without a word and laid it on the table! She looked
at me and at the revolver (note that the revolver was already an
object familiar to her. I had kept one loaded ever since I opened
the shop. I made up my mind when I set up the shop that I
would not keep a huge dog or a strong manservant, as Mozer
does, for instance. My cook opens the doors to my visitors. But

in our trade it is impossible to be without means of self-defence in case of emergency, and I kept a loaded revolver. In early days, when first she was living in my house, she took great interest in that revolver, and asked questions about it, and I even explained its construction and working; I even persuaded her once to fire at a target. Note all that). Taking no notice of her frightened eyes, I lay down on the bed, half-undressed. I felt very much exhausted; it was by then about eleven o'clock. She went on sitting in the same place, not stirring, for another hour. Then she put out the candle and she, too, without undressing, lay down on the sofa near the wall. For the first time she did not sleep with me—note that too. . . .

CHAPTER VI

A Terrible Reminiscence

Now for a terrible reminiscence. . . .

I woke up, I believe, before eight o'clock, and it was very nearly broad daylight. I woke up completely to full consciousness and opened my eyes. She was standing at the table holding the revolver in her hand. She did not see that I had woken up and was looking at her. And suddenly I saw that she had begun moving towards me with the revolver in her hand. I quickly closed my eyes and pretended to be still asleep.

She came up to the bed and stood over me. I heard everything; though a dead silence had fallen I heard that silence. All at once there was a convulsive movement and, irresistibly, against my will, I suddenly opened my eyes. She was looking straight at me, straight into my eyes, and the revolver was at my temple. Our eyes met. But we looked at each other for no more than a moment. With an effort I shut my eyes again, and at the same instant I resolved that I would not stir and would not open my eyes, whatever might be awaiting me.

It does sometimes happen that people who are sound asleep suddenly open their eyes, even raise their heads for a second and look about the room, then, a moment later, they lay their heads again on the pillow unconscious, and fall asleep without understanding anything. When meeting her eyes and feeling the revolver on my forehead, I closed my eyes and remained motionless, as though in a deep sleep—she certainly might have supposed that I really was asleep, and that I had seen nothing, especially as it was utterly improbable that, after seeing what I had seen, I should shut my eyes again at such a moment.

Yes, it was improbable. But she might guess the truth all the same—that thought flashed upon my mind at once, all at the same instant. Oh, what a whirl of thoughts and sensations rushed into my mind in less than a minute. Hurrah for the electric speed of thought! In that case (so I felt), if she guessed the truth and knew that I was awake, I should crush her by my readiness to accept death, and her hand might tremble. Her determination might be shaken by a new, overwhelming impression. They say that people standing on a height have an impulse to throw themselves down. I imagine that many suicides and murders have been committed simply because the revolver has been taken in the hand. It is like a precipice, with an incline of an angle of forty-five degrees, down which you cannot help sliding, and something impels you irresistibly to pull the trigger. But the knowledge that I had seen, that I knew it all, and was waiting for death at her hands without a word—might hold her back on the incline.

The stillness was prolonged, and all at once I felt on my temple, on my hair, the cold contact of the iron. You will ask: did I confidently expect to escape? I will answer you as God is my judge: I had no hope of it, except one chance in a hundred. Why did I accept death? But I will ask, what use was life to me after that revolver had been raised against me by the being I adored? Besides, I knew with the whole strength of my being that there was a struggle going on between us, a fearful duel for life and death, the duel fought by the coward of yesterday, rejected by his comrades for cowardice. I knew that and she knew it, if only she guessed the truth that I was not asleep.

Perhaps that was not so, perhaps I did not think that then, but yet it must have been so, even without conscious thought, because I've done nothing but think of it every hour of my life since.

But you will ask me again: why did you not save her from such wickedness? Oh! I've asked myself that question a thousand times since—every time that, with a shiver down my back, I recall that second. But at that moment my soul was plunged in dark despair! I was lost, I myself was lost—how could I save any one? And how do you know whether I wanted to save any one then! How can one tell what I could be feeling then?

My mind was in a ferment, though; the seconds passed; she still stood over me—and suddenly I shuddered with hope! I quickly opened my eyes. She was no longer in the room: I got out of bed: I had conquered—and she was conquered for ever!

I went to the samovar. We always had the samovar brought into the outer room and she always poured out the tea. I sat down at the table without a word and took a glass of tea from her. Five minutes later I looked at her. She was fearfully pale, even paler than the day before, and she looked at me. And suddenly . . . and suddenly, seeing that I was looking at her, she gave a pale smile with her pale lips, with a timid question in her eyes. "So she still doubts and is asking herself; does he know or doesn't he know; did he see, or didn't he?" I turned my eyes away indifferently. After tea I closed the shop, went to the market and bought an iron bedstead and a screen. Returning home, I directed that the bed should be put in the front room and shut off with a screen. It was a bed for her, but I did not say a word to her. She understood without words, through that bedstead, that I "had seen and knew all," and that all doubt was over. At night I left the revolver on the table, as I always did. At night she got into her new bed without a word: our marriage bond was broken, "she was conquered but not forgiven." At night she began to be delirious, and in the morning she had brain-fever. She was in bed for six weeks.

PART II

CHAPTER I

The Dream of Pride

Lukerya has just announced that she can't go on living here and that she is going away as soon as her lady is buried. I knelt down and prayed for five minutes. I wanted to pray for an hour, but I keep thinking and thinking, and always sick thoughts, and my head aches—what is the use of praying?—it's only a sin! It is strange, too, that I am not sleepy: in great, too great sorrow, after the first outbursts one is always sleepy. Men condemned to death, they say, sleep very soundly on the last night.[9] And so it must be, it is the law of nature, otherwise their strength would not hold out. . . . I lay down on the sofa but I did not sleep. . . .

. . . For the six weeks of her illness we were looking after her day and night—Lukerya and I together with a trained nurse whom I had engaged from the hospital. I spared no expense—in fact, I was eager to spend money for her. I called in Dr. Shreder and paid him ten rubles a visit. When she began to get better I did not show myself so much. But why am I describing it? When she got up again, she sat quietly and silently in my room at a special table, which I had bought for her, too, about that time. . . . Yes, that's the truth, we were absolutely silent; that is, we began talking afterwards, but only of the daily routine. I purposely avoided expressing myself, but I noticed that she, too, was glad not to have to say a word more than was necessary. It seemed to me that this was perfectly natural on her part: "She is too much shattered, too completely conquered," I thought, "and I must let her forget and grow used to it." In this way we were silent, but every minute I was preparing myself for the future. I thought that she was too, and it was fearfully interesting to me to guess what she was thinking about to herself then.

I will say more: oh! of course, no one knows what I went through, moaning over her in her illness. But I stifled my moans in my own heart, even from Lukerya. I could not imagine, could not even conceive of her dying without knowing the whole truth. When she was out of danger and began to regain her health, I very quickly and completely, I remember, recovered my tranquillity. What is more, I made up my mind to defer our future as long as possible, and meanwhile to leave things just as they were. Yes, something strange and peculiar happened to me then, I cannot call it anything else: I had triumphed, and the mere consciousness of that was enough for me. So the whole winter passed. Oh! I was satisfied as I had never been before, and it lasted the whole winter.

You see, there had been a terrible external circumstance in my life which, up till then—that is, up to the catastrophe with my wife—had weighed upon me every day and every hour. I mean the loss of my reputation and my leaving the regiment. In two words, I was treated with tyrannical injustice. It is true my comrades did not love me because of my difficult character, and perhaps because of my ridiculous character, though it often happens that what is exalted, precious and of value to one, for some reason amuses the herd of one's companions. Oh, I was never liked, not even at school! I was always and everywhere disliked. Even Lukerya cannot like me. What happened in the regiment, though it was the result of their dislike to me, was in a sense accidental. I mention this because nothing is more mortifying and insufferable than to be ruined by an accident, which might have happened or not have happened, from an unfortunate accumulation of circumstances which might have passed over like a cloud. For an intelligent being it is humiliating. This was what happened.

In an interval, at a theatre, I went out to the refreshment bar. A hussar called A—— came in and began, before all the officers present and the public, loudly talking to two other hussars, telling them that Captain Bezumtsev, of our regiment, was mak-.

ing a disgraceful scene in the passage and was, "he believed,
drunk." The conversation did not go further and, indeed, it was
a mistake, for Captain Bezumtsev was not drunk and the "disgraceful scene" was not really disgraceful. The hussars began
talking of something else, and the matter ended there, but next
day the story reached our regiment, and then they began saying
at once that I was the only officer of our regiment in the refreshment bar at the time, and that when A—— the hussar, had
spoken insolently of Captain Bezumtsev, I had not gone up to
A—— and stopped him by remonstrating. But on what
grounds could I have done so? If he had a grudge against
Bezumtsev, it was their personal affair and why should I interfere? Meanwhile, the officers began to declare that it was not a
personal affair, but that it concerned the regiment, and as I was
the only officer of the regiment present I had thereby shown all
the officers and other people in the refreshment bar that there
could be officers in our regiment who were not over-sensitive
on the score of their own honour and the honour of their regiment. I could not agree with this view. They let me know that
I could set everything right if I were willing, even now, late as
it was, to demand a formal explanation from A——. I was not
willing to do this, and as I was irritated I refused with pride.
And thereupon I forthwith resigned my commission—that is
the whole story. I left the regiment, proud but crushed in spirit.
I was depressed in will and mind. Just then it was that my sister's husband in Moscow squandered all our little property and
my portion of it, which was tiny enough, but the loss of it left
me homeless, without a farthing. I might have taken a job in a
private business, but I did not. After wearing a distinguished
uniform I could not take work in a railway office. And so—if it
must be shame, let it be shame; if it must be disgrace, let it be
disgrace; if it must be degradation, let it be degradation—(the
worse it is, the better) that was my choice. Then followed three
years of gloomy memories, and even Vyazemsky's House. A year
and a half ago my godmother, a wealthy old lady, died in
Moscow, and to my surprise left me three thousand in her will.
I thought a little and immediately decided on my course of

action. I determined on setting up as a pawnbroker, without apologizing to any one: money, then a home, as far as possible from memories of the past, that was my plan. Nevertheless, the gloomy past and my ruined reputation fretted me every day, every hour. But then I married. Whether it was by chance or not I don't know. But when I brought her into my home I thought I was bringing a friend, and I needed a friend so much. But I saw clearly that the friend must be trained, schooled, even conquered. Could I have explained myself straight off to a girl of sixteen with her prejudices? How, for instance, could I, without the chance help of the horrible incident with the revolver, have made her believe I was not a coward, and that I had been unjustly accused of cowardice in the regiment? But that terrible incident came just in the nick of time. Standing the test of the revolver, I scored off all my gloomy past. And though no one knew about it, she knew, and for me that was everything, because she was everything for me, all the hope of the future that I cherished in my dreams! She was the one person I had prepared for myself, and I needed no one else—and here she knew everything; she knew, at any rate, that she had been in haste to join my enemies against me unjustly. That thought enchanted me. In her eyes I could not be a scoundrel now, but at most a strange person, and that thought after all that had happened was by no means displeasing to me; strangeness is not a vice—on the contrary, it sometimes attracts the feminine heart. In fact, I purposely deferred the climax: what had happened was, meanwhile, enough for my peace of mind and provided a great number of pictures and materials for my dreams. That is what is wrong, that I am a dreamer: I had enough material for my dreams, and about her, I thought she could wait.

So the whole winter passed in a sort of expectation. I liked looking at her on the sly, when she was sitting at her little table. She was busy at her needlework, and sometimes in the evening she read books taken from my bookcase. The choice of books in the bookcase must have had an influence in my favour too. She hardly ever went out. Just before dusk, after dinner, I used to take her out every day for a walk. We took a constitutional, but we were not absolutely silent, as we used to be. I tried, in fact, to make a show of our not being silent, but talking harmoniously, but as I have said already, we both avoided letting ourselves go. I did it purposely, I thought it was essential to "give her time." Of course, it was strange that almost till the end of the winter it did not once strike me that, though I loved to watch her stealthily, I had never once, all the winter, caught her glancing at me! I thought it was timidity in her. Besides, she had an air of such timid meekness, such weakness after her illness. Yes, better to wait and—"she will come to you all at once of herself. . . ."

That thought fascinated me beyond all words. I will add one thing; sometimes, as it were purposely, I worked myself up and brought my mind and spirit to the point of believing she had injured me. And so it went on for some time. But my anger could never be very real or violent. And I felt myself as though it were only acting. And though I had broken off our marriage by buying that bedstead and screen, I could never, never look upon her as a criminal. And not that I took a frivolous view of her crime, but because I had the sense to forgive her completely, from the very first day, even before I bought the bedstead. In fact, it is strange on my part, for I am strict in moral questions. On the contrary, in my eyes, she was so conquered, so humiliated, so crushed, that sometimes I felt agonies of pity for her, though sometimes the thought of her humiliation was actually pleasing to me. The thought of our inequality pleased me. . . .

I intentionally performed several acts of kindness that winter. I excused two debts, I gave one poor woman money without any pledge. And I said nothing to my wife about it, and I didn't do it in order that she should know; but the woman came herself to thank me, almost on her knees. And in that way it became public property; it seemed to me that she heard about the woman with pleasure.

But spring was coming, it was mid-April, we took out the double windows and the sun began lighting up our silent room with its bright beams. But there was, as it were, a veil before my eyes and a blindness over my mind. A fatal, terrible veil! How did it happen that the scales suddenly fell from my eyes, and I suddenly saw and understood? Was it a chance, or had the hour come, or did the ray of sunshine kindle a thought, a conjecture, in my dull mind? No, it was not a thought, not a conjecture. But a chord suddenly vibrated, a feeling that had long been dead was stirred and came to life, flooding all my darkened soul and devilish pride with light. It was as though I had suddenly leaped up from my place. And, indeed, it happened suddenly and abruptly. It happened towards evening, at five o'clock, after dinner. . . .

CHAPTER II

The Veil Suddenly Falls

Two words first. A month ago I noticed a strange melancholy in her, not simply silence, but melancholy. That, too, I noticed suddenly. She was sitting at her work, her head bent over her sewing, and she did not see that I was looking at her. And it suddenly struck me that she had grown so delicate-looking, so thin, that her face was pale, her lips were white. All this, together with her melancholy, struck me all at once. I had already heard a little dry cough, especially at night. I got up at once and went off to ask Shreder to come, saying nothing to her.

Shreder came next day. She was very much surprised and looked first at Shreder and then at me.

"But I am well," she said, with an uncertain smile.

Shreder did not examine her very carefully (these doctors are sometimes superciliously careless), he only said to me in the other room, that it was just the result of her illness, and that it wouldn't be amiss to go for a trip to the sea in the spring, or, if that were impossible, to take a cottage out of town for the summer. In fact, he said nothing except that there was weakness, or something of that sort. When Shreder had gone, she said again, looking at me very earnestly—

"I am quite well, quite well."

But as she said this she suddenly flushed, apparently from shame. Apparently it was shame. Oh! now I understand: she was ashamed that I was still *her husband*, that I was looking after her still as though I were a real husband. But at the time I did not understand and put down her blush to humility (the veil!).

And so, a month later, in April, at five o'clock on a bright sunny day, I was sitting in the shop making up my accounts. Suddenly I heard her, sitting in our room, at work at her table, begin softly, softly . . . singing. This novelty made an overwhelming impression upon me, and to this day I don't understand it. Till then I had hardly ever heard her sing, unless, perhaps, in those first days, when we were still able to be playful and practise shooting at a target. Then her voice was rather strong, resonant; though not quite true it was very sweet and healthy. Now her little song was so faint—it was not that it was melancholy (it was some sort of ballad), but in her voice there was something jangled, broken, as though her voice were not equal to it, as though the song itself were sick. She sang in an undertone, and suddenly, as her voice rose, it broke—such a poor little voice, it broke so pitifully; she cleared her throat and again began softly, softly singing. . . .

My emotions will be ridiculed, but no one will understand why I was so moved! No, I was still not sorry for her, it was still something quite different. At the beginning, for the first minute, at any rate, I was filled with sudden perplexity and terrible amazement—a terrible and strange, painful and almost vindictive amazement: "She is singing, and in my presence; *has she forgotten about me?*"

Completely overwhelmed, I remained where I was, then I

suddenly got up, took my hat and went out, as it were, without thinking. At least I don't know why or where I was going. Lukerya began giving me my overcoat.

"She is singing?" I said to Lukerya involuntarily. She did not understand, and looked at me still without understanding; and, indeed, I was really unintelligible.

"Is it the first time she is singing?"

"No, she sometimes does sing when you are out," answered Lukerya.

I remember everything. I went downstairs, went out into the street and walked along at random. I walked to the corner and began looking into the distance. People were passing by, they pushed against me. I did not feel it. I called a cab and told the man, I don't know why, to drive to Politseysky Bridge. Then suddenly changed my mind and gave him twenty kopeks.

"That's for my having troubled you," I said, with a meaningless laugh, but a sort of ecstasy was suddenly shining within me.

I returned home, quickening my steps. The poor little jangled, broken note was ringing in my heart again. My breath failed me. The veil was falling, was falling from my eyes! Since she sang before me, she had forgotten me—that is what was clear and terrible. My heart felt it. But rapture was glowing in my soul and it overcame my terror.

Oh! the irony of fate! Why, there had been nothing else and could have been nothing else but that rapture in my soul all the winter, but where had I been myself all that winter? Had I been there together with my soul? I ran up the stairs in great haste, I don't know whether I went in timidly. I only remember that the whole floor seemed to be rocking and I felt as though I were floating on a river. I went into the room. She was sitting in the same place as before, with her head bent over her sewing, but she wasn't singing now. She looked cursorily and without interest at me; it was hardly a look but just an habitual and indifferent movement upon somebody's coming into the room.

I went straight up and sat down beside her in a chair

abruptly, as though I were mad. She looked at me quickly, seeming frightened; I took her hand and I don't remember what I said to her—that is, tried to say, for I could not even speak properly. My voice broke and would not obey me and I did not know what to say. I could only gasp for breath.

"Let us talk . . . you know . . . tell me something!" I muttered something stupid. Oh! how could I help being stupid? She started again and drew back in great alarm, looking at my face, but suddenly there was an expression of *stern surprise* in her eyes. Yes, surprise and *stern*. She looked at me with wide-open eyes. That sternness, that stern surprise shattered me at once: "So you still expect love? Love?" that surprise seemed to be asking, though she said nothing. But I read it all, I read it all. Everything within me seemed quivering, and I simply fell down at her feet. Yes, I grovelled at her feet. She jumped up quickly, but I held her forcibly by both hands.

And I fully understood my despair—I understood it! But, would you believe it? ecstasy was surging up in my head so violently that I thought I should die. I kissed her feet in delirium and rapture. Yes, in immense, infinite rapture, and that, in spite of understanding all the hopelessness of my despair. I wept, said something, but could not speak. Her alarm and amazement were followed by some uneasy misgiving, some grave question, and she looked at me strangely, wildly even; she wanted to understand something quickly and she smiled. She was horribly ashamed at my kissing her feet and she drew them back. But I kissed the place on the floor where her foot had rested. She saw it and suddenly began laughing with shame (you know how it is when people laugh with shame). She became hysterical, I saw that her hands trembled—I did not think about that but went on muttering that I loved her, that I would not get up. "Let me kiss your dress . . . and worship you like this all my life." . . . I don't know, I don't remember—but suddenly she broke into sobs and trembled all over. A terrible fit of hysterics followed. I had frightened her.

I carried her to the bed. When the attack had passed off, sitting on the edge of the bed, with a terribly exhausted look, she took my two hands and begged me to calm myself: "Come, come, don't distress yourself, be calm!" and she began crying again. All that evening I did not leave her side. I kept telling her I should take her to Boulogne to bathe in the sea now, at once, in a fortnight, that she had such a broken voice, I had heard it that afternoon, that I would shut up the shop, that I would sell it to Dobronravov, that everything should begin afresh and, above all, Boulogne, Boulogne! She listened and was still afraid. She grew more and more afraid. But that was not what mattered most for me: what mattered most to me was the more and more irresistible longing to fall at her feet again, and again to kiss and kiss the spot where her foot had rested, and to worship her; and—"I ask nothing, nothing more of you," I kept repeating, "do not answer me, take no notice of me, only let me watch you from my corner, treat me as your dog, your thing. . . ." She was crying.

"*I thought that you would leave me like that*," suddenly broke from her unconsciously, so unconsciously that, perhaps, she did not notice what she had said, and yet—oh, that was the most significant, momentous phrase she uttered that evening, the easiest for me to understand, and it stabbed my heart as though with a knife! It explained everything to me, everything, but while she was beside me, before my eyes, I could not help hoping and was fearfully happy. Oh, I exhausted her fearfully that evening. I understood that, but I kept thinking that I should alter everything directly. At last, towards night, she was utterly exhausted. I persuaded her to go to sleep and she fell sound asleep at once. I expected her to be delirious, she was a little delirious, but very slightly. I kept getting up every minute in the night and going softly in my slippers to look at her. I wrung my hands over her, looking at that frail creature in that wretched little iron bedstead which I had bought her for three rubles. I knelt down, but did not dare to kiss her feet in her sleep (without her consent). I began praying but leapt up again. Lukerya kept watch over me and came in and out from the kitchen. I went in to her, and told her to go to bed, and that to-morrow "things would be quite different."

And I believed in this, blindly, madly.

Oh, I was brimming over with rapture, rapture! I was eager for the next day. Above all, I did not believe that anything could go wrong, in spite of the symptoms. Reason had not altogether come back to me, though the veil had fallen from my eyes, and for a long, long time it did not come back—not till to-day, not till this very day! Yes, and how could it have come back then: why, she was still alive then; why, she was here before my eyes, and I was before her eyes: "To-morrow she will wake up and I will tell her all this, and she will see it all." That was how I reasoned then, simply and clearly, because I was in an ecstasy! My great idea was the trip to Boulogne. I kept thinking for some reason that Boulogne would be everything, that there was something final and decisive about Boulogne. "To Boulogne, to Boulogne!" . . . I waited frantically for the morning.

CHAPTER III

I Understand Too Well

But you know that was only a few days ago, five days, only five days ago, last Tuesday! Yes, yes, if there had only been a little longer, if she had only waited a little—and I would have dissipated the darkness!—It was not as though she had not recovered her calmness. The very next day she listened to me with a smile, in spite of her confusion. . . . All this time, all these five days, she was either confused or ashamed. She was afraid, too, very much afraid. I don't dispute it, I am not so mad as to deny it. It was terror, but how could she help being frightened? We had so long been strangers to one an-

other, had grown so alienated from one another, and suddenly
all this. . . . But I did not look at her terror. I was dazzled by the
new life beginning! . . . It is true, it is undoubtedly true that I
made a mistake. There were even, perhaps, many mistakes.
When I woke up next day, the first thing in the morning (that
was on Wednesday), I made a mistake: I suddenly made her my
friend. I was in too great a hurry, too great a hurry, but a confession was necessary, inevitable—more than a confession! I did
not even hide what I had hidden from myself all my life. I told
her straight out that the whole winter I had been doing nothing but brood over the certainty of her love. I made clear to her
that my money-lending had been simply the degradation of
my will and my mind, my personal idea of self-castigation and
self-exaltation. I explained to her that I really had been cowardly that time in the refreshment bar, that it was owing to my
temperament, to my self-consciousness. I was impressed by
the surroundings, by the theatre: I was doubtful how I should
succeed and whether it would be stupid. I was not afraid of a
duel, but of its being stupid . . . and afterwards I would not
own it and tormented every one and had tormented her for it,
and had married her so as to torment her for it. In fact, for the
most part I talked as though in delirium. She herself took my
hands and made me leave off. "You are exaggerating . . . you
are distressing yourself," and again there were tears, again almost hysterics! She kept begging me not to say all this, not to
recall it.

I took no notice of her entreaties, or hardly noticed them:
"Spring, Boulogne! There there would be sunshine, there our
new sunshine," I kept saying that! I shut up the shop and transferred it to Dobronravov. I suddenly suggested to her giving all
our money to the poor except the three thousand left me by my
godmother, which we would spend on going to Boulogne, and
then we would come back and begin a new life of real work. So
we decided, for she said nothing. . . . She only smiled. And I believe she smiled chiefly from delicacy, for fear of disappointing
me. I saw, of course, that I was burdensome to her, don't imagine I was so stupid or egoistic as not to see it. I saw it all, all, to

the smallest detail, I saw better than any one; all the hopelessness of my position stood revealed.

I told her everything about myself and about her. And about
Lukerya. I told her that I had wept. . . . Oh, of course, I
changed the conversation. I tried, too, not to say a word more
about certain things. And, indeed, she did revive once or
twice—I remember it, I remember it! Why do you say I looked
at her and saw nothing? And if only this had not happened,
everything would have come to life again. Why, only the day
before yesterday, when we were talking of reading and what
she had been reading that winter, she told me something herself, and laughed as she told me, recalling the scene of Gil Blas
and the Archbishop of Granada.[10] And with what sweet, childish laughter, just as in old days when we were engaged (one
instant! one instant!); how glad I was! I was awfully struck,
though, by the story of the Archbishop; so she had found
peace of mind and happiness enough to laugh at that literary
masterpiece while she was sitting there in the winter. So then
she had begun to be fully at rest, had begun to believe confidently that I should leave her *like that*. "I thought that you
would leave me *like that*," those were the words she uttered then
on Tuesday! Oh! the thought of a child of ten! And you know
she believed it, she believed that really everything would remain *like that*: she at her table and I at mine, and we both should
go on like that till we were sixty. And all at once—I come forward, her husband, and the husband wants love! Oh, the delusion! Oh, my blindness!

It was a mistake, too, that I looked at her with rapture; I
ought to have controlled myself, as it was my rapture frightened
her. But, indeed, I did control myself, I did not kiss her feet
again. I never made a sign of . . . well, that I was her husband—
oh, there was no thought of that in my mind, I only worshipped her! But, you know, I couldn't be quite silent, I could
not refrain from speaking altogether! I suddenly said to her
frankly, that I enjoyed her conversation and that I thought her
incomparably more cultured and developed than I. She flushed
crimson and said in confusion that I exaggerated. Then, like a

fool, I could not resist telling her how delighted I had been
when I had stood behind the door listening to her duel, the
duel of innocence with that low cad, and how I had enjoyed her
cleverness, the brilliance of her wit, and, at the same time, her
childlike simplicity. She seemed to shudder all over, was mur-
muring again that I exaggerated, but suddenly her whole face
darkened, she hid it in her hands and broke into sobs. . . . Then
I could not restrain myself: again I fell at her feet, again I began
kissing her feet, and again it ended in a fit of hysterics, just as
on Tuesday. That was yesterday evening—and—in the morning. . . .

In the morning! Madman! why, that morning was to-day,
just now, only just now!

Listen and try to understand: why, when we met by the
samovar (it was after yesterday's hysterics), I was actually struck
by her calmness, that is the actual fact! And all night I had been
trembling with terror over what happened yesterday. But suddenly she came up to me and, clasping her hands (this morning, this morning!) began telling me that she was a criminal,
that she knew it, that her crime had been torturing her all the
winter, was torturing her now. . . . That she appreciated my
generosity. . . . "I will be your faithful wife, I will respect
you . . ." Then I leapt up and embraced her like a madman. I
kissed her, kissed her face, kissed her lips like a husband for the
first time after a long separation. And why did I go out this
morning, only for two hours . . . our passports for abroad. . . .
Oh, God! if only I had come back five minutes, only five minutes earlier! . . . That crowd at our gates, those eyes all fixed
upon me. Oh, God!

Lukerya says (oh! I will not let Lukerya go now for anything. She knows all about it, she has been here all the winter,
she will tell me everything!), she says that when I had gone out
of the house and only about twenty minutes before I came
back—she suddenly went into our room to her mistress to ask
her something, I don't remember what, and saw that her ikon
(that same ikon of the Mother of God) had been taken down
and was standing before her on the table, and her mistress

seemed to have only just been praying before it. "What are you doing, mistress?" "Nothing, Lukerya, run along." "Wait a minute, Lukerya." "She came up and kissed me." "Are you happy, mistress?" I said. "Yes, Lukerya." "Master ought to have come to beg your pardon long ago, mistress. . . . Thank God that you are reconciled." "Very good, Lukerya," she said. "Go away, Lukerya" and she smiled, but so strangely. So strangely that Lukerya went back ten minutes later to have a look at her. "She was standing by the wall, close to the window, she had laid her arm against the wall, and her head was pressed on her arm, she was standing like that thinking. And she was standing so deep in thought that she did not hear me come and look at her from the other room. She seemed to be smiling—standing, thinking and smiling. I looked at her, turned softly and went out wondering to myself, and suddenly I heard the window opened. I went in at once to say: 'It's fresh, mistress; mind you don't catch cold,' and suddenly I saw she had got on the window and was standing there, her full height, in the open window, with her back to me, holding the ikon in her hand. My heart sank on the spot. I cried, 'Mistress, mistress.' She heard, made a movement to turn back to me, but, instead of turning back, took a step forward, pressed the ikon to her bosom, and flung herself out of window."

I only remember that when I went in at the gate she was still warm. The worst of it was they were all looking at me. At first they shouted and then suddenly they were silent, and then all of them moved away from me . . . and she was lying there with the ikon. I remember, as it were, in a darkness, that I went up to her in silence and looked at her a long while. But all came round me and said something to me. Lukerya was there too, but I did not see her. She says she said something to me, I only remember that workman. He kept shouting to me that "Only a handful of blood came from her mouth, a handful, a handful!" and he pointed to the blood on a stone. I believe I touched the blood with my finger, I smeared my finger, I looked at my finger (that I remember), and he kept repeating: "a handful, a handful!"

"What do you mean by a handful?" I yelled with all my might, I am told, and I lifted up my hands and rushed at him.

Oh, wild! wild! Incomprehensibility! Improbability! Impossibility!

CHAPTER IV

I Was Only Five Minutes Too Late

Is it not so? Is it likely? Can one really say it was possible? What for, why did this woman die?

Oh, believe me, I understand, but why she died is still a question. She was frightened of my love, asked herself seriously whether to accept it or not, could not bear the question and preferred to die. I know, I know, no need to rack my brains: she had made too many promises, she was afraid she could not keep them—it is clear. There are circumstances about it quite awful.

For why did she die? That is still a question, after all. The question hammers, hammers at my brain. I would have left her like that if she had wanted to remain like that. She did not believe it, that's what it was! No—no. I am talking nonsense, it was not that at all. It was simply because with me she had to be honest—if she loved me, she would have had to love me altogether, and not as she would have loved the grocer. And as she was too chaste, too pure, to consent to such love as the grocer wanted she did not want to deceive me. Did not want to deceive me with half love, counterfeiting love, or a quarter love. They are honest, too honest, that is what it is! I wanted to instil breadth of heart in her, in those days, do you remember? A strange idea.

It is awfully interesting to know: did she respect me or not?

I don't know whether she despised me or not. I don't believe she did despise me. It is awfully strange: why did it never once enter my head all the winter that she despised me? I was absolutely convinced of the contrary up to that moment when she looked at me with *stern surprise*. Stern it was. I understood on the spot that she despised me. I understood once for all, for ever! Ah, let her, let her despise me all her life even, only let her be living! Only yesterday she was walking about, talking. I simply can't understand how she threw herself out of window! And how could I have imagined it five minutes before? I have called Lukerya. I won't let Lukerya go now for anything!

Oh, we might still have understood each other! We had simply become terribly estranged from one another during the winter, but couldn't we have grown used to each other again? Why, why, couldn't we have come together again and begun a new life again? I am generous, she was too—that was a point in common! Only a few more words, another two days—no more, and she would have understood everything.

What is most mortifying of all is that it is chance—simply a barbarous, lagging chance. That is what is mortifying! Five minutes, only five minutes too late! Had I come five minutes earlier, the moment would have passed away like a cloud, and it would never have entered her head again. And it would have ended by her understanding it all. But now again empty rooms, and me alone. Here the pendulum is ticking; it does not care, it has no pity. . . . There is no one—that's the misery of it!

I keep walking and walking. I know, I know, you need not tell me; it amuses you, you think it ridiculous that I complain of chance and those five minutes. But it is evident. Consider one thing: she did not even leave a note, to say, "Blame no one for my death," as people always do. Might she not have thought that Lukerya might get into trouble. "She was alone with her," might have been said, "and pushed her out." In any case she would have been taken up by the police if it had not happened that four people, from the windows, from the lodge, and from the yard, had seen her stand with the ikon in her hands and jump out of herself. But that, too, was a chance, that the people were standing there and saw her. No, it was all a moment, only an irresponsible moment. A sudden impulse, a fantasy! What if she did pray before the ikon? It does not follow that she was facing death. The whole impulse lasted, perhaps, only some ten minutes; it was all decided, perhaps, while she stood against the wall with her head on her arm, smiling. The idea darted into her brain, she turned giddy and—and could not resist it.

Say what you will, it was clearly misunderstanding. It would have been possible to live with me. And what if it were anæmia? Was it simply from poorness of blood, from the flagging of vital energy? She had grown tired during the winter, that was what it was. . . .

I was too late!!!

How thin she is in her coffin, how sharp her nose has grown! Her eyelashes lie straight as arrows. And, you know, when she fell, nothing was crushed, nothing was broken! Nothing but that "handful of blood." A teaspoonful, that is. From internal injury. A strange thought: if only it were possible not to bury her? For if they take her away, then . . . oh, no, it is almost incredible that they should take her away! I am not mad and I am not raving—on the contrary, my mind was never so lucid—but what shall I do when again there is no one, only the two rooms, and me alone with the pledges? Madness, madness, madness! I worried her to death, that is what it is!

What are your laws to me now? What do I care for your customs, your morals, your life, your state, your faith! Let your judge judge me, let me be brought before your court, let me be tried by jury, and I shall say that I admit nothing. The judge will shout, "Be silent, officer." And I will shout to him, "What power have you now that I will obey? Why did blind, inert force destroy that which was dearest of all? What are your laws to me now? They are nothing to me." Oh, I don't care!

She was blind, blind! She is dead, she does not hear! You do not know with what a paradise I would have surrounded you. There was paradise in my soul, I would have made it blossom around you! Well, you wouldn't have loved me—so be it, what of it? Things should still have been like that, everything should have remained like that. You should only have talked to me as a friend—we should have rejoiced and laughed with joy looking at one another. And so we should have lived. And if you had loved another—well, so be it, so be it! You should have walked with him laughing, and I should have watched you from the other side of the street. . . . Oh, anything, anything, if only she would open her eyes just once! For one instant, only one! If she would look at me as she did this morning, when she stood before me and made a vow to be a faithful wife! Oh, in one look she would have understood it all!

Oh, blind force! Oh, nature! Men are alone on earth—that is what is dreadful! "Is there a man alive on the battlefield?"[11] cries the Russian hero. I cry the same, though I am not a hero, and no one answers my cry. They say the sun gives life to the universe. The sun is rising and—look at it, is it not dead?[12] Everything is dead and everywhere there are dead. Men are alone—around them is silence—that is the earth! "Men, love one another"—who said that?[13] Whose commandment is that? The pendulum ticks callously, heartlessly. Two o'clock at night. Her little shoes are standing by the little bed, as though waiting for her. . . . No, seriously, when they take her away to-morrow, what will become of me?

THE DREAM OF
A RIDICULOUS MAN

A FANTASTIC STORY

I

I am a ridiculous man. Now they call me a madman. That would be a promotion if it were not that I remain as ridiculous in their eyes as before. But now I do not resent it, they are all dear to me now, even when they laugh at me—and, indeed, it is just then that they are particularly dear to me. I could join in their laughter—not exactly at myself, but through affection for them, if I did not feel so sad as I look at them. Sad because they do not know the truth and I do know it. Oh, how hard it is to be the only one who knows the truth! But they won't understand that. No, they won't understand it.

In old days I used to be miserable at seeming ridiculous. Not seeming, but being. I have always been ridiculous, and I have known it, perhaps, from the hour I was born. Perhaps from the time I was seven years old I knew I was ridiculous. Afterwards I went to school, studied at the university, and, do you know, the more I learned, the more thoroughly I understood that I was ridiculous. So that it seemed in the end as though all the sciences I studied at the university existed only to prove and make evident to me as I went more deeply into them that I was ridiculous. It was the same with life as it was with science. With every year the same consciousness of the ridiculous figure I cut in every relation grew and strengthened. Every one always laughed at me. But not one of them knew or guessed that if there were one man on earth who knew better than anybody else that I was ridiculous, it was myself, and what offended me most of all was that they did not know that. But that was my own fault; I was so proud that nothing would have ever induced me to tell it to any one. This pride grew in me with the years; and if it had happened that I allowed myself to confess to any one that I was ridiculous, I believe that I should have blown out my brains the same evening. Oh, how I suffered in my early youth from the fear that I might give way and confess it to my schoolfellows. But since I grew to manhood, though I acknowledged my awful characteristics more fully every year, for some unknown reason I have become calmer. I say "unknown," for to this day I cannot tell why it was. Perhaps it was owing to the terrible misery that was growing in my soul through something which was of more consequence than anything else about me: that something was the conviction that had come upon me that *nothing in the world mattered*. I had long had an inkling of it, but the full realisation came last year almost suddenly. I suddenly felt that it was all the same to me whether the world existed or whether there had never been anything at all: I began to feel with all my being that there was *nothing existing*. At first I fancied that many things had existed in the past, but afterwards I guessed that there never had been anything in the past either, but that it had only seemed so for some reason. Little by little I guessed that there would be nothing in the future either. Then I left off being angry with people and almost ceased to notice them. Indeed this showed itself even in the pettiest trifles: I used, for instance, to knock against people in the street. And not so much from being lost in thought: what had I to think about? I had almost given up thinking by that time; nothing mattered to me. If at least I had resolved my questions! Oh, I had not resolved one of them, and how many were there? But I gave up caring about anything, and all the questions disappeared.

And it was after that that I found out the truth. I learnt the truth last November—on the third of November, to be precise—and I remember every instant since. It was a gloomy evening, one of the gloomiest possible evenings. I was going home at about eleven o'clock, and I remember that I thought that the evening could not be gloomier. Even physically. Rain had been falling all day, and it had been a cold, gloomy, almost menacing rain, with, I remember, an unmistakable spite against mankind. Suddenly between ten and eleven it had stopped, and was followed by a horrible dampness, colder and damper than the rain, and a sort of steam was rising from everything, from every stone in the street, and from every by-lane if one looked down it as far as one could. A thought suddenly occurred to me, that if all the street lamps had been put out it would have been less cheerless, that the gas lamp made one's heart sadder because it lighted it all up. I had had scarcely any dinner that day, and had been spending the evening with an engineer, and two other friends had been there also. I sat silent—I fancy I bored them. They talked of something rousing and suddenly they got excited over it. But nothing mattered to them, I could see that, and only made a show of being excited. I suddenly said as much to them. "My friends," I said, "nothing matters to you one way or the other." They were not offended, but they all laughed at me. That was because I spoke without any note of reproach, simply, because it did not matter to me. They saw that nothing mattered to me, and it amused them.

As I was thinking about the gas lamps in the street I looked up at the sky. The sky was horribly dark, but one could distinctly see tattered clouds, and between them fathomless black patches. Suddenly I noticed in one of these patches a star, and began watching it intently. That was because that star gave me an idea: I decided to kill myself that night. I had firmly determined to do so two months before, and poor as I was, I bought a splendid revolver that very day, and loaded it. But two months had passed and it was still lying in my drawer; it mattered so little to me that I wanted to seize a moment when it would not matter so little—why, I don't know. And so for two months every night that I came home I thought I would shoot myself. I kept waiting for the right moment. And so now this star gave me a thought. I made up my mind that it should certainly be that night. And why the star gave me the thought I don't know.

And just as I was looking at the sky, this little girl took me by the elbow. The street was empty, and there was scarcely any one to be seen. A cabman was sleeping in the distance in his cab. It was a child of eight with a kerchief on her head, wearing nothing but a wretched little dress all soaked with rain, but I noticed particularly her wet broken shoes and I recall them now. They caught my eye particularly. She suddenly pulled me by the elbow and called me. She was not weeping, but was spasmodically crying out some words which she could not utter properly, because she was shivering and shuddering all over. She was in terror about something, and kept crying,

"Mommy, mommy!" I turned facing her, I did not say a word
and went on; but she ran, pulling at me, and there was that note
in her voice which in frightened children means despair. I
know that sound. Though she did not articulate the words, I understood that her mother was dying, or that something of the
sort was happening to them, and that she had run out to call
some one, to find something to help her mother. I did not go
with her; on the contrary, I had an impulse to drive her away. I
told her first to go to a policeman. But clasping her hands, she
ran beside me sobbing and gasping, and would not leave me.
Then I stamped my foot, and shouted at her. She called out "Sir!
sir! . . ." but suddenly abandoned me and rushed headlong
across the road. Some other passer-by appeared there, and she
evidently flew from me to him.

I mounted up to my fifth storey. I have a room in a flat where
there are other lodgers. My room is small and poor, with a gar-
ret window in the shape of a semicircle. I have an oilskin couch,
a table with books on it, two chairs and a comfortable armchair, as old as old can be, but nonetheless Voltairean.[1] I sat
down, lighted the candle, and began thinking. In the room next
to mine, through the partition wall, a perfect Sodom was going
on. It had been going on for the last three days. A retired captain lived there, and he had half a dozen visitors, gentlemen of
doubtful reputation, drinking vodka and playing *stoss* with old
cards. The night before there had been a fight, and I know that
two of them had been for a long time engaged in dragging each
other about by the hair. The landlady wanted to complain, but
she was in abject terror of the captain. There was only one other
lodger in the flat, a thin little regimental lady, on a visit to Petersburg, with three little children who had been taken ill since
they came into the lodgings. Both she and her children were in
mortal fear of the captain, and lay trembling and crossing themselves all night, and the youngest child had a sort of fit from
fright. That captain, I know for a fact, sometimes stops people
in the Nevsky Prospect and begs. They won't take him into the
service, but strange to say (that's why I am telling this), all this
month that the captain has been here his behaviour has caused

me no annoyance. I have, of course, tried to avoid his acquaintance from the very beginning, and he, too, was bored with me from the first; but it never matters to me how much they shout the other side of the partition nor how many of them there are in there. I sit up all night and forget them so completely that I do not even hear them. I stay awake till daybreak, and have been going on like that for the last year. I sit up all night in my armchair at the table, doing nothing. I only read by day. I sit—don't even think; ideas of a sort wander through my mind and I let them come and go as they will. A whole candle is burnt every night. I sat down quietly at the table, took out the revolver and put it down before me. When I had put it down I asked myself, I remember, "Is that so?" and answered with complete conviction, "It is." That is, I shall shoot myself. I knew that I should shoot myself that night for certain, but how much longer I should go on sitting at the table I did not know. And no doubt I should have shot myself if it had not been for that little girl.

II

You see, though nothing mattered to me, I could feel pain, for instance. If any one had struck me it would have hurt me. It was the same morally: if anything very pathetic happened, I should have felt pity just as I used to do in old days when there were things in life that did matter to me. I had felt pity that evening. I should have certainly helped a child. Why, then, had I not helped the little girl? Because of an idea that occurred to me at the time: when she was calling and pulling at me, a question suddenly arose before me and I could not resolve it. The question was an idle one, but I was vexed. I was vexed at the reflection that if I were going to make an end of myself that night, nothing in life ought to have mattered to me. Why was it that all at once I did not feel that nothing mattered and that I was sorry for the little girl? I remember that I was very sorry for her, so much so that I felt a strange pang, quite incongruous in my position. Really I do not know better how to convey my fleeting sensation at the moment, but the sensation persisted at home when I was sitting at the table, and I was very much irritated as I had not been for a long time past. One reflection followed another. I saw clearly that so long as I was still a human being and not nothing, I was alive and so could suffer, be angry and feel shame at my actions. So be it. But if I am going to kill myself, in two hours, say, what is the little girl to me and what have I to do with shame or with anything else in the world? I shall turn into nothing, absolutely nothing. And can it really be true that the consciousness that I shall *completely* cease to exist immediately and so everything else will cease to exist, does not in the least affect my feeling of pity for the child nor the feeling of shame after the contemptible act I had committed? I stamped and shouted at the unhappy child as though to say—not only do I feel no pity, but even if I behave inhumanly and contemptibly, I am free to, for in another two hours everything will be extinguished. Do you believe that that was why I shouted that? I am almost convinced of it now. It seemed clear to me that life and the world somehow depended upon me now. I may almost say that the world now seemed created for me alone: if I shot myself the world would cease to be at least for me. I say nothing of its being likely that nothing will exist for any one when I am gone, and that as soon as my consciousness is extinguished the whole world will vanish too and become void like a phantom, as a mere appurtenance of my consciousness, for possibly all this world and all these people are only me myself. I remember that as I sat and reflected, I turned all these new questions that swarmed one after another quite the other way, and thought of something quite new. For instance, a strange reflection suddenly occurred to me, that if I had lived before on the moon or on Mars and there had committed the most disgraceful and dishonourable action and had there been put to such shame and ignominy as one can only conceive and realise in dreams, in nightmares, and if, finding myself afterwards on earth, I were able to retain the memory of what I had done on the other planet and at the same time knew that I should never, under any circumstances, return there, then looking from the earth to the moon—would it matter to me or not? Should I feel shame for that action or not? These were idle and superfluous questions for the revolver was already lying before me, and I knew in every fibre of my being that it would happen for certain, but they excited me and I raged. I could not die now without having first resolved something beforehand. In short, the child had saved me, for I put off my pistol shot for the sake of these questions. Meanwhile the clamour had begun to subside in the captain's room: they had finished their game, were settling down to sleep, and meanwhile were grumbling and languidly winding up their quarrels. At that point I suddenly fell asleep in my chair at the table—a thing which had never happened to me before. I dropped asleep quite unawares.

Dreams, as we all know, are very strange things: some parts are presented with appalling vividness, with details worked up with the elaborate finish of jewellery, while others one gallops through, as it were, without noticing them at all, as, for instance, through space and time. Dreams seem to be spurred on not by reason but by desire, not by the head but by the heart, and yet what clever tricks my reason has played sometimes in dreams, what utterly incomprehensible things happen to it! My brother died five years ago, for instance. I sometimes dream of him; he takes part in my affairs, we are very much interested, and yet all through my dream I quite know and remember that my brother is dead and buried. How is it that I am not surprised that, though he is dead, he is here beside me and working with me? Why is it that my reason fully accepts it? But enough. I will begin about my dream. Yes, I dreamed a dream, my dream of the third of November. They tease me now, telling me it was only a dream. But does it matter whether it was a dream or reality, if the dream made known to me the Truth? If once one has recognised the truth and seen it, you know that it is the truth and that there is no other and there cannot be, whether you are asleep or awake. Let it be a dream, so be it, but that real life of which you make so much I had meant to extinguish by suicide, and my dream, my dream—oh, it revealed to me a different life, renewed, grand and full of power!

Listen.

III

I have mentioned that I dropped asleep unawares and even seemed to be still reflecting on the same subjects. I suddenly dreamt that I picked up the revolver and aimed it straight at my heart—my heart, and not my head; and I had determined beforehand to fire at my head, at my right temple. After aiming at my chest I waited a second or two, and suddenly my candle, my table, and the wall in front of me began moving and heaving. I made haste to pull the trigger.

In dreams you sometimes fall from a height, or are stabbed, or beaten, but you never feel pain unless, perhaps, you really bruise yourself against the bedstead, then you feel pain and almost always wake up from it. It was the same in my dream. I did not feel any pain, but it seemed as though with my shot everything within me was shaken and everything was suddenly dimmed, and it grew horribly black around me. I seemed to be blinded and benumbed, and I was lying on something hard, stretched on my back; I saw nothing, and could not make the slightest movement. People were walking and shouting around me, the captain bawled, the landlady shrieked—and suddenly another break and I was being carried in a closed coffin. And I felt how the coffin was shaking and reflected upon it, and for the first time the idea struck me that I was dead, utterly dead, I knew it and had no doubt of it, I could neither see nor move and yet I was feeling and reflecting. But I was soon reconciled to the position, and as one usually does in a dream, accepted the facts without disputing them.

And now I was buried in the earth. They all went away, I was left alone, utterly alone. I did not move. Whenever before I had imagined being buried the one sensation I associated with the grave was that of damp and cold. So now I felt that I was very cold, especially the tips of my toes, but I felt nothing else.

I lay still, strange to say I expected nothing, accepting without dispute that a dead man had nothing to expect. But it was damp. I don't know how long a time passed—whether an hour, or several days, or many days. But all at once a drop of water fell on my closed left eye, making its way through a coffin lid; it was followed a minute later by a second, then a minute later by a third—and so on, regularly every minute. There was a sudden glow of profound indignation in my heart, and I suddenly felt in it a pang of physical pain. "That's my wound," I thought; "that's the bullet. . . ." And drop after drop every minute kept falling on my closed eyelid. And all at once, not with my voice, but with my whole being, I called upon the power that was responsible for all that was happening to me:

"Whoever you may be, if you exist, and if anything more rational than what is happening here is possible, suffer it to be here now. But if you are revenging yourself upon me for my senseless suicide by the hideousness and absurdity of this subsequent existence, then let me tell you that no torture could ever equal the contempt which I shall go on dumbly feeling, though my martyrdom may last a million years!"

I made this appeal and held my peace. There was a full minute of unbroken silence and again another drop fell, but I knew with infinite unshakable certainty that everything would change immediately. And behold my grave suddenly was rent asunder, that is, I don't know whether it was opened or dug up, but I was caught up by some dark and unknown being and we found ourselves in space. I suddenly regained my sight. It was the dead of night, and never, never had there been such darkness. We were flying through space far away from the earth. I did not question the being who was taking me; I was proud and waited. I assured myself that I was not afraid, and was thrilled with ecstasy at the thought that I was not afraid. I do not know how long we were flying, I cannot imagine; it happened as it always does in dreams when you skip over space and time, and the laws of thought and existence, and only pause upon the points for which the heart yearns. I remember that I suddenly saw in the darkness a star. "Is that Sirius?" I asked impulsively, though I had not meant to ask any questions.

"No, that is the star you saw between the clouds when you were coming home," the being who was carrying me replied.

I knew that it had something like a human face. Strange to say, I did not like that being, in fact I felt an intense aversion for it. I had expected complete non-existence, and that was why I had put a bullet through my heart. And here I was in the hands of a being not human, of course, but which is, which exists. "And so there is life beyond the grave," I thought with the strange frivolity one has in dreams. But in its inmost depth my heart remained unchanged. "And if I have got to be again," I thought, "and live once more under the control of some irresistible power, I don't want to be vanquished and humiliated."

"You know that I am afraid of you, and you despise me for that," I said suddenly to my companion, unable to refrain from the humiliating question which implied a confession, and feeling my humiliation stab my heart as with a pin. He did not answer my question, but all at once I felt that I was not despised, but that I was being laughed at and that there was no compassion for me, and that our journey had an unknown and mysterious object that concerned me only. Fear was growing in my heart. Something was mutely and painfully communicated to me from my silent companion, and penetrated my whole being. We were flying through dark, unknown space. I had for some time lost sight of the constellations familiar to my eyes. I knew that there were stars in the heavenly spaces the light of which took thousands or millions of years to reach the earth. Perhaps we were already flying through those spaces. I expected something with a terrible anguish that tortured my heart. And suddenly I was thrilled by a familiar feeling that stirred me to the depths: I suddenly caught sight of our sun! I knew that it could not be our sun, that gave life to our earth, and that we were an infinite distance from our sun, but for some reason I knew with my whole being that it was a sun exactly like ours, a repetition of it, its double. A sweet, thrilling feeling resounded with ecstasy in my heart: the kindred power of the same light which had given me light stirred an echo in my heart and resurrected it, and I had a sensation of life, my former life for the first time since I had been in the grave.

"But if that is the sun, if that is exactly the same as our sun," I cried, "where is the earth?"

And my companion pointed to a star twinkling in the distance with an emerald light. We were flying straight towards it.

"And are such repetitions possible in the universe?[2] Can that be the law of nature? . . . And if that is an earth there, can it be just the same earth as ours . . . just the same, as poor, as unhappy, but precious and beloved for ever, arousing in the most ungrateful of her children the same poignant love for her that we feel for our earth?" I cried out, shaken by irresistible, ecstatic love for the old familiar earth which I had left. The image of the poor girl whom I had repulsed flashed before me.

"You shall see it all," answered my companion, and there was a note of sorrow in his voice.

But we were rapidly approaching the planet. It was growing before my eyes; I could already distinguish the ocean, the outline of Europe; and suddenly a feeling of a great and holy jealousy glowed in my heart.

"How can it be repeated and what for? I love and can love only that earth which I have left, stained with my blood, when, in my ingratitude, I extinguished my life with a bullet in my heart. But I have never, never ceased to love that earth, and perhaps on the very night I parted from it I loved it more than ever. Is there suffering upon this new earth? On our earth we can only love with suffering and through suffering. We cannot love otherwise, and we know of no other sort of love. I want suffering in order to love. I long, I thirst, this very instant, to kiss with tears the earth that I have left, and I don't want, I won't accept life on any other!"

But my companion had already left me. I suddenly, quite without noticing how, found myself on this other earth, in the bright light of a sunny day, fair as paradise. I believe I was standing on one of the islands that make up on our globe the Greek archipelago,[3] or on the coast of the mainland facing that archipelago. Oh, everything was exactly as it is with us, only everything seemed to have a festive radiance, the splendour of some great, holy triumph attained at last. The caressing sea, green as emerald, splashed softly upon the shore and kissed it with manifest, almost conscious love. The tall, lovely trees stood in all the glory of their blossom, and their innumerable leaves greeted me, I am certain, with their soft, caressing rustle and seemed to articulate words of love. The grass glowed with bright and fragrant flowers. Birds were flying in flocks in the air, and perched fearlessly on my shoulders and arms and joyfully struck me with their darling, fluttering wings. And at last I saw and knew the people of this happy land. They came to me of themselves, they surrounded me, kissed me. The children of the sun, the children of their sun—oh, how beautiful they were! Never had I seen on our own earth such beauty in mankind. Only perhaps in our children, in their earliest years, one might find some remote, faint reflection of this beauty. The eyes of these happy people shone with a clear brightness. Their faces were radiant with the light of reason and fulness of a serenity that comes of perfect understanding, but those faces were gay; in their words and voices there was a note of childlike joy. Oh, from the first moment, from the first glance at them, I understood it all! It was the earth untarnished by the Fall; on it lived people who had not sinned. They lived just in such a paradise as that in which, according to all the legends of mankind, our first parents lived before they sinned; the only difference was that all this earth was the same paradise. These people, laughing joyfully, thronged round me and caressed me; they took me home with them, and each of them tried to reassure me. Oh, they asked me no questions, but they seemed, I fancied, to know everything without asking, and they wanted to make haste and smoothe away the signs of suffering from my face.

IV

And do you know what? Well, granted that it was only a dream, yet the sensation of the love of those innocent and beautiful people has remained with me for ever, and I feel as though their love is still flowing out to me from over there. I have seen them myself, have known them and been convinced; I loved them, I suffered for them afterwards. Oh, I understood at once even at the time that in many things I could not understand them at all; as an up-to-date Russian progressive and contemptible Petersburger, it struck me as inexplicable that, knowing so much, they had, for instance, no science like ours. But I soon realised that their knowledge was gained and fostered by intuitions different from those of us on earth, and that their aspirations, too, were quite different. They desired nothing and were at peace; they did not aspire to knowledge of life as we aspire to understand it, because their lives were full. But their knowledge was higher and deeper than ours; for our science seeks to explain what life is, aspires to understand it in order to teach others how to live, while they without science knew how to live; and that I understood, but I could not understand their knowledge. They showed me their trees, and I could not understand the intense love with which they looked at them; it was as though they were talking with beings like themselves. And perhaps I shall not be mistaken if I say that they conversed with them. Yes, they had found their language, and I am convinced that the trees understood them. They looked at all nature like that—at the animals who lived in peace with them

and did not attack them, but loved them, conquered by their
love. They pointed to the stars and told me something about
them which I could not understand, but I am convinced that
they were somehow in touch with the stars, not only in
thought, but by some living channel. Oh, these people did not
persist in trying to make me understand them, they loved me
without that, but I knew that they would never understand me,
and so I hardly spoke to them about our earth. I only kissed in
their presence the earth on which they lived and mutely worshipped them themselves. And they saw that and let me worship
them without being abashed at my adoration, for they themselves loved much. They were not unhappy on my account
when at times I kissed their feet with tears, joyfully conscious
of the love with which they would respond to mine. At times I
asked myself with wonder how it was they were able never to
offend a creature like me, and never once to arouse a feeling of
jealousy or envy in me? Often I wondered how it could be that
I, a boaster and a liar, never talked to them of what I knew—of
which, of course, they had no notion—that I was never
tempted to do so by a desire to astonish or even to benefit
them.

They were as gay and sportive as children. They wandered
about their lovely woods and copses, they sang their lovely
songs; their fare was light—the fruits of their trees, the honey
from their woods, and the milk of the animals who loved them.
The work they did for food and raiment was brief and not laborious. They loved and begot children, but I never noticed in
them the impulse of that *cruel* sensuality which overcomes almost every man on this earth, all and each, and is the source of
almost every sin of mankind on earth. They rejoiced at the arrival of children as new beings to share their happiness. There
was no quarrelling, no jealousy among them, and they did not
even know what the words meant. Their children were the children of all, for they all made up one family. There was scarcely
any illness among them, though there was death; but their old
people died peacefully, as though falling asleep, giving blessings
and smiles to those who surrounded them to take their last

farewell with bright and loving smiles. I never saw grief or tears on those occasions, but only love, which reached the point of ecstasy, but a calm ecstasy, made perfect and contemplative. One might think that they were still in contact with the departed after death, and that their earthly union was not cut short by death. They scarcely understood me when I questioned them about immortality, but evidently they were so convinced of it without reasoning that it was not for them a question at all. They had no temples, but they had a real living and uninterrupted sense of oneness with the whole of the universe; they had no creed, but they had a certain knowledge that when their earthly joy had reached the limits of earthly nature, then there would come for them, for the living and for the dead, a still greater fulness of contact with the whole of the universe. They looked forward to that moment with joy, but without haste, not pining for it, but seeming to have a foretaste of it in their hearts, of which they talked to one another.

In the evening before going to sleep they liked singing in musical and harmonious chorus. In those songs they expressed all the sensations that the parting day had given them, sang its glories and took leave of it. They sang the praises of nature, of the sea, of the woods. They liked making songs about one another, and praised each other like children; they were the simplest songs, but they sprang from their hearts and went to one's heart. And not only in their songs but in all their lives they seemed to do nothing but admire one another. It was like being in love with each other, but an all-embracing, universal feeling.

Some of their songs, solemn and rapturous, I scarcely understood at all. Though I understood the words I could never fathom their full significance. It remained, as it were, beyond the grasp of my mind, yet my heart unconsciously absorbed it more and more. I often told them that I had had a presentiment of it long before, that this joy and glory had come to me on our earth in the form of a yearning melancholy that at times approached insufferable sorrow; that I had had a foreknowledge of them all and of their glory in the dreams of my heart and the visions of my mind; that often on our earth I could not look at

the setting sun without tears . . . that in my hatred for the men
of our earth there was always a yearning anguish: why could I
not hate them without loving them? why could I not help for-
giving them? and in my love for them there was a yearning
grief: why could I not love them without hating them? They listened to me, and I saw they could not conceive what I was saying, but I did not regret that I had spoken to them of it: I knew
that they understood the intensity of my yearning anguish over
those whom I had left. But when they looked at me with their
sweet eyes full of love, when I felt that in their presence my
heart, too, became as innocent and just as theirs, the feeling of
the fulness of life took my breath away, and I worshipped them
in silence.

Oh, every one laughs in my face now, and assures me that
one cannot dream of such details as I am telling now, that I only
dreamed or felt one sensation that arose in my heart in delirium and made up the details myself when I woke up. And when
I told them that perhaps it really was so, my God, how they
shouted with laughter in my face, and what mirth I caused! Oh,
yes, of course I was overcome by the mere sensation of my
dream, and that was all that was preserved in my cruelly
wounded heart; but the actual forms and images of my dream,
that is, the very ones I really saw at the very time of my dream,
were filled with such harmony, were so lovely and enchanting
and were so actual, that on awakening I was, of course, incapable of clothing them in our poor language, so that they were
bound to become blurred in my mind; and so perhaps I really
was forced afterwards to make up the details, and so of course
to distort them in my passionate desire to convey some at least
of them as quickly as I could. But on the other hand, how can
I help believing that it was all true? It was perhaps a thousand
times brighter, happier and more joyful than I describe it.
Granted that I dreamed it, yet it must have been real. You know,
I will tell you a secret: perhaps it was not a dream at all! For
then something happened so awful, something so horribly
true, that it could not have been imagined in a dream. My heart
may have originated the dream, but would my heart alone have

been capable of originating the awful event which happened to me afterwards? How could I alone have invented it or imagined it in my dream? Could my petty heart and my fickle, trivial mind have risen to such a revelation of truth? Oh, judge for yourselves: hitherto I have concealed it, but now I will tell the truth. The fact is that I . . . corrupted them all!

V

Yes, yes, it ended in my corrupting them all! How it could come to pass I do not know, but I remember it clearly. The dream embraced thousands of years and left in me only a sense of the whole. I only know that I was the cause of their sin and downfall. Like a vile trichina, like an atom of the plague infecting whole kingdoms,[4] so I contaminated all this earth, so happy and sinless before my coming. They learnt to lie, grew fond of lying, and discovered the beauty of lying. Oh, at first perhaps it began innocently, with a jest, coquetry, with amorous play, perhaps indeed with an atom, but that atom of lying made its way into their hearts and pleased them. Then sensuality was soon begotten, sensuality begot jealousy, jealousy—cruelty. . . . Oh, I don't know, I don't remember; but soon, very soon the first blood was shed. They marvelled and were horrified, and began to be split up and divided. They formed into unions, but it was against one another. Reproaches, upbraidings followed. They came to know shame, and shame brought them to virtue. The conception of honour sprang up, and every union began waving its flags. They began torturing animals, and the animals withdrew from them into the forests and became hostile to them. They began to struggle for separation, for isolation, for individuality, for mine and thine. They began to talk in different languages. They became acquainted with sorrow and loved sorrow; they thirsted for suffering, and said that truth could only be attained through suffering. Then science appeared. As they became wicked they began talking of brotherhood and humanitarianism, and understood those ideas. As they became criminal, they invented justice and drew up whole legal codes in order to observe it, and to ensure their being kept, set up a guillotine. They hardly remembered what they had lost, in fact refused to believe that they had ever been happy and innocent. They even laughed at the possibility of this happiness in the past, and called it a dream. They could not even imagine it in definite form and shape, but, strange and wonderful to relate, though they lost all faith in their past happiness and called it a fairy tale, they so longed to be happy and innocent once more that they succumbed to this desire like children, made an idol of it, set up temples and worshipped their own idea, their own "desire"; though at the same time they fully believed that it was unattainable and could not be realised, yet they bowed down to it and adored it with tears! Nevertheless, if it could have happened that they had returned to the innocent and happy condition which they had lost, and if some one had shown it to them again and had asked them whether they wanted to go back to it, they would certainly have refused. They answered me:

"We may be deceitful, wicked and unjust, we know it and weep over it, we grieve over it; we torment and punish ourselves more perhaps than that merciful Judge Who will judge us and whose name we know not. But we have science, and by means of it we shall find the truth and we shall arrive at it consciously. Knowledge is higher than feeling, the consciousness of life is higher than life. Science will give us wisdom, wisdom will reveal the laws, and the knowledge of the laws of happiness is higher than happiness."

That is what they said, and after saying such things every one began to love himself better than any one else, and indeed they could not do otherwise. All became so jealous of the rights of their own personality that they did their very utmost to curtail and destroy others' personalities, and made that the chief thing in their lives. Slavery followed, even voluntary slavery; the

weak eagerly submitted to the strong, on condition that the latter aided them to subdue the still weaker. Then there were saints
who came to these people, weeping, and talked to them of their
pride, of their loss of harmony and measure, of their loss of
shame. They were laughed at or pelted with stones. Holy blood
was shed on the threshold of the temples. Then there arose men
who began to think how to bring all people together again, so
that everybody, while still loving himself best of all, might not
interfere with others, and all might live together in something
like a harmonious society. Regular wars sprang up over this
idea. All the combatants at the same time firmly believed that
science, wisdom and the instinct of self-preservation would
force men at last to unite into a harmonious and rational society; and so, meanwhile, to hasten matters, "the wise" endeav-
oured to exterminate as rapidly as possible all who were "not
wise" and did not understand their idea, that the latter might
not hinder its triumph. But the instinct of self-preservation
grew rapidly weaker; there arose men, haughty and sensual,
who demanded all or nothing. In order to obtain everything
they resorted to evildoing, and if they did not succeed—to suicide. There arose religions with a cult of non-existence and self-
destruction for the sake of the everlasting peace in annihilation.
At last these people grew weary of their meaningless toil, and
signs of suffering came into their faces, and then they proclaimed that suffering was a beauty, for in suffering alone was
there meaning. They glorified suffering in their songs. I moved
about among them, wringing my hands and weeping over
them, but I loved them perhaps more than in old days when
there was no suffering in their faces and when they were innocent and so lovely. I loved the earth they had polluted even more
than when it had been a paradise, if only because sorrow had
come to it. Alas! I always loved sorrow and tribulation, but only
for myself, for myself; but I wept over them, pitying them. I
stretched out my hands to them in despair, blaming, cursing
and despising myself. I told them that all this was my doing,
mine alone; that it was I had brought them corruption, con-
tamination, and lying. I besought them to crucify me, I taught

them how to make a cross. I could not kill myself, I had not the
strength, but I wanted to suffer at their hands. I yearned for suffering, I longed that my blood should be drained to the last
drop in these agonies. But they only laughed at me, and began
at last to look upon me as a holy fool. They justified me, they
declared that they had only got what they wanted themselves,
and that all that now was could not have been otherwise. At last
they declared to me that I was becoming dangerous and that
they should lock me up in a madhouse if I did not hold my
tongue. Then such grief took possession of my soul that my
heart was wrung, and I felt as though I were dying; and
then . . . then I awoke.

It was morning, that is, it was not yet daylight, but about six
o'clock. I woke up in the same arm-chair; my candle had burnt
out; every one was asleep in the captain's room, and there was
a stillness all round, rare in our flat. First of all I leapt up in great
amazement: nothing like this had ever happened to me before,
not even in the most trivial detail; I had never, for instance,
fallen asleep like this in my arm-chair. While I was standing and
coming to myself I suddenly caught sight of my revolver lying
loaded, ready—but instantly I thrust it away! Oh, now, life, life!
I lifted up my hands and called upon eternal truth, not with
words but with tears; ecstasy, immeasurable ecstasy flooded my
soul. Yes, life and preaching! Oh, I at that moment resolved to
preach, and resolved it, of course, for my whole life. I go to
preach, I want to preach—of what? Of the truth, for I have seen
it, have seen it with my own eyes, have seen it in all its glory.

And since then I have been preaching! Moreover I love all
those who laugh at me more than any of the rest. Why that is
so I do not know and cannot explain, but so be it. I am told that
I am straying, and if I have already strayed even now, what will
happen later? It is true indeed: I stray, and perhaps with time it
will get even worse. And of course I shall stray many times before I find out how to preach, that is, find out what words to
say, what things to do, for it is a very difficult task. I see all that
as clear as daylight, but, listen, who does not stray? And yet, you

know, all are making for the same goal, all are striving in the same direction anyway, from the sage to the lowest robber, only by different roads. It is an old truth, but this is what is new: I cannot stray far. For I have seen the truth; I have seen and I know that people can be beautiful and happy without losing the ability to live on earth. I will not and cannot believe that evil is the normal condition of mankind. And it is just this faith of mine that they laugh at. But how can I help believing it? I have seen the truth—it is not as though I had invented it with my mind, I have seen it, seen it, and the living image of it has filled my soul for ever. I have seen it in such full perfection that I cannot believe that it is impossible for people to have it. And so how can I stray? I shall make some slips no doubt, and shall perhaps talk in others' words, but not for long: the living image of what I saw will always be with me and will always correct and guide me. Oh, I am full of courage and freshness, and I will go on and on even for a thousand years! Do you know, at first I meant to conceal the fact that I corrupted them, but that was a mistake— that was my first mistake! But truth whispered to me that I was lying, and preserved me and corrected me. But how establish paradise—I don't know, because I do not know how to put it into words. After my dream I lost command of words. All the chief words, anyway, the most necessary ones. But never mind, I shall go and I shall keep talking, I won't leave off, for anyway I have seen it with my own eyes, though I cannot describe what I saw. But the scoffers do not understand that. It was a dream, they say, delirium, hallucination. Oh! As though that meant so much! And they are so proud! A dream! What is a dream? And is not our life a dream? I will say more. Suppose that this paradise will never come to pass (that I understand), yet I shall go on preaching. And yet how simple it is: in one day, in one hour everything could be arranged at once! The main thing is to love others as oneself,[5] that's the main thing, and that's everything; nothing else is needed—you will find out at once how to arrange it all. And yet it's an old truth which has been repeated and retold a billion times—but it has not formed part of our lives! "The consciousness of life is higher than life, the knowledge of the laws of happiness is higher than happiness"—that is what one must contend against. And I shall. If only every one wants it, it can all be arranged at once.

And I sought out that little girl . . . and I shall go on and on!

ENDNOTES

"The Double"

1. (p. 5) *a titular councillor:* The Table of Ranks, established by Tsar Peter the Great in 1722 and lasting until 1917, listed fourteen ranks for the military, the civil service, and the court, and provided opportunity for advancement; nobility was bestowed on those who successfully climbed the ladder of ranks. A titular councillor was the ninth civilian rank in the Table of Ranks and the lowest rank to confer personal nobility; nobility became hereditary at the fourth rank. The ranks for civil service were: (1) chancellor; (2) actual privy councillor; (3) privy councillor; (4) actual state councillor; (5) state councillor; (6) collegiate councillor; (7) court councillor; (8) collegiate assessor; (9) titular councillor; (10) collegiate secretary; (11) secretary of naval constructions; (12) government secretary; (13) provincial secretary; (14) collegiate registrar.

2. (p. 6) *"if something were amiss, if some intrusive pimple had made its appearance, or anything else unpleasant had happened":* Dostoevsky reminds readers of Nikolay Gogol's story "The Nose" (1835), in which a civil servant, newly arrived in Moscow and hoping to advance his career, wakes up one morning to discover that his nose is missing.

3. (p. 6) *Probably the roll of green, grey, blue, red and particoloured notes:* This is slang terminology for various monetary units: Green refers to a 3-ruble note, grey to a 50, blue to a 5, and red to a 10.

4. (p. 11) *Krestyan Ivanovich Rutenspitz:* The doctor's name recalls *spitzruteny;* "cat-o'-nine-tails" is the closest English equivalent for this instrument of punishment that was essentially a bundle of rough sticks. Moreover, its German roots suggest the tip of a penis and thus Freudian penetration.

5. (p. 22) *Gostiny Dvor:* The Gostiny Dvor is an indoor mall with lots of small shops.

6. (p. 24) *peacefully settled down to an emaciated nationalist paper:* Dostoevsky is referring to *Severnaya pchela* (The Northern Bee, 1825–1859), a conservative newspaper founded by the Russian journalist and novelist Faddey Venediktovich Bulgarin and aimed at a middle-

class readership; the newspaper was quite influential until the mid-1840s.

7. (p. 31) *a dinner more like some Balthazar's feast:* The name differs slightly, but perhaps Dostoevsky was thinking of the biblical book of Daniel, 5:1–30, which tells of King Belshazzar, who hosted a fabulous feast during which his death was foretold.

8. (p. 31) *oysters and fruit from Eliseyev's and Milyutin's:* In Dostoevsky's time, these produce stores, named for their owners, were the largest in St. Petersburg.

9. (p. 32) *the congratulatory glass of sparkling wine—brought from a distant kingdom:* "A distant kingdom" is a tongue-in-cheek reference to France; the reference occurs in a three-page paragraph full of ironic quotations from Russian literature and illustrates the exaggeratedly high style Dostoevsky uses to emphasize the pretentiousness of this bureaucratic ball.

10. (p. 35) *French minister, Villesle:* Count Joseph Villesle (1773–1854) was a French reactionary and royalist who served as prime minister (1821–1827) for Louis XVIII and Charles X.

11. (p. 35) *the Turkish Vizier, . . . the beautiful Marquess Louisa:* Golyadkin is thinking of characters from a popular pulp novel by the Russian author Matvei Komarov titled *The Tale of the Adventures of the English Milord George and the Brandenburg Marquess Frederika Louisa with the Additional Story of the Former Turkish Vizier Martsimiris and the Sardinian Princess Teresa* (1782). By 1840 the novel was in its eighth edition.

12. (p. 47) *boom of a cannon shot:* Dostoevsky is evoking Aleksandr Pushkin's narrative poem *The Bronze Horseman,* in which cannons announce the rising of flood waters.

13. (p. 63) *"The box has been opened . . . that Krylov, and a great fable-writer!":* Ivan Krylov (1768–1844) was Russia's greatest fable writer. The reference here is to his fable "The Box."

14. (p. 70) *Bryullov's picture:* Painted in Italy by Karl Bryullov (1799–1852), "The Last Day of Pompeii" (1833) was exhibited at the St. Petersburg Academy of Arts and provoked much press commentary both in Russia and abroad.

15. (p. 70) *about Baron Brambeus:* Brambeus was the pseudonym of Osip Senkovsky (1800–1858), editor from 1834 to 1847 of the commercially successful Russian journal *Biblioteka dlia chteniia* (Library

for Reading). His fiction, published under the name Baron Brambeus, was extremely popular.

16. (p. 71) *"If thou forget me . . . Do not thou forget me"*: These lines, frequently repeated in young ladies' albums, were popular at the time.

17. (p. 73) *disagreeing with certain learned professors in the slanders they had promulgated against the Turkish prophet Muhammad*: This is a reference to the 1840s debates about Islam and the prophet Muhammad. Dostoevsky may have read the Koran in French translation in the 1840s; he definitely studied it in the 1850s while working as a civil engineer in Siberia. As an epileptic, Dostoevsky was particularly interested in Muhammad's supposed epilepsy.

18. (p. 86) *"Grishka Otrepyov was the only one, sir, who gained by imposture"*: Grishka Otrepyov, a renegade monk, was widely believed to be the First False Dmitry. (False Dmitry was the name given to three imposters claiming to be the son of Tsar Ivan IV; the real Dmitry was assassinated in 1591.) In addition to evoking the theme of impostorship, the name also played a role in Russian literature, particularly Pushkin's historical play *Boris Godunov*.

19. (p. 86) *crush the snake gnawing the dust in contemptible impotence*: Dostoevsky is parodying Salieri's monologue from scene 1 of Pushkin's tragedy *Mozart and Salieri* (1830).

20. (p. 125) *"He's our Russian Faublas"*: Faublas, a calculating, skillful seducer, was the protagonist of *Les Amours du chevalier de Faublas*, a novel by the French author Jean-Baptiste Louvet de Couvray (1760–1797).

21. (p. 144) *"I used to be in service at General Stolbnyakov's"*: This name, and the other names Petrushka drops a few sentences later, are satiric tag names: General Stolbnyakov's last name means "stupor" in Russian, Prince Svinchatkin's means "loaded die," Colonel Pereborkin's means "surplus receipts," and General Nedobarov's means "unpaid debts."

22. (p. 148) *"an émigrée, a Madame Falbalas"*: Madame "Frills" is the French boarding school mistress in Pushkin's 1825 poem "Count Nulin." *Falbalas* is French for "frills."

23. (p. 161) *"the day of Jean Jacques Rousseau is over"*: Jean-Jacques Rousseau (1712–1778) was known for advocating sentiment as an educa-

tional tool. Golyadkin shallowly presumes sentiment to mean compliments.

"White Nights"

1. (p. 178) *The inhabitants of Kamenny and Aptekarsky Islands or of the Peterhof Road. . . . Visitors to Pargolovo; . . . the tripper to Krestovsky Island:* The summer homes of high-ranking officials were on Kamenny and Aptekarsky Islands in St. Petersburg, and along the road to Peterhof west of St. Petersburg. Low-ranking bureaucrats and the poor vacationed at Pargolovo. Krestovsky Island was known for its large park.

2. (p. 179) *My way lay along the canal embankment:* The action of "White Nights" occurs on the embankment of the Ekaterinsky Canal (today known as the Griboedov Canal).

3. (p. 191) *"I am like the djinn of King Solomon when, . . . those seven seals were at last taken off":* The dreamer refers here to "The Fisherman's Tale" from the fifteenth-century collection of tales, *The Arabian Nights' Entertainments* (better known as *1001 Arabian Nights*).

4. (p. 192) *"Now 'the Goddess of Fancy' . . . if you have read Zhukovsky":* The "Goddess of Fancy" is a reference to the 1809 poem "My Goddess," by the Russian poet Vasily Zhukovsky (1783–1852); the poem was a loose translation of Johann Wolfgang von Goethe's 1780 poem "Meine Göttin" (My Goddess).

5. (p. 193) *"You ask, perhaps, what he is dreaming of":* Dostoevsky added the romantic reading list that follows when he revised the story in 1860, providing his dreamer with a cultural genealogy. E. T. A. Hoffman (1776–1822) was a writer and composer known for his fantastic tales. St. Bartholomew's Night refers to the August 24, 1572, massacre of French Protestants, or Huguenots, by Catholics in Paris; the massacre became the subject of works by the French authors Prosper Mérimée and Alexandre Dumas pére and the German-born composer Giacomo Meyerbeer. Diana Vernon is the heroine of Sir Walter Scott's novel *Rob Roy* (1817). After a long siege, the Russian city of Kazan was taken by Tsar Ivan the Terrible in 1552; the story of the battle was recounted in Mikhail Kheraskov's epic poem *Rossiada* (1779), the sixth volume of Nikolay Polevoy's *History of the Russian People* (1829–1833), and Nikolay

Karamzin's *History of Russia* (1819–1829), one of Dostoevsky's favorite books. Clara Mowbray is the heroine of Sir Walter Scott's novel *St. Ronan's Well* (1824), and Effie Deans is the heroine of his novel *The Heart of Midlothian* (1818). Jan Hus (1369?–1415) was a leading Czech religious reformer who was burned at the stake as a heretic. *Robert le Diable* (Robert the Devil) was an 1831 opera in five acts by Meyerbeer. Minna and Brenda are the heroines of Sir Walter Scott's novel *The Pirate* (1821). The battle of Berezina was a decisive battle fought in 1812 during Napoleon's retreat from Moscow, which led to the destruction of Napoleon's army. Countess Vorontsova-Dashkova (1744–1810), the president of both the Academy of Sciences and the Russian Academy, was renowned as a salon hostess. Georges-Jacques Danton (1759–1794) was a French revolutionary leader often credited with the overthrow of the monarchy and the establishment of the First French Republic; he is the subject of Georg Büchner's 1835 play *The Death of Danton*. "Cleopatra *ei suoi amanti*" refers to a scene in Aleksandr Pushkin's "Egyptian Nights" (1835). *The Little House in Kolomna* (1833) is the title of a Pushkin tale in verse.

6. (p. 195) *"so long and so fondly"*: This quotation comes from the Russian author Mikhail Lermontov's 1841 translation of Heinrich Heine's poem "Sie liebten sich beide" (literally, They Loved Each Other; 1823). Dostoevsky's dreamer mixes images from this poem with scenes from Gothic novels such as *Neuhausen Castle* (1823), by the Russian author Aleksandr Marlinsky (the pseudonym of Aleksandr Aleksandrovich Bestuzhev).

7. (p. 203) The Barber of Seville: The comic opera *The Barber of Seville* (1816) was composed by Gioacchino Rossini. Rosina is the heroine of the opera.

8. (p. 209) "R, *o*—Ro; s, *i*—si; n, *a*—na": The dreamer refers to a scene in act 2 of *The Barber of Seville*, in which Figaro advises Rosina to write to her lover and she hands him the letter she's already written.

"Notes from Underground"

1. (p. 235) *I am a collegiate assessor*: Collegiate assessors are the eighth rank in Peter the Great's Table of Ranks (see note 1 for "The Double," which explains the table more fully).

2. (p. 236) *"beautiful and sublime"*: By quoting this phrase from the German philosopher Immanuel Kant's 1764 essay "Observations on the Feeling of the Beautiful and the Sublime," the underground man reveals his 1840s education; by the 1860s this phrase had become a cliché.

3. (p. 240) *There may even be a greater accumulation of spite in it than in l'homme de la nature et de la vérité*: The French means "the man of nature and of truth" and is Dostoevsky's distortion of the French author Jean-Jacques Rousseau's self-portrait in the preface to his *Confessions* (1782–1789), a work Dostoevsky frequently attacked.

4. (p. 242) *As soon as they prove to you . . . that you are descended from a monkey*: The underground man refers here to Charles Darwin's *On the Origin of Species by Means of Natural Selection* (1859), which was translated into Russian in 1864.

5. (p. 243) *in spite of all possible Vagenheims*: Vagenheim was a common name among St. Petersburg's dentists.

6. (p. 244) *"divorced from the soil and one's national origins"*: Dostoevsky mockingly paraphrases his native soil philosophy, which found expression in both journals he coedited with his brother Mikhail, *Vremya* (Time, 1861–1863) and *Epokha* (Epoch, 1864–1865). While Dostoevsky acknowledged the benefits of Peter the Great's modernization drive, he felt that it greatly deepened the divide between the educated classes and rest of the Russian people; his native soil philosophy advocated a merger of the best both had to offer.

7. (pp. 246–247) *But what is to be done*: The underground man is making an oblique reference to Nikolay Chernyshevsky's novel *What Is to Be Done?* (1863).

8. (p. 248) *a picture worthy of Ge*: Dostoevsky despised the work of the Russian artist Nikolay Ge (1831–1894) and sharply criticized his painting *The Last Supper*, which was exhibited in St. Petersburg in 1863.

9. (p. 248) *As you will*: Mikhail Saltykiv-Shchedrin (1826–1889), a satirical writer and journalist, published a sympathetic review of Ge's painting. Dostoevsky attacks him here by taking the title of his review literally.

10. (p. 251) *following Buckle, that through civilization mankind becomes softer, and*

consequently less bloodthirsty and less fitted for warfare: In his History of Civilization in England (1857–1861), the English historian Henry Thomas Buckle (1821–1862) argued that the development of civilization necessarily leads to the end of all wars.

11. (p. 252) *Take the whole of the nineteenth century . . . Schleswig-Holstein:* These are references to contemporary wars. Napoleon III, nephew of the "Great" Napoleon, not only joined the Crimean War against Russia (1854–1856), he also captured Cochin China for France (1859–1862), fought on the losing side of the emperor Maximilian in Mexico, and became involved in the war on Prussia (1870); the Civil War was being fought in America; and Prussia was at war with Denmark over the province of Schleswig-Holstein.

12. (p. 252) *to whom the Attilas and Stenka Razins could not hold a candle:* Attila (406?–453), king of the Huns, fought fierce wars against the Roman Empire; Stenka Razin (1630?–1671) was a Cossack and subsequently a folk hero who led peasant uprisings (1667–1671) against Russia.

13. (p. 252) *They say that Cleopatra . . . derived gratification from their screams and writhings:* Here Dostoevsky alludes to a journalistic polemic that arose over a dramatic reading of Cleopatra's monologue from Aleksandr Pushkin's *Egyptian Nights* (1835).

14. (p. 252) *the nature of a piano-key or the stop of an organ:* Dostoevsky took this analogy from the French encyclopedist Denis Diderot's 1769 dialogue with Jean Le Rond D'Alembert: "We are instruments endowed with sense and memory. Our senses are piano keys upon which surrounding nature plays, and which often play upon themselves."

15. (p. 253) *crystal palace:* The reference here is both to the building designed by Sir Joseph Paxton for the Great Exhibition in London (1851) and to Vera Pavlovna's fourth dream in Nikolay Chernyshevsky's novel *What Is to Be Done?* (1863).

16. (p. 255) *I have made a fig at some one:* A "fig" is a rude gesture made by placing the thumb between the second and third fingers of a closed fist.

17. (p. 257) *the Colossus of Rhodes . . . Mr. Anaevsky:* The Colossus of Rhodes, a 100-foot-tall bronze statue of the mythological sun god Helios located in Rhodes, Greece, was one of the seven wonders

of the world; it was erected in 282 B.C., but destroyed by an earthquake about sixty years later. A. E. Anaevsky (1788–1866) was a
much ridiculed hack writer.

18. (p. 266) *Heine . . . considers that Rousseau certainly told lies about himself in
his confessions, and even intentionally lied, out of vanity:* In his book *On Germany,* the poet Heinrich Heine (1797–1856) writes that no man
is capable of telling the truth about himself. He argues that the
French writer Jean-Jacques Rousseau (1712–1778), in his *Confessions,* hides his real intentions behind false avowals.

19. (p. 269) *A Propos of the Wet Snow:* In 1849 the Russian literary critic
Pavel Annenkov (1813?–1887) wrote that "raw rain and wet
snow" were invariant elements of the Petersburg landscape in the
works of Natural School writers and their imitators. Dostoevsky
evokes the period (the late 1840s) and the naive assumptions of
the Natural School writers, which he had shared. Dostoevsky's
Poor Folk was published in *A Petersburg Collection* (1846), one of two
collections that became identified with the Natural School. The
stories in the collection presented sketches from the life of St. Petersburg and often featured petty clerks, the movement's favorite
character, depicted as one might draw sketches from nature.

20. (p. 269) *"When from dark error's subjugation . . . At memories of foul disgrace":* The poet and journalist Nikolay Nekrasov (1821–1878)
was known for writing poetry with civic themes. These lines were
from one of his famous poems about redeeming a prostitute,
something Nekrasov himself did in real life.

21. (p. 273) *always on the look out for Kostanzhoglos and Uncle Pyotr Ivanichs:*
Dostoevsky evokes two positive characters from the Russian liter-
ary tradition: Kostanzhoglo from part 2 of Nikolay Gogol's *Dead
Souls* (1852) and Pyotr Ivanovich (Ivanich is the abbreviated
form) Aduev from Ivan Goncharov's novel *An Ordinary Story*
(1847).

22. (p. 274) *by preference in Weimar or the Black Forest:* Weimar, Germany,
was an important intellectual center mainly because the poet Johann Wolfgang von Goethe (1749–1832) lived there. The Black
Forest of southwestern Germany was considered a "romantic" re-
gion.

23. (p. 274) *At most, they would take him to the lunatic asylum as "the King of*

Spain": The copy clerk hero of Gogol's "Diary of a Madman" (1835) goes mad and believes that he is the King of Spain.

24. (p. 277) *like Gogol's Lieutenant Pirogov:* Pirogov, one of the protagonists of Gogol's story "Nevsky Prospect" (1835), considers complaining to the authorities after being thrashed soundly by a German tradesman whose wife he tried to seduce, but he quickly forgets his injury. Here and elsewhere, Dostoevsky uses him as a symbol of shamelessness and frivolity.

25. (p. 277) *of the point of honour* (point d'honneur): Dostoevsky here refers to a Russian dueling ritual borrowed from the West. (For more on duels, consult Reyfman, *Ritualized Violence Russian Style;* see "For Further Reading.")

26. (p. 278) *to describe this officer in an exposé . . . sent the story to Fatherland Notes:* By having his underground man misspell "exposé," Dostoevsky makes fun of the investigatory journalism popular in the 1860s. *Fatherland Notes* was an important Russian literary journal (1839–1884) known for its liberal tendency.

27. (p. 285) *"good and beautiful," something in the Manfred style:* This is a reference to the deeply tormented, world-weary, romantic hero of "Manfred" (1817), a verse drama by the English poet Lord Byron.

28. (p. 285) *the Pope would agree to retire from Rome to Brazil; . . . the neighbourhood of Rome:* Pope Pius VII excommunicated Napoleon in 1809, after which the emperor held him virtually captive until 1814; in 1806 the Villa Borghese, a summer house on the outskirts of Rome, belonged to Camillo Borghese, who married Napoleon's sister Paulette. Lake Como is situated in the Italian Alps.

29. (p. 305) *all this was out of Pushkin's Silvio and Lermontov's Masquerade:* Silvio is the revengeful hero of Aleksandr Pushkin's short story "The Shot" (1830); *Masquerade,* a romantic drama (1835) by Mikhail Lermontov (1814–1841), features a similarly vengeful character named Incognito.

30. (p. 314) *"Yes, in the Haymarket":* The Haymarket Square, located in a poor neighborhood, abounded in taverns and houses of ill repute.

31. (p. 330) *he is witty, charming, a regular Lovelace:* Lovelace is Clarissa's seducer in the novel *Clarissa; or the History of a Young Lady* (1747–1748), by English author Samuel Richardson. Lovelace's name has become synonymous with "seducer."

32. (p. 334) *European, inexplicably lofty subtleties à la George Sand:* George

Sand was the pseudonym of Amandine-Aurore-Lucile Dupin (1804–1876), the French woman author of many popular novels whose strong female protagonists garnered much sympathy for women's rights and social reform.

33. (p. 334) *"Into my house come bold and free, / Its rightful mistress there to be"*: These are the last two lines of the Nikolay Nekrasov poem that serves as an epigraph to part II of this story (see note 20, above).

"The Meek One"

1. (p. 357) *advertising in the* Voice: The *Voice* was a liberal Russian weekly (1863–1884).

2. (p. 358) *"Sternness, sternness, and sternness!"*: Here Dostoevsky introduces an inexact quotation from a government official in Nikolay Gogol's story "The Overcoat" (1842) to illustrate the pawnbroker's insensitivity.

3. (p. 359) *she was kind and meek*: The word Dostoevsky uses for "kind" is the Russian word dobra, which also means "good," as in "good and evil." Dostoevsky thus underlines the story's ethical dimension.

4. (p. 361) *"I am part of that part of the Whole that seeks to do ill, but does good. . . . Faust"*: The pawnbroker is showing off his education here by paraphrasing this line of Mephistopheles, the devil figure who tempts Faust in part 1 of the poetic drama Faust (1808, 1832), by the German author Johann Wolfgang von Goethe.

5. (p. 369) *"first impressions of existence"*: As he reproaches his wife for her generosity, the pawnbroker misquotes a line from Aleksandr Pushkin's narrative poem Demon (1823). By applying Pushkin's line, which refers to a metaphysical awakening, to the meek one's introduction to the pawnbroking business, the narrator reveals the narrowness of his life and concerns.

6. (p. 370) *We went three times and saw* The Hunt after Happiness, *and* Singing Birds: The Hunt after Happiness may be a drama by P. I. Yurkevich (d. 1884), which passed the censors on October 2, 1876, early in the month Dostoevsky wrote this story; or it may be an adaptation of Francis Talfourd's 1854 play Abon Hassan, or The Hunt After Happiness, a semi-original fairy extravaganza in rhyme in one act. *La Périchole* (Songbird, 1868) was an operetta by Jacques Offenbach (1819–1880).

7. (p. 371) *Truth is truth, and even Mill is no use against it!*: John Stuart Mill (1806–1873) was an English positivist philosopher who advocated for women's rights. Dostoevsky's journalistic collaborator, the literary critic Nikolay Strakhov, reviewed Mill's 1869 essay "The Subjection of Women" in the journal *Dawn* in 1870.

8. (p. 376) *Vyazemsky's House*: Vyazemsky's was an infamous flophouse in St. Petersburg's Haymarket Square.

9. (p. 385) *Men condemned to death, they say, sleep very soundly on the last night*: Here Dostoevsky reminds his readers of Victor Hugo's 1829 novel *The Last Day of a Condemned Man*, the source of his fantastic frame for the story.

10. (p. 397) *recalling the scene of Gil Blas and the Archbishop of Granada*: Dostoevsky loved this scene from Alain-René Lesage's novel *L'Histoire de Gil Blas de Santillane* (1715–1736); encouraged to give his opinion about one of the Archbishop's sermons, Gil Blas gives an honest reply by criticizing the sermon mildly; scandalized, the Archbishop fires him.

11. (p. 403) *"Is there a man alive on the battlefield?" cries the Russian hero*: Dostoevsky is probably referring to the words of Beltov, the hero of *Who Is to Blame?* (1846), a novel about a love triangle written by the Russian author Alexander Herzen. In complaining that his life has been a failure, Beltov compares himself to the Russian hero left alone on the battlefield.

12. (p. 403) *The sun is rising and—look at it, is it not dead?*: Dostoevsky takes this image from the Bible, Revelation 16:8–9, in which the sun scorches the earth with fire.

13. (p. 403) *"Men, love one another"—who said that?*: Dostoevsky here stresses the Western-educated pawnbroker's alienation from God by showing his ignorance of the Gospels. The reference is to the Bible, John 15:12.

"The Dream of a Ridiculous Man"

1. (p. 410) *a comfortable arm-chair, as old as old can be, but nonetheless Voltairean*: By recalling the French writer Voltaire (1694–1778), Dostoevsky stresses the ridiculous man's western, atheistic education. He also

evokes Voltaire's *Micromegas*, a philosophical tale that recounts the interplanetary travels of the title character, a young inhabitant of Sirius.

2. (p. 417) *"And are such repetitions possible in the universe?"*: Dostoevsky gives a mystical tint to the philosophical concept of other worlds, an idea he develops with the Elder Zosima in his novel *The Brothers Karamazov* (1879–1880).

3. (p. 418) *found myself on this other earth, in the bright light of a sunny day, fair as paradise . . . the Greek archipelago*: The ridiculous man's dream of the Golden Age is a recurrent image in Dostoevsky's work. It not only resembles the classical model portrayed by the French landscape artist Claude Lorrain in his painting *Acis and Galatea* (one of Dostoevsky's favorites); it also resembles the French socialist utopias from the 1840s that influenced him so heavily.

4. (p. 423) *Like a vile trichina, like an atom of the plague infecting whole kingdoms*: A trichina is a parasitic worm. The image comes from the epilogue to Dostoevsky's 1866 novel *Crime and Punishment*, in which Raskolnikov dreams of a terrible plague caused by microbes that causes madness.

5. (p. 427) *The main thing is to love others as oneself*: The ridiculous man turned prophet proclaims Christ's teaching from the Gospel of Mark (see the Bible, Mark 12:31).

INSPIRED BY NOTES FROM UNDERGROUND, THE DOUBLE AND OTHER STORIES

"The Metamorphosis"

Dostoevsky's "The Double" was an inspiration for the Austrian writer Franz Kafka's best-known story, "The Metamorphosis" (1915). Kafka modeled much of his narrative, about a man transformed into an insect, on Dostoevsky's strange tale of the lowly civil servant Golyadkin. "The Double" opens with the disoriented Golyadkin lying in his bed as he struggles to determine whether what he sees is dream or reality. The scene is a precursor for the beginning sentence of "The Metamorphosis": "As Gregor Samsa awoke from unsettling dreams one morning, he found himself transformed in his bed into a monstrous vermin."

In "The Metamorphosis," Gregor Samsa is a traveling salesman; he loathes his profession but must work to provide for his dependent and demanding family. Like the morbidly oversensitive Golyadkin, Gregor feels intimidated by his supervisor but morally and intellectually superior to him. The protagonists of both stories have "doubles," but whereas Golyadkin's double is adroit and enviable, Gregor's double is a monstrous, verminous insect, less capable of succeeding in the real world than Gregor himself. When Gregor changes into an insect, even his family turns against him. Both protagonists are hidden away by the end of the story: Golyadkin in a madhouse and Gregor in his insect shell, where he ultimately expires.

Invisible Man

The notion of a subterranean man isolated from society is not new to fiction; it can be traced back to the early eighteenth century and Daniel Defoe's shipwrecked hero Robinson Crusoe, who took up residence in a cave. In "Notes from Underground," Dostoevsky depicts isolation from society as a psychological rather than a physical phenomenon. Ralph Ellison takes Dostoevsky's theme a step further in Invisible Man (1952).

The underground man of Ellison's novel becomes a symbol for African-Americans and their position within a predominately white society. The nameless young black narrator of *Invisible Man* resides in a burrow beneath the streets of New York City. In recalling the events of his life that led him underground, he notes both black and white people who do not see him; they "see only my surroundings, themselves, or figments of their imagination." Ellison combines in his main character the fierce paranoia of Dostoevsky's underground man and an almost supernatural quality.

Saul Bellow, in his review of *Invisible Man* in *Commentary* (June 1952), lauded Ellison's accomplishment:

> What a great thing it is when a brilliant individual victory occurs, like Mr. Ellison's, proving that a truly heroic quality can exist among our contemporaries. People too thoroughly determined and our institutions by their size and force too thoroughly determined can't approach this quality. That can only be done by those who resist the heavy influences and make their own synthesis out of the vast mass of phenomena, the seething, swarming body of appearances, facts, and details.

Invisible Man quickly established Ellison as a preeminent twentieth-century novelist and existentialist thinker, on a par with the well-known French existentialists Albert Camus and Jean-Paul Sartre.

The Fall

Novelist, essayist, and playwright Albert Camus was devoted to Dostoevsky throughout his literary career. Camus, who won the Nobel Prize for Literature in 1957, adapted Dostoevsky's novel *The Possessed* for the stage with *Les Possédés* (1959). But the Russian novelist's influence went much deeper than inspiring adaptations of his work: It can be said that Dostoevsky's underground man was the father of existentialism itself.

In Camus's 1956 novel *La Chute* (*The Fall*), the underground man's confessional tenor is echoed in the voice of Jean-Baptiste Clamence. The book, whose title evokes humanity's fall from grace and consequent discovery of shame, explores the inadequacy of traditional values—indeed an entire social ethos that held sway before alienation became widespread—as a basis for solving the problems of modern man. Throughout the novel, Clamence holds a one-sided conversation with a stranger in an Amsterdam bar. By confessing his own deeds, and alluding to the sins of all humans, Clamence hopes to alleviate his shame by sharing it. Written in Camus's elegant, lucid style and skillfully structured, *The Fall* delineates Clamence's search for meaning in his life—a fruitless exercise, Camus seems to say, to which every human is necessarily committed.

COMMENTS & QUESTIONS

In this section, we aim to provide the reader with an array of perspectives on the text, as well as questions that challenge those perspectives. The commentary has been culled from sources as diverse as reviews contemporaneous with the work, letters written by the author, literary criticism of later generations, and appreciations written throughout history. Following the commentary, a series of questions seeks to filter Fyodor Dostoevsky's Notes from Underground, The Double and Other Stories through a variety of points of view and bring about a richer understanding of these enduring works.

Comments

FRIEDRICH NIETZSCHE

Dostoevsky [is] the only psychologist, incidentally, from whom I had something to learn; he ranks among the most beautiful strokes of fortune in my life.

—from *Twilight of the Idols* (1888)

THE SPECTATOR

"Look well at the face of Dostoievsky, half a Russian peasant's face, half a criminal physiognomy, flat nose, small penetrating eyes beneath lids that quiver with a nervous affection; look at the forehead, lofty, thoroughly well-formed; the expressive mouth, eloquent of numberless torments, of abysmal melancholy, of infinite compassion and envy!—An epileptic genius, whose exterior speaks of the mild milk of human kindness, with which his temperament was flooded, and of the depth of an almost maniacal acuteness which mounted to his brain." These words of Dr. Brandes, which occur in a letter to Nietzsche, written in 1888, express with force and precision the view of Dostoievsky, both as a man and as a writer, which probably every reader of the extraordinary works now being translated by Mrs. Garnett would naturally be inclined to take. To the English reader, no less than to the Norwegian critic, what must first be apparent in those works is the strange and poignant mixture which they contain of "an almost maniacal acuteness"

445

with "the mild milk of human kindness"—of the terrible,
febrile agitations reflected in those penetrating eyes and their
quivering lids, with the serene nobility and "infinite compassion" which left their traces in the expressive mouth and the
lofty brow. These conflicting and mingling qualities are, in fact,
so obvious wherever Dostoievsky's genius reveals itself in its
truly characteristic form, that there is some danger of yet another, and no less important, element in this complex character
escaping the notice which it deserves—the element of humour. . . . This mood of pure comedy disappears in The Double—
a singular and highly interesting work, containing a study of
the growth of madness in a feeble intellect overcome by extreme self-consciousness—where the ridicule is piled up till it
seems to topple over upon itself, and the furious laughter ends
in a gnashing of teeth. . . . But Dostoievsky's humour [is] the
key to his sympathetic treatment of character. There are many
ways of laughing at one's fellow-creatures. One may do so with
the savage fury of Swift, or the barbed mockery of Voltaire, or
the caressing mischief of Jane Austen; but Dostoievsky, in his
latest works, uses another sort of laughter—the laughter of lov-
ingkindness. Such laughter is very rare in literature; Shakespeare
has some for Falstaff (though there it is complicated by feelings
of genuine contempt); it inspired Sterne when he created Uncle
Toby, and, of course, there is the classic instance of Don
Quixote. Dostoievsky's mastery of this strange power of
ridicule, which, instead of debasing, actually ennobles and en-
dears the object upon which it falls, is probably the most remarkable of all his characteristics.

—April 11, 1914

J. D. BERESFORD
The supposed autobiographer (his name does not appear) in
Notes from Underground is, perhaps, too intelligently aware of his
own condition, but it is evident that Dostoevsky's purpose
could only be fully served by the form of a personal confession.
It is, indeed, a confession that holds no reserves. In the earlier
part of the story we see the assumed writer of the notes suffer-

ing agonies from the consciousness of his humiliation. This is followed by two attempts to assert himself, both futile. We then see him in a contest with his servant, Apollon, whose condition is a reflex of his own. And, finally we get the representative instance of a brutal use of temporary superiority of position in his dealings with the unfortunate little prostitute, Liza. Moreover, the title is conclusive. The "underground" is clearly indicated as that of the mind, and if the story had been written within the last ten years the author would have been accused by the reviewers of having steeped himself in the writings of the psycho-analysts. . . .

We come to the consideration of his jealousy of Turgenev, and of the unfortunate meeting of the two men in Switzerland. All Dostoevsky's resentment and his behaviour at the meeting in question are readily explicable by the theory of his neurosis, but the need for impartiality demands that we should ask if a perfectly normal explanation is forthcoming. Personally I have failed to find one that is consistent with an unprejudiced interpretation of Dostoevsky's general character. Apart from his prepossession, he exhibits traits of gentleness, affection, and tolerance that do not appear to me consonant with his treatment of Turgenev. He did not seek to belittle his other contemporaries. But, in this instance, like the hero of Notes from Underground, he could not resist the unconscious desire to try and jostle his superior from the pavement.

—from the London Mercury (February 1920)

THOMAS MANN
The tortured paradoxes which Dostoevsky's "hero" hurls at his positivistic adversaries, antihuman as they sound, are spoken in the name of and out of love for humanity: on behalf of a new, deeper, and unrhetorical humanity that has passed through all the hells of suffering and of understanding.

—on Notes from Underground, from his Introduction
to The Short Novels of Dostoevsky (1945)

Questions

1. There are "family resemblances" among the women in these stories. First, summarize the resemblances. Second, evaluate them: Do they denigrate or elevate women?

2. The male protagonists of these stories suffer from extreme self-consciousness (for starters). Does Dostoevsky provide or at least imply historical reasons for the malign form of this state of mind?

3. There is often a religious component to Dostoevsky's fiction, though it is not always directly expressed. Could religion save his male characters from themselves?

4. Would you say that among the components of a modern person's character there is almost always an underground man of the type in Dostoevsky's novella? Can you think of any public figures who defiantly assert what the rest of us see as defects? Who display their vices as though they were virtues?

FOR FURTHER READING

Biography

Frank, Joseph. *Dostoevsky: The Seeds of Revolt, 1821–1849.* Princeton, NJ: Princeton University Press, 1976.

———. *Dostoevsky: The Years of Ordeal, 1850–1859.* Princeton, NJ: Princeton University Press, 1983.

———. *Dostoevsky: The Stir of Liberation, 1860–1865.* Princeton, NJ: Princeton University Press, 1986.

———. *Dostoevsky: The Miraculous Years, 1865–1871.* Princeton, NJ: Princeton University Press, 1995.

———. *Dostoevsky: The Mantle of the Prophet, 1871–1881.* Princeton, NJ: Princeton University Press, 2002.

Kjetsaa, Geir. *Fyodor Dostoyevsky: A Writer's Life.* Translated by Siri Hustvedt and David McDuff. New York: Viking, 1987.

Mochulsky, Konstantin. *Dostoevsky: His Life and Work.* Translated and with an introduction by Michael A. Minihan. Princeton, NJ: Princeton University Press, 1967.

Rice, James L. *Dostoevsky and the Healing Art: An Essay in Literary and Medical History.* Ann Arbor, MI: Ardis Publishers, 1985.

Criticism and Cultural Studies

Anderson, Roger B. *Dostoevsky: Myths of Duality.* University of Florida Humanities Monograph series, no. 58. Gainesville: University Press of Florida, 1986.

Bakhtin, Mikhail M. *Problems of Dostoevsky's Poetics.* Edited and translated by Caryl Emerson, with an introduction by Wayne C. Booth. Theory and History of Literature series, Vol. 8. Minneapolis: University of Minnesota Press, 1984.

Gibson, A. Boyce. *The Religion of Dostoevsky.* Philadelphia: Westminster Press, 1973.

Jackson, Robert Louis. *Dostoevsky's Quest for Form.* New Haven: Yale University Press, 1966.

─────. *The Art of Dostoevsky: Deliriums and Nocturnes.* Princeton, NJ: Princeton University Press, 1981.

Knapp, Liza. *The Annihilation of Inertia: Dostoevsky and Metaphysics.* Evanston, IL: Northwestern University Press, 1996.

Jones, Malcolm V. *Dostoyevsky after Bakhtin: Readings in Dostoyevsky's Fantastic Realism.* Cambridge and New York: Cambridge University Press, 1990.

Leatherbarrow, William J., ed. *The Cambridge Companion to Dostoevskii.* Cambridge and New York: Cambridge University Press, 2002.

Morson, Gary Saul. "Introductory Study: Dostoevsky's Great Experiment." In *A Writer's Diary,* Vol. 1: 1873–1876, pp. 1–117. Translated and annotated by Kenneth Lantz. Evanston, IL: Northwestern University Press, 1993, pp. 1–117.

Paperno, Irina. *Suicide as a Cultural Institution in Dostoevsky's Russia.* Ithaca, NY: Cornell University Press, 1997.

Peace, Richard. *Dostoyevsky: An Examination of the Major Novels.* Cambridge: Cambridge University Press, 1971.

Reyfman, Irina. *Ritualized Violence Russian Style: The Duel in Russian Culture and Literature.* Stanford, CA: Stanford University Press, 1999.

Scanlan, James P. *Dostoevsky the Thinker.* Ithaca, NY: Cornell University Press, 2002.

Works Cited in the Introduction

Bakhtin, Mikhail M. *Art and Answerability: Early Philosophical Essays.* Translated by Vadim Liapunov; edited by Michael Holquist and Vadim Liapunov. Austin: University of Texas Press, 1990, p. 22.

Belknap, Robert L. "The Unrepentant Confession." In his edited volume *Russianness: Studies on a Nation's Identity: In Memory of Rufus Wellington Mathewson.* Studies of the Harriman Institute series. Ann Arbor, MI: Ardis Publishers, 1989, pp. 113–123.

─────. "*The Gentle Creature* as the Climax of a Work of Art that Almost Exists." *Dostoevsky Studies, New Series,* Vol. 4 (2000), pp. 35–42.

James, William. *The Varieties of Religious Experience*. 1902. Introduction by Reinhold Niebuhr. New York: Simon and Schuster (Touchstone Books), 1997.

Lewis, Michael. *Shame: The Exposed Self*. New York: Free Press, 1992.

Meerson, Olga. "Old Testament Lamentation in the Underground Man's Monologue: A Refutation of the Existentialist Reading of *Notes from Underground*." *Slavic and East European Journal*, 36:3 (1992), pp. 317–322.

Miller, Robin Feuer. "Dostoevsky and Rousseau: The Morality of Confession Reconsidered." In *Dostoevsky: New Perspectives*, edited by Robert Louis Jackson. Englewood Cliffs, NJ: Prentice-Hall, 1984, pp. 82–98.

Scanlan, James P. *Dostoevsky the Thinker*. Ithaca, NY: Cornell University Press, 2002.

Adventures of Huckleberry Finn	Mark Twain	1-59308-000-X	$4.95
The Adventures of Tom Sawyer	Mark Twain	1-59308-068-9	$4.95
Aesop's Fables	Aesop	1-59308-062-X	$5.95
The Age of Innocence	Edith Wharton	1-59308-074-3	$4.95
Alice's Adventures in Wonderland and Through the Looking Glass	Lewis Carroll	1-59308-015-8	$5.95
Anna Karenina	Leo Tolstoy	1-59308-027-1	$8.95
The Art of War	Sun Tzu	1-59308-016-6	$3.95
The Awakening and Selected Short Fiction	Kate Chopin	1-59308-001-8	$4.95
The Call of the Wild and White Fang	Jack London	1-59308-002-6	$4.95
Candide	Voltaire	1-59308-028-X	$4.95
A Christmas Carol, The Chimes and The Cricket on the Hearth	Charles Dickens	1-59308-033-6	$5.95
The Collected Poems of Emily Dickinson	Emily Dickinson	1-59308-050-6	$5.95
The Complete Sherlock Holmes, Volume I	Sir Arthur Conan Doyle	1-59308-034-4	$7.95
The Complete Sherlock Holmes, Volume II	Sir Arthur Conan Doyle	1-59308-040-9	$7.95
The Count of Monte Cristo	Alexandre Dumas	1-59308-088-3	$5.95
Cyrano de Bergerac	Edmond Rostand	1-59308-075-1	$3.95
David Copperfield	Charles Dickens	1-59308-063-8	$7.95
The Death of Ivan Ilych and Other Stories	Leo Tolstoy	1-59308-069-7	$7.95
Don Quixote	Miguel de Cervantes	1-59308-046-8	$9.95
Dracula	Bram Stoker	1-59308-004-2	$4.95
Emma	Jane Austen	1-59308-089-1	$4.95
Ethan Frome and Selected Stories	Edith Wharton	1-59308-090-5	$5.95
Frankenstein	Mary Shelley	1-59308-005-0	$3.95
Great Expectations	Charles Dickens	1-59308-006-9	$4.95
Grimm's Fairy Tales	Jacob and Wilhelm Grimm	1-59308-056-5	$7.95
Gulliver's Travels	Jonathan Swift	1-59308-057-3	$3.95
Heart of Darkness and Selected Short Fiction	Joseph Conrad	1-59308-021-2	$4.95
The House of Mirth	Edith Wharton	1-59308-104-9	$4.95
Howards End	E. M. Forster	1-59308-022-0	$6.95
The Hunchback of Notre Dame	Victor Hugo	1-59308-047-6	$5.95
The Idiot	Fyodor Dostoevsky	1-59308-058-1	$7.95
The Importance of Being Earnest and Four Other Plays	Oscar Wilde	1-59308-059-X	$6.95
The Inferno	Dante Alighieri	1-59308-051-4	$6.95
Jane Eyre	Charlotte Brontë	1-59308-007-7	$4.95

Jude the Obscure	Thomas Hardy	1-59308-035-2	$6.95
The Jungle	Upton Sinclair	1-59308-008-5	$4.95
The Last of the Mohicans	James Fenimore Cooper	1-59308-065-4	$4.95
Les Misérables (ABRIDGED)	Victor Hugo	1-59308-066-2	$9.95
Little Women	Louisa May Alcott	1-59308-108-1	$6.95
Main Street	Sinclair Lewis	1-59308-036-0	$5.95
The Metamorphosis	Franz Kafka	1-59308-029-8	$6.95
Middlemarch	George Eliot	1-59308-023-9	$8.95
My Ántonia	Willa Cather	1-59308-024-7	$4.95
Moby-Dick	Herman Melville	1-59308-018-2	$9.95
Narrative of the Life of Frederick Douglass, an American Slave	Frederick Douglass	1-59308-041-7	$4.95
Notes From Underground, The Double and Other Stories	Fyodor Dostoevsky	1-59308-037-9	$4.95
O Pioneers!	Willa Cather	1-59308-019-0	$4.95
The Odyssey	Homer	1-59308-009-3	$5.95
Oliver Twist	Charles Dickens	1-59308-030-1	$4.95
The Origin of Species	Charles Darwin	1-59308-077-8	$7.95
Persuasion	Jane Austen	1-59308-048-4	$4.95
The Picture of Dorian Gray	Oscar Wilde	1-59308-025-5	$4.95
The Portrait of a Lady	Henry James	1-59308-096-4	$7.95
A Portrait of the Artist as a Young Man and Dubliners	James Joyce	1-59308-031-X	$7.95
Pride and Prejudice	Jane Austen	1-59308-020-4	$4.95
The Prince and Other Writings	Niccolò Machiavelli	1-59308-060-3	$5.95
The Red Badge of Courage and Selected Short Fiction	Stephen Crane	1-59308-010-7	$3.95
Robinson Crusoe	Daniel Defoe	1-59308-011-5	$4.95
The Scarlet Letter	Nathaniel Hawthorne	1-59308-012-3	$3.95
Selected Stories of O. Henry	O. Henry	1-59308-042-5	$5.95
Sense and Sensibility	Jane Austen	1-59308-049-2	$4.95
Sons and Lovers	D. H. Lawrence	1-59308-013-1	$7.95
The Souls of Black Folk	W. E. B. Du Bois	1-59308-014-X	$5.95
The Strange Case of Dr. Jekyll and Mr. Hyde and Other Stories	Robert Louis Stevenson	1-59308-054-9	$3.95
A Tale of Two Cities	Charles Dickens	1-59308-055-7	$4.95
The Three Musketeers	Alexandre Dumas	1-59308-079-4	$6.95
The Time Machine and The Invisible Man	H. G. Wells	1-59308-032-8	$4.95
Uncle Tom's Cabin	Harriet Beecher Stowe	1-59308-038-7	$5.95
The Varieties of Religious Experience	William James	1-59308-072-7	$7.95
Walden and Civil Disobedience	Henry David Thoreau	1-59308-026-3	$4.95
The War of the Worlds	H. G. Wells	1-59308-085-9	$3.95

ℬ

BARNES & NOBLE CLASSICS

If you are an educator and would like to receive an
Examination or Desk Copy of a Barnes & Noble Classic edition,
please refer to Academic Resources on our website at
WWW.BN.COM/CLASSICS

or contact us at
B&NCLASSICS@BN.COM.

All prices are subject to change.